The Forever Girl

ALSO BY JILL SHALVIS

Wildstone Novels

Mistletoe in Paradise (novella)

The Summer Deal

Almost Just Friends

The Lemon Sisters

Rainy Day Friends

The Good Luck Sister (novella)

Lost and Found Sisters

Heartbreaker Bay Novels

Wrapped Up in You

Playing for Keeps

Hot Winter Nights

About That Kiss

Chasing Christmas Eve

Accidentally on Purpose

The Trouble with Mistletoe

Sweet Little Lies

Lucky Harbor Novels

One in a Million

He's So Fine

It's in His Kiss

Once in a Lifetime

Always on My Mind

It Had to Be You

Forever and a Day

At Last

Lucky in Love

Head Over Heels

The Sweetest Thing

Simply Irresistible

Animal Magnetism Novels

All I Want

Still the One

Then Came You

Rumor Has It

Rescue My Heart

Animal Attraction

Animal Magnetism

The Forever Girl

A Novel

Jill Shalvis

HARPER LARGE PRINT
An Imprint of HarperCollinsPublishers

THE FOREVER GIRL. Copyright © 2021 by Jill Shalvis. All rights reserved. Printed in the United States of America. No part of this book may be used or reproduced in any manner whatsoever without written permission except in the case of brief quotations embodied in critical articles and reviews. For information, address HarperCollins Publishers, 195 Broadway, New York, NY 10007.

HarperCollins books may be purchased for educational, business, or sales promotional use. For information, please e-mail the Special Markets Department at SPsales@harpercollins.com.

FIRST HARPER LARGE PRINT EDITION

ISBN: 978-0-06-306247-4

Library of Congress Cataloging-in-Publication Data is available upon request.

21 22 23 24 25   LSC   10 9 8 7 6 5 4 3 2 1

The Forever Girl

Prologue

Three years ago

Maze Porter was good at pretending to be fine, but since no one could see her, she dropped all pretense and stopped twenty-five yards short of her goal, unable to so much as swallow past the lump stuck in her throat.

For nine years now, since she'd been sixteen, she'd made this annual pilgrimage, but her legs refused to go another step. As far as her eyes could see, green grass spread out in front of her like a blanket over gently rolling hills, dotted with aged, sweeping oaks.

And myriad gravestones.

Above her, the sky churned moodily. Thunder rumbled, and a part of her heart smiled, because Michael had always loved a good storm.

Buoyed by the idea of her onetime foster sibling sitting on a cloud creating weather to amuse her, she managed to coax herself closer and let the strap of her beach chair slip off her shoulder. She tried to open it, but it was more stubborn than . . . well, her. "Not today, Satan," she muttered. Not when she'd paid way too much for it at the touristy general store in Wildstone, but finally, after a two-minute battle of the wills, swearing the air blue the whole time, she got the thing open. Feeling righteous, she plopped down—only to have the chair jerk beneath her weight, making her gasp dramatically and throw her hands out, braced to fall on her ass.

She didn't.

Relieved to have something go her way, she pulled a can of soda from her purse, cracked it open, and toasted to the grave. "Happy birthday. Hope that was entertaining."

"Oh, hugely," said an amused female voice behind her. "*And* you beat us here."

"Of course she did," a second female voice said. "Maze's far too perfect to be late. There's a reason I always wanted to be her when I grew up."

Maze snorted. *Perfect.* Right. Just one of many roles she'd played. She looked up as Caitlin and Heather moved into her view, two of the only people on earth who could both make her laugh and drive her insane— almost as if they were a real family.

It felt like they were, thanks to the year they'd spent together running wild and free at the beach, at the lake, in the hills, having the sort of innocent kid adventures that bonded people for a lifetime . . . But in reality, Caitlin and Michael Walsh had been the only actual blood siblings. Maze and Heather, and a whole bunch of others, had been just the foster kids.

As they'd done for nine years now, Caitlin and Heather began taking things from a big bag: a HAPPY BIRTHDAY streamer, balloons, and a small cake—all superhero themed, of course.

Tradition for Michael's birthday. Today would've been his eighteenth birthday. He'd loved birthdays, but he'd only gotten nine of them. Chest tight with memories and an almost paralyzing sense of loss, Maze stood, pulled a Deadpool action figure from her pocket, and set it on Michael's headstone. He'd been too young for Deadpool, but she knew it would've been his favorite, hands down. He'd been mischievous, sharp as a tack, and had loved to laugh, and just thinking about him made it hard to breathe.

Heather smiled at her through eyes shining with unshed tears and produced a Thor action figure.

Cat was next with—no big surprise—Catwoman, and she took the longest, standing in front of her brother's grave until, finally, she sniffed, wiped her eyes, and turned back to them with a smile and a nod. She was in charge of her emotions and their world, as always.

Of course she and Heather got *their* beach chairs open without incident, setting them up in an informal semicircle facing Michael's grave, leaving space for a fourth chair.

The last member of their ragtag group hadn't yet arrived. Hell, maybe he'd be a no-show this year. The thought made Maze ache. She'd given a quick thought to not showing up either, but guilt was a huge burden, and no one felt the weight of it more than she did, seeing as she was the one responsible for Michael's death.

"Stop," Caitlin said quietly, carefully balancing the cake in her lap as she cut it into three pieces. "I can hear your self-destructive thoughts from here."

Like Caitlin knew about self-destructive thoughts—she'd never had a moment of doubt in her life. *She* was the perfect one, the *real* deal perfect. Two years older than Maze, Cat had her shit together. She'd been *born* with her shit together. Her hair was a long, shiny blond silk that never frizzed, her smile could draw in even the most hardened soul, and she had the sort of willowy body that looked good in every damn thing, even though her idea of exercise was lifting her Starbucks coffee cup to her lips. Maze could hate her for that alone . . . except Cat was one of the most intensely loyal, fiercely protective, caring people who had ever come into her life.

"You can't just tell someone to stop angsting," Heather said, taking a piece of cake. Heather was petite, barely coming up to Maze's chin. But what she lacked in height, she made up for in grit. Today her black hair had bright magenta highlights that gave her an implied attitude to mask the fact that she was the sweetheart kitten of the group, the one who never used her claws.

She didn't have to. Maze used hers enough for everyone. People said it was her red hair. It wasn't red, it was *auburn*, thank you very much, but still, there was no getting around the fact that her hair—a bunch of uncontrollable waves and the bane of her existence—did tend to match her bad 'tude. She hadn't needed the shrink from Child Protective Services to tell her it was because she'd never really had a sense of belonging. That's what happened when you were raised like a wild tumbleweed in the wind, tossed in directions against your will. Whatever. She was long over it and took another pull of her soda to hide all the annoying feelings bombarding her.

Caitlin, their self-appointed den mother, handed her a piece of cake. Maze had just taken her first bite when she felt it, a shift in her force field, along with an awareness tingling at the back of her neck. Her body knew what that meant even if her brain pretended not to, and the frosting went down the wrong pipe. While she went about choking up a lung, Heather pounded her on the back until she could suck in air again.

Walker Scott hadn't made a sound in his approach. No footsteps, no rustling, nothing. The man was silent as the night.

Walker the boy hadn't been silent. He'd been feral, and there'd been nothing calm or quiet about him.

Maze should know. They'd all spent a year together in Caitlin's parents' Wildstone home, and if she was being honest with herself, that year had been the best of her life.

And the very worst.

She watched as Walker set out his chair. It didn't dare misbehave, opening for him with a flick of a forearm. He then set a Batman action figure next to the others on the gravestone and, with a hand braced on the granite, stood still for a moment, staring down at Michael's name.

When he finally turned to them, both Caitlin and Heather lifted their arms in greeting, and he obligingly bent to hug them one at a time, murmuring something too low for Maze to hear. Whatever it was seemed to comfort them both, and it did something deep inside Maze to see their honest emotion, something she herself had a hard time revealing on the best of days—which this wasn't. Didn't stop her from soaking up the sight of Walker. He wore dark jeans, work boots, an untucked blue button-down stretched taut over broad shoulders . . . and a sling holding his left arm tight to his body. Dark aviator sunglasses covered his eyes, but she didn't need to see them. That sky-blue gaze of his was burned onto her soul.

There'd been a time when he'd smiled at her with warmth, affection, and hunger. There'd been even more times when he'd made her laugh—back in the days when she still could. All of it long gone now, as around them the air went thick with memories.

Maze did not lift her arms in invitation.

And he did not reach for her.

"Maze," he said simply, and gave her a single curt nod. She got it, but even after all that had happened between them, a small part of her yearned to see that old spark of pure trouble in his eyes, accompanied by that bad-boy smile, the one that promised a thrill and had never failed to deliver. It never got easier to see him, but Cat gestured them in like they were her ducklings for birthdays and holidays and anything else she could think of. Maze pretended to hate being dragged back into their tight circle, but the honest-to-God truth was that she didn't know what she'd do without them.

Caitlin pulled something from her bag.

A bran muffin.

Walker didn't do cake—or any junk food, for that matter—never had. He ate to fuel his body, which of course showed, since he looked like a lean, hard-muscled fighting machine. Food wasn't a pleasure button for him like it was for her. Nope, Walker had other pleasure buttons, ones she sometimes relived in the deep dark of the night.

Taking the muffin, he let out an almost inaudible sound of amusement before turning to stare at the gravestone while slowly, and clearly painfully, lowering himself to the chair.

"What happened to you?" Maze asked him softly.

He shrugged with his good shoulder and took a bite of the muffin.

She turned to look at Heather and Caitlin.

Caitlin looked pained but said nothing.

Heather was biting her lower lip like she was trying to hold back, but finally burst out with "He got shot." Then she slapped her hand over her mouth.

Maze sucked in air. "*Shot?* When?"

"Two weeks ago, on the job," Heather said from between her fingers. "He's on leave."

Walker sent Heather a long look, and she tossed up her hands.

"Whatever, Walk. You all know I don't keep secrets anymore, not for anyone." She began to chew on her fingernails, painted black and already down to the nubs. She switched to waving a hand in front of her face. "And now I'm sweating."

Heather, Maze, and Walker had all come from vastly different, but equally troubled, backgrounds by the time they'd landed in the same foster home at ages nine, fifteen, and sixteen, respectively. Caitlin's parents had welcomed them with open arms for one perfect year, until the Event, which had scattered them all far and wide. Still minors, Heather and Maze had been fostered by new, fairly decent families within a few months of each other. Walker had ended up in a group home, aging out of the system when he turned eighteen. From there, he'd gone into the military and then the FBI. The rigorous discipline had molded him, given him a sense of purpose and a way to channel his demons. It'd toughened and hardened the already toughened, hardened kid.

But Maze knew him better than most, or at least she had. Very few understood that beneath the edgy shell he wore like armor beat a heart that would lay itself down for the people it beat for. Once upon a time, *she'd* been one of those people.

"The leave is temporary," Walker said. "I'm going back next week."

Heather's eyes filled. "You almost died."

"But I didn't."

Maze's gut clenched. As kids, they'd all had hopes and visions of what they wanted to be when they grew up. Walker had wanted to run a bar or restaurant. He'd wanted to be surrounded by friends and be able to take care of them by feeding them. Simple dream, really, but it spoke of his deep-seated need to have those few trusted people in his life close to him. That was all that mattered.

He'd ended up going in a very different direction. Maze wasn't sure why exactly, but her working theory had always been that he figured giving a shit had never gotten him anywhere, so why try.

"You almost died?" she asked softly.

He looked pained as he swallowed the last of his muffin. "I'm fine."

"But—"

"Drop it, Maze," he said in a warning tone that she imagined probably had all the bad guys' balls retreating north.

She opened her mouth to tell him that very thing, but Heather pointed to the carefully tended gravesite and said quietly, "I love the wildflowers you planted last year, Cat, they're all blooming now." Ever their peacemaker. At nineteen, Heather was the youngest and therefore remembered the least about that long-ago night. She'd never been able to process bad stuff, and the rest of them always shielded her the best they could.

Caitlin smiled at Heather, but it wasn't her usual two-hundred-watt. If Heather was the group's soul, Caitlin was its heart, and she'd been the closest to Michael. His loss had changed her immeasurably, taking her from sweet and fun loving . . . to sweet and completely, unbendingly bossy and tyrannical with those she loved—quite the combo.

"I was out here last week to pull the weeds," Cat said, "*without* using Daddy's tractor."

Everyone looked at Maze, who sighed. "One time. Jeez. You *borrow*"—still holding her fork in one hand

and the paper plate in the other, she managed to use air quotes for the word *borrow*—"a guy's tractor one time, and no one lets you forget it."

"That's because thanks to you, it's now illegal to drive a tractor without a permit in the state of California," Walker said.

Maze would've sworn she'd heard a dry amusement in his tone, but she couldn't tell past his dark sunglasses. "That's a total exaggeration. I didn't even get arrested." Though his implication that she'd been wild and impulsive wasn't exactly wrong.

Caitlin smiled and reached out for both Heather's and Maze's hands, waiting for Heather to take Walker's so they were all connected. "Damn. It's been what, like two months since we were all together for Heather's birthday? Missed you guys. I love you."

"I love you too," Heather said softly.

"Love you," Walker murmured in his low baritone without a single beat of hesitation.

There was a beat of silence, and when it wasn't filled, once again everyone looked at Maze.

"Me too," she said.

Heather shook her head.

Caitlin rolled her eyes.

Walker didn't react at all.

"*What?*" Maze said defensively.

"You never say the actual words," Caitlin said.

"Of course I do."

"Never," Heather said.

Fine. She didn't. But as she'd learned the hard way growing up with an emotionally unavailable mom, no dad, and a few too many foster homes, those three little words held *way* too much power.

Caitlin eyed her watch and craned her neck to look behind them at the parking lot a good hundred yards back.

"What are you looking for?" Maze asked.

"Mom and Dad should've been here by now."

Maze's stomach dropped. "You invited them?"

Heather raised her hand. "Actually, that was me. I was checking in with them the other day and I mentioned our annual thing."

"You mean our *secret* annual thing?" Maze asked.

"Again," Heather said slowly and clearly, "I don't keep secrets anymore. And you know why."

The cake soured in Maze's belly. Yeah, she certainly did know why Heather no longer kept secrets. She turned to Caitlin. "Why didn't you tell me Jim and Shelly were coming?"

At the use of her parents' first names, annoyance flickered over Caitlin's face. She probably thought Maze was still mad at them, but that wasn't it. It was more that she felt like she didn't *deserve* to call them Mom and Dad.

"I didn't tell you they were coming," Cat said, "because I knew then *you* wouldn't."

Was she that stubborn? Unfortunately, yes. "It should've been my choice to make, not yours." And great, now her voice was trembling. "You don't get to boss me around and make choices for me anymore." It was a low blow and she knew it. But she wasn't sweet like Heather, and she sure as hell couldn't be rational like Caitlin.

"Michael was their son," Cat said. "Their baby."

See? Rational. "Believe me," Maze said, chest too tight to breathe. "I get that."

Disappointment joined the annoyance on Caitlin's face. "You know that's not what I meant. I'm just saying that they have every right to be here at their son's grave."

While Maze did not have that same right. Got it. She started to stand up, but Caitlin tugged on her arm. "Don't you dare go. They'll want you to be here. And Michael would want that too."

"Did you ask them?" Maze met her gaze. "Or is this a complete surprise for them as well?"

Caitlin winced, giving her away. Dammit. Maze shook her head.

"See, *this* is why it's easier to not be part of a family."

"*A* family?" Caitlin asked. "Or *this* family?"

Contrary to popular belief, Maze did have a few social skills and could read a room. She knew she was treading in dangerous territory here and was about to seriously piss off the only people who'd ever remained at her back. But a funny thing happened to her when she felt cornered. It made her . . . *feel,* which in turn made her even more stubborn than usual, and that was saying something.

Heather was already crying. But to be fair, Heather cried at the drop of a hat.

Maze closed her eyes to her pain. "Heather," she murmured. "Don't."

But then Caitlin sniffed too, and when a tear ran down her perfect cheek, it shook Maze to the core, because Caitlin almost never cried.

"Stop that. You're all just proving my point."

Caitlin swiped angrily at her face. "Let me guess. You suck at meaningful relationships, so why bother, right?"

"Something like that." But the real truth was Maze didn't just suck at them, she destroyed them. That was what she did: sabotage her own happiness. And she was good at it.

"Bullshit," Caitlin snapped. "You just don't like needing anyone."

Maze drew a deep breath. "Look, I didn't come here to ruin this for you guys. But we all know that we're here because of me. I'm the one. This is all my fault."

At that, Caitlin stood, vibrating with fury. "No. You don't get to own this, Maze." She began shoving everything back into her bag, her movements jerky with anger. "We all made decisions we regret that night."

Maze was vibrating too, with sorrow and angst. "I'm not a kid anymore, Cat. You don't have to protect me, and I don't need your misplaced sympathy. You should hate me."

Heather was still crying, and Caitlin put her hand on her shoulder as she stared at Maze. "Is that what you want? Us to hate you?"

Okay, so she'd backed herself into a corner, and as always she was going to start swinging, taking out only herself. "Yes," she said. "That's what I want."

Everyone stared at her in shock. Except Walker. He was still showing nothing.

"I refuse to believe that," Caitlin finally said. "You're part of this family, whether you like it or not. You can't just run away. Love doesn't work like that and I thought you knew it." She nodded to Heather. "Come on, honey, let's go wait for Mom and Dad in the parking lot."

Maze didn't watch them go. She closed her eyes and tried to think of something else. The ocean. Puppies. Thai takeout. But it didn't work. She strained to hear their retreat, but they must've already gone because all that came to her was the rumble of not-too-distant thunder.

Good to know she could still clear an area without even trying. Feeling sick, she opened her eyes and stared up at the churning, turbulent sky, which was in exact accord with her mood. Telling herself to get over it, she wiped her tears on the hem of her shirt before reaching for her chair to try to close it. When it fought back and pinched her finger, she gave it a good kick.

A low male snort came from behind her and she froze. Why was it that Walker of all people always got to witness her most humiliating moments? Was it karma? Was it because she'd once forgotten to say thank you, or maybe very slightly cheated on her taxes? *Lied about not wanting to be a part of the only family she'd ever truly wanted as her own?*

"Nicely done, Mayhem Maze." Walker, of course.

Rolling her eyes at the old nickname that she'd definitely earned—"borrowing" that tractor notwithstanding—she glared at her chair, now upside down on the grass but still fully opened. When Walker reached for it, she stopped him.

"No, I've got it," she said, practically choking on her stubborn pride. The theme of her life, of course: being stupidly, doggedly stubborn, because being perceived as helpless or needy made her nuts.

Walker pushed his sunglasses to the top of his head and eyed her. "You going to kick it again?"

"Probably."

There was a small smile on his mouth, but not in his eyes, those sharp blue orbs that saw everything and revealed nothing. "You never change."

Aware that this wasn't exactly a compliment, she looked away, because facing Caitlin's parents was nothing compared with facing Walker. Forget the chair. She needed to be anywhere but here. Even a root canal without meds would be preferable.

"Walking off for the win," he said to her back. "Shocking."

She whirled around. "*You're* the one who's always gone."

"For work. Not because I'm running scared."

A direct hit. "Yeah, well, your work doesn't deserve your dedication. It nearly killed you." She barely managed to get the words out.

"What do you care? You've been ignoring me for years now."

Yep, for four years and two months, but who was counting? "I'm *trying*," she said, tossing up her hands. "For all the good it's done since you're still talking to me."

He just looked at her for a long moment, then folded her chair with annoying ease—one handed—and set the strap on her shoulder. "Always good to know I still irritate the shit out of you, Maze."

He was so clearly favoring his right shoulder, and her heart hurt. "It's time for a new job," she said quietly. "You know that, right? At some point, you're going to run out of your nine lives."

He just shook his head, either at the truth of her statement or because he just didn't want to hear her opinion. Both were entirely possible.

"There are lots of other jobs," she said. "You don't have to put your life on the line for a paycheck."

His smile was grim as another rumble of thunder sounded. Ignoring the rain as it started to fall, he shook his head. "It's what I know. I can't jump around like you do."

The rain cooled her skin but not her anger. Yes, she'd jumped around, doing a huge variety of jobs before landing on bartending while working her way through business school, but she felt she finally had it right. Not that that was any of his beeswax. "Still a total asshole, I see."

"Maybe I just care."

And maybe once upon a time, she'd believed that to be true. "Screw you, Walker."

"You already did that. Didn't work out so well for me."

Since that was the shameful truth, she should've been wise and kept her mouth shut. But when had she ever been wise? "Just . . . stay the hell away from me." Then, as she had the morning after they'd gotten hitched by an Elvis impersonator on one shockingly memorable drunken night in Vegas four years and two months ago, she turned and walked away.

Chapter 1

Now

You've got this, Cat told herself. But note to self: she so did not in fact have this. Her nerves had taken over—her own fault, of course. She'd done a thing. A big thing. And though her heart had been in the right place when she'd done that thing, butterflies were revolting in her gut, telling her she'd be the only one who'd see it that way. It was times like this that she missed Michael the most, because he would've been her ally in this, she was sure. Back then, even at half her height and weight, he'd been her shadow. The cutest shadow on the planet. Over time, she'd gotten used to being without him, but it'd never gotten easier.

Twin piglet-like snorts distracted her, and she looked down at her fiancé's "babies." The pug brothers had huge buggy black eyes and little round bodies and vibrated like they needed their batteries changed. Roly was black and Poly tan, both with black faces, black curly tails, and little black feet.

They snorted at her until she gave in and scooped them up, one in each arm, having to smile at their smushed-in faces. "Okay, guys, listen up. We've got a lot to do today." She took a good, hard look around the old cabin that had been in her family's possession since the early 1900s. It sat right on Rainbow Lake, about twenty minutes outside of Wildstone, a small ranching community on California's central coast. She had a lot of good memories here: visiting her grandparents, learning to swim . . . she'd even run away here a few times in her dramatic teens.

Her grandparents were gone, and her parents now lived in South Carolina, where both of them were college professors. They were thinking of selling this place, but had agreed to let her live here until her wedding. At least that was the official reason. The unofficial one was that she was losing her collective shit and had needed the safety net.

The problem was that there were still a few vital pieces missing from the puzzle of Caitlin's life: the most important pieces, the corner pieces, the ones you couldn't do without. And since Michael was an angel now—and damn, her heart still squeezed painfully every time she thought about him, which was a *lot*—she was really counting on the wedding to bring the other vital pieces back to her. Those pieces named Heather, Walker, and Maze.

The estrangement between them all felt like a huge, gaping hole. It'd started at Michael's grave three years ago and had only gotten worse. Hence the *thing* she'd done.

No one was going to thank her. And it was entirely possible it would all blow up in her face. But she'd had to try. Just thinking about it had the butterflies in her belly escaping and taking flight in her nervous system, giving her the shakes.

But that might have been the five cups of coffee she'd consumed.

She set down the pugs, much to their snorting, squealing displeasure, and got to it. Running around like a madwoman for the next few hours, she changed the sheets on the beds in the spare bedrooms, swept the wood floors, washed the towels so they'd smell fresh . . . all while fielding call after call from her boss, Sara. Cat managed the Wildstone deli that Sara owned. Cat also made all the hot food, which was actually the only part of her job she enjoyed, because the deli itself was a nightmare. She'd taken three weeks off for the wedding, but Sara, who'd missed her calling as the passive-aggressive queen of the universe, had been in contact almost every day in the guise of needing something, while really just wanting Caitlin to know of her every little mistake or misstep.

So when her phone buzzed in her pocket yet again while Cat was folding clothes in the laundry room, she ignored it.

"Caitlin?" came Dillon's voice. "Can you bring me my laptop?"

She transferred another load into the dryer, turned it on, blew a stray hair off her sweaty face, and poked her head out of the laundry room to find Dillon sitting on the couch in the living room, feet up on the coffee table, Roly and Poly curled up on his lap. "Are you kidding me?"

He flashed her the charming smile that had caught both her attention and her heart a year ago. "Sorry," he said. "But my ankle's bothering me again. Do you mind?"

Hard to, when his twisted ankle was actually her fault. She'd seen a *Cosmo* post online titled "The Top Ten Ways to Spruce Up Your Sex Life." Feeling ambitious, she'd gone with number one: "Seduce Your Man in the Shower." What could she say? The illustrations had looked intriguing.

Turned out attempting intriguing things in the shower was dangerous.

Feeling guilty, she ran up the stairs and got his laptop, stopping to straighten out the mess he'd left on the desk. When she got back downstairs, he was standing at the front door with his golf bag slung over his shoulder.

"What are you doing?" she asked.

"Just got a call from Mom. Her golf date bailed and she needs me to do the back nine with her."

"But your ankle."

"We've got a cart." He handed her the pugs.

Juggling the soft sausage loaves while trying to avoid the inevitable face kisses—a big no-thank-you, since they had a fondness for licking each other's butts—she stared at Dillon. "You said that you'd be here to meet my family and have dinner with us."

"Babe." His face softened. "*I'm* your family. Me and my mom, and your parents."

"You know that's only technically true," she protested. She and Heather and Walker and Maze might not be blood, but they were something even deeper. A self-made family, and yeah, okay, maybe it was a very dysfunctional one, but it felt more real than anything else in her life.

"Come on," Dillon said, putting his hands on her hips and giving her a frustrated smile. "When's the last time you heard from Maze or Heather"—he set a finger against her lips when she tried to speak—"where you didn't contact them first. I mean, have they offered to help you with the wedding? They're in it—you insisted on them over your local friends—so . . . where have they been?"

She could admit that he had a point. They hadn't been together since their fight in front of Michael's grave. Heather had vanished, just gone dark for a whole year before suddenly responding to Caitlin's texts again as if nothing had happened. But she still hadn't been back to Wildstone and wouldn't give Caitlin much information other than that she was okay and "working on things." Whatever that meant.

Caitlin hadn't seen Maze either, and not for a lack of trying. But they'd texted and had a few strained calls. And to give Maze credit, she always responded when Caitlin reached out, even with her busy life that was now in Santa Barbara, two hours south of Wildstone.

But Caitlin had, however, seen Walker. Sparingly, but he'd been gone on the job nearly nonstop the past three years. She missed him.

She missed all of them and wanted them back together. And as the self-appointed bossy older sister of the fam, she was determined—and, okay, also slightly desperate—to make it happen. And yeah, maybe, *maybe,* she'd rushed her wedding along, knowing it was the one thing that could bring her siblings of the heart back together. She couldn't help herself. For whatever reason, the four of them had synced and melded into a core family that long-ago year, but they were losing each other, and that scared her. She'd already lost Michael; hell if she'd lose the others too. She needed this so badly she couldn't even explain it to Dillon. But the truth was the last time she'd felt vibrantly alive had been when they'd all been in her life, and she was just desperate enough to play with fate to make it happen. "*Please* stay, Dillon."

He studied her face and sighed, his eyes lit with affection as he cupped her jaw. "I promised Mom, but I'll get back asap. Take care of my babies?"

It was the best she was going to get, so she nodded. He brushed a nice, warm kiss across her lips, and then he was gone.

Caitlin blew out a breath and eyed his "babies." They stared up at her with those googly eyes and she had to laugh. She'd grown up with big dogs, so she didn't quite get the appeal of the little ones. They yipped. They had a Napoleon complex. Last week at the dog park, they'd terrorized a big dog into peeing on them.

But Dillon loved them. When the two of them had first started getting serious, they'd talked about their future. As an investment banker, he had a solid job and made a great living. He was fun and sexy. But she hadn't fallen in love until she'd seen his "Life" list on his Notes app: wife, kids, big house, and a big pension.

And the past year had been . . . really good. They traveled, they laughed, and she'd felt so lucky. But lately there'd been missed dates. Fewer and fewer late-night talks beneath the stars. Less time spent together. She'd decided it was wedding stress, on both their parts.

Because if Dillon was pulling away, she could admit that she'd let him.

She'd kept all this bottled up because . . . well, that's what she did, always. There were lots of corked bottles of emotion deep inside her. But this, with Dillon . . . for the first time in her life she didn't know what to do. She couldn't tell her parents, because they'd asked her—begged her—more than once to *please* think about dating Dillon longer before saying yes to a ring.

She hadn't.

Her friends Charlene and Wendy were each very happily married and sickeningly in love, and Wendy was a coworker of Dillon's. They *loved* him for her, said he was the best thing to ever happen to her. So maybe she just didn't do sickeningly in love?

Maybe it would catch up with her.

When she'd finally finished her manic nesting, she critically eyed the cabin. She'd done everything she could to make it look homey and inviting. Exhausted, she jealously eyed Roly and Poly, now snoozing in their fancy beds, but before she could even think about taking a nap herself, she heard a car drive up.

Her stomach jangled uncomfortably as she hurried out front in time to see Heather getting out of an old, beat-up two-door Civic. She was twenty-two now and had made it clear she no longer needed a big sister, but Caitlin couldn't help but still see the sweet, terrified, neglected nine-year-old Heather had been when she'd first come into Caitlin's childhood home. Her hair had grown out a bit, straight and blunt to her collarbone, still black, but with pretty metallic blue streaks. At the sight of her cute, petite self, Caitlin felt her heart melt as she rushed over. "You made it!"

Heather laughed. "Did I have a choice?"

"Nope." Caitlin pulled her in and hugged her tight.

"Wow." Heather patted her on the back. "Okay. Hi to you too."

Caitlin didn't let go. She couldn't. This was her baby sister, and Michael would've been Heather's age now, still Caitlin's shadow, she was sure of it, but also being her backup boss.

"Um . . ." Heather patted her some more. "Not sure we can do this all day, so . . ."

Nope. Caitlin still couldn't let her go, not yet.

Heather laughingly caved, hugging Caitlin back. "Okay, okay, all day it is."

Caitlin gave a little snort to beat back the threat of tears and reluctantly released her. "I missed you." To hide just how much, she peered into the empty front seat of Heather's car. "Your text said your plus-one was someone named Sam."

"Oh. About that . . ." Heather's smile went a bit forced, the way it always had when she'd stolen food from the pantry to secretly hoard, even though Caitlin's parents had made it clear that everyone in their house could eat as often and as much as they needed.

Heather pressed a lever on the driver's-side seat so that it slid forward, then reached in and pulled out a little girl from a toddler car seat. "So . . ." Heather said softly, nervously. "This is Sammie."

Caitlin's mouth fell open. "A baby? You had a baby?"

"I *big* girl!" the "baby" said proudly.

Heather cupped the back of Sammie's head and kissed her chubby cheek. "Yes," she said, smiling at the little girl's face. "You're a big girl."

Caitlin was still gaping. "You . . . had a baby."

"I did."

Caitlin absorbed this blow, and yes, it was a blow, because once upon a time, she'd known everything—every single little thing—about her people. That was what she did: she was the center of their universe and kept them all connected. It gave her purpose and made her feel important in a world where she often felt invisible. The truth was she *needed* to be needed by them.

And yet she was now so unnecessary that Heather had gotten pregnant and had a baby without a word. Feeling like she'd just been hit by a freight train, she swallowed hard. "Is Sammie's daddy coming too?"

"No." Heather reached back into the car for a duffel bag, which she slung over her shoulder. Her jeans were torn in a few spots, and not by design. The rest of her clothing seemed ragged too, and now that the shock was wearing off, Caitlin noticed that Heather's face was wan and tight, and it made her heart hurt. "You're . . . on your own? No baby daddy?"

Something crossed Heather's face. Pride. "We're not together, but we're friends and he helps. I'm good, Cat."

"But—"

Heather's smile fell. "Please, can we save the twenty questions thing for later? I'm working on zero sleep and enough stress to take down a buffalo. If I lose it now, I'll never find it again."

"Sure," Caitlin managed, trying not to take offense, because she did always ask way too many questions, but how was she supposed to help herself? These were her people and she wanted them back. Shelving that for the moment, she smiled at Sammie.

Sammie stared at her with the biggest brown eyes she'd ever seen, but didn't return the smile.

Caitlin tried another smile, because seriously, *everyone* liked her, even cats, which, along with roses, she was allergic to. Being liked was kind of her thing.

But Sammie's deadpan expression never changed.

"Don't take it personally," Heather said. "She's just super shy. Probably because it's been just her and me."

Caitlin had a million questions, starting with why, if the baby daddy was around, had it been just Heather and Sammie? And also, why hadn't it been *Cat* and Heather and Sammie? But just then another car pulled up the driveway. She and Heather turned in unison, but Caitlin was pretty sure she was the only one whose heart was suddenly threatening to explode from her chest, because Maze was getting out of the passenger seat, followed by a guy from behind the wheel. He reached for Maze's hand and smiled down at her. "Ready, sweetness?"

Maze's gaze had locked on Caitlin, face grim. "As I'll ever be."

"Hey," Caitlin called out. "Weddings are *fun*, dammit!"

Maze's mouth twitched, but her eyes remained wary . . . and nervous, Caitlin realized, which softened her in a big way. Of all of them, Maze was the toughest nut to crack, even more so than Walker, and that was saying something because she was pretty sure Walker had been born and immediately dipped in Kevlar.

"Okay," she said. "So weddings aren't always fun, but *mine* will be."

Next to her, Heather gave a low laugh. "She decrees it so."

Maze smiled at that and walked up to them, stopping in front of Caitlin.

"Hi," Caitlin said softly.

"Hi," Maze said back, just as softly.

"Good to see you."

"Same."

"You brought a guy," Caitlin said.

"If you'll remember, you demanded I do so. You said, and I quote, 'Don't you dare show up without your boyfriend.'"

"Yeah, but that was a few months ago. You don't have relationships that last weeks, let alone months."

"Thanks for the reminder." Maze turned and hugged Heather before coming back to Caitlin.

"Are we okay?" Caitlin asked quietly.

"As okay as we ever are."

"That's not saying much."

Maze touched her finger to the tip of her nose and then sighed dramatically when Caitlin could no longer stop herself and pulled her in for a tight hug.

"Don't waste your energy trying to escape," Heather said. "Just give in. It's easier, trust me."

Maze gave a small laugh, relaxed against Caitlin, and finally hugged her back.

And since that was what Caitlin had been waiting on, she let go. "See, was that so bad?" She looked up at Maze's boyfriend, whom she knew nothing about. Getting info out of Maze was harder than infiltrating the CIA.

"Hi," he said with an affable smile as he held out a hand. "I'm Jace."

He was tall, lanky, good-looking, and at ease, which gave him brownie points. Clearly, he didn't yet realize he'd just joined the circus.

"I'm Caitlin," she said, "and this is Heather and Sammie."

Jace turned to little Sammie and gave her a big grin.

She gave him a big, sticky-looking grin back and held out her arms, the universal demand for *up*.

Caitlin blinked in surprise.

So did Heather.

Without missing a beat, Jace obliged Sammie and scooped her up, making her giggle and adding about a bazillion points to his pro column. He bounced Sammie a few times and poked her in the belly, making her giggle some more, and the sweet baby laughter made Caitlin's ovaries turn over and weep.

So did the sight of Dillon's BMW turning the corner. He'd hurried and returned, just like he'd told her he would, and gratitude and affection filled her. She smiled and waved, and he waved back . . . and then pulled into the garage, shutting the door behind him and going directly inside without coming out to be introduced.

And just like that, Caitlin's anxiety was back. "So." She gave her best pageant smile. "Who needs a drink?"

Chapter 2

Maze's to-do list:
—Remember to zip your mouth instead of
run it. Sometimes it's okay to just shh . . .

Maze had lots of pleasure buttons. Skinny-dipping. Off-roading just a little too fast. Online shopping. Romance novels. But nowhere on that list were reunions or weddings, so this had potential disaster written all over it—from a personal standpoint anyway.

And then there was the fact that she was back in Wildstone. If anyone ever asked what she'd thought of her time in the small California beach and ranching community, she'd have said it was a good place to grow up.

In truth, it was the best place to grow up and the only place she'd ever considered home.

So coming back was . . . hard. But this was about Cat, not her. Not that that stopped her from jumping on Cat's offer of a drink.

And despite everything, damn, it was good to see Heather and Cat's bossy-ass self. So good. But she'd stayed away on purpose, and even after ten minutes she knew leaving again on Sunday would kill her.

Jace handed Sammie back to Heather and took Maze's hand like a loving boyfriend as they moved toward the cabin. He leaned in. "You do realize you could scare the devil himself with that fake smile, right?"

Shit. She shook herself and tried again, curving her lips, trying to will a smile into her eyes. "Better?"

"Sure. For filming a horror flick."

She rolled her eyes and made him laugh. And in turn, his laugh made her smile, a real one this time. They both lived in Santa Barbara, Jace in a small boutique hotel he also owned and ran, Maze in a teeny-tiny studio apartment just outside of town—because she liked to be close to everything she needed, but not too close.

She really did like Jace—as a friend and also as her boss, since she worked as a bartender in his hotel. There was a lot of genuine affection between them, but happily absolutely zero chemistry, which had allowed a real friendship to take hold, rare for Maze. She didn't like to let people in. Jace was one of the few.

His own bad luck, because when Caitlin had asked Maze if she'd be bringing a date to the wedding, she'd stupidly made up a boyfriend. Since in reality, she hadn't had a date in too long to remember, and since Jace had recently been dumped by his last girlfriend for being "too nice," Maze had recruited him for the role.

"Better," he said about her so-called smile. "Now you just look like you're in the mood to kill only puppies, not the whole planet. So . . ." He looked around, taking in the lake, the cabin, the rolling hills all around them. "Where is he?"

"He who?"

He gave her a *come on* look. "You know who. The one you wanted to see me be especially attentive to you."

"I didn't say that."

"It was implied in your utter desperation to get me here."

Hard to argue the truth. Harder still to admit the truth, that she was indeed hoping to show off in front of Walker, making sure he knew he no longer mattered to her.

A lie, of course. But *she* no longer mattered to *him*, and her pride—the big, fat ball of it stuck in her chest—would allow nothing less than for her to show up here happy, successful, and unavailable.

Lies on lies . . . But she'd always been good at digging her own grave.

Sammie was teetering around at top speed, giggling as she tipped first one way and then the other, looking like a staggering, happy drunk. When she headed for the street instead of the front porch, Heather gasped, but Jace got there first, quickly scooping her up. "Gotcha!"

As most females did, Sammie stared up at him dreamily. She was a total mini-Heather, and Maze shook her head in marvel. "I can't believe you have a kid."

Heather shrugged and smiled. Maze recognized the smile, as it was the same as hers.

Forced.

Caitlin moved ahead of them to open the door, but Maze held back and eyed Heather. "You okay?"

"Better now." Heather watched Jace hold Sammie, keeping her safe. "It's a lot to handle on my own."

"I can't even imagine. There are days I can hardly manage taking care of myself, much less be in charge of another tiny, admittedly adorable little human."

Caitlin, with her catlike hearing, turned back to them. "But you didn't have to do it alone."

Heather looked stricken, and Maze slipped an arm around her. "Cat," she murmured in soft reproach.

"I know. God . . ." Caitlin shook her head. "I'm sorry. I just wish you'd have let me help." She softened the words with a sad smile. "I feel like we're all strangers and I hate that. Let's go inside."

The cabin was an A-frame, with big windows and a porch for a stunning lake view. Maze had been here several times before, during that year they'd spent with Caitlin's parents in Wildstone. She hadn't had the best of luck with foster homes up to that point, but she'd finally started to relax, knowing there would always be food if she was hungry and no one was going to yell at her.

Or worse.

What she remembered most about this place was Cat's mom baking a lot of cookies in the small, cozy kitchen. She'd even tried to teach Maze to bake. That part had been an utter failure, mostly because all Maze had wanted was to eat the cookies. Well, that and spend time with Cat's mom, which, if she was being honest, was the real prize. Her own mom had considered Maze an afterthought. There'd been a huge emotional disconnect for her own daughter, something Maze hadn't realized she'd felt keenly until landing in the Walsh home.

She could remember one time in particular with Cat's mom. Maze had loved to lick the spoon when

Cat's mom made cookies, and once she'd also sneaked a lick of the bowl as well. Nothing had ever been more like her secret fantasy family life than that little act of defiance. Of course, Shelly, Cat's mom, had caught her, head in the bowl, tongue swiping the last of the batter. Maze had frozen, deer in the headlights, certain that she'd get in trouble. And trouble for a foster kid usually meant stuffing your belongings into a trash bag and getting a one-way ride to a new place.

But Cat's mom had simply laughed softly, handed her a paper towel to wipe the batter from her nose, and hugged her. "Sometimes I do that too," she'd confessed.

The memories were some of the best of her shitty childhood, and she felt herself relaxing as Caitlin gestured them inside. From the depths of the house came a fierce snarling and snorting sound. "Oh my God," Cat said to the unseen growlers. "Put a cork in it. We come in peace." And with that, she swung the door open wide, revealing two teeny . . . well, it was hard to tell, actually. They looked like bowling balls with faces. Smashed-in faces.

Caitlin glanced back with an apologetic smile. "The pugs are Dillon's. Don't worry, they don't bite—unless you're a big dog and they need to establish their dominance, aka small-man syndrome. And even then, all they can reach are ankles."

Heather picked up Sammie.

A lanky, lean guy sat on the couch holding the remote, wearing plaid golf pants and a pale blue shirt, looking like he'd just walked off the cover of *Golf* magazine.

"Everyone," Caitlin said, "meet Dillon."

Dillon stood up. "Come here, babies," he said to the pugs, and scooped them up, gently setting them on the couch. Then he very formally shook everyone's hand. Maze was last, and he eyed her over their handshake. "You're Mayhem Maze."

She thought she did a great job of not wincing at her old nickname, which, okay, yeah, she'd earned. Sneaking into the principal's private bathroom and looping plastic wrap around the toilet beneath the seat (evil, okay, yes, but he'd yelled at her in front of everyone for stealing—which she hadn't done—and called her a hoodlum, so she figured she might as well live up to the name, right?). Adding green food coloring to the water dispenser in a dentist's reception area (she'd heard him refer to her as a typical punk-ass foster kid, and hey, there was nothing "typical" about her). Blowing up her chemistry lab volcano (accidentally, honest!) . . .

"Guilty," she said to Dillon.

She figured he'd smile or say something teasingly. Instead, he remained serious as he leaned in and whispered, for her ears only, "Don't mess this up for her, okay? The wedding's very important to her, and she's important to me."

Then he turned away and sank back to the couch and his game.

Okaaaay. Maze let out a shaky breath and turned to the door with some half-baked idea of running for the hills, except she nearly barreled into Caitlin.

Caitlin lifted a beautiful green plant with white flowers in a ceramic container. "Remember this? We painted this container at a ceramics class that summer, and I've kept the plant alive this whole time. I thought maybe after the wedding you could take it home and babysit it while I'm on my honeymoon."

Maze lifted her hands. "I've got a black thumb. I'll kill it."

"In a week?"

She thought about how quickly she'd managed to get off on the wrong foot with Caitlin's future husband. "You'd be surprised how fast I can kill things."

Cat sighed and Maze felt like a jerk. Cat had offered her an olive branch. It was also a blatant attempt to make sure they saw each other again when Maze would have to give the plant back.

"Sure," Maze said, and took the plant. "Just don't expect it to be alive."

Cat smiled. "I know you'll do your best. That's all I can ask."

Maze's chest hurt.

Heather had given Sammie a piece of banana, and she had it smashed in both hands as she ran around doing her staggering drunk impression again, happily chattering in baby speak. Her bright eyes landed on the pugs, now in Dillon's lap, and she beelined straight for them with an excited scream.

The pugs screamed back, but in alarm. Dillon cuddled them in close. *"Caitlin."*

Sammie kept coming at him.

"The couch is linen," Dillon said to the little girl.

"It's okay," Caitlin told him. "I bought Tide pens at Costco."

Dillon frowned, but Jace snagged Sammie before she executed her destroy-the-couch mission. "Hey, you. Let's go wash your hands while your mama sits down and puts her feet up."

Heather looked at him like he was the god of all men. "You've got the best boyfriend on the planet," she whispered to Maze. Maze thought she managed to hide her grimace, but Heather cocked her head. "What?"

"Nothing."

Heather nodded, but she still studied Maze for a long beat. Without Michael, Heather was the youngest and the most intuitive. "So. Santa Barbara? How do you like living there versus Wildstone?"

Wildstone had been . . . well, home. But Santa Barbara worked. It was warm, not too small a town, but not too big either, and being sandwiched between the Pacific Ocean and beautiful rolling hills made it feel familiar and deceptively safe. She had a good job and an even better boss. She had friends, both on the job and in the building where she lived. She dated. Sometimes. Okay, so she didn't tend to date the same guy more than a few times, but she found herself reluctant to form close ties, especially since apparently she had never really learned how to do that successfully.

But she was fine, even happy. Or happy enough, anyway. She spent her free time volunteering at a women's shelter, mostly just cleaning and doing whatever needed to be done, but it gave her a sense of something she'd never had before—that she was worthy enough to be able to give something back.

She liked that. A lot.

She was also going to school online at night. All of it added up to an almost very full life, and it was . . . nice. Really nice. Definitely a quieter life than she'd ever imagined for herself, but fulfilling.

Well, it *had* felt like it was fulfilling, until she'd stepped foot in here again.

"Love it," she said.

"Hmm," Heather said. "You do realize that I know your trying-to-pull-one-over-on-me smile. I also know you still think of me as the baby here. But trust me, I've grown up fast these past few years. Also, I've missed you like hell. I'm not going to push you, but I'm here if you ever want to talk." She paused, eyes on Maze. "Please want to talk. I really did miss you, and frankly, I need my big sister back in my life."

A gut punch. And a heart punch. "I should've—"

Heather shook her head. "I didn't say that to make you feel guilty. Or maybe I did. Did it work?"

Maze let out a rough laugh, feeling a little bit lucky that the front door opened just then.

Unluckily, it was Walker, and her chest tightened, restricting air. *Chin up. You've got this.* But her heart was tripping all over itself as her eyes soaked up the sight of him. No current bullet holes, at least that she could see, which had relief rolling through her. Nothing but that long, leanly muscled body, the one that still played a starring role in all her secret fantasies. She'd even tried replacing him with Liam Hemsworth, but it hadn't worked.

Walker looked at Dillon on the couch. "Hey, you're in the same spot as you were last time I saw you."

Wait, they knew each other?

"Funny," Dillon said. "So funny."

Walker hugged Heather, then pulled back to look at her face. "You're better," he said.

"Yep, flu's all gone, thankfully."

And he and Heather had seen each other? What's going on?

Caitlin took her turn at hugging Walker, squeezing so hard he grunted, but he let her hold on for as long as she wanted. "You need another haircut already," she said, reaching up to ruffle his dark hair, making him laugh and shrug.

Caitlin too? Maze stood there feeling . . . stupid. And a whole bunch of other things that reminded her of being a kid. Once, in a long-ago foster home, she'd been woken up by a nightmare and had gotten out of bed—a big no-no in that house. She'd wandered into the living room to find the entire family watching TV, eating ice cream, and playing games. She'd felt so unimportant, but worse than that, she'd felt invisible, unwanted, like she was someone no one remembered existed.

Shrugging that off, she decided to obsess about other things. Like how it *really* pissed her off that Walker was even better looking now at almost thirty than he'd ever been. He was six feet plus of solid perfection, smelling deliciously male and rocking a rough five o'clock shadow and finger-tousled hair that gave him an undeniable bad-boy look that had always drawn her in.

Caitlin was still hugging Walker, and honestly? Maze had to fight the urge to do the same. Then she remembered the last time she'd been in his arms, which had been amazing but had also been immediately followed by the harshest heartbreak of her life, and the urge vanished.

Jace came out of the kitchen with Sammie wrapped around him like a monkey, which reminded her that he was her pretend boyfriend for the weekend. Probably not great for the role if she got caught mentally jumping another man's bones.

Jace set Sammie down and she immediately began to run in circles, apparently enjoying the sound of her voice as she sang gibberish.

Walker hunkered down to Sammie's level and she stopped on a dime to smile at him.

"Wow, you got big," he said.

"*Big!*" she repeated jubilantly, and went back to running in circles.

Walker rose back to his full height and *finally* looked at Maze. Her first urge was to do the same as all the other females had and fawn over him, dammit. Her second urge was to throw something at him.

He'd made sure to stay a part of everyone's life but hers.

She tried really hard to not do stupid, immature shit anymore, but she definitely felt a regression coming on and turned to Jace. "Hey, honey," she said in her best sex-kitten voice. "Need anything?"

Jace stepped closer and smiled down at her face—his mischievous smile, not that anyone but her knew that. "No, baby. I'm good," he said, and gave her a little pat on the ass.

Her back to the rest of the room, she narrowed her eyes.

He just grinned. "How about you, baby? Can I get *you* anything?"

A lobotomy would be great. She looked away from him, and her eyes—the traitors—sliced back to Walker.

He was watching her in that quiet, assessing way he had.

Dammit. He'd always had a high bullshit meter, and she didn't need it going off here. So she took a deep breath, accessed her genuine affection for Jace, and went up on tiptoes to brush a kiss to his jaw.

"How about I get you all drinks while you guys put your stuff away in your rooms?" Caitlin asked. "What does everyone want?"

"My usual," Dillon said, still on the couch.

Walker sent the guy a look that should've had Dillon losing control of his bladder. "Seriously?"

"What?"

"Is there a problem with your legs that keeps you from getting your own damn drink?"

"Actually, yes. Sprained my ankle. Ask me how."

Walker shifted his expression to his patented *don't make me kick your ass* look.

Dillon wisely shut up.

Maze picked up her bag and handed it to Jace. "We're upstairs, second bedroom on the left. You okay for a few? I'm going to help Caitlin."

Jace eyed Walker, who was also heading into the kitchen. "Sure," he said. "You go help Caitlin."

"Jace . . ."

"Don't worry, Maze. I get it." He leaned in closer. "But you skipped a bunch of pieces to the puzzle when you dragged me up here to pretend to be in love with you, including the fact your once-almost-husband would be here, so you owe me a long bedtime story later."

"It's not what you think."

"Hmm." But he gave her a reassuring smile. "Later, Maze."

"Thanks." And this time when she kissed his cheek, it wasn't for a role; it was in gratitude.

She moved into the kitchen and found . . . great . . . only Walker. Suddenly her heart didn't fit inside her rib cage, and she realized she'd only been fooling herself about moving on. She hadn't moved on at all. She'd been faking it, even to herself.

Normally, he had a good five inches on her, but she was in boots today. Kick-ass boots with three-inch heels, which she'd worn on purpose in case she had to go toe-to-toe with him. She peered into those sky-blue eyes of his, the ones that could be ice or fire depending on his mood. Given the chill she felt now, it wasn't exactly a mystery as to how he was feeling. She let a beat go by and then another, hoping Caitlin would materialize, but as it turned out, a few seconds with a man who'd seen you naked felt like years. Deciding she wasn't up for this, even with her boots, she turned to go.

"Chicken?" he asked, voice low. Taunting.

She turned back, eyes narrowed. "Never."

That got her the genuine Walker smile, which made her blow out a sigh.

"Look," she said, "we've been doing such a great job of avoiding each other, why stop now?"

"I'm not avoiding you," he said.

"Fine. I'm avoiding you." She craned her neck. The kitchen was freshly renovated and homey and warm, but no high-strung, mastermind blonde named Caitlin anywhere. "Where is she?"

"In the wine cellar."

"There's a wine cellar?"

He shrugged. "It's that, or she got smart and is running for the hills."

He'd already had her full attention, but at this, she put her own emotions aside as protective feelings welled up inside of her for Caitlin. "Why? Do you think she's making a mistake marrying Dillon?"

He didn't answer this. He wouldn't. Walker believed in letting people make their own mistakes without commentary or judgment. He'd certainly been witness to plenty of hers.

"You don't like him?" she pressed.

Again, nothing, but there was a grim set to his mouth now.

"You don't," she whispered, and leaned against the counter, worried. "Do we need to step in? Kill him and hide the body? What?"

"You've been gone for three years," he said in a mild tone, but the censure was in the words themselves. "What does it even matter to you?"

Here was the thing about guilt: she already carried so much of it, there was nothing he could say to make her feel worse than she already did. "We fought the last time I was with all of you," she said. "I upset everyone. I thought it was best to give you all the gift of time away from me. You are welcome."

He shook his head. "At least be honest. You found it easier to walk away than to stick. You always have. You only connect and stay connected if you're chased. And that's some serious bullshit right there, Maze."

God, the way he said her name. It brought up more of those memories she'd buried deep for her own sanity. "I'm not the one of us who disconnected," she said.

"And there you go rewriting history to suit yourself again."

She frowned at the fighting words because *oh, hell no.* "What's that supposed to mean?"

Stepping close, he braced his hands on the counter on either side of her hips, caging her in as he lowered his head to look her in the eyes. "You know damn well what happened in Vegas. And it sure as hell wasn't me doing the disconnecting."

At the unwanted memories involving rum, Walker, and a quickie wedding simply because she'd wanted so desperately to belong to someone, her breath hitched, and suddenly she was afraid she'd lose it in front of him. At least their Elvis impersonator officiant had never filed the papers, so there was that. She sucked in a big breath. "I don't remember much about that night."

This made him frown as he searched her gaze for honesty. Since she couldn't give it, she turned away and said, "Okay, how about this . . . we do each other a favor and leave the past in the past where it belongs. Let's just get through this weekend for Caitlin, okay?"

Pulling her back around, he stared at her for a long beat before finally shaking his head, disgusted, possibly at the both of them. "Fine."

Annoyed by his tone, the one that said maybe she was an unfathomable pain in his ass, she poked a finger into his pec, hard. *"Fine."*

Catching her finger, he tugged until she stumbled against him. And in that brief second when she had no balance, not physically or mentally, he caught her and held her steady.

Just like he used to do.

She froze, and so did he, and their eyes locked on to each other. She wanted to shove him. She also wanted to yank his head close and put her mouth on his. Confused, she closed her eyes briefly, then opened them and spoke quietly but firmly. "Look, in a few days, this'll be over and we can forget that we had to see each other again. Until then, we have a truce. We work together for Caitlin's sake. Nothing more. No talking . . ." Remembering the feel of his hands on her, she added,

"And no touching. After the wedding, you go your way and I'll go mine. Deal?"

Something flashed deep in his eyes as they stood staring at each other. A beat went by. Two. And then, still standing too close, he finally broke the silence. "We're going to have to talk eventually, Maze."

She shook her head. "No." She'd messed up once, big time, by letting her walls down and falling for him. But that part of her life was in the past and that's where it would stay. "Not a chance."

Just then, Caitlin came back into the room loaded down with six bottles of wine. "I brought everything," she said as Maze surreptitiously shifted away from Walker. "Red, white, rosé . . ." She finally looked up, then paused.

Maze smiled, like *nothing to see here . . .*

"Did I miss something?" Caitlin asked.

"Nope." Maze shook her head. "Not a thing." She glanced over at Walker, who was looking at her like she'd yet to make a single decision he approved of.

Well, he could join the damn club then, because she often didn't approve of her decisions either, but for better or worse, no play on words intended, they had a truce, and that was a relief.

Chapter 3

Walker's man of honor to-do list:
—Survive the weekend.

Walker Scott had never been a huge people person, so the fact that he was doing nothing but peopling for the next few days didn't exactly thrill him. The only thing that made it tolerable was that, for the most part, it was *his* people. Luckily, he didn't have many. In fact, he could count them on one hand and they were all here in the cabin. Caitlin, Heather . . . Maze—though he hadn't been face-to-face with her for three years.

And yet here they were, standing in Caitlin's kitchen, staring at each other. Problem was, looking at

Maze had always been like looking into the sun. Heart-stopping and . . . lethal.

And she'd brought a boyfriend . . .

Good times ahead.

The sound of a cork popping had him turning in time to see Caitlin taking a swig right from one of the bottles of wine. She swiped her forearm over her mouth and offered him the bottle.

He took it, but instead of drinking from it, he set it down out of her reach. "What's going on, Cat?"

She sighed and seemed to relax slightly at his use of her nickname. "Nothing."

"Come on," he said. "You're never anything but calm and in charge."

"Calm? I'm not calm. Name one time I've been calm."

That was an easy one for him. "The day your parents started fostering me. Even though at seventeen you were only one year older than me, you still took me by the hand and told me that I was yours now and that it was all going to be okay." He shook his head at the memory. "I was shaking in my boots."

She snorted. "You've never shaken in your boots, not a single day of your life."

She was wrong. He'd been given up at age two. CPS had rehomed and rehomed him like he was a dog at the shelter. Not a puppy, because everyone wanted a puppy, but a complete-with-disciplinary-problems adolescent dog.

No one ever wanted to keep those.

By the time he'd landed at the Walsh house, he'd been scared plenty, his biggest fear being that people would always be able to walk away from him. "Shaking in my boots," he repeated. "But not you. You commandeered my stuff and unpacked me even though I never unpack, anywhere. Before I knew what was happening, you took me apart—just like my backpack—and civilized me."

Maze snorted. She'd hitched herself up and was sitting on the counter, taking a swig out of the forgotten wine bottle. Her hair was longer than it'd ever been, falling past her shoulders in wild fiery-red waves that were as uncontained as the woman herself. She was in faded Levi's that fit like a second skin and some seriously hot boots, both showing off her mile-long legs. Her soft scoop-necked tee said: SHE BELIEVED SHE COULD, BUT SHE WAS REALLY TIRED SO SHE DIDN'T.

Everything about her sitting there with a *dare me* expression on her face teased at his memories of her. He might've been moved by that, but she'd been one of those who'd been able to walk away from him.

"'Civilized'?" she echoed, brows raised.

"Okay, so 'civilized' is probably a stretch," he admitted. "Human then. She made me human. Michael too. He used to make me hold his hand, told me he was nervous about whatever it was we were doing. Didn't realize until years later that I was the shaky one and he had my back. At nine." His voice thickened. "He had a way of reaching right inside someone and squeezing their heart for every emotion in it."

Cat drew a deep, shaky breath and nodded.

Thinking about Michael was hard enough. Speaking about him was almost impossible, and Walker too had to take a deep breath. "Actually, you all made me human."

"Same," Maze whispered. "You've done so much for us, Cat, always. But something's wrong, I can feel it. I want to help."

"You've had a funny way of showing it."

Maze looked stricken for a beat, then nodded, owning it. "I know," she said quietly. "I've got a lot to make up for, so please let me."

Cat sighed. "No, it's fine. I'm fine. I mean, am I overreacting to everything and wanting to kill people? Yes. Do I maybe need professional help? Also yes. But I'm a stressed-out bride, so whatever." She pointed at Walker. "You. You never seem to show when you're angry or frustrated and never overreact about anything. What's your secret?"

His secret wasn't any secret at all. For most of his younger years, showing anything had brought him nothing but trouble. "Anger and frustration are unproductive emotions," he said. "Let them go."

"Seriously? That's it? That doesn't help me at all."

"Because you've never let go of anything," he said.

Cat tossed up her hands in frustration. "Duh."

He let out a low laugh. "Try this. When you feel yourself ramping up, count to five. Chances are, you'll have lost the murderous urge by then."

"One, two, three, four, five," she said quickly, and then shook her head. "Nope, I still want to shake you both."

Walker shrugged. "Better than wanting to kill us."

Maze looked surprised. And insulted. "Us? What have we done?"

"I'm not sure," Caitlin said, "but something was going on when I walked in here. It seemed like you were about to fight."

Walker knew better than to react, but Maze couldn't seem to help herself. For all she'd been through—and she'd been through a lot, through hell, even more so than him—she still wore her heart on her sleeve, which was maybe his favorite thing about her. She sucked in a breath, then seemed to realize that she'd given herself away with the sound, so she rolled her eyes.

"Nothing's going on with me, but you're right." She jabbed her thumb in his direction. "He's been annoying since he arrived."

Walker laughed; he couldn't help it. "You do know that you still wrinkle your nose when you lie, right?"

Maze rubbed her nose and glared at him.

"See, neither of you is denying it," Caitlin said, hands on hips. "Something's wrong. I don't know what it is, but I want it fixed. *Now.* Before my wedding. You can consider it one of my wedding presents, but to be clear, I still want real presents."

"This is ridiculous," Maze said. "There's nothing—"

"Maze, you can't even look at him. And he hasn't *stopped* looking at you."

So much for being stoic and impenetrable. But she was right. He couldn't stop looking at Maze. Mostly because he wanted to wrap his hands around her neck. Sometimes he also wanted to squeeze. But other times he just wanted to slide those hands north into her hair. Or south, to slowly peel her out of those sexy jeans and remind her why they'd been magic together the one time she'd let her walls down with him.

Since he couldn't do any of that, he shook his head at Caitlin. "This weekend's about you, not us."

"That's right," Maze chimed in, backing him up. Which, for the record, she'd never done before. Typically, she'd argue with him even if he said the sky was blue. He was pretty sure she enjoyed it.

And once upon a time, he'd enjoyed it too.

A lot.

Maze hopped off the counter and headed to the door. "I'll just go check on the others—oomph," she said as she ran into Jace. Heather was right on his heels, holding Sammie.

Jace caught Maze and used the excuse to wrap his arms around her. Not surprising, since the guy was her boyfriend. But what *was* surprising was that Maze jumped, like she wasn't used to being touched by him.

Interesting.

"Aw," Heather said to Maze. "You two are a cute couple. Have you been together long?"

"A year," Maze said, at the exact same time Jace said, "A week."

Awkward silence.

"He means a year," Maze said, her nose wrinkling.

Jace smiled easily. "Right. How time flies . . ."

Sammie let out a stream of cheerful baby garble, and Walker suddenly felt almost cheerful too. Because if

Jace was really Maze's boyfriend, Walker would eat his own shorts.

Dillon came into the kitchen, followed by a parade of Roly and Poly trotting along behind him, all three looking surprised to find the room full.

Roly and Poly immediately circled Sammie, sniffing at her—probably because she smelled like banana and had Cheerios stuck to her pants.

"What's for dinner?" Dillon asked.

"Whatever you're cooking yourself," Walker said.

Dillon laughed. "Like Caitlin would let me cook in her kitchen."

"*Piz!*" Sammie yelled.

Roly and Poly both squealed in terror, eyes bugging out as they turned tail and ran out of the room as fast as they could, which, due to the fact that they couldn't get purchase on the linoleum floor with their paws, wasn't all that fast. Roly—or was it Poly?—fell over like a tipped cow, legs straight up in the air.

Walker scooped up and righted the little guy and got a snort for a thank-you.

"She means pizza," Heather translated for Sammie. "It's the only food she approves of. Nobody judge me, all right? You'll see when you have kids, this gig is not for the faint of heart."

Dillon took in Sammie with her wild hair, banana-streaked face, and sticky hands and grimaced. Walker was surprised he didn't go running out of the room like his "babies" had.

"You're not going to have kids?" Heather asked Dillon.

"Of course we are," Caitlin said. "We can't wait. It's on our life list."

"Maybe just not any time soon," Dillon said.

Caitlin blinked in surprise, and the silence fell as hard as Roly just had.

Heather turned awkwardly to Maze. "What about you and Jace?"

Maze looked like she might be allergic to the question, but Jace came through for her, giving an easy laugh as he gently squeezed her in a one-armed hug. "She's shy about it because she's been to one of my family dinners. Five siblings, lots of bickering. It'd send anyone running screaming into the night."

The thing about getting to know someone when you were kids was that you got to know them on a level you couldn't easily achieve as adults. Add in ugly childhoods and a shockingly traumatic event that forever changed your lives, and the connection deepened whether you liked it or not. Walker knew Maze. She was as tough as they came. *Nothing* scared her.

"I'm sorry," Caitlin said, shaking her head. "But . . ." She looked at Dillon. "'Not any time soon'?"

"We're a little busy right now, don't you think?"

"Only until the wedding."

Dillon looked pained. "Maybe this is a topic for another time. Without an audience."

Caitlin nodded, but looked deeply unsettled. She tried to recover, though, Walker could tell. She turned to Sammie, smiled, and opened her arms.

Sammie ran right at her, and Caitlin beamed—until Sammie passed her by and leaped at Walker, crashing into his legs, giving him a fiercely intense command in baby speak, using both her voice and *gimme* hands.

Caitlin sighed.

"She'll come around," Heather promised.

Walker gave in to the demands of the cutest little tyrant on the planet and scooped her into his arms.

Sammie sweetly patted his cheeks with her sticky hands.

Two-plus years ago he'd stopped in on Heather and found her pregnant, exhausted, and clearly at the end of her rope. He'd ended up staying a few days, filling her fridge and cabinets with food, taking care of things while she caught up on sleep. He'd continued to visit whenever he could, sometimes just being an extra adult in a very tiny and very overwhelmed apartment.

So yeah, Sammie felt comfortable around him and vice versa. She gave a sigh and laid her head on his shoulder, smelling like bananas and hopes and dreams. He rarely allowed himself the luxury of hopes and dreams—hadn't for a long, long time. But he found himself pulling her tiny body to his, dropping his jaw to the top of her head, and closing his eyes just for a beat, wondering what it might be like to have kids of his own and be a positive force in their lives in a way he'd never had himself.

Maze watched Sammie completely melt against Walker and felt herself react to the look on his face, a soft expression she'd never seen on him before. "She knows you," she said, doing her best to keep the jealously out of her voice.

He didn't respond. Maybe because Sammie had gone back to playfully patting his face with her chubby hands, specifically his mouth. Maze would bet her last dollar that little Sammie was enjoying the feel of his scruffy jaw, or maybe the game he made out of pretending to bite her fingers so she'd squeal in delight.

Tired of waiting for the answer he was clearly not going to give her, Maze turned to Heather for an explanation.

"I couldn't have made it these past few years without him," Heather said. "He'd somehow just magically show up when I needed something. Money, a shoulder to cry on, someone to talk me off the ledge."

Caitlin looked as devastated as Maze felt. "But . . . I called, I texted, I emailed . . . you'd gone dark and I couldn't reach you at all. I finally got the gist—you didn't want contact. But I swear, if I'd known, I'd have been there in a heartbeat, no matter what."

Maze took Heather's hand. "I *didn't* call, text, or email, and that's on me. But if I'd been able to get out of my own way enough to hear what was going on in your life, I'd have been there too."

"It's not on you, not on either of you." Heather shook her head. "I couldn't . . . I couldn't tell either of you. I'd made a huge mess out of my life, and it all fell apart, completely. I was ashamed and needed to handle it on my own. But the truth is, I *wasn't* handling it. I was sinking. And then Walker just showed up one day and did his usual strong, silent thing, taking care of whatever needed to be taken care of, whether I wanted help or not."

Cat looked at Walker. "You should've told me."

"No," Heather said quickly. "I made him promise on Michael's grave that he wouldn't. I'm sorry, I really am, but I needed to grow up—without you guys at my back, fixing my mistakes."

Maze hated that Heather had been so alone. Hated even more that it had happened because she had been selfishly down her *own* rabbit hole. "I'm sorry," she said softly. "I failed you. I won't let that happen again."

"*We* won't let that happen again," Caitlin said firmly.

Heather nodded, eyes suspiciously bright. "Me either."

Cat turned on Walker and punched him in the arm. "Ow!" she said, shaking out her hand. "Dammit. You're a brick wall."

"I taught you how to hit," he told her. "You can't tuck your thumb in like that. And set your feet and put your weight into it."

Cat hit him again, the right way. "That's for not telling me what Heather was going through."

"Not my story to tell."

Sammie was squirming to be free, so Walker set her down. Again Cat held out her arms to the little girl, but Sammie shook her head and yelled, "I'm this many!" She held up three fingers, dropping a small stuffed giraffe she'd just picked up.

Heather shook her head. "She's not three, she just likes to say it. She's two and a half, and yeah, the math adds up to me being pregnant at Michael's gravesite. I planned on telling all of you there, but everything blew up so quickly, and before I knew it, so much time had gone by that I was too embarrassed."

Maze picked up the giraffe off the floor. "So there was one last secret," Maze murmured.

"Yes." Heather winced. "I'm sorry."

Maze shook her head. "No. You don't owe me an apology. Ever. This was on all of us."

Sammie was staring up at Maze with Heather's pretty brown eyes. She had her mama's expressive smile too.

"She's so sweet, and she looks just like you." Maze didn't know much about kids, but this one drew her in, probably because she was Heather's and therefore all of theirs. She held out the giraffe to Sammie.

The little girl looked at her very seriously, clearly not a fan of strangers. But this was something Maze understood all too well, so she just smiled.

"It's okay. Whenever you're ready."

And like melting butter, Sammie shifted close and took the giraffe with a shy smile.

Caitlin sighed. "Seriously? *Everyone* always likes me. What am I doing wrong?"

"You're trying too hard. And you," Maze said to Sammie, "are as pretty as your mama, you know that?"

Sammie nodded, making them all laugh.

Dillon headed to the fridge. "So glad Caitlin wasn't the only one holding a secret. For the record, I was totally against hers. I told her she needed to tell you guys that the wedding's not this weekend but *next* weekend."

Everyone froze—except Caitlin, that is. She swiveled her head so fast that Maze got dizzy just looking at her as she glared at her fiancé. "Oh my God. Are you kidding me?"

Dillon looked around at their shocked faces and gave a low laugh. "You didn't tell them yet? Babe, they need to know for their jobs if they're going to stay all of next week like you want."

"Wow," Caitlin said. "You suck at apologies."

"Wait." Maze shook her head. "*What?*"

"She wanted you guys here for the whole week," Dillon said. "Her hope was to"—he used air quotes here—"'re-create the good old days.'"

"Do you want to know my hope for you?" Cat asked him with venom dripping off her overly sweet tone. "It's that you'll be uncomfortable on the couch tonight."

With a drawn-out sigh, Dillon grabbed a container of something from the fridge, then a fork from a drawer, and walked out.

"He's kidding, right?" Heather asked.

Caitlin drew a deep breath. "No. Look, I'm sorry. I know it's selfish and a big ask, but I wanted time with you guys before the wedding insanity began. Just us, like it used to be, for the whole week before the circus."

"Circus?" Heather asked. "You mean your wedding?"

"That," Cat said.

Huh. Interesting word choice for supposedly the best day of a woman's life, Maze thought, and from the look on Walker's face, he felt the same.

"But it's not just us," he said. "You've got Dillon, Heather has Sammie, and Maze has . . . Joe."

"Jace," Jace said.

Maze glared at Walker. "And what about who *you* brought—your bad attitude."

"Huh," he said, nodding. "You know what? It really is suddenly starting to feel like the good old days."

Maze shook her head at Caitlin. "You should've told us."

"Really?" Cat asked. "Look me in the eye and say you'd have come for a whole week, Ms. Apparently Has Forgotten How to Use Her Phone."

Maze shifted guiltily. "You could've tried it anyway."

"You do realize you never come home anymore, right?"

"Yes, because *I'm* the one who blew us all up."

"Wrong." Caitlin grabbed her hands and squeezed until Maze looked at her. "But if you're so intent on taking blame, fine. Take the blame for starting the fight at Michael's grave. But it was a highly emotional day, Maze. Someone was bound to light the fire. And whatever, we've had a million fights. It never mattered because we're always still a unit. But you used it as an excuse to back off. So yeah, I did what I had to in order to get you here, and now you're staying and that's that."

"I can't just stay, Cat. I've got to work this next week."

"But your boss is right here." Caitlin pointed at Jace. "You don't even have to call him since he's also your boyfriend."

Maze squelched her grimace. "How did *you* get the week off?" she asked, misdirecting. "Your boss is the Grinch."

"Yes, and she's calling every hour on the hour asking for stuff, even though this is personal leave, not paid leave. I'm dealing with it."

Heather bit her lower lip. "I work two part-time jobs, one waitressing, one doing some accounting under the table for a bookie." She was a tech genius. Even back at nine years old, she could hack into anything. She was a wiz . . . with very little actual drive. "I could maybe get the time off, but Sammie . . . well, she's not nearly as easy as she is cute. I couldn't burden you all with her for a whole week."

"Neither of you is a burden," Caitlin said. She looked at Walker.

He shook his head. "I can't stay either."

He didn't give a reason. While Maze wondered about that, Caitlin threw herself at the back door, arms spread wide to keep them inside. "Okay, now you all listen to me. I'm having a bad bridal moment here. I can't find shoes for my wedding dress. Dillon's aunt threw me a bridal shower and all the gifts are at Dillon's mom's house, which means I have to go over there and see her to get them. She's going to ask me if I'm stress eating. And yes, FYI, I'm definitely stress eating. In fact, I ate *all* the things and I'm not sure I'll fit into my wedding dress, *and* I've got a zit on the end of my nose making me look like the Wicked Witch of the West." She paused. "Or is it the east?" She shook her head. "It doesn't matter! None of it matters if you guys are with me. You're all damn well staying because I'm already doing this without Michael. I won't do it without you too, you hear me? I can't do this without you. I *can't!*" She exhaled deeply, smoothed her hair, and straightened her shoulders. "Now. Who besides me needs a drink?" She turned to the bottles lined up on the counter.

Heather looked at Walker, eyes wide, brows up.

He shook his head. The man could say more with a head shake than anyone Maze had ever met. It could mean *don't worry,* or *it's not worth the argument,* or *I've got this.* Maze was pretty sure that this particular head shake meant the last one, because he stepped closer to Caitlin and took her hand. "Hey," he said to her softly. "It's going to be okay."

"No, it's not!"

It wasn't like she was screaming, but . . . it was definitely an outside voice, which was shocking. Caitlin *never* used her outside voice and was always the epitome of calm and in control.

"Oh my God," Caitlin said when they all just stared at her. "I'm allowed to lose my shit, you know! I'm allowed the bridal moment that all the books say I'm entitled to!"

Walker put his hands on her shoulders. "First," he said, "breathe."

Wrapping her hands around his wrists, Caitlin stared into his eyes. "One, two, three, four, five . . . Nope." She shook her head. "I can't go on unless you're staying. *All* of you. We used to be BFFs, remember? Because I do. I remember everything." Her eyes filled. "But at the moment, I don't feel like I have any BFFs at all, and I hate that. I miss you guys, dammit. And the least you could do is *pretend* to miss me just as much."

Maze's chest went tight and she stepped to Walker's side to face the woman she wanted back as her BFF as well, even though she didn't deserve her after failing her so badly. "We're staying," she said, ignoring the feel of Walker's surprised gaze on her. "We'll stay as long as you need."

"We will?" Heather asked.

"Yes," Maze said.

"Okay," Heather agreed, nodding like a bobblehead. "We will."

Maze looked at Walker.

The man wasn't afraid of much. Maybe nothing, and certainly not her. But she gave him her hardest *do this* gaze, and apparently even he knew when to go up against her and when to let the tide take him. "Yeah," he said. "We're staying."

Maze nodded at him. Then she turned back to Caitlin. "Do I still have the crazy eyes?" Caitlin asked.

"No," Maze said.

A total lie. Caitlin definitely still had the crazy eyes, and Maze got it. Cat was afraid they'd all take off on her, as if any of them could. She'd held them together all these years single-handedly, and Maze knew they'd be nothing without Caitlin Walsh.

Which meant whatever the bride wanted, whatever she needed, Maze would do. She'd make this right; she'd give everything she had, which admittedly wasn't much. "Where's your lip gloss? You're never without lip gloss."

"In my pocket," Caitlin whispered.

Maze pulled it from Cat's pocket and handed it to her. "Time to get it together, babe. We're all right here and not going anywhere."

Caitlin gripped Maze's arms, eyes a little wild. "Promise?"

"Promise on Michael's grave," she whispered.

"Okay then." Caitlin let out a shaky breath and nodded. "We're going to need more wine from the cellar."

Of that, Maze had no doubt.

Chapter 4

Caitlin's to-do list:
—Get Sammie to love me.
—Stop going to the kitchen in the middle
of the night to forage.
—Buy wedding shoes that will make me
look gorgeous and confident.

For the first time in weeks, Caitlin woke up without heartburn. This was due to two reasons. First, her house was full of her people. Sure, she'd had to trick them into being here, and Dillon had almost blown everything by outing her the way he had, but everyone had called off work for the next week.

Surprisingly, Dillon was reason number two. Last night, he'd started off on the couch, but somewhere around the time she'd brewed Sleepytime tea to help get sleepy, and which she might've added her last swig of brandy to, he'd shown up in the kitchen, said, "The couch sucks because you're not on it," and then promised to go to the store and buy her more alcohol in the morning. He'd probably buy the wrong stuff, but he was trying and that meant something. So had the way he'd kissed her as if he could do that for the rest of his life.

Nights like that reminded her of why she loved him.

She tried to roll over but couldn't. Opening her eyes, she realized the answer for that. Roly was on her chest and Poly on her legs. She couldn't feel her toes. She tried to move the dogs, but somehow they'd turned themselves into tiny sacks of cement, as always refusing to budge until their master, Lord Dillon, awoke and told them it was time to eat. "Dillon," she said. "Help, I'm trapped."

Dillon stretched and opened his dark eyes, taking in the problem in an instant. He chuckled warmly, and the tender amusement in his gaze made her toes curl. With a kiss to her nose, he said, "Time for breakfast, babies."

The pugs replied with snuffles and snorts, wriggling in sheer pleasure as he scooped them off of Caitlin and gently plopped them on the floor.

"That should buy us a few minutes," he said, and pulled her to him. "Hey."

"Hey."

With a sexy smile she'd never managed to resist, he pinned her beneath him. "I liked that look in your eyes," he murmured. "What are you thinking about?"

"Wishing that we could live our life right here in bed, since it's where we get along the best."

She smiled to soften the words, but he didn't smile back. In fact, he rolled off her onto his back with a heavy sigh.

"I'm not still mad at you," she said.

"Maybe I'm still mad at you."

She blinked and came up on an elbow. "What? Why? You're the one who almost screwed everything up."

"And you never do?"

"Hey, I'm a delight. Ask anyone."

He snorted and sat up too, shoving his fingers through his hair. "My mom said you haven't called her back. She's left three messages for you."

"She wants to talk about the wedding, Dillon. Specifically the flowers, the food, and the fact that I didn't ask your cousin to be a bridesmaid. The cousin who hates me almost as much as your mom does."

"Neither of them hates you."

"Your mom thinks this is her wedding and wants to do what she wants, not what I want."

He sighed. "Maybe you could just give in on something? Anything?"

She gaped at him. "She wants roses at the ceremony, which I'm allergic to. She also wants an open bar—something we can't afford because we both decided on an expensive honeymoon to Bali instead. And your cousin is *not* going to be in the wedding. Hello, she tried to set you up with her best friend."

"That was before she knew I was serious about you."

"It was last month!" Caitlin took a deep breath. The two of them had been bickering so much lately, and here they were, doing it again before they'd even brushed their teeth. She exhaled slowly. "I'm sorry, but your mom finds fault with everything I do, and then she tells you about it and it puts a strain on us. She hasn't liked me from day one, when she learned I didn't finish college."

"Okay, so maybe she thought you were looking for your M.R.S. degree at first," he admitted.

"My what?"

He grimaced, like he wished he'd kept his mouth shut. "She thought your career goals were to be *Mrs.* Dillon Beckman."

Caitlin stared at him. "Is that what you think?"

"No." He sighed. "But I wish you'd find a career job, so you're happy with your work like I am."

Needing to be *not* naked for this conversation, she got out of bed and pulled on the pj's he'd stripped her out of last night. "I love what I do, Dillon."

He snorted. "You love making sandwiches?"

"Wow. Okay," she said slowly, suddenly mad all over again. "First of all, I make a lot more than sandwiches. And second, I get that it's nothing high-powered like what you do, but cooking fulfills me. You know that."

"You're managing a deli and have a boss who micro-manages *you*, even when you're not at work. You complain about that job all the time. We both know you could do better for yourself. I thought you wanted to do better."

She paused, unable to deny a lot of that. "Is that why you told everyone you don't want kids right now, because I don't have the right job to please your family? Because you've never said that before. Kids are on your list, and you led me to believe it's something you wanted too."

"We're just not in a place to have kids yet."

Her heart sank. "Since when? We have dogs. How much harder can a baby be?"

"Babe . . . babies are expensive and require plan-ning. We haven't even started. First we need to create our retirement fund, build an education fund, beef up our savings accounts, and buy a house. And with me the only one bringing in any substantial money, that isn't going to happen any time soon."

Okay, don't overreact. You've jumped on him and it's early. He hates early. He hates anything before his req-uisite five-mile run, shower, and coffee. But apparently, she couldn't help herself. "My parents had me early and they never regretted a thing."

"I'm not sure I want a big, crazy houseful like you had. Kids coming and going, and don't even try to tell me that your parents prioritizing saving all the foster kids in the land didn't affect you. You're upending your life for them—still."

She chewed on that for a moment. "I know you don't understand this, but my parents felt they had enough love and resources to make a difference, and they did. And I'd hoped to do the same."

"You can't save the world, Cat."

Maybe not, but she could save the people in her orbit. "So is that list of yours just generic then, or specific to me?" she asked.

"What difference does it make?"

"A *huge* difference," she said.

He got out of the bed and pulled on sweats.

"Are you going somewhere?" she asked.

"I need caffeine to deal with you. Lots of it."

"Dillon."

With a sigh, he turned back.

"We're getting married in eight days," she said softly. "Now would be a good time to tell me that you've changed your mind."

"I haven't changed my mind," he said. "On anything."

She looked into his eyes and had to admit, he was right. It was her. She was the one who'd pushed the relationship into serious territory, then further pushed for a ring. She was the one who'd pushed for all of it, and yet somehow she felt like she was the one just being carried downstream for this wedding. Yes, she'd wanted to be Dillon's wife, but she'd also wanted to elope to Bali, not just honeymoon there. Just the two of them, without his family's influence. But his mother, a widow, had had very different plans for her only son.

And then, instead of using her backbone, or even slowing down the momentum, she'd jumped into the wedding plans with both feet, focusing on how it would reunite her with Maze and Heather and get them back into her life. No one could refuse a wedding, right?

And here she was . . .

"Look," Dillon said, not unkindly, "I don't want to argue. We're both under a lot of stress with the wedding, and the full house here is adding even more pressure. I think it's just too early for this. It's too early for anything, unless"—his face softened—"you're feeling like a repeat of last night?"

She gave him an *are you kidding me?* look, and he gave a low, mirthless laugh.

"Right. No way in hell." He headed for the door. "Need to clear my head, babe. Going on a run."

Chapter 5

Walker's man of honor to-do list:
—Don't kill the groom. Or the maid of honor.

At breakfast, Walker watched—and found himself reluctantly impressed by—Maze. She'd made Caitlin hand over the wedding to-do list, saying that as the maid of honor, she'd make sure everything got done. He was even more impressed when Caitlin did, with only one demand of her own: that they all take this one day for fun first and go on a family hike.

Which was exactly what Caitlin's parents had done with the lot of them that summer. Walker hadn't appreciated the outing then, the one that had forced them into acting like a family. In fact, he'd resented the hell out of it.

At first.

But it'd taken a shockingly short amount of time for him to fall for Caitlin's parents and want them as his own. Shelly had fed him home-cooked meals and Jim had taken him to ball games with Michael, and for the first time in his life, he'd belonged. He'd spent the best year of his life with them up until the house had burned to the ground . . .

. . . killing Michael in the process.

All of their lives had been plunged into chaos. The Walshes had to relocate and needed time to grieve and put their lives back together. Because that had involved staying in a hotel at first, then renting a smaller place until they could get back on their feet, CPS had taken the fosters. That had scattered him and Heather and Maze far and wide. Under normal circumstances, they probably wouldn't have seen one another again. But Caitlin and her parents had treated them as part of the family, taking them everywhere, ensuring that they knew they were important, even vital, to the core group, each of them, and as a result, they'd become important and vital to each other. Going through the tragedy of the fire together had only deepened that unbreakable bond, and the ragtag motley crew had fought to stay in one another's lives.

Until three years ago at Michael's grave.

Now, for better or worse, Caitlin had gathered them together again. After breakfast, they all stood on the back porch applying sunscreen. February in California had the potential to be the best weather for the whole year. Today was no exception at a sunny seventy-eight degrees. Cat came at Walker with a can of sunscreen and sprayed him until he felt like a greased-up pig. "Stop."

"You never protect yourself."

Actually, he *always* protected himself. Grabbing the can, he returned the favor, laughing when she squealed at the icy coldness of the spray. "Payback's a bitch," he said, and turned to help Heather with Sammie, but Jace was already there. Stepping off the porch, Walker found Maze staring at him. "What?"

She shook her head.

"Come on," he said. "I'm giving you a free pass here. Talk."

"Wow, a free pass. Those used to be sacred."

When he'd first landed in the Walsh home at age sixteen, a fifteen-year-old Maze had already been there for a few weeks. She'd been feisty and mouthy, and he'd been drawn to that from the start. Then one night he'd heard whimpering and had followed the heartbreaking sounds to Maze's bedroom. He'd flipped on the light, but her bed had been empty. Another soft whimper had led him to the closet, where he'd found her cowering in a laundry basket. He'd coaxed her out by offering her a free pass—anything she wanted—if she'd tell him what was wrong.

She'd taken the free pass and given him some bullshit story about being afraid of storms. She wasn't afraid of storms—she *loved* storms—but he'd let her have the lie, and in return she'd given him all of her chores for the week.

There'd been many more "free passes" over that year, mostly relating to covering each other's asses when they'd found trouble, which they'd done readily enough.

But she'd never told him what really haunted her. Truth was, she hadn't had to. He'd found her in the midst of enough nightmares to put her broken words together with what he knew of her past—that she'd been removed from her mom's custody because of a string of abusive boyfriends.

Maze had learned to hide in closets for a damn good reason. It'd killed him then, and still did.

"A free pass," he said again now. "Whatever you want. Just tell me what's wrong."

"All right." She drew a deep breath. "I want to know why you clearly managed to keep in touch with Caitlin and Heather and not . . ." Breaking off, she looked away.

He shifted to see her face. "And not you?"

"You know what? Never mind." She turned to move off, but he pulled her back around to face him.

"Do you remember what your last words were to me?" he asked.

"'Fuck you'?" she asked sweetly.

He smiled grimly. "Close. You told me to stay the hell away from you."

"I didn't mean literally."

He arched a brow. "Noted. But you need to be very careful what you say to me, Maze. We're grown-ups now. I'm going to always take you at your word."

She looked away. "What if only one of us is an actual grown-up?"

He smiled. "You missed me."

She snorted. "You're about to get a repeat of my so-called last words to you."

"You missed me," he said again. "And for the record, I missed you too. And now *I* get a question."

"That was *not* part of the bargain. *I'd* never be stupid enough to give *you* a free pass."

"Humor me. Please?"

The "please" seemed to boggle her, and he got it. He rarely allowed himself to show vulnerability. There were only a few people who could expose that side of him, and they were all here, stuck together at the lake for a week. "Fine," she said. "One question."

"Why did you stay away from Caitlin and Heather so long?"

"I discovered I'm easier taken in small doses."

That gave him a pang for her. "Maze—"

"Hey, let's go," Caitlin called out. She headed across the front yard to the small trail that wound around the lake.

And like good little minions, everyone followed.

A light breeze had chased away all the clouds so that nothing marred the eye-popping blue sky. The trail was rocky but flat, and dry foliage crunched beneath their feet as they moved along the water's edge. Maze was in front of Walker in a pair of black shorts that showed off her sexy long legs, every single inch of which he'd once taken his mouth on a tour of. She wore a tight white tank top and an oversized plaid button-down tied at the waist, exposing some skin between that and the waistband of her shorts every time she moved, which was all the time because Maze was in constant motion. She was frying his brain cells left and right, and he'd like to not think about her at all, but apparently that was beyond his control.

It helped that Jace walked alongside her. Whether he was her boyfriend or not, she wasn't available, and that was absolutely the best thing for both of them.

Caitlin was wearing a huge backpack like she was going on a five-day wilderness excursion. There was a weight to her shoulders that spoke of more than just the weight of whatever she was carrying. Dillon walked at her side, coaxing Roly and Poly along, both of whom were lagging on their leashes.

"Come on, babies. I know you guys can get your little booties up to this beach," he said when they stopped, refusing to walk farther. He crouched down and looked them in the eyes. "We talked about this. I can't carry you around all the time."

They snorted and whined, and with a laugh, he scooped them up, tucking one beneath each arm. "Roly, man, you're getting . . . *roly.*"

The pug wheezed and licked his face.

Walker lifted the backpack from Caitlin's shoulders. "What the hell's in here? Rocks?"

"It's everything but the kitchen sink," Dillon said. "But she likes to be prepared, and God help anyone who wants to help her."

"Because I can do it myself," Caitlin said, playing tug-of-war with Walker for the pack.

"But you don't have to," Walker said.

"Dude, don't even try." Dillon sighed, set the dogs down, and swooped up the backpack from both of them. "I've got it."

Caitlin huffed out a breath, took the leashes from Dillon's hand, and marched off in front of them.

"She's stubborn," Walker said.

"You think?"

The lake was a deep blue, dotted with whitecaps flashing with each swell. A few boats were scattered across the water. Winter fishing was a big sport here. Halfway around the lake, they came to a place Walker remembered well: a small cove, complete with a tire swing hanging from an ancient, gnarled, beautiful oak.

"Wa-wa!" Sammie yelled, pointing to the lake.

"Yes, baby, *water*," Heather said, "but we're not going swimming today. The water's chilly."

Sammie nodded sagely.

Roly plopped onto the sand and stared at the water lapping about ten feet from him. Poly barked once and ran straight for the water, not stopping when he hit it, plowing into it.

And vanished.

Everyone gasped. Dillon stood at the water's edge. "Poly!" he yelled.

Nothing.

Walker started for the water, but Maze was already there, running past Dillon. In up to her thighs, she looked down, reached beneath the water, and came up with Poly.

"Oh my God," Caitlin said as Maze strode out of the water, drenched. "Thank you! Dillon, she saved Poly!"

Dillon took Poly from Maze and, in a move that seemed to shock everyone, hugged Maze tight with his free arm. "Thank you," he said, and kissed her on top of her head.

Maze, never comfortable with affection, not to mention feelings, didn't seem to know what to do with herself. Walker might have laughed, except she was now shrugging out of the damp plaid overshirt, leaving her in that equally damp white tank top, which had him feeling things no one should be feeling at a family picnic. Stripping out of his sweatshirt, he tossed it to her and got a few seconds of enjoyment watching her try to decide between her pride and freezing her ass off. In the end, she pulled on his sweatshirt, and damn, she looked good in it.

"Time for food!" Caitlin declared with an overabundance of cheer that had Walker taking a second look at her. "Just give me a few minutes to set up," she said.

When Caitlin needed a minute, it was usually to give herself a time-out in order to avoid bloodshed. Walker headed over to where she was setting up a rather elaborate picnic. "What's up?"

Caitlin downed a glass of wine. "Nothing."

"You're running around like a chicken without a head trying to please everyone, and you're day drinking. So try again."

Even though she didn't have anywhere near the same life experience he did, Caitlin had always treated him like she was the big sister. She was the warmest, sweetest person he'd ever met and had come into his life during a time when he hadn't known much warmth or sweetness. He'd never felt anything but gratitude and a brotherly sense of protectiveness for her, and that shit went deep with him. Soul deep. She was his family for life, and he'd do anything for her.

Same for Heather.

He glanced at the third musketeer. Maze was a different story. Not that he wouldn't throw himself in front of a train for her, because he would. But if she wanted his heart and soul . . . well, they weren't available. She'd already had them.

And destroyed them.

"Done," Caitlin said, gesturing to the spread. "Think it's okay?"

She'd thought of everything, including Dillon's favorite beer, Heather's favorite cookies, and a container of dry cereal in which Sammie was already up to her elbows. Pieces of the cereal were stuck to her cheeks and chin.

"Delicious?" Walker asked the kid.

She beamed at him and drooled. Heather laughed and kissed her baby's face all over, much to Sammie's utter delight. Caitlin tried to join in the fun and Sammie's smile faded.

"Honestly," Caitlin said, and *that* made Sammie laugh.

Maze and Jace were sitting on an old log sharing a sandwich, looking annoyingly cozy. Walker tried to find something in their body language to prove his gut theory that they weren't sleeping together, but he got nothing. For the first time ever, his famed instincts failed him.

"Sorry," Caitlin said to Walker, breaking his attention. "The stuff I packed for you is far more boring. Turkey on wheat with sprouts. But don't worry, it'll keep your body pure."

Maze choked on a bite. "Sorry," she muttered, carefully not looking at him. Which was how he found his first genuine grin of the day. He sat with Sammie, and though she offered to share her cereal, he passed and ate his sandwich.

A bit later, he saw Maze by herself sitting on the tire swing, staring out at the water.

Because he couldn't seem to help himself, he followed. When he was at her back, he took a hold of the swing and gave her a gentle nudge.

"That all you got?" she asked, and threw her weight into it so she went higher.

"You do know you don't always have to go five hundred miles an hour, right?"

She flashed him a look as she swung by him. "And right back at you."

Touché. "I saw that you won that bartending competition in San Francisco," he said.

She leaned back, her feet up to the sky as she pumped for more speed. "And you saw that where?" she asked.

He shrugged. "After the five hundredth time that Facebook recommended we be friends, I decided to check it out and see what you were up to."

"You keeping tabs on me, Walk?"

Actually, he'd kept track of all of them; it was a part of his obsessive need to keep safe the few people who had keys to his heart. Maze had been a challenge, since he'd had to do his protective thing from afar and quietly. Of all of them, not only wouldn't she thank him for watching out for her, she'd be pissed off. And it bugged the hell out of him that she'd been content to have nothing to do with him at all, when he felt the opposite.

She'd been broken when Michael died. Broken when he'd stupidly married her *far* before she'd been ready for any such thing. And broken three years ago when she'd walked away from all of them rather than face down her pride and admit she needed anyone. "Yeah," he said. "I've kept tabs on you."

She held his gaze for a long beat, shocking the hell out of him when she nodded and quietly said, "Thanks. And I'm not just a bartender."

"I know," he said. "You're still in night school for your bachelor's degree. But even if you weren't, if there's anyone who can make being a bartender a hotshot career, it's you. Because, Maze?"

"Yeah?"

"You've never been 'just' anything in your life."

She blinked, like she didn't know what to do with the compliment. Which kind of broke his heart.

"What do you want to do after you graduate?" he asked.

"Run a bar and grill and keep bartending. I like it," she said. "But I want to be the boss. I think I'll like that even better."

He laughed and nodded.

"I got that dream from you, you know," she said softly. "You always wanted to run your own restaurant so you could feed all your people."

Funny how their dreams had aligned but not their lives. Heather and Sammie were sitting in the grass. Caitlin was feeding Dillon a bite of her sandwich. Roly and Poly were collapsed in front of their portable water bowl. Roly was asleep. Too tired to stand up, Poly lay there, chin resting on the lip of the water dish, lapping up water. Jace was sitting with them. No one was paying them any attention. "You and Jules doing okay?" he asked.

Maze snorted, then jumped off the swing. "Yeah. We're fine." And with that, she headed off to the picnic table, perusing the assortment of desserts Caitlin had brought. Walker followed and grabbed an apple and a wedge of cheese. He began cutting them up.

Diverted from the cookies, Maze paired a piece of apple with a slice of cheese. "I see what you're doing, you know." She bit into the snack. Chewed. Swallowed. "Trying to change me. Many have tried. None have succeeded."

"I wouldn't change a thing about you."

She choked on her apple and cheese, and he rubbed her back until she wheezed out an *"I'm fine!"*

"That too."

She shook her head and took another bite. He waited her out, knowing that was the only way to get her to talk. Maze didn't like silence and tended to fill it. And sure enough, she sighed and spoke. "You asked why I lost touch with Caitlin and Heather. I pulled back," she admitted. "Caitlin thinks she did something wrong, but she didn't. It was all me. I got locked into a cycle of guilt I couldn't shake."

"Maze," he said, aching for her. The fire that had taken out the Walshes' house and killed their son had begun in the basement, where the older kids had been working on their plans to sneak out.

Maze had been the ringleader on that particular adventure. Caitlin's parents had never blamed her for the fire, or for Michael's death, but she'd blamed herself. When the Walshes could no longer take on foster kids, Maze had felt abandoned. And honestly? Walker 100 percent got that, irrational as it was.

"A few months after Vegas," Maze said softly, "Caitlin threw herself a birthday party. I didn't go. I blew her off, no warning."

"Because of me," he said quietly, remembering. "Because you didn't want to see me."

She lifted a shoulder in a possible admission to that. "I didn't think about how it would affect her. It was selfish. But then, because I'm me, I made it even worse."

"How?"

"Remember Caitlin's surprise anniversary party for her parents that same year?"

He nodded.

"I was supposed to get them there. Caitlin asked me, said it was my only job."

"A pretty big job, seeing as you were estranged from them by that time," Walker said.

"It's true that we hadn't spoken much," she said. "They'd been busy rebuilding their lives, and me . . . well, I still had some things to work through. But Caitlin wanted me to do it, to make up with them. I agreed, even knowing deep down I'd only make things worse. But I picked them up . . ." She trailed off, eating the last pieces of apple and cheese.

Walker cut up some more, giving her a minute.

"We had a . . . disagreement in the car on the way to the party," she finally said. "Because that's what I do, right? Ruin things. Mayhem Maze . . . I wear the nickname well, as we all know."

He instantly felt sick that he'd ever let that nickname stick to her. "Maze—"

"I was still so angry," she said, "even though I had no right to be. They asked how I was doing. And I said . . ." She closed her eyes. "I said, 'My real parents are the only ones allowed to inquire about my life.' I said they'd given me up just like everyone else, so my life didn't concern them." She opened her eyes, and they were filled with regret and pain. "Even though of course I had no idea who my birth dad was and my mom hadn't bothered with me in years."

"You were hurting—"

"Right, and we know how much I like to share my pain." She shook her head. "But they kept it classy. Shelly said she might not be my birth mom, but she'd brought me into her house and thought of me as a daughter. Still did." Maze paused. "Which of course was one of the sweetest things I'd ever heard."

"What happened?" he asked quietly.

"I behaved predictably. I said, 'If you loved me so much, you'd have found a way to keep me.'" She shook her head. "I'll never forget the look on Shelly's face. I feel so badly about that and what came next."

"Which was?"

"When I got out of the car, I saw your truck. Vegas had only been a few months before that. We hadn't seen each other or talked, and it was like all my mistakes were in one place mocking me. So I compounded my errors and left. And then I guess they went inside, and when everyone yelled 'Happy anniversary,' Caitlin's mom burst into tears. And not the happy ones."

Walker nodded. Caitlin had been furious with Maze.

He hadn't been, because unlike Caitlin, who'd looked at this from the other side, he understood how Maze had felt, though as usual, she'd let her emotions get the best of her. Back then, she hadn't yet learned how to temper herself. But at some point, she'd clearly figured that out. She could now hide herself in plain sight.

"A few years ago, I realized only I held the power to make myself miserable about the past," she said, "but I also had the power to *stop* making myself miserable. So I reached out. They responded right away, and I tried to apologize but they wouldn't let me. They were super kind and happy to hear from me, and I was my usual weird and awkward."

"Those are two of my favorite things about you."

She snorted and he smiled.

"What did they say?"

"They wanted to meet."

"And?"

She closed her eyes. "And . . . I didn't show."

"Why?"

"Because I was overwhelmed, afraid, nervous . . . hell, I don't know, pick one."

"What were you nervous about?"

She shrugged, but he knew. She'd been nervous that she'd be rejected. She hadn't been able to trust them when they'd said it was all fine because it hadn't been fine the last time they'd said that, when they'd had to move into the hotel without the fosters. They'd promised to come back for her, for all three of them, but that hadn't happened. "I get it, Maze."

She opened her eyes and looked at him. "You do?"

"Yeah. I do. And I wish you'd stop beating yourself up for things that weren't just on you."

She took that in for a beat. "I guess I'll be seeing them at some point this week," she said uneasily.

He looked into her eyes, saw the fear. The shame. "But this time you won't be alone."

Their gazes held and he did his best to send encouraging vibes, but it wasn't his strong suit.

"I should've found a way to see them before now so it wouldn't be so uncomfortable. I blame Past Maze. Past Maze is the worst."

"No, she isn't, and neither is Present Maze."

She slid him a look. "Would you still say that if you knew that Present Maze's plan is to avoid them until the last possible moment, adding stress and anxiety to every day that goes by? I mean, it is how I operate best."

"Maze. It really will be okay."

"Easy for you to say. You don't have to face your past."

Ha. Little did she know.

Caitlin called them over and tried to get everyone involved in some games. First up was Ultimate Frisbee. She put Maze, Heather, and Walker on one team, and Dillon, herself, and Jace on the other. Then she smiled at Sammie. "Would you like to be on my team?"

Sammie shook her head.

"You know," Cat said, "one of these days I'm going to win you over. You don't know this, but when I first met Maze, she tried to resist me too."

Maze smiled. "True story."

Walker smiled too. When he'd come into the house all those years ago, Maze had been doing her damnedest to ignore Caitlin. A few weeks later, Caitlin came home from dance camp with a black eye. She'd gotten into a fight with a boy who'd been picking on some girl, and after that Maze decided Caitlin was her person for life.

"I won her over," Caitlin said to Sammie, skipping the part where she'd had to club some boy in the face to do it. "Just like I'm going to do with you."

Sammie ran back to Heather.

Caitlin sighed.

The teams went off to separate sides of the beach to strategize, and Heather eyed Maze. "We're going to play nice."

Maze studied her fingernails.

"*Maze*," Heather said.

"I'm always nice. I'm a peach!"

Walker laughed. Maze was super competitive, always had to win at any cost, and *never* played nice.

Maze pointed at him to shut it.

Heather looked at Walker. "She's not going to play nice."

Walker shook his head. "Nope."

Maze threw up her hands. "The point of a game is to win. What does that have to do with being nice?"

Heather shook her head. "We should let Caitlin win. She's so stressed."

"Letting her win isn't going to help," Maze said.

"Then what will?"

Maze scrunched her lips together like she was trying to bite back an answer not suitable for public consumption.

Again, Heather looked at Walker. "I'm counting on you to play fair because I've never known you to *not* be fair."

Maze rolled her eyes. "Don't let that pretty face fool you, he's no Boy Scout."

This was true. He was no Boy Scout.

Caitlin blew her whistle—yes, she'd brought a whistle—and the game started. Maze sent the Frisbee flying in a beautiful, perfect arc . . . and beaned Dillon right in the face. As far as throws went, it was pretty impressive. So was the blood spurt that came from Dillon's nose. But the most impressive thing of all was the sheer high pitch of the guy's scream.

When everyone stood still in shock, Walker jogged over to take a look. "Probably not broken," he said, and while Caitlin doctored Dillon up from her first-aid kit, everyone else moved back to the food, looking for dessert.

Except Maze. She remained at Walker's side while he looked over Dillon's nose.

"I'm sorry," she said softly to Dillon, eyes filled with genuine remorse as she apologized.

And here Walker had thought her in her wet tank top was the hottest thing he'd ever seen, but Maze accessing her emotions and acting on them definitely moved to first place.

Dillon waved her off. "We're even," he said, sounding very nasal. "You saved Poly."

Maze nodded and, with an unreadable look at Walker, walked off. She went straight for the cookies.

"What?" she asked defensively when he caught her double-fisting a pair of snickerdoodles.

"Those things'll kill ya."

She shrugged, like she wasn't sure she had a long life span coming anyway. "At least I'll go happy."

"Will you?"

Her eyes landed on his. "I'll have you know I'm *very* happy."

"With John."

"*Oh my God,*" she said, and narrowed her eyes at him. "You damn well know his name, you've got the memory of an elephant."

Something he wouldn't mind *not* having when it came to her, because remembering every detail was painful. "The opposite of you, apparently," he said lightly.

She scowled and went back to ignoring him.

Once Dillon stopped bleeding, the groom-to-be claimed fun lake time over, and they all began the walk back. They were spread out on the trail, Dillon and Caitlin in the lead. Dillon had the backpack this time and Caitlin had Roly and Poly on their fancy leashes. She was telling a story that was making Dillon laugh and restoring his good humor.

He really did appear to love her, Walker had to admit, at least in his own way. And who the hell was he to judge anyway, when he couldn't seem to manage the sort of intimacy that a relationship like that required.

Footsteps came up behind him, and he knew who it was without looking because his blood pressure rose. "Nice shot back there, Tex."

Maze blew out a breath. *End of conversation,* he thought. But then she slowed down so they were side by side. "I didn't mean to do that," she said.

"Your life motto."

She gave him a shoulder nudge that was really more like a shove as she passed him, which suited him just fine because . . . short shorts.

"Are you staring at my ass?" she asked.

"Yes."

She tripped over her own feet.

Heather came along and grinned at them, looking far more carefree than she had when she'd arrived yesterday. The reason for that was apparent. Jace had Sammie on his back, piggyback style.

"Look, isn't it beautiful out?" Caitlin called back, pointing to the green rolling hills. "To our right are the bluffs, where ten thousand years ago, glaciers from the ice age melted and created craters that eventually became Rainbow Lake. And if you look to our left, there's a perfect specimen of a ponderosa, can you believe it?"

Dillon laughed and hooked an arm around her neck. "She narrates like that in bed too. It's cute. 'This here is your funny bone, and then south, we come to a bone that isn't funny at all, it's perfectly hard and—'"

Maze, who'd been walking and munching on a PowerBar, made a face like she was gagging. "Hey, trying to eat here."

Jace, his palms on little Sammie's legs as he held her firmly on his shoulders, ducked a little to look into Maze's eyes. "Everything okay here?"

"Yep."

Jace took her hand and pulled her in closer. "Sure?"

Maze gave the guy a smile. "Yes, I'm sure, you goof. I'm fine."

Jace nodded, brushed a kiss over her lips, sent Walker a long gaze that held some sort of warning in it, and moved off.

Maze waited until Jace was out of earshot. "I've got a problem," she said.

The smile that crossed Walker's mouth happened all on its own. He liked Maze a lot of different ways, but whenever she had a problem, it made her good and pissed off, and a good and pissed off Maze was one of his favorites. All that defiant energy and scorching attitude really did it for him. The only thing better was Maze in his bed. Because a turned-on Maze was adventurous, curious, single-minded, generous, and holy-shit hot. "So dump him."

She blinked. "What?"

"Dump the asshole if you don't like him. Jeff seems like the kind of guy who'll move on without issue."

She rolled her eyes at the "Jeff" and shook her head. "I'm not talking about *Jace*."

He shrugged. It'd been worth a try. "Okay, so what's the problem?"

"I don't like Dillon."

"You don't like ninety-nine percent of the population."

"I'm serious, Walk."

He met her gaze. "We both know this is Caitlin's call."

Maze drew a deep breath. "Even if we think she's making a mistake?"

We. The last time they'd been a "we," she'd had his ring on her finger and he'd thought his life couldn't get more perfect. "Probably we shouldn't be throwing stones from glass houses."

Her mouth tightened at the truth of that, and they walked some more.

"I feel awful about lying low for so long," she said quietly. "I owe Heather and Caitlin both. Seeing Caitlin so stressed and on the verge of a breakdown is killing me. She did so much for us." Her eyes went fierce. "It's my turn to be the strong one. I just hope I can fake it." She pasted on a smile. "Gotta fake it to make it, right?"

"Maze, you're the strongest woman I know."

She blinked, looking so surprised that he grabbed her hand and squeezed it.

"Believe it. Because I absolutely do."

She let out a shaky breath. "I wish I could be as confident about that as you."

"Then do what you just said. Fake it until you make it. Maybe then you'll realize the truth about yourself."

"Which is?"

"You've got all the power, you always did. Once you realize it, you'll be able to do anything you want."

Chapter 6

Maze's maid of honor to-do list:
—Take Frisbee off the list of reception
  activities.

Years ago, one of Maze's favorite things to do at the lake had been to sit waterside by moonlight with a firepit warming her toes. So it felt surreal to find herself doing that very thing with the same people all these years later.

Surreal and . . . nice.

They'd made a fire on the beach and ate s'mores while listening to the tune of the water hitting the shoreline and crickets singing.

Correction: they all ate s'mores except for Walker, because his body was a temple. Trying to block the memories of how she'd once worshipped at the temple of Walker, she looked away from him and her gaze locked on Jace's. He pulled her to her feet and then off to the side. "So I'm going to go to bed to give you guys some time alone."

"You don't have to do that." She searched his gaze. "Unless you're too tired to stay up?"

He gave her a small smile. "I'm too tired to stay up."

She could hear the lie in his voice and started to say something, but he shook his head and bent to give her a sweet kiss on the lips and a look that said he'd be just upstairs if she needed him.

When she walked back to the fire, all eyes were on her. Heather's. Caitlin's.

Walker's . . .

"What?" she said. "Never seen a couple kiss good night before? And who's bogarting the marshmallows?"

"I remember the last time we did this," Heather said. "Coyotes came down from the hill and were making hungry noises and howling. I cried."

"You were nine," Maze said. "You were scared."

"I know. And you stood up, grabbed a few big sticks we hadn't put in the fire yet, and started to head out to scare them off." Heather smiled. "You were so badass, Maze. And protective. You always had our backs."

"It was Walker who saved us, though." He'd taken the sticks from her and gone after them himself.

"Because it takes a village," Heather said. "And I love our village."

"Me too," Cat said.

Walker didn't say anything and Cat elbowed him.

"Ow. And what?"

"You love our village too."

"Of course I do," he said easily.

Maze rolled her eyes. "If we're going to get mushy, I'm out of here."

"If you leave now," Cat said, "no more s'mores for you. Ever."

Not about to risk that, Maze stayed. They were quiet, but it was a comfortable silence. Well, at least on everyone else's part. Maze was never comfortable, not in silence or otherwise.

When they ran out of supplies, they scattered. Maze went inside and passed Jace having a Netflix marathon in the den.

So much for his being tired. But she sure as hell was, so she waved and kept going, up the stairs and into her room. She climbed over the makeshift bed on the floor where she and Jace were taking turns sleeping and crawled into the comfy bed.

She had no idea how much later it was when she jerked at the sound of someone trying to open the bedroom door. She was no longer in the cabin. She was in her mother's old apartment, which she knew from the scent of old weed and bad booze.

She was dreaming.

Her relief was short-lived, because she couldn't wake up. The light slanting in through the broken shutters was just enough to see the bedroom doorknob turning. The lock caught and so did the sob in her throat.

Back and forth the knob turned, but the lock held.

"Just dreaming," she whispered to herself. It'd been years since the last nightmare and even more years since it had been reality and not a nightmare at all. Her mom had a weakness for men, all of them. But one in particular had been fond of preteen girls. She'd been a handy target.

He'd gotten into her bedroom twice, and the second time she'd been ready with a baseball bat. He'd never tried again.

But that first time . . . Sometimes she could still feel his hands on her. She'd screamed bloody murder and had finally managed to wake up her passed-out mom, who'd come stumbling down the hallway to see what the commotion had been about.

Asshole Boyfriend—Maze refused to ever use his name—had been smart enough to get out of her bedroom and play innocent.

When she'd finally been removed from her mom's custody by CPS, they'd put her through mandatory counseling. All these years later, that night of horror still pissed her off whenever she thought about it, but she didn't feel scarred. She knew it hadn't been her fault, she didn't hate all men, and she could enjoy sex when she was in the mood.

She considered herself lucky more than a survivor.

But it turned out sometimes the brain played nasty tricks. Apparently, it didn't matter how much time had passed—terror was terror, even in dreams. She hardly even registered grabbing her pillow and running for the closet, shutting the door behind her to curl up into the tiny space on the floor, the pillow over her head.

When the closet door opened, she cried out and shrank back against the wall, lost in the confusion between the dream and reality.

Strong, warm arms gathered her up against a broad chest. "Maze."

She recognized the safety of that rough voice. It was embarrassing, but she clutched at Walker like he was her personal teddy bear.

"I've got you," he said quietly, calmly, pressing his jaw to her, holding her tight to him, better than any teddy bear she'd ever had. "You're safe and I've got you."

And then he sat on the floor of the closet, his back to the wall, and held her while she cried herself out.

His big hand stroked her hair. "Want to talk about it?"

"No."

"You're not alone, Maze. You're never alone. We're all right here at your six."

"Are you?" she whispered thickly.

"I might not be the most open guy, but I've never lied to you."

That much *was* true. He'd always been honest, down to that long-ago Vegas morning when he'd woken up married to her and said, "I'll take care of this, I'll fix it." At the memory, she closed her eyes tight.

The next time she woke up, she was back in bed, alone, and it was morning. She sat straight up and looked around. Jace was asleep on the floor.

Had it actually happened?

She looked at the closet. The door was open, a pillow on the floor in there.

Yep. It'd happened.

She covered her face and took in a deep breath, remembering the feel of Walker's arms around her, holding her tight to him. He hadn't pressed her to talk. He'd just chased away her nightmares and held her until she'd fallen asleep.

It embarrassed her that he knew everything about her, even the things she never talked about, when she knew only a few stark details of his past, nothing but the bare minimum. She didn't know what to do with that. With any of it. So she did what she did best: lived in the land of denial. Stepping over a sleeping Jace, she got dressed.

You're not alone, Maze. You're never alone. We're all right here at your six.

Walker's words were stuck in her brain. Because she wanted to be at their backs too. It was time to give back to the people who'd given her so much, *past* time.

She found Caitlin in the kitchen mainlining coffee and frosting a pan of cinnamon rolls. Maze held out her hand.

"Touch this pan before I'm done and die."

"Not the cinnamon rolls. I want your *real* to-do list. That's right, I know you gave me just a few of the million things you've still got on your plate. I want the whole thing."

"What? No." She shook her head. "I don't want to overwhelm you, Maze."

"Woman, give me your list. I'm the maid of honor and your best friend, and it's time I act like it. You're drowning and I want to help."

"Because . . . you love me?" Caitlin asked, brows up.

"Yes. Now hand it over."

Caitlin laughed. "One of these days you're going to say the words."

Maze just gave her the *gimme* hands.

Caitlin pushed a huge three-ring binder across the table to Maze. It was stuffed to the gills with sticky notes and little pieces of paper sticking out of it at all angles.

"Funny," Maze said.

Caitlin didn't laugh.

Maze stared at her. "*That's* your to-do list?"

"Yep."

"It's bigger than the Bible, Cat."

Caitlin sighed. "I know, I know. Look, I used to dream about my wedding and what it would be like. I had it all planned out in my head for years. But let me tell you something, the reality of putting a wedding together is *nothing* like the fantasy. And leaving things to chance is not in my nature. Practice makes perfect." She paused. "But to be honest . . . if I could go back and do it all over again, I'd elope."

Maze caught the real emotion in Caitlin's voice and her own heart squeezed. "Cat, you haven't done it yet. If it's making you this unhappy, it's not too late."

"I'm not unhappy," Caitlin said. "I'm *not*," she repeated when Maze seemed doubtful. "Ugh, don't listen to me, okay? I'm just tired. I'm worried. It's a lot to plan. I mean, we get a wedding rehearsal, but there's no rehearsal for the reception and it's starting to freak me out. Anything could go wrong. Hold on. I can fix that." She wrote on a napkin: *Have a practice reception.*

Maze stared at the napkin. "You want to rehearse for what is basically a party?"

"With a lot of people who are all *really* different from each other, so yes, I want to rehearse so that it goes off without a hitch. Did you hear about that wedding in San Francisco last weekend? The bride's family and the groom's family started a fight with each other—over cake. They ended up in a huge cake fight and the bride got frosting in her eye and needed to wear an eye patch on her honeymoon."

Maze blew out a breath. "Look me in my cake-free eyes and tell me you really want to do this."

Cat met her gaze. "I want to do this."

Maze nodded. "Okay. Then let's do this." She paused. "Um, you might want to shower before the day's activities because you've got some frosting in your hair."

"Shit."

"Hey, it could be worse, it could be in your eye."

"Smart-ass."

When Caitlin was gone, Maze sat alone at the table with the binder. It was impressive. There were lists for the lists. The daily list began with: *Clear the washer and dryer or you'll get mold and then get sick and die.*

Not on Maze's watch. So she went to the small laundry room off the kitchen. She was pulling a load out of the dryer when she felt a change in the force field. The only warning she had of who it was came from the deep thrum that began low in her belly. Only one person had ever affected her that way.

Walker came in with a basket of clothes, which he dumped in the washer, lights and darks together in one load. Looking her over, he carefully took her in. "You okay?"

She realized she was so tense that her shoulders were hunched up to her ears, so she purposefully relaxed them. "I'm good, but your clothes are probably screwed."

He gave a small smile but didn't stop looking at her, and she realized he was asking because of last night, when he'd found her in the closet, when she'd cried all over him.

"I'm fine," she said with a sigh. "And . . . um, thanks. For being there." She paused, not sure she really wanted an answer but unable to stop herself from asking, "How did you know I was . . . having a rough night?"

"I couldn't sleep. I was heading for the kitchen when I thought I heard you."

Damn. How she hated that.

"I knew Jace had fallen asleep in the den watching TV and that you were alone. How often does it happen, Maze?"

"Almost never," she said honestly, but when he didn't seem to buy that, still eyeing her with an intense protectiveness she recognized, she shook her head. "It only happens when I get really tired or stressed."

"You know you've got nothing to fear from him anymore, right?"

She nodded, because she'd found out years ago that the guy had been killed in a bar fight. "Yeah, and I get that the closet thing doesn't make any sense, but it's kinda like mac and cheese. Comfort, you know?" She stopped and cocked her head. "Wait. How do you know that I've got nothing to fear from him anymore?"

His face gave nothing away as he turned back to his laundry, but she stopped him.

"No," she said. "Don't give me that blank expression. Spill it. How and why would you know that?"

In typical Walker fashion, he stated the facts like he was talking about the weather. "I tracked him down and found out he's dead. Which saved me from killing him."

She gaped at him because she knew he wasn't kidding. *"When?"*

"The group home I went to after the fire was run by a woman whose husband was a cop. He had search programs on his computer."

Shockingly touched, and also far too close to tears for comfort, she drew a shaky breath and redirected by pointing her chin at the laundry basket.

"That's . . . surprisingly domestic of you," she said.

"I'm good at throwing things into the washer."

"Are you, though?"

He smiled. "Smart-ass."

"That's the second time today I've been called that already."

"Cuz it's true," he said. "As for what I'm doing, Caitlin was struggling yesterday, so I told her I'd help. She didn't have a full load so I added some of my stuff, along with some clothes I found on the bathroom floor."

She reached into the washer and pulled out a pair of her own pale pink lace undies. "These are mine."

"Are you sure? Cuz I've got a pair just like them."

She rolled her eyes but also laughed, and in return, he smiled. A real smile. *Note to self: Never look directly into Walker's eyes, especially pre-caffeination.* "Your undies shouldn't be touching my undies."

He laughed, the sound rubbing at a whole bunch of her good spots, damn him. "Why not?"

She searched for a valid reason that wasn't *Because it makes me remember how good we were in bed.* "It's just not done," she said lamely.

Walker moved in, his mouth brushing her ear when he spoke in a husky whisper. "You do realize that your undies have touched my undies before. In fact—"

"Oh my God." She set a few fingers against his lips. "Don't say it."

His eyes were heated and flat-out laughing at the same time. "Don't say what?"

"You know what! That our . . . *parts* have touched too."

"And what parts might that be, Maze?"

Taking a sharp breath, she pointed at him. "You know what parts, you just want me to talk dirty."

He grinned.

She shoved her undies in her pocket before jabbing a finger at him again. "I'm onto you."

"If that was true, we'd both be a lot more relaxed right now."

She didn't know whether to laugh or push him. Before she could decide, Jace walked by the laundry room, followed by Sammie, who was literally dripping Cheerios with each step, and then both pugs, snorting and squeaking as they cleaned up after Sammie like they were her personal vacuums. "Apparently, I'm the Pied Piper," Jace said, then paused and took a second to look at Maze. "You okay?"

"Yep."

Jace slid his gaze to Walker briefly, but then kept moving, his parade in line behind him.

Walker shook his head. "Your boyfriend's a good guy, but I'm not sure how smart he is."

"Why do you say that?"

"Because he lets me get close to you." He shifted even closer and looked her in the eyes. "Unless, of course, he's not really your boyfriend."

Maze narrowed her eyes. "What he is is none of your business, especially for a guy who's got a girlfriend of his own."

"Do I?"

"Yes, that tall brunette with the smallest bikini on the planet."

Walker laughed softly.

"What's so funny?"

"The only way you saw a pic of her is if you took a deep, *deep* dive online. Face it, you've been stalking me too."

Dammit. Caught. "Hey, I stumbled on that pic by accident."

"That picture wasn't on my Instagram, it was on Boomer's," he said smugly.

Boomer owned and ran the Whiskey River Bar and Grill in Wildstone, and in the old days, he and Walker had found lots of trouble together. She crossed her arms and ignored the fact that she could feel her face flaming. "So I was curious, so what? Why aren't you bringing her to the wedding?"

"Because I went out with her a total of two times. Two *years* ago."

"So . . . you're not into long relationships?"

Suddenly, his eyes were no longer shining with merriment. Or anything. Walker was in shutdown mode. "Not anymore," he said.

Caitlin pressed her forehead to the cool glass of her bedroom window and stared out at the night. The day had gone . . . shockingly well. Maze had sent the guys to check in on the equipment rental company, and the girls had gone shoe shopping. She'd finally found the right shoes for her dress. They were gorgeous silvery goodness with four-inch heels that would put her eye to eye with Dillon.

Around her, the house was finally quiet. Everyone was sleeping, Dillon included—no doubt thanks to the orgasm she'd just given him. If there was one place where the two of them meshed and all her needs were met, it was in bed. He was just the right level of adventurous, and he made her feel sexy.

But as had been happening lately, when they weren't in bed, little tendrils of doubt filled her. Earlier, she'd given him a compatibility test she'd found on BuzzFeed. He hadn't remembered the color of her toothbrush, her favorite pizza topping, or what her secret fantasy was—which, by the way, was for the man in her life to vacuum the entire house without being asked. When he'd thought her crazy for being annoyed that he hadn't known this in spite of her telling him at least once a week, she'd gotten annoyed right back.

Because what woman *didn't* have that fantasy?

With a sigh, she shook it off and reminded herself to concentrate on the house being filled with the people she loved above all else. Walker. Maze. Heather. And Sammie! She still couldn't believe that she hadn't known about her, that she hadn't been trusted to know.

But the truth is, that was on her. "You're too bossy," she told her reflection in the window. "Too judgmental."

"Hmm," Dillon agreed sleepily from the bed, not moving a single inch, eyes still closed. "All true, but I do love it when you're bossy in bed."

Caitlin thunked her forehead on the window while Dillon laughed softly.

"What do you think of them?" she asked quietly.

"Your friends?"

"My *family.*"

"You never mentioned Heather having a kid."

It was too embarrassing to admit she'd not known. "She's adorable, though, right?"

"Hmm."

She turned to look at him. "You don't think so?"

"Didn't realize kids were so . . . messy."

Caitlin smiled. That was one of her favorite parts. "Having her here really brings it home how much I want one of my own," she said softly.

"Caitlin . . ." He sighed and flopped onto his back. "We talked about this. I love you. I love you so much that I want to be selfish and have it just be us."

She sent him a warm smile, but she couldn't help but need more info. "For how long?"

"I don't know. But I do know we're not ready. We've got my student loans to pay off. A retirement portfolio to build. Careers to stoke."

"I want my career to be food and kids."

"You want to be a stay-at-home mom?"

"Not necessarily," she said. "I still want to work. Maybe I can start my own home delivery meal service."

"Really?" he asked doubtfully.

She was starting to get the feeling that he was forgetting a few pieces of *her* hopes and dreams. "Why do you sound surprised?"

"The only thing I'm surprised by is how much we've been arguing lately," he said.

"Me too. But I don't know why we're doing it."

"It's wedding stress," he said. "*Your* wedding stress."

"And you're not stressed?"

"Only when you are."

"Maybe counseling would help," she suggested quietly.

"What kind of couple needs counseling before they're even married?" He patted the mattress. "Come back to bed, Caitlin."

"In a minute."

"You're doing it again, aren't you? Running through all the details of the wedding."

Actually, for once, she wasn't. She was running through the details of her life. So she had no idea why she answered the way she did. "Yes," she said. "Caught me. I'm thinking about the meeting at the florist we have this week. My mom and dad aren't flying in until Friday, just before the rehearsal dinner, but your mom's coming. That means you and I need to get on the same page."

"I hear you," he said.

She straightened when she saw a shadow cross the yard. When it moved beneath the slash of blue light from the moon, she realized it was Maze and relaxed.

At the water's edge, Maze stepped onto the dock, walked to the end, and plopped herself down, lying back to stare up at the sky.

Caitlin couldn't see her expression from here, but there was a sense of anxiety and nerves vibrating from her that caught at her heart. She rose to her feet and was about to grab a pair of sweats to go out there, when another shadow emerged from the house. A tall, leanly muscled shadow, bare chested, barefoot, striding down the dock with ease of movement and a sense of purpose.

Walker.

Caitlin stilled, watching as he approached Maze, who was still lying flat on her back, feet hanging over the edge of the dock, seemingly unaware of his approach. He said something and Maze jerked in surprise.

Caitlin leaned closer as if maybe, if she tried hard enough, she could hear them. And she wanted to. Desperately. Once upon a time, they'd all been so close, so important to each other. Actually, *everything* to each other.

But then they'd all had that fight three years ago at Michael's graveside and had scattered far and wide. As far as she knew, Walker and Maze hadn't had any interaction in those three years.

Interesting then that his body language seemed . . . determined. And . . . familiar? Something else too. *Intimate.* She pressed a hand to the glass as if she could call out to them and be a part of their conversation, but suddenly Dillon's warm arm encircled her from behind, his mouth landing just beneath her ear.

"Come to bed," he said again, and then took her there himself. But for the first time—at least in bed— he couldn't get her where she wanted to go.

Chapter 7

Maze's maid of honor to-do list:
—Pull off a reception rehearsal without a
   frosting fight.

"You're going to get bit up by mosquitos."

Maze nearly jumped out of her skin and off the dock into the lake at the sound of Walker's disembodied, sleep-husky voice in the dark night somewhere behind her. Lifting her head, she sent a glare in his direction, which was undoubtedly wasted on him because of the low visibility. "I came out here to be *alone*."

He didn't say anything to this, and she craned her neck to get a better look at him. He wore a pair of running sweats and nothing else. *Gulp.*

"And *you're* gonna be the one to get bit up by mosquitos."

"I never get bit."

"Because you're not sweet enough," she said.

"No doubt."

He crouched low at her side and looked her over. She did her best not to squirm in her pj's: sweat bottoms, oversized T-shirt, and let's not forget the fake UGGs. She used the cover of relative darkness to study him too. He'd always been fit, but there was a lean hardness to his body that felt new. An edge. Her eyes caught on the sizable scar above his left pec where the bullet had pierced his chest three years ago.

His chest.

"Turn around," she whispered.

He paused for a full beat, then reluctantly turned. Yep, there they were, the burn scars across the broad expanse of his back, shoulder to shoulder, from running into the Walshes' burning house to try to save Michael. They'd faded a lot, but they were still clear enough to have the fear and terror bubble up inside her again.

"Do they hurt?"

"Not anymore."

"And the bullet wound?"

"Sometimes, with the wrong pressure."

She closed her eyes, feeling overwhelmingly grateful he was still alive. Even if she had mixed emotions about the man, and oh, she did, she couldn't picture life without him on the planet somewhere.

Which meant he wasn't the problem. She was. Walker emitted a sexual pull that was hard to resist. When he entered her field of vision, she got a rush, and up close? He was deadly. The second she caught a hint of his scent or felt his body heat, she was as good as gone.

"Why aren't you sleeping?" he asked.

She shrugged and concentrated on the night around her. The moon was a little sliver in the sky; the water lapped gently against the rocky beach and dock pylons. She felt . . . overwhelmed, but it wasn't from seeing Caitlin and Heather again. No matter how much time they went without seeing one another, they fell back into their same old rhythm, and even with all the things between them that hadn't been said, it was an odd comfort.

She supposed that was the meaning of family.

But seeing Walker . . . that wasn't comfortable at all. She'd told herself she wouldn't react to seeing him again, that she wouldn't let his presence get to her, that she could ignore him.

She'd failed on all counts.

He, of course, didn't appear to be having any of these same issues. He'd remained cool, calm, stoic, even amused by the fact Caitlin had tricked them into spending all this time together. Amused and . . . sweet. At least to Caitlin and Heather and Sammie.

Maze could remember a time when he'd been sweet with her as well. How even drunk in Vegas that night, she'd felt cared for. She'd felt safe with him. Safe and protected, two things she'd rarely, if ever, felt in her life, because she more than anyone knew safe and protected were nothing but illusions. And yet Walker had a way of making the illusion seem real, more real than anything else in her life.

She needed to keep her guard up so she didn't accidently fall again. Because this wasn't about her and Walker. It was about Caitlin, whom Maze wanted to protect, the same way Caitlin had always protected her. It was Maze's turn now, and she wanted to keep Caitlin from experiencing any heartbreak.

Because as far as she could tell, there was *always* heartbreak with love.

"Maze."

"I'm sleeping fine."

He nodded. "Okay, so if you don't want to talk about that, then there's something else."

"What?"

He tossed a folder down at her side.

She stared at the file and then craned her neck to try to see his face more clearly. "What is this?"

"Our divorce papers," he said.

"Excuse me?"

He lifted a shoulder. "Turns out drunk Elvis *did* file the papers, which sealed the deal."

She blinked once, slow as an owl. "'Sealed the deal,'" she echoed slowly.

"He made our wedding legit," Walker said. "We're married."

She sat up so fast she got dizzy. "You can't be serious."

"Do you think I'd joke about this?"

Mind racing, she stared at him. "Are you telling me that we've been married this whole time?"

"Yes."

Having a hard time processing, she shook her head. "How long have you known?"

"Maze—"

"How long, Walker?"

"Six months."

"Six *months*?" Here was the thing about having your stomach hit your toes: it made you feel like you were going to throw up. Or maybe that was just her life. *"Six months?"*

"I found out when I went to get a loan for a piece of property I was thinking of buying," he said. "The lender needed my wife's info so he could check her credit as well as mine."

"Whoa." She could only imagine the shock of that call. "That must have been a surprise."

He let out a low laugh. "Yeah."

"Six months . . ." she whispered again.

"Are you going to just keep repeating that?"

"I think I am, yeah." She got to her feet too fast and wobbled. There was a clanging in her head and her vision went wonky. "Dammit."

"Maze?"

"Hold on. There's three of you, and while once upon a time I'd have loved to have three of you at once, right now I'm going to throw up."

He moved efficiently and quickly, and before she could so much as blink, he'd pushed her to sit again and had palmed the back of her clammy neck. "Push against my hand."

She had no idea why she did what he'd directed. Maybe it was his surprisingly gentle, but absolutely authoritative, tone. Or because she was starting to feel like she was drowning, and at the moment, like it or not, he was her only lifeline. Dropping her head to her knees, she closed her eyes.

"So you want three of me, huh?"

She kept her eyes closed. "*Wanted,* past tense. And only in bed."

He laughed.

Lifting her head, she glared at him. "How is it that you've known for six months and you're only just now telling me?"

"I wanted to get you the solution before I told you the problem," he said.

"And that took six months?"

"I got my attorney on it right away, but then I was away on a job. I knew I'd see you here, and I thought this would go over better if I told you in person."

She turned her head and stared out at the water. "You don't have to tiptoe around me. You should know that."

He didn't answer, which had her looking at him again.

His eyes were dark. Serious. "I don't know much about you anymore, Maze."

"Other than we're married."

A very small hint of a smile curved his mouth. "Other than that. And the fact that you're committing adultery with Josh."

She let out a reluctant laugh, but other than that ignored the "Josh" thing. "Are you going to tell me that in the past six months you haven't gotten busy with anyone?"

The hint of a smile turned into the real thing. "I take my vows seriously."

She rolled her eyes. "So . . . we're really married."

"Yep."

"Who knows?"

"Just you and me, and Elvis apparently—if he remembers."

"You haven't told Heather or Caitlin?" she asked, unable to keep the slight bitterness from her voice. "I mean, you *did* keep in touch with both of them."

He studied her for a long beat, during which she did her best to hold eye contact and keep her chin up. Not easy when she felt so off-balance. But one thing she knew about Walker: he expected her to go toe-to-toe with him. He wasn't attracted to wallflowers.

And why she was worried about *that,* she had zero idea . . .

"I don't care if anyone finds out," he finally said. "But I felt you should know first."

"And you couldn't tell me six months ago because you were on a job."

He nodded.

"You went back in the field after you got shot."

He shrugged. "Turns out I'm not suited for a desk job."

"Why do you keep tempting fate?" she asked, bog-gled. "Do you *want* to die on the job?"

"You asked me that three years ago and the answer is still the same. Why do you care?"

The question pissed her off enough to not answer him. "We've been here for three days. Three days, Walker. Why didn't you tell me sooner?"

"And when should I have done that?" A note of ir-ritation came into his voice. "On the hike with your boyfriend that you've been dating a year? Or is it a week?"

She told herself to bite her tongue, to not get drawn in by those eyes, that body, or the way he made her skin hum with anticipation. But she'd never been any good at holding her tongue. "Is it that hard for you to believe that someone might want me in his life?"

"Actually, that someone would want you in his life is easy to believe," he said. "What's harder to believe is that you'd let it happen."

She stared at him, her chest suddenly too tight to talk. She rose to her feet, pushed past him, and headed back to the house, quite certain if there'd been any light at all, she could've seen the steam coming out of her own ears. "He drives me insane," she snapped as she entered her bedroom.

Jace jerked upright from the floor. He'd clearly been sleeping, as he stared at her befuddled for a beat. "What?"

"He drives me insane!"

"Ah." He nodded and drew a deep breath, awareness coming fully into his heavy-lidded, sleepy eyes. "Warren."

"*Walker!* And what is that between you two anyway?"

Jace snorted. "If you don't know, I can't help you."

"You're not jealous of him," she said slowly. "Because you and me have never been a thing. Probably because you're my boss and you don't like hanky-panky going on between your employees."

"That's true," he agreed. "But that's not why we're not a thing. It took me six months to even get you to talk to me. You've got trust issues."

"Hey."

"Plus you friend-zoned me before I could blink," he said, looking amused but also serious.

He was trying to make a point, she realized. "Jace, we're not attracted to each other like that."

"Okay, first, *any* straight man with blood flowing through his veins would be attracted to you, but you're right," he said, "we're not a thing, and before you freak out, I don't want to be a thing." He smiled. "Mayhem Maze."

She blew out a breath. "She's *way* in my past."

"If that's true, it's a shame. And second," he went on, "protectiveness and possessiveness are two traits that don't really have a lot of logic attached to them. I see the way he looks at you, Maze."

"Like he wants to strangle me?"

"Like you're lunch. *And,*" he went on when she opened her mouth, "I don't want you hurt."

"I'm not going to get hurt. I'm fire retardant." She stepped over him and climbed into the bed. "Thanks for giving me the bed for a second night in a row. You can have it tomorrow—"

The knock at the door stopped her cold. It was immediately accompanied by a low, unbearably familiar voice. *"Maze."*

"Oh my God, it's him." She jumped up to shove the blanket and pillow Jace had been using under the bed, then hopped back in between the sheets. "Come on," she hissed at Jace.

But instead of getting into the bed with her, he moved to the door.

"Wait—*where are you going? No, don't answer it!*" she whisper-yelled just as he opened the damn door.

Jace looked at Walker for a long beat. "I'm going to take a shower," he finally said. "A long one. After, I'm going to go down to the dock to stargaze."

"You want to go stargazing now, in the middle of the night?" Maze asked in disbelief.

Jace turned to her. "No, Maze. I want to give you and Walker a moment. Because clearly it needs to happen. You two are just too stupid to figure that out for yourselves."

"Hey," she said, automatically defensive at the "stupid" comment, but she slid a look at Walker, who was eyeing Jace with an interesting expression she couldn't quite place.

The door shut and then she was alone with her husband. She yanked the covers up to her chin. *"What?"*

He leaned back against the door. "Something you want to tell me?"

"Nope. Having secrets is more *your* thing."

He gave her an impressive eye roll, sauntered closer, and sat at the edge of the bed near her hip.

She raised her hands in the universal *what?* gesture.

"There are some things I want to say."

"Then say them and get out."

"Yes, I kept in touch with Caitlin and Heather," he said. "Actually, Caitlin kept tabs on *me*. Made me come into town for every excuse under the sun. Then she'd boss me into sticking around for a few days. Against all understanding, she loves me, treats me like I belong to her, and has expectations that go with it." His smile faded. "Heather was different. I had to go after her and butt my way in and pretty much figure out for myself she was in trouble."

Maze's chest hurt thinking about Heather being alone, pregnant, scared, and in pain. "I'm glad she had you," she said softly. "And that neither she nor Caitlin was ever really alone."

"And like I told you last night, neither were you."

She met his gaze.

"I always knew where you were," he said. "When you worked on that cruise ship for one whole cruise, quitting because you were seasick the whole time. When you moved to San Jose and got a job at a new club, then punched out one of the patrons for getting handsy. When you tried San Francisco but couldn't really find your place."

She gaped at him. "Two years ago," she said, "when my car died and I couldn't afford a new one, I got cash in the mail. Two grand. That was you, wasn't it?"

He just looked at her.

"Oh my God. It was." Her chest felt like it was caving in on itself. "Why didn't you just show up at my door?"

"You'd made it clear you didn't want to see me or need my help."

And yet he'd helped anyway. "Why?"

"You know why."

"Because you felt obligated," she said.

"Wrong."

"Then what?"

"I think I'll let you wrestle with that one." He tossed the file with the divorce papers into her lap. "You forgot those. You need to sign them." He glanced at the pillow on the floor and then at the closed bedroom door. "Unless, of course, you don't want to."

She chucked one of her pillows at him, but he easily ducked it.

"I wouldn't sleep with your eyes closed if I were you," she said.

He flashed a smile at that. "Never do."

"You're impossible."

"Guilty." He picked up her hand and studied it.

"What are you looking for?"

"A diamond. A year is a long time to be with some-one. Any smart man would've locked it down with you by now."

Her stomach went a little squishy. "I'm not the type of woman a guy wants to keep."

His fingers tightened around hers. "You're wrong about that, Maze."

Right. She had a long history of not being good enough, and he was a big part of that history. "Go away, Walk."

When he didn't move fast enough to suit her, she picked up her other pillow and aimed it at him. He flashed her a grim smile and slipped out of the room before it could hit her intended target: his smug face.

Chapter 8

Maze's updated maid of honor to-do list:
—Don't kill the man of honor.

M aze was still awake the next morning because . . .
She.

Was.

Married?

Good God. She rolled out of bed and . . . oh yeah, tripped over her pretend boyfriend, Jace.

Her life was officially a sitcom.

"Hey," Jace grumbled sleepily, and sat up. "There's no acceptable reason for waking me up at . . ." He blinked at the clock. ". . . Jesus, five A.M.—unless morning sex is on the table."

"Dream on."

"I was dreaming just fine, thank you very much—"

A knock came at the door. Maze froze for a beat, then tore off her sweatpants, leaving her in just the oversized T-shirt and cheeky panties. "Get up here," she demanded as she leaped back into bed. "He doesn't believe that we're together and I need him to."

"Why?"

"So he won't be able to melt my cold, hard heart. There. Are you happy?"

When Jace just looked at her in disbelief, she waved her hands frantically.

"Come on, come on!"

"You're unhinged, you know that?"

"Yeah, yeah, now get your ass up here and fake being into me. I know, I know, but just pretend I'm whoever you were dreaming about," she said.

"I wasn't—"

"Right. So that's a gun in your shorts then?"

"Shit," he muttered, getting into bed with her. "This is awkward."

"It's only awkward if it's for me."

He adjusted "it." "Trust me, it's not. You're too mean."

There was another knock and an accompanying teeny-tiny demanding voice. *"Jace!"*

Maze relaxed and smiled. "Sammie!" she called out, shoving Jace away from her. He was laughing so hard, he hit the floor. "Come on in, baby!"

The door opened. Sammie was bouncing up and down like the Energizer Bunny, but she wasn't alone. Behind her was Heather in a matching pj set with little kitties on them. Her hair was wild, and a pillow crease ran across a cheek. She looked like she was twelve. "It's a pajama party. Remember when we had those?"

Caitlin appeared next to her wearing a pretty silk robe and slippers, with perfect hair and . . .

"Are you wearing mascara already?" Maze asked in disbelief.

"Of course," Caitlin said.

Maze laughed, but it dried up in her throat when she realized Walker was behind Cat, wearing his sweat bottoms from last night. He'd added a T-shirt from— she stopped breathing—the dive bar in Vegas where their problems had all begun.

They all came in. Walker eyed the pillow and blanket on the floor with Jace.

"Fell out of bed," Jace said easily, and rose to his feet.

"With your blanket and pillows?" Heather asked.

"Yep."

Maze slid her gaze to Jace's boxer shorts as he got into bed next to her. Luckily, morning wood was no longer a problem. Good thing too, because before she knew it *everyone* was on the bed—except Walker. He walked slowly into the room, purposely eyeing the pillow and blanket on the floor before meeting Maze's eyes.

Dammit.

She was now sandwiched in between Heather and Caitlin, with Jace at her feet and Sammie trying to climb on top of him, but for a second, all that craziness faded away. It was only her and Walker in the room, which both gave her a secret thrill and pissed her off.

"Up!" Sammie yelled at Walker.

"Yeah," Heather said to him, patting a corner of Maze's bed. "Up."

"I'm good." But he scooped up Sammie and, to her screaming delight, hung her upside down off the back of his shoulders. Then he playfully tossed her to the bed. She bounced and squealed and gave a sweet belly laugh. Caitlin leaned in to tickle her . . . and Sammie stopped laughing and gave her a deadpan look.

Walker laughed.

"It's not funny! I want her to love me. I *need* her to love me."

"She will," Heather promised, ever the peacemaker. "Sammie, remember those brownies we make? Caitlin taught me how to make them. She also tells the best stories. I used to crawl into her bed at night when I got scared and she'd read to me. You like being read to."

Sammie remained unconvinced.

"It's okay," Caitlin said with false cheer. "I guess I can't be loved by everyone."

Everyone but Maze laughed. She was just too aware of Walker standing bedside while Jace was actually in the bed and under the covers with her. Seriously, how did she manage to get herself into these situations? She sighed and forced herself to check into the conversation going on around her.

"I mean, I don't get why wanting to be a mom with a simple job is so strange," Cat was saying. "He has a life list, and children are on it." She turned her head to look at Maze. "What do you think?"

She thought she was currently too busy having a freak-out to speak intelligently. But since Caitlin could spot a freak-out from ten miles away, she smiled and nodded. "You need to follow *your* dreams. You want to be a mom sooner than later."

"But that's not crazy, right? I'd make a good mom. I mean, I really think that raising kids, my own or otherwise, is the most important thing I'll ever do. Like my parents did."

"They were good at it," Heather said. "And you would be too. We learned a lot from them, they're amazing. I mean, I never thought I'd have a kid, but now I can't imagine my life any other way."

"But what if Dillon's not on board?"

"Cat, you should do what you want," Maze said.

"Yeah, that's not exactly how healthy relationships work," Caitlin said dryly. "Healthy relationships are about the three Cs."

"Calamity, cluelessness, and catastrophe?" Maze asked.

Jace laughed, and she glared at him.

"Communication, commitment, and compromise," Caitlin said.

"Well, *compromise* means he has to give something up as well," Maze said.

Cat gave her a look. "I'm not sure you understand how these things go. I mean, you barely committed to keeping a plant alive for a week."

Maze opened her mouth and then shut it. Because what Cat said was true.

"Not everyone's known since they were a five-year-old what they wanted to be, Cat," Walker said with a slight censure in his voice.

Surprised by his defense, Maze looked at him. He met her gaze—his unreadable, of course. But he knew her, maybe better than anyone. He certainly knew her better than she knew herself, or so it seemed at times.

She had no idea what the hell she wanted out of her life, but she did know one thing for sure. "Very few people get a real shot at happiness," she said carefully. "I just want to make sure you get a shot at yours."

Caitlin looked at her, like, really looked at her. "Are you okay?"

At that, everyone craned their necks and stared at her. Awesome. And no, she wasn't okay. She was *never* okay. "I'm great. And *starving*." She rolled off the bed, not so accidentally kicking Walker in the shins while she was at it.

Five minutes later she was in the kitchen, watching Caitlin working on a huge spread while everyone else showered and dressed for the day. It was shockingly impressive. The girl had been born to take care of people.

Maze was definitely missing that gene. But in spite of Cat liking to do everything herself, she stepped in to make toast.

Cat smiled. "Just like the old days. You making toast."

"It's the only thing you'd ever let me do."

"Because you hate to cook."

Maze smiled. "But I do love to eat."

Cat smiled too and set her head on Maze's shoulder for a beat. "I'm sorry about before. I know sometimes I sound bitchy."

"Sometimes?"

Caitlin laughed and hugged her. "Missed this," she whispered. "Missed you. So much."

Maze wrapped her arms around her. "Me too."

"Today's going to be a busy day. Wedding errands and chores, et cetera."

"We'll help," Maze said.

"Thanks."

They pulled apart.

"Do you ever miss those days?" Cat asked. "When we were little and lived at Mom and Dad's house and had no worries?"

Maze *always* had worries. But the answer was simple: "Yes."

Her eyes fell on the two small framed pics hanging by the fridge. The first one was of Cat sitting at the lake's edge with a laughing Michael. Maze remembered that day. She and Cat had been tasked with babysitting Michael, which had never been a task in Maze's eyes. Playing tag with him on the edge of the water had been more fun than anything else, and she'd loved being with him. Caitlin too. Because the two of them had been so . . . normal. They had no idea what the big, bad world was like, and when she was with them, Maze could pretend she didn't know either.

Hungry for those days, she looked closer at the pic. Cat was laughing too, looking open and happy. And carefree. Seeing it made her realize something: she hadn't seen carefree Cat since . . . *since* . . . After Michael's death, Cat had taken everything on as her personal responsibility. Making sure her parents got through losing their son. Making sure to keep in touch with Walker and Heather and Maze when they'd all been separated. She'd become Head In Charge of Everything, and as a result, carefree Cat had been buried with her brother.

Feeling an ache in her chest for all Cat had been through, Maze turned to the second pic. It was of Cat's parents, looking vibrant and happy. "I've never seen that picture," she murmured.

"It was two years ago, right before Dad's diagnosis."

Maze sucked in a breath. "Diagnosis?"

"Cancer. It appears to all be gone now, though. We're holding our breath." Caitlin pointed at her with the whisk. "You'd have heard about it from me before now if you'd asked about them even once."

Maze cringed. "I know. I'm so sorry. It's . . . complicated."

"Complicated how? They loved you and doted on you all the time. Hell, my mom favored you over both me *and* Michael. You could do no wrong. They did everything they could for you, got you into the same classes as me, offered to help you stay in contact with your mom if you wanted, clothed and fed you, kept you safe—which you didn't care about, I know, but my point is they cared. So much, Maze."

Until the fire, that is, after which they'd moved on without her.

Actually, that wasn't fair. They'd reached out to her just a few months after the fire, asking how she was. She'd responded, and a part of her had hoped it meant they'd be coming for her. But at that point, they still hadn't had a big enough place. Maze could admit that at the time, she hadn't understood the depths of what they'd been through. All she'd known or thought about was what she'd been through.

A few years or so later, she'd texted them, just a breezy "hi, thinking of you, hope you're well" sort of thing. They'd responded sweetly and suggested that they meet up for lunch sometime.

Maze had stared at their response for days, before ultimately deleting the text rather than replying. She still didn't know why exactly.

Wait. That was a lie. She did know. It was called hurt. She was still acting like that abandoned teenager.

Then she'd further screwed up at the anniversary party, the last nail in the coffin of that relationship.

"Well?" Caitlin asked.

"You don't get it."

"Why? Because I'm the real kid?"

"Well . . . yeah."

Caitlin was slicing cheese now with a very big knife. "Yes," she said stiffly. "I was the real kid who did her best to keep everyone happy. Michael too. We shared our parents, willingly, but it's not like it was easy, Maze. I worked my ass off to always be okay and take care of everyone."

And when Michael passed away, Cat had changed forever, something Maze was just starting to see. More guilt settled in her chest. "I never asked that of you."

"Of course not, because you're allergic to asking for help."

Maze turned to walk away, but Heather was in the doorway. "Morning!" she said with way too much morning cheer, telling Maze she was here as the peacemaker, as usual.

"Hope you're hungry," Caitlin said.

Heather nodded. "Starving. Walker took Sammie outside to see the birds. She was a little cranky. He's got a way with her."

That was because Walker had a way with *all* women.

"So where's the boyfriend?" Heather asked Maze.

She was buttering the toast and took an embarrassingly long moment to realize Heather was talking to her. "Um . . . maybe he went back to bed?" She sniffed. "Wait, is something burning?"

"Oh my God." Caitlin yanked open the oven. Smoke curled up to the ceiling. "It's the biscuits. Dammit!" She pulled out the charred mounds and stared at them. "You know what? It's fine. Totally *fine*. I can make more. It's all fine."

Dillon came into the kitchen. "What burned?"

"Nothing! I'm fine!"

Dillon lifted his hands. "Okay then." He started to head back to the living room.

Maze shook her head at him. "Dude, when a woman says she's fine, it's code for she's *not* fine."

"Caitlin and I don't speak in code, we speak our minds like adults," he said, and walked out of the kitchen.

Still holding the cookie sheet, smoke curling up from each individual biscuit, Caitlin pushed out the back door and dumped the biscuits onto the ground. Roly and Poly ran through the kitchen and outside, snorting and squealing. They took one sniff of the charred mess and vanished back into the house.

Maze peeked out. "You okay?"

"Everything is totally one hundred percent *fine!*" she yelled.

A few birds flocked to the biscuits, pecked at them, then flew off.

"Great, even animals won't eat them." Cat sagged. "It's a metaphor for my life."

Maze stepped out and shut the door behind her. She used a towel she'd grabbed to take the hot cookie sheet from Caitlin, which she set aside before wrapping her arms around the sister of her heart. "It was just a few biscuits, Cat."

"It's more than the biscuits!" she wailed.

Maze sighed. "I know."

Cat hugged her back tight and held on. "Are you getting hives from the prolonged hug?"

"Yes."

Caitlin let out a watery laugh and tightened her grip like a true sister. "You're avoiding me."

"Are you kidding me? You've kidnapped me and are holding me—literally—against my will for a week. How in the world can I avoid you? Please tell me, so I can do it."

"You know what I mean." Cat pulled back and wiped her tears. "You're avoiding being alone with me. You don't want to be here."

"It's not that." Maze tried to collect her thoughts. "It's not you, and I'm sorry if I let you think that."

"You won't talk to me, which means it *is* about me. I want this all out in the open, it's past time. Just talk to me, dammit."

Now Maze sighed. "Fine. I'm worried you're rushing this whole marriage thing."

Caitlin's mouth fell open. "What?"

"The wedding. You've only been with Dillon for what, a year? I've got things that have been growing in my fridge for longer than that. What's the rush? I mean, they say you don't really know someone until you've been with them for well *over* a year, and even then you have to see them in a variety of emotional situations to make sure you can deal with their reactions."

Cat's eyes had narrowed. "What kind of emotional situations?"

"Like . . . say if a toddler is coming at your pristine, fancy white couch with sticky fingers."

Caitlin sighed. "He loves that couch. Look, I know what this is really about. It's because I'm getting married before you."

Oh, the irony of that statement. "No, it's not. And wow. Is that what you think? That I'd be jealous because you're getting married?"

Cat tossed up her hands. "I don't know what to think, you don't talk to me. Do you think you're the only one who's struggling to find her place? Who feels like she doesn't belong? Do you know I feel guilty because my childhood was damn good and I know it?"

"You lost your brother and childhood home in one fell swoop, Cat. You're allowed to be as fucked up as the rest of us."

Caitlin sighed, and a lot of the air seemed to go out of her sails. "I just want you to consider my family yours. I wanted to give that to you."

Suddenly Maze's throat was burning like the biscuits. "I've always admired how you keep people in your life," she managed. "You keep people, even when they don't always deserve to be kept."

Caitlin was clearly astonished. "If you're about to tell me that you don't think you deserve to be kept, I'm going to hurt you, Maze. I mean it. Oh my God. You're so stupid." She yanked her back in for another hug and this one hurt.

"Can't. Breathe." Maze tried to tap out, but Cat just tightened her grip.

"So, so, so, so stupid," Cat repeated, sounding tearful. "I love you, you stupid, stupid girl, and I know damn well you love me back."

Maze shrugged. "Maybe. When you're not yelling at me or trying to strangle me."

Caitlin pushed her away with a teary laugh. "Okay, fine. But seeing as you do love and adore me, it turns out there's something you can do to make me feel better."

"Anything except hug you again."

"Haha. All you've got to do is answer one question."

"Oh boy," Maze said warily.

"No, don't be scared."

Maze laughed a little. "Right. You do know you're scary as hell, yeah?"

"One question, Maze, and you *can't* lie."

Oh, but she could. And had . . .

Caitlin looked her right in the eye. "Is there something going on between you and Walker? And before you answer, I want you to know it's a nonjudgmental question. I've always thought the two of you would bring out the best in each other. He'd help you realize how amazing you are, and you'd—"

"What? Scare him off women entirely?" she asked dryly, pretending her heart wasn't pounding.

"No," Caitlin said, not joking. "You'd soften him."

Maze snorted, because she could attest to the fact that there wasn't any softness to Walker, not a single inch of his leanly muscled bod. The man was a rock.

Inside and out.

"You know what I mean," Caitlin said earnestly. "He's always had a soft spot for you. Different from what he feels for me or Heather. He takes care of the two of us. But with you, he . . ." She shook her head, smiled. "It's like he admires your strength and knows he can stand at your side. He doesn't have to watch your back all the time, he can just . . . enjoy you. If that makes sense."

If that had been true, he'd never have let her go. But he had. "You're wrong."

"Maybe," Caitlin replied in a tone that said she didn't believe that for a hot second.

"Pick another question," Maze said flatly.

Caitlin nodded so easily that Maze felt certain she'd been tricked.

"I was thinking," Caitlin said, "maybe while you're here, you could stay . . . open. Like really open. And don't even bother looking at me like I've just suggested a gyno exam in the middle of Main Street. You know what I mean by open."

Yes, but she wished she didn't. "That's not a question."

"Will you stay open? Just for the week?" Caitlin asked. "And thank you. It's a lovely present. I won't even regift it."

"How about this?" Maze asked. "I will if you will."

Some of Cat's smugness left. "Maze—"

"I will if you will," she repeated softly, and Cat slowly nodded.

Chapter 9

Maze's maid of honor to-do list:
—Call the caterer to add alcohol for the
*   bride's dressing room ahead of the*
*   ceremony.*

That night, Maze didn't have a nightmare, but she did have one hell of a weird dream. Elvis was chasing her around the lake, and she was in a wedding dress. She sat straight up in bed with a horrified laugh. It was certainly an improvement over her last nightmare, but no thank you.

It was still dark. A glance at the clock told her it was four thirty in the morning. What the heck? She peeked over the side of the bed, but Jace was out like a light. So she stepped over him, stole the sweats he'd left on the floor, and left. In the hallway, she paused in front of Walker's room. His door was ajar, so she took a peek.

He lay on his back in the center of the bed, breathing steadily and evenly. She knocked lightly on the doorjamb, but he didn't move. Biting her lower lip, she squeezed in and shut the door behind her. "Hey," she whispered.

Nothing. The sheet was pooled dangerously low on his hips, revealing a mouthwatering chest and abs that she suddenly wanted to lick.

"*Walk.*" This time she added a poke to his chest.

"Shh. He's sleeping," he murmured.

"It's almost morning."

He cracked an eye and looked at her before smiling. "You're right. We should hurry. Come here." And he lifted the sheet in open invitation.

He wasn't wearing anything except testosterone and pheromones, and her heart stopped. "Oh my God."

"It bodes well for me that you're already saying 'oh my God.' But I'm going to need you to lose your boyfriend's sweats first."

"You and I are not going to—" She drew in a deep breath. *How did he always derail her?* "I'm only here to tell you that I'm going to sign the papers."

He paused a beat. "Okay."

"I just haven't yet because I want to read through them first."

"Don't worry. I'm still leaving my vinyl collection to you."

"You think this is funny?" she asked in disbelief.

"Your reaction to it is."

"You know what? I'm going now. People are going to hear us."

"They're not awake. They're lucky enough to be sleeping."

She turned to go, but he caught her, wrapping his fingers around her wrist. His eyes were open but heavy lidded, his jaw beyond a five o'clock shadow, mouth almost curved. "You're up before dawn. What am I missing?"

"Nothing."

He sat up with a frown. "Did you have another nightmare?"

"Yes. Elvis was chasing me around the lake." She left off the part where she'd been in a wedding dress because that was just too embarrassing.

"Want me to make you forget about the dream?"

"No!" her mouth said, but her other body parts quivered and cried, *Yes!* "I'm going now because we don't want anyone to see me and think I'm making the walk of shame back to my room."

"We don't?"

"No, because right now no one knows about Vegas. And if we keep it quiet, no one will ever have to know."

He studied her for a long beat. "And that would bother you, if anyone knew."

"Yes!"

He let go of her and slid out of bed. Naked. He walked to a duffel bag on a chair, where he took his time pulling on a pair of jeans over a world-class ass.

No underwear.

The denim looked soft and well worn. He grabbed a shirt next, covering up that scrumptious body. When he caught her staring, his lips twitched.

"What?" she asked. "I like to look."

"Good to know. The ball's in your court, tough girl. On both counts." Then he headed toward the door.

"Wait. What does that mean, 'on both counts'?"

He gave her a long look, smiled . . . and walked out of the room.

Tossing up her hands, she went back to her room. Jace was gone. She climbed into bed and was just closing her eyes when Jace came back, showered and fully dressed. "Sleep well?" he asked.

The question and his tone were mild, but she studied him closely. "Yes," she said. "Like a log."

"A log who dreams about wedding dresses, Elvis, Vegas, and, near as I can piece together, the best sex you ever had? Tell me you weren't having sex with Elvis."

With a groan, she lay back and pulled her pillow over her face.

Jace laughed, and when he didn't say anything else, she pushed the pillow off her face to look at him. His face was serious now. *"What?"*

He sat at her hip. "Why are we really pretending to be together?"

"I already told you. Everyone else was bringing a plus-one and I didn't want to be a loser."

"Except Heather's plus-one is Sammie, and Walker didn't bring anyone."

"Other than his bad attitude," she muttered.

"Yeah, see, you keep saying that, but the only one with a bad attitude that I've seen is you." That he said this in a calm, quiet, even gentle tone saved his life. "Talk to me, Maze."

Stay open. That had been Caitlin's request, and she'd asked so little of Maze and yet given so much. "He . . . hurt me," she said.

Jace's eyes went dark and dangerous. "He put his hands on you?"

"No. *No*," she repeated when he remained tense. "He would never. Look, it was all a very long time ago and it's a long story."

"I'm listening."

She blew out a sigh. "You know I grew up in foster homes."

"Because your dad left before you were born and your mom was fond of assholes."

She blinked in surprise.

"Heather and I were talking about how all of you met when you were fostered by Caitlin's parents, after each suffering some pretty shitty childhoods."

"What else did she tell you?"

"Nothing. Just that you're all bonded for life, but she was sparse on the details of why."

She let out a rough breath, because she did her best to never think about that year she'd spent in the Walsh home, but she'd let herself fall into those memories while here because some of them were the best of her entire life. But not the story she was going to tell Jace now. "Caitlin's parents were really great," she started. "Heather, Caitlin, Michael—Cat's younger brother—and Walker and I got really close that year. Their home wasn't too far from here, actually. It was in town. The problem was . . ." She closed her eyes. *"Me,"* she admitted. "I was fifteen and wild and impulsive. I rebelled against the rules, because . . . well, I don't know why really, probably because I had an issue with authority and also was an angry punk ass. And that's what started the whole thing."

"What thing?"

"A carnival came to Wildstone," she said. "Caitlin's parents took us during the day, but we had to leave at dark. I wanted to go back later that night and see all the lights, but that wasn't allowed. Shelly and Jim gave us a lot of freedom, but they still had rules and I thought a lot of them were dumb." She drew a deep, shuddering breath. "So Mayhem Maze came up with the brilliant idea of sneaking out that night. Just me and Caitlin and Walker. We'd done it a few times before, so I thought no big deal. We didn't tell Heather or Michael—they were too young to go. The deal was we'd meet in the basement and climb out one of the windows, walk the two miles to the carnival, and have a great time."

"I take it that didn't happen," Jace said.

She shook her head. "Caitlin didn't want to go. She didn't like to break the rules. So it was a cluster from the start, and it only got worse when Heather showed up in the basement. She loved to eavesdrop and then tattle, but on that night her tactic had been to blackmail us." She managed a rough laugh. "She promised she'd keep our secret *if* we took her along."

He smiled. "So she was smart, even back then."

"Oh yeah," Maze said with a laugh. "And adorable. Irresistible, really. Still is, though she will no longer keep anyone's secret."

Jace smiled and Maze cocked her head.

"Wait. What was that?"

"What?"

"That look in your eye," she said. "That's the look you get when you like someone. The last time I saw it on you was right before you started dating that cute blond beverage distributor. Daisy, right?"

"There's no look," he said.

"There's totally a look, Jace."

A muscle in his jaw clenched, and then he nodded. "Okay, maybe there's a look. But it's not going anywhere. Clearly."

Because he was still her "boyfriend." More guilt slashed through her. "Jace—"

"This isn't about me. Heather promised not to tell. So what happened?"

Maze sighed. "I turned on a little portable heater to warm the basement while we were all arguing. Millie, the Walsh's dog, always followed us everywhere. She'd come down the stairs after Heather. Her tail knocked over the heater and the rug caught on fire. The whole house was engulfed in flames in like five minutes. It was an inferno."

"Jesus. Were you hurt?"

She gave a bitter laugh. "No. Not even a little. Caitlin, Heather, Walker, Millie, and I all got out through the high, narrow basement window." Suddenly there was a huge lump in her throat—pure grief and survivor's guilt. She couldn't swallow past it. "Caitlin and Michael's parents were gone for the evening and already out of the house. We were standing on the grass staring in horror at the fire when I realized Walker was running back inside. To get Michael." She shook her head. "The firefighters arrived and had to drag him out—he wouldn't go without Michael. But he'd hit his head and had a concussion, plus smoke inhalation and some second- and third-degree burns."

"And Michael?"

All she could do was shake her head.

"Ah, Maze." Jace pulled her to him and squeezed, pressing his cheek to the top of her head. "I'm so sorry, honey."

"It was the smoke that got him. He never even woke up." She sniffed and choked back the emotion, shaking it off the best she could. "The house couldn't be saved.

So Caitlin and her parents had to move. And Heather, Walker, and I were sent to other foster homes. Thanks to Caitlin, we managed to stay in contact."

"And then Vegas happened."

She nodded.

"Heather said you two were always close. She didn't know much about his early years. She said if anyone knew, it'd be you."

Maze knew shockingly little as well, not for a lack of asking. Walker had coaxed much of her story from her over the years but had always shrugged off his own. "He's a closed book."

"Were you . . . seeing each other?"

"No. Just here and there with the others, but a few years before, we'd had a near miss at one of Caitlin's holiday parties." She'd never forget it. They'd been out back beneath a starry night sky and a huge tree—and a sprig of mistletoe. It'd been a joke really, when she'd gone up on tiptoe to kiss him, but it had quickly escalated.

"Near miss?" Jace asked.

Maze bit her lower lip. "Look, there was eggnog involved. We . . . kissed."

"Wow. You heathens."

"Hey, it was a big deal, okay?"

"Why?"

She shrugged, trying to find the words. "There'd always been a tension between us that was different than with the others. And it wasn't until then"—when they'd nearly taken each other up against the tree but had come to their senses—"that either of us realized it was a physical chemistry. But we caught ourselves in time. I think because we knew it would ruin everything. Which means I was a lot smarter when I was still in my teens than I was at twenty-one." She pulled the divorce papers from beneath her pillow and tossed them into his lap.

Jace opened the file and read, his eyes widening in surprise. "So Elvis *did* file."

"Go figure. A man doing something he promised he wouldn't."

Jace grimaced and ran a hand down his face. "You really didn't know?"

She shook her head. "Walker didn't either. Not until he went for a loan for some property he wanted to buy. That's when he had these papers drawn up."

"And now all you have to do is sign."

"Yep."

He met her gaze. "And yet you haven't signed."

"I don't have a pen."

He rolled his eyes.

"I'm going to sign!"

He stood. "You know, suddenly everything's crystal clear." He laughed. "You're still into him and you're acting like you're also still in high school. You do realize all you have to do is tell him how you feel, right?"

"And you do realize you know nothing, right?" She stood too. "It was over the next morning, Jace. Remember the part where I said he hurt me? Well, he didn't want me, not really. So no, I'm not going to tell him a damn thing. I'm going to sign these papers and move on with my damn life!"

His smile had vanished. "Look, I realize I don't know shit about this—"

"Damn right you don't."

"But I do know *you*. You don't choose people lightly, Maze. Ever. And from what I can tell about Walker, he's a stand-up guy with a solid but tough job, and he keeps the people he cares about in his life close. And . . ."

She narrowed her eyes. "And what?"

"You're one of those people."

"I'm a pain in his ass."

"No doubt," he said. "But it's more than that and I think you know it."

And then he was gone, leaving her alone with the thoughts she didn't want to have. So she grabbed some clothes and headed into the bathroom. It was steamy from a shower . . . and not empty.

"Oh," she said, an involuntary exclamation at the sight of Walker in nothing but a towel, leaning over the bathroom sink shaving. "Sorry. I was just going to shower . . ."

"No problem." He gestured to the shower behind him. "Help yourself."

She might have, but to get past him, she'd have to brush up against him.

He gave her a smile via the mirror.

"What?" she asked a little defensively.

"You're trying to decide whether you want to touch me or shove me," he said, still shaving.

She went hands on hips. "Let's go with shove."

"Which means you *do* want to touch, you just don't want me to know it," he said smugly.

"You know what? I'll come back later," she said, annoyingly breathless for no reason, but definitely *not* from the sight of him in just a towel, still damp from his shower.

He gave a low laugh, and she narrowed her eyes.

"Look," he said, "we both have a busy day ahead with wedding errands and chores."

This was true. There were errands to run, lots of them. And she also had to go check out the wedding venue, which was a property just outside of town in the middle of ranch land and wineries. It had a restaurant and wide-open patio that led to a gorgeous view of rolling green hills dotted with oaks. It was on her list to stop by and familiarize herself with it so that she could run the wedding rehearsal on Friday night just before the rehearsal dinner.

"So I'm sure we can be grown-ups about this. Plus, we've both seen it all."

"Yes, but . . ." She squirmed. "It's been a while."

He smiled. "Has anything changed?"

"Maybe." When his gaze met hers in the mirror, she lifted a shoulder. "I'm not exactly the cute young twenty-one-year-old anymore."

"No, you're something even better."

Her breath caught, and again their gazes met and held in the mirror. "Are you taking your sweet-ass time on purpose?" she asked.

"You think I've got a sweet ass?"

She crossed her arms but couldn't resist giving the body part in question a long look-over in the towel, which made her go damp in places that had no business going damp. "You already know damn well you've got the best ass on the West Coast."

"But not the East Coast?"

"Are you *flirting* with me?"

"Not if you have a boyfriend," he said easily.

They stared at each other for a long beat before he rinsed off his razor and went back to shaving. "But to be clear," he said, "*your* ass is the sweetest on the planet. In case you were wondering."

She locked her wobbly knees and let out a shaky breath. "Could you possibly hurry up?"

"And miss the expression on your face when you have to try to squeeze past me to the shower?"

She made a big point of sucking it all in to get past him without touching. Or shoving.

He just laughed and kept on shaving. "It's okay," he said. "I've got the memories of the last time you touched me on repeat."

"I'd have thought your legions of women since then would've erased the memories of me."

"I don't know about legions," he said, all teasing aside now. "But it could be the entire female race and the memories of you from that night will never fade."

Then he turned off the sink, wiped his face with a towel, and, when he looked up and found her just staring at him, smiled and left her alone to shower.

So how ridiculous was it when a small—and maybe actually not so small at all—part of her wished he'd stayed?

Chapter 10

Walker's man of honor to-do list:
—Do not sleep with, marry (again), or kill
Caitlin's maid of honor.

After the surprisingly revealing conversation with Maze, Walker headed downstairs. Since it was early, he doubted anyone else was up, but it was actually late for him. Apparently habits were habits. Getting up early . . . tangling with Maze . . .

He really didn't want to be pulled into her force field, but hell if that had stopped him. The only thing that helped was the certainty she was feeling it too, because when she thought no one was paying attention, she watched him. And then if he managed to catch her eye, she'd either roll hers or turn away.

Denial had always been her best friend.

He'd been curious to see how quickly she'd sign the divorce papers. He'd expected to feel closure, but at the moment, he was regretting even handing her the docs, because he knew the truth now.

He was never going to find closure with her.

But there was no going back, which meant that once again, there was something out of his control and he was left waiting to see if she was going to pass on him like a bad habit.

Other than the group right here in this house, people didn't walk toward him, they walked away. Hell, they ran. Even in his job, when people saw him coming, they ran. Granted, those were usually the bad guys. But his birth parents had walked. None of his foster families had kept him, including Caitlin's parents. Okay, so their house had burned down and they literally couldn't foster anymore, but still. Even the system had walked away the day he turned eighteen. But none of them had hurt him more than Maze.

No matter how hard he tried, he was always left standing alone with no one to count on except himself. But at least now he was choosing to be alone. *His* choice, *his* control, and he was okay with that. Or he had been.

Until he'd seen Maze again.

In the kitchen, he was surprised to find Heather at the table, head down, fast asleep. Sammie was in a *Frozen* princess nightgown, sitting in front of an open cupboard, empty food containers spread out before her. With one hand, she was gnawing on a piece of toast; the other was happily banging on a container with a wooden spoon. Roly and Poly were her avid audience, their buggy eyes locked in on her toast. Sammie grinned up at Walker and lifted both arms at him in silent, drooling demand.

There weren't a lot of people who could get him to bend to their will, but this little thing could do it without trying. When he scooped her up, Heather's head jerked upright. "Who? What? Where?"

Walker put a hand on her shoulder. "Why don't you go back to bed?"

Heather got to her feet. "No, I've gotta dress Sammie and then run to Home Depot for stuff for the reception. Maze's been working her ass off, so I offered to take her list and do the store run."

"The list?"

Heather fumbled in her jeans pocket and pulled out a piece of paper.

Walker took it, kissed her on the top of her head, and nudged her out of the kitchen. "Go back to bed," he repeated. "I've got Sammie and we'll go to Home Depot."

"They don't open until six A.M."

"It's six thirty."

Heather blinked sleepily. "Oh . . ." She smiled, but it turned into a yawn. "Time flies when you have a kid. But I can't let you do this, it's too much."

She looked so exhausted that he didn't want her on the road. "It's okay, I've got this."

"You only *think* you've got this. Trust me, running errands with her is a nightmare."

Maybe, and granted, he knew zip about having a kid. But he did know a little something about being one. His childhood was a blur of never belonging or being wanted. He knew Heather's past wasn't all that different. The fact that she was raising Sammie on her own gutted him, but he was trying to stay a presence in their lives, for Sammie's sake as well as Heather's. And his own, if he was being honest. Besides . . . "How hard can it be?"

Heather snorted. "You'll see, and bless you. Oh, and pro tip? She's more cooperative if you play the *Frozen* soundtrack on repeat. Do you have it on your Spotify?"

Walker gave her a blank look.

Heather shook her head. "Never mind. Take my car. It's got her car seat anyway, and the CD's already loaded."

Five minutes later Walker had Heather's keys and was trying to get Sammie into the car seat. But Sammie didn't want to get in the car seat, and apparently her superpower was the inhuman ability to turn herself into a limp noodle while screaming bloody murder at the same time.

"What's going on?"

Walker turned and found Maze standing behind him, looking cool and calm, sipping coffee and looking vastly amused.

"Having fun?" she asked over Sammie's screaming.

"Heather was too tired to adult," he said. "So I said I'd go to Home Depot and get the stuff you needed."

"And you got conned into babysitting while you were at it?"

"More like bamboozled. I actually volunteered."

She laughed out loud, and damn, she had a great laugh. She bent to look into the back seat at Sammie, who was still using her vocal cords to their full extent. "Hey, kiddo, I'll make you a deal. You let me buckle you in and I'll buy you something at the store."

Sammie went from crying to smiling in a single heartbeat. "Toy!" she squealed in delight, and let Maze buckle her in.

Maze straightened and gave Walker a victory smile.

"Doesn't count," he said. "You bribed her."

"Doesn't matter how, what matters is it worked." She got into the passenger seat.

He slid behind the wheel and gave her a look. "You're coming along?"

"Don't want to miss you getting your ass kicked by a two-and-a-half-year-old."

"There'll be no ass kicking. It's about setting expectations and having rules."

She laughed again. "This isn't the military, Walk. She's not your little soldier."

"It's about logic and common sense."

Maze just shook her head. "You poor, ignorant man."

He decided to overlook this. But he was having trouble overlooking her thin, lacy see-through sweater over a cami, both topping denim shorts that showed off her legs. He wasn't sure he was going to be able to concentrate on anything else, but then the *Frozen* CD started playing and Sammie began to sing. At high volume and off-key. He turned the music down, but she just got louder.

Halfway to Home Depot, while Walker's ears were already starting to bleed, Sammie yelled, "Potty!"

"We're almost there," he told her.

"There's a gas station on the corner," Maze said. "Maybe you should stop."

"I'm not taking her to a gas station bathroom," Walker said.

"Potty!"

"We're hurrying," he said via the rearview mirror. "Two minutes."

He pulled into the Home Depot parking lot. There was a light cool wind, but hell if he wasn't sweating. He got out, pulled Sammie from her car seat and set her down. He stripped off his sweatshirt, and before he could toss it into the driver's seat, he heard water splashing.

Sammie had hiked up her princess nightgown and spread her legs, and had her head bent, watching herself pee through her Wonder Woman undies.

In the parking lot.

A woman got out of the car across from them and tsked at him.

Maze was grinning. "Tried to tell you." She crouched next to Sammie, they did some quick maneuvering, and then Maze was carrying Sammie toward the entrance.

Walker, who rarely, if ever, felt clueless and uncertain of his next move, but who felt both of those things now, strode after them. When he caught up, he looked at Maze. "How we doing?"

"Well, Sammie's commando since her babysitter didn't listen to her, and I need some more caffeine, but other than that, we're both hanging in there."

Three aisles in, Walker was holding Sammie in one arm, pushing the cart with his free hand, and trying to keep up with Maze, who was deep in her list and concentrating. Sammie was crying again because he wouldn't let her have any of the mountain of bags of M&Ms they'd just passed, done up for Valentine's Day.

"Ms!" Sammie sobbed, staring despondently over his shoulder with an arm outstretched dramatically as they passed them by.

"Bad for your teeth," he said.

Sammie sobbed through three more rows until he caved and gave her a bag of M&Ms for each hand to keep her from ripping random shit off the shelves.

He could hear Maze, out in front of them, laughing her ass off. He set Sammie in the cart and came up behind a still-chortling Maze, where she was facing a row of unfinished frames. "What the hell is so funny?"

"Not supposed to swear around impressionable ears."

"Trust me, she can't hear me over her own inhaling of the M&Ms."

"Maybe I meant me," she said.

Now he laughed. "I've never made a single impression on you."

"Wanna bet?"

He wanted to give some brainpower to that confusing response, but he was distracted because she'd reached up to a high shelf, her perfectly shaped ass about an inch from his—

"Ms!" Sammie yelled at him. *"More!"*

What felt like five lifetimes later, Maze finally had everything on her list. By the time they checked out and got a commando, chocolate-covered Sammie back to the car, Walker was also covered in chocolate and wanted to stab himself in the eye with a stick. Repeatedly.

"You smell like candy."

He sent a death glare at Maze, who just laughed at him again. He didn't get it. In his world, he was feared. Men backed down whenever he gave them this same look.

Not Maze. She actually moved *into* his personal space, piercing his armor with nothing but that smile. "I can't tell you how much fun I just had."

He crossed his arms and stared down at her.

Not intimidated in the least, she just grinned. "Poor big, tough, untouchable Walker. Taken down by a little girl."

"By two girls, actually . . ." he said with a rough laugh. "I seriously underestimated and under-appreciated parenthood."

Sammie fell asleep in her car seat as he and Maze loaded the trunk.

"That was like taking your most badly behaved buddy out when he's shit-faced," he said. "No filter, wanting every ridiculous thing he sees, crying and getting mad over nothing, singing nonsense at the top of his lungs . . . I kept expecting to get kicked out and banned from the store for life."

"Hmm." She sipped the coffee he'd bought her. "You do realize we were that level of annoying ourselves in Vegas."

He stared at her, surprised. It was damn hard to surprise him, but she'd never once brought up the subject of Vegas first. Stepping toward her, he trapped her up against the car, an arm on either side of her head, palms flat on the roof of the vehicle. Her breath caught, and as a result, so did his, but he ignored that and met her gaze. "Thought you didn't remember a thing about that night."

"I remember you getting into our hotel room minibar."

"That was all you, babe. You said you had big plans for the chocolate."

She took a deep breath and her breasts brushed against his chest. He closed his eyes and dropped his forehead to her shoulder, almost weak in the knees at just being this close to her.

"I'd *never* open a minibar," she said. "Everything in it costs a million dollars. And I talk a big game when I'm drunk."

"Actually, you came through on every promise you made that night. Well, except one."

She pushed at him until he backed up and then strode angrily around the car and got in.

Chapter 11

Maze's to-do list
—Never ever have a big circus of a wedding.

Maze's emotions were still far too close to the surface when she and Walker and a commando Sammie got back to the house. It felt like a week had gone by, but it was only eight thirty. In the morning.

Getting up early was not all it was cracked up to be. Neither was tackling Cat's to-do list, which was no joke. Maze had gone through the binder several times now, and though it made her eyes cross, she was on it. There was only one thing in her favor: Cat's parents weren't coming in until Friday. A stay of execution—but even just the thought made her feel guilty. They'd buried a child, and now their firstborn was getting married and they were facing the fact that not only would Michael miss it, he'd never experience his own wedding.

Maze drew a deep breath and pushed that aside. She didn't bury it; she couldn't. Truthfully, Michael was never far from her mind. But she locked it up in a box for later. Her plan for today was simple. She was going to wake everyone and hand out tasks. She put bacon in the oven and brewed coffee. Feeling domestic, she texted everyone to get their asses downstairs. Well, everyone but the bride-to-be. Maze wanted Caitlin to take it easy today. She also wanted to prove herself, because for so long Caitlin had taken care of her chicks.

It was Maze's turn.

Thirty minutes later, she'd fed everyone bacon and toast, ignoring their exaggerated shock at her kitchen skills, and then bustled them all outside.

In the field of wild grass on one of the two picnic benches between the house and the lake, she got everyone staining the newly purchased reclaimed-wood picture frames in various sizes that Caitlin wanted scattered on the reception tables.

Walker was the exception. He'd gotten a call and stood off to the side, his back to everyone.

Dillon was actually helping too, and the pugs slept under everyone's feet, napping like they owned the joint. "You always do this," he said to them. "You say you want to do stuff, but you don't mean it." He picked them up, one under each arm, and carried them inside.

"I can't," Walker was saying to whomever he was talking to. "I told you, something came up this week. Don't worry, I promise when I get back we'll have some us time." He paused, clearly listening, and then laughed.

Laughed.

Maze hadn't heard that sound in a damn long time. And as if he sensed her watching, he turned his head and locked gazes with her. She started to back away but bumped right into an oak tree, so then she had to stand there like she'd meant to lean on it.

"I've gotta go," he said into the phone, still looking at Maze as he slid it into his pocket.

"You've got to shut down your live screen," she said, "or you'll end up butt dialing her, and that'll make you look pathetic and get you dumped."

And here was the thing about Walker. When he was amused, something interesting happened to his face. His eyes twinkled. Not just with merriment but with sheer mischief. On any given day, he practically *leaked* bad boy, but when he was in a good mood, it multiplied.

Exponentially.

Which is what happened now as he came toward her. She actually got dizzy from looking at him. Most people understood personal space boundaries, but Walker did not. At least not with her. He came at her until they were toe-to-toe.

"So you *do* have a girlfriend," she said.

He was so close he had to tilt his head to look into her face. And of course he didn't answer the question. Instead he had one of his own. "You sign those papers yet?"

"You tell her that you're still married?" she countered, chin up.

Reaching out, he set a big hand on the tree beside her head. "Worried about me?"

"Worried about *her*," she managed, her body doing traitorous things. Like wanting to brush up against him just to see if their bodies still combusted when they touched, wondering if he still gave that heart-stopping rough male groan whenever she made a sexual move on him, telling herself she needed to know if a single brush of his lips would still set her afire . . .

He smiled down at her with that mouth she already knew could do diabolically delicious things to her. "You're cute when you're jealous."

She sputtered because she wasn't sure which was worse, him saying she was *cute*—which she most definitely was not—or him thinking she was actually jealous, which was beyond stupid. "I'm not either of those things."

"Liar." He tugged on a strand of her hair. "As for me, I've already told you, I'm not the one breaking our vows every night."

At that, and the reminder of her deception with Jace, she looked away. But Walker cupped her jaw and brought her face back to his. The smile was gone now, replaced by an expression of intensity, and she was viscerally reminded what it felt like to be in his crosshairs.

Exhilarating and terrifying.

"That was my boss on the phone," he said softly. "So I'm going to ask you again. Is there something you want to tell me?"

He wanted her to come clean about Jace. But remembering how quickly he'd forgotten her, she knew her pride wasn't going to let him off the hook. No way, no how. So she pulled free and said, "Absolutely not." And with her nose in the air, she went to join the others.

"The frames have to be perfect," she called out. "They're going to be filled with pics of Caitlin's favorite people. If you stain them wrong, you won't be one of those people."

Jace laughed.

"Trust me," Heather whispered. "She's actually not kidding."

After, they put together some other wood accents for the reception, centerpieces for the tables, and cute signs designating different areas, like a food and drink station and a photo booth. Maze ticked everything off in the wedding bible, and afterward she took Caitlin for her last dress fitting—with a pit in the bottom of her stomach. Cat's mom was going to FaceTime at the dress shop, which had Maze sweating in uncomfortable places and blood rushing through her veins. On a scale of one to passing out from a panic attack, she was at a nine-point-nine.

The shop was a cute, fancy place in San Luis Obispo, about thirty minutes from the lake house. Cat was quiet on the drive. Maze too. She knew why she wasn't saying much: she couldn't, because anxiety was blocking her air passage. But the quiet was definitely out of character for Cat. "Are you okay?"

"Sure," Cat said.

"Sure?" Maze slid her a look. "That doesn't sound like you. What's wrong?"

"This week's going too fast."

Maze risked another look. "You want to push the wedding? Just say the word, babe. I'll handle the rest, no worries."

Cat's eyes filled and she turned away to stare out the window. "That's not it."

"Then what?"

"You'll all leave after the wedding," Cat said quietly.

This caused an actual stab of pain straight through Maze's chest. Taking one hand off the wheel, she set it on Cat's and entwined their fingers. "I'm a dickhead," she said.

Cat gave a startled laugh and wiped a tear away. "Yes."

"Huh." Maze let out a small smile. "Thought you might at least pretend to argue that one. Look . . ." She drew a deep breath as she pulled into the dress shop parking lot, parked, and turned to Cat. "I might physically leave because, well, I have a job and I like to have a roof over my head. But I'll never vanish on you again. I'll pick up a phone, answer a text, and come see you— *and* have you come see me—as often as possible. You can see my work, meet my friends—"

"You have friends?"

"Haha," Maze said. "And yes. I mean, not like you and Heather, of course. But I have work friends, and also a few in my apartment building, and where I volunteer at the women's shelter—"

"Wait. You volunteer? At a women's shelter?"

Maze shrugged. "I had some extra time and—"

"You volunteer. You help people, maybe even kids who were like you and needed a place to go so they couldn't get hurt by some asshole—"

"I mostly just clean, so don't make me into some kind of hero," Maze grumbled, but it was too late.

Cat leaned over the console and hugged her tight. "Oh, Maze. You're amazing, you know that, right?"

"Look, you can come with me when you visit. You can clean a few toilets and then see if you think it's so amazing. It's only a two-hour drive. We can even FaceTime—"

Cat grabbed Maze by the front of her shirt and gave her a smacking kiss right on the lips.

"Wow. Okay. But I don't put all the way out unless you buy me a meal first."

Cat kissed her again, her eyes shimmering with tears. "You mean it, right?"

"I mean it," she vowed, her own throat tight. "Now, are we going in, or do you want to make out?"

Cat was laughing as they walked into the shop. If only Maze could feel as carefree at the moment, but she was incredibly aware that in a few minutes she was going to see Cat's mom again.

They were served champagne and cookies, and were enjoying them, when Cat got a text.

"Oh no," she murmured. "Mom's stuck in a meeting. Her boss is as mean as mine."

"It's okay," Maze assured her while trying not to show her sheer relief. "I've got you. I'll take pics for her."

The tailor first brought out Maze's bridesmaid dress for her to pick up since Heather had already gotten hers. Maze thought she managed to hide her cringe at the color of the dress, which was supposed to be peach but looked more like a sort of unhealthy orange.

"Dillon's mom loved that color," Caitlin said.

"It's . . ." Maze managed to smile. ". . . great."

Caitlin nodded doubtfully, looking very distracted as she was ushered into a dressing room.

When she hadn't come out five full minutes later, Maze knocked on the door. "Need help?"

"I need something."

"Come out or I'm coming in."

Caitlin slowly came out and moved wordlessly to the pedestal in front of three huge mirrors.

The dress was gorgeous but clearly too tight to zip. Caitlin stared at herself in the mirrors and burst into tears.

Maze waved off the horrified tailor and sat on the pedestal next to Caitlin.

"It's my fault," Caitlin sobbed. "I ate the entire bag of frozen Costco Bagel Bites, and it was five servings."

"Everyone knows the serving size doesn't count with Bagel Bites. And you're perfect, by the way. It's your dress that needs to adjust, just a little. No biggie."

Caitlin sniffed. "You think I'm perfect?"

"One hundred percent perfect."

Caitlin half laughed, half cried. "That's the sweetest thing you've ever said to me."

"Okay, but we don't have to—"

Too late. Caitlin threw her arms around Maze and squeezed tight.

"—hug," Maze said with a sigh. But in the end, she went with it and hugged Caitlin back. "You're a nut."

"A *perfect* nut, though . . ."

"Cat?"

"Yeah?"

"Why are your boobs vibrating?"

Cat sniffed and pulled back. "I've got my phone in my bra. It's my boss. She calls all the time to either tell me she can't figure something out or blame me for something going wrong."

"But it's your wedding week."

"Oh, she knows."

Maze took in the unhappiness in Cat's eyes and wanted more than anything to bring back the carefree, happy Cat, because she deserved it more than anyone she knew. But short of going back in time to make sure Michael didn't die, she had no idea how to help. "You need a new job, babe."

"I like what I do."

"Then you need to do it for someone else, someone who'll appreciate your talents more. You're amazing, Cat, and you deserve better."

The bride sniffed some more. "You really do love me."

"Duh."

After surviving yet another long hug, Maze got the tailor, who took some measurements and promised to fix the dress. Then Maze got Cat changed and back to the lake house. She hadn't even set her bag down when Heather caught her alone in the hallway, pulling her aside, looking around them to make sure no one was listening.

"What now?" Maze asked with dread.

"Um." Heather paused. "Is everything okay?"

Loaded question. "Yes. Why?"

"No reason," Heather said casually. "I just wanted to apologize that you guys keep getting interrupted or stuck with Sammie."

"Oh, no worries." Maze smiled. "She was great this morning at Home Depot. She even got chocolate all over Walker and everything."

"Actually, when I asked if everything's okay, I meant with you and Jace."

Oh. Oh shit.

Heather bit her lower lip. "Listen, it's none of my business, but Jace is clearly sleeping on the floor of your room. Are you two in a fight?"

"Um . . ."

"Because . . ." Heather paused long enough that Maze met her gaze. "I think he's flirting with me,

Maze. I mean, I can't tell for sure because my radar's broken. But if he is, then he's a jerk, which I really need to know."

Dammit. "No, he's not a jerk. He's a good guy." She paused. "One who's just here as a favor."

"What?"

Maze grimaced. "Look, I heard everyone was coming here with a plus-one, so I panicked. After a lot of begging, Jace—my boss and also one of my best friends—agreed to be my pretend boyfriend."

Heather stared at her and then laughed. "So . . . he's available?"

"One hundred percent. But I need to keep this between us."

"'This' being a big, fat lie?" Heather asked, very amused.

Maze blew out another breath. "Yes. It's embarrassing."

"You mean when you panicked thinking that Walker was bringing a plus-one because you're still totally one hundred percent over the moon in love with him?"

Maze nearly fell over. "What?"

Heather grimaced. "Um, what?"

"Heather."

"Yeah, so let's scrap my last question from the record, on account of it being based on decade-old information."

Maze was staring at her, heart pounding. "Oh my God. I *knew* I recognized the 'totally one hundred percent over the moon' part. You and your hacking abilities. You broke into my password-protected journal on that laptop we all used to share, didn't you?"

"I was bored."

"You were nine."

"And curious!"

Maze covered her face, remembering some of the whiny teenage details she'd spent long hours languishing on and on about in that journal back in the day.

"And anyway," Heather said, "if you'd all just let me play with you guys back then, I wouldn't have been forced to spy on you. And it's not like I didn't understand your crush on Walker. Even then, he was one of the best guys I'd ever known. He understands what he missed out on growing up, and loyalty and connections mean something to him. He'd never turn his back on a single one of us, ever."

Oh, but he had . . .

Heather looked away. "Not like I did. I just . . ." She shook her head. "After that time at Michael's grave, knowing we all had so much we were dealing with, I knew I couldn't burden you guys with the mess I'd made of my life. I'm so sorry I vanished like that."

"Please don't put this all on you, we all did it. We all let our own shit put doubts into our heads, and then let those doubts tell us we were better off alone. Which is never the case. I get that now. I think you do too."

Heather turned to her. "I don't ever want to be without you guys again. Ever." She pulled the baby monitor off her hip to eye the screen. Sammie was still out cold, sleeping peacefully, a small smile on her perfect face.

"She's amazing," Maze said softly. "I'm proud of you, Heather."

Heather looked up, surprised. "You are?"

"Yeah. You were dealt a bad hand and you turned it into a win. It's a sweet life you've got there." She nodded toward Sammie.

"It doesn't feel sweet without you guys in it. I'm really so sorry. I feel like I can't say it enough, but I didn't realize until I saw you all again how much I needed you in my life."

"Me too." Maze took her hand. "I wish I'd known you were in trouble, but that I didn't was on me. But I promise that me vanishing like I did wasn't about you, ever. I missed you so much."

They were hugging it out when Caitlin came down the hall. "What are we doing? Group hug without me?" Dropping her purse to the floor, she insinuated herself into the middle and joined in. "What did I miss?"

"How stupid we are for vanishing," Heather said, "for not keeping up with each other's lives. Never again."

"Agreed," Caitlin said. "Never again. You guys are the mac to my cheese."

They sealed the vow with a glass of wine that turned into a couple of bottles. The rest of the evening was a pleasant blur for Maze as the three of them sat up late doing Cat's favorite thing, making lists, in this case for what else still needed to be done for the wedding.

"Oh, and I've got to pick up Dillon's wedding band at the jeweler's and make the final payment," Caitlin said, and grimaced. "*Without* letting Dillon know, since I was supposed to do it two weeks ago. And also I need to let his mom know I picked out the flowers with my mom during an appointment when she FaceTimed in. There are no decisions left to be made, even though she's insisting on coming with me to make *that* final payment in a few days." She thunked her head on the table. "Oh my God, *why didn't I elope*?"

"I can handle the jeweler for you," Maze said.

"You've done so much already."

"Don't you know?" Maze took her hand. "I'd do anything for you. Well, anything except deal with your scary-sounding future mother-in-law. You need to find your backbone, babe."

When Caitlin teared up, Maze pointed at her.

"No. No more tears. I've used up my quota."

"Fine," Caitlin said. "But hugs are endless."

"Oh my God. No—" But it was futile. Caitlin already had her in an arm hold.

The next morning came way too quickly. Maze stood in the shower trying to steam her hangover away. It wasn't working.

"Tell me again why I have to be in here with you while you're in the shower?" Jace asked through the shower curtain from his perch on the counter.

"Because you had one job, to be my boyfriend, and so far no one's buying it. You need to yell out my name. Or moan *really* loud. No, wait! Do both!"

The curtain was yanked back a few inches. "You can't be serious," he said.

"Hey! Do you mind? Naked in here!" She put a wet hand to his face and pushed his head out of the shower.

"I didn't look. Also, nice tat."

"You said you didn't look!"

"I lied. See, *that's* how you do it, Maze. You make the lie believable."

She glared at him and then closed the curtain again in a huff.

"And anyway, I think Walker really cares about you," Jace said quietly.

She yanked the curtain open. "For the last time, he's done with me, okay? He came here with divorce papers, so please, tell me one more time that he cares about me . . ."

He shook his head. "How about I tell you something else instead. You two need to figure this out sooner than later, because I've got a problem."

She turned off the water and wrapped a towel around herself. "I can't handle any more problems."

"I've got a thing for Heather."

"Because she's awesome."

"So . . . you're okay with it?" he asked slowly, cautiously.

"Very. She deserves a good guy and you're the best of them."

He stilled, then gave a small smile. "Thanks. I'd like to get to know her better, but that's difficult when your husband is constantly eyeballing me like he wants to kill me. And FYI, he probably could in a thousand and one different ways with his bare hands."

"He doesn't care if I'm with you."

"Okay, let's pretend for one second that's true—which it isn't. But if it was, then why are we having pretend sex in the shower?"

"I don't know. It's ridiculous." She covered her eyes for a beat to think. "*I'm* ridiculous. I have no idea why this all is getting to me."

"Don't you?"

She dropped her hand and looked at him, completely confused, and he visibly softened.

"Maze, you're one of the smartest people I've ever met. Put it together."

She realized he was trying to tell her that this was getting to her because she still had feelings for Walker. And while she suspected deep, deep down that it *might* be true, there was no way in hell she was going to admit it.

"You need to tell him," he said.

"Why?"

"Because I'm a stand-up guy, and I hate this. I hate making everyone here think we're together when we're not. I was wrong to agree. And you're wrong too, because in case you've forgotten, you're a stand-up chick as well."

Maze walked out of the bathroom and ran right into the brick wall that was Walker.

His hands came up to her arms, holding her steady while she got her feet beneath her. Flustered, she took a step back. "Were you eavesdropping?" she asked, wincing at how annoyingly breathless she sounded.

"Didn't you want me to be?"

"Of course not."

"Hmm. You forget . . ." He dipped his head so that his mouth brushed her ear. "I know what you sound like when you're *not* faking."

Why on earth had she thought bringing Jace as her boyfriend would ever work? Because Walker was right. He knew the real thing between them had been heart-stopping and emotional, and *nothing* had ever been like it. And if that didn't drive her nuts . . .

Sammie came barreling down the hall and threw herself at Walker's legs. "Birds!"

"You want to go see the birds?" he asked, hoisting her up.

She nodded vehemently.

"You got it." He looked at Maze. "See how it works? You ask for what you want. You use your words, Maze. It's not magic."

When she didn't say anything—because what was there to say?—he gave her a long look and left with Sammie.

Chapter 12

Caitlin's to-do list:
—Figure out how to lose fifteen pounds in
*   four days.*

I t was noon and Caitlin was already too exhausted for the reception rehearsal. But Maze had everyone all lined up outside like good little soldiers, and she was trying to pay attention while obsessing over things like would her wedding dress really fit? And did she need a wax? Anything to avoid thinking about how Michael would've loved this week and how she shouldn't have to do this without him.

"Participation is mandatory and you *will* have fun," Maze commanded.

Caitlin had to laugh. Clearly, her refound BFF was channeling the bossy bride herself. Maze was in running gear that had most likely never seen so much as a jog, but she looked impressively in charge as she strode back and forth in front of them, the binder tucked under one arm, her iPad under her other. The only thing she was missing was a whistle. Even Dillon was there, though Caitlin had to promise him his favorite sexual favor to get him out here.

"So," Maze said loudly with fanfare, "today's mission: we're going to run through and practice all the reception activities. Quickly. I call it a speed reception rehearsal." She paused, clearly expecting excitement.

Everyone just stood there looking at her with varying degrees of boredom. Well, except for Roly and Poly, who were in their fancy outdoor beds napping in the sun.

"Hey!" Maze said, pointing at them all. "This is going to be fun, dammit! Now, look alive, people. I've divided up the itinerary. I estimate the real thing on Saturday will take three hours, but we're going to run through it in one hour today. Hence the 'speed' part of the speed reception rehearsal. Get it?"

Deadpan looks.

"Ugh." Maze tossed up her hands. "Fine, we'll just get on with it. Everyone go to your designated table, where there's an itinerary. First up is the introduction of the bride and groom. Then drinks—that should cheer all you lushes up. Food's next, which for today's purposes is Taco Bell takeout because I didn't have time to cook."

"Didn't have time or *can't* cook?" Jace asked.

Walker laughed.

"Nice to see you two bonding," Maze said, heavy on the sarcasm. "After food, we dance. Then the cutting of the cake and more dancing. Oh, and there's also a game going on the whole time, called Secret Mission. Your instructions are taped beneath the seat of your individual chairs. Be discreet. Don't share. It's called *Secret* Mission for a reason. Now go!"

Caitlin moved to Maze. "I'm impressed," she said, sincerely touched. This was more than she could have imagined asking Maze for. "You've gone over and above."

"Don't thank me yet. I plan to embarrass the hell out of you with my maid of honor speech."

Cat turned Maze to face her. "You know how you think *I'm* perfect?"

"Well, not *totally* perfect," Maze said. "You've got a hair out of place here." She patted the side of Caitlin's head, making her laugh.

"You know how you think I'm perfect?" Caitlin asked again softly.

"Yeah."

"Well, I think *you're* perfect, Maze. Just as you are."

Maze's eyes got misty, but she then quickly rolled them. "And I think you're wearing your rose-colored glasses again."

"Nope," Caitlin said. "I'm allergic to roses, remember? Just like you're allergic to compliments."

Maze laughed and strode off to check on her minions. She'd set up the mock reception in the grass. Talking and laughing among themselves, they had read their secret missions and, to Caitlin's relief, they seemed to be taking the game seriously. Except for Dillon. He was sitting quietly, looking at his card with resigned annoyance.

It'd been her idea to do the game. She'd seen it on Pinterest. At the real reception, everyone would be given a secret mission, written specifically for them and stuck under their chair—things like hug a friend or relative you haven't seen in a long time, each task designed to encourage mingling. The first five people to drop their completed mission into a basket at the head table would win a prize.

For today, she'd created fun, easy missions for Maze to hand out. There'd been a brief debate on this issue because Maze had wanted to come up with the missions herself, but Cat had thought that . . . dangerous. Maze had sighed but ultimately agreed—she couldn't be trusted.

Heather's mission was to get someone to swear. Walker's was to make someone laugh out loud. Dillon needed to get Caitlin to swoon (okay, so that one was self-serving, sue her). Jace's mission was to get someone to rumba with him. And Maze . . . all she had to do was smile at someone unprompted.

Maze, as acting DJ, called Caitlin and Dillon up for their first dance.

Dillon came for Caitlin with his charming smile, the one that always disarmed her. He tugged her to him, his hands going straight to her ass.

"Hey," she said. "This dance is supposed to be classy."

"But this is just practice."

"Yes. For the *real thing*."

Dillon sighed.

"What?"

"Nothing."

"It's something," she insisted.

"I thought this wedding would be fun, is all."

She stared at him. "Are you kidding me? I wanted a small family-only wedding. Having a big three-ring-circus wedding for basically your mother because you're an only child and all she's ever wanted was a huge wedding for you—not nearly as much. But I'm trying to make the most of it."

He sighed again. "It's not all my mom's fault. You haven't really ever tried with her."

Caitlin bit back her automatic defensive response and counted to five, like Walker had taught her. And damn if she didn't realize in those five seconds that Dillon might be a *little* bit accurate. Or a lot. "Fine," she said. "You're right. I could try harder with your mom."

He blinked in surprise. "Thank you. That means a lot."

Feeling a surge of affection for him, she forced a smile. "Besides, we're going to Bali for a week, so who knows, maybe we'll get started on something from your life list."

"Like . . . planning out our retirement?" he asked.

"I was thinking one of the other things."

He accidentally danced on her toes.

"Ouch!"

"I'm sorry!"

Maze quickly came to cut in and Caitlin happily let her. From the corner of her eye she caught sight of Heather and Jace dancing the rumba, looking far more like a bride and groom than she and Dillon had looked.

She turned to watch Dillon and Maze dancing very stiffly, silent. Awkward with each other.

But that's not what bothered her. Maze might be hard on the people in her life, but she generally liked everyone.

And yet she didn't like Dillon.

Walker didn't like him either. At first she'd attributed that to the brotherly feelings Walker had for her, and as the brother of her heart, he didn't feel anyone was good enough for her. But she'd come to realize he specifically didn't think *Dillon* was good enough for her.

So to realize that straight shooter Maze felt the same way threw her off. If Maze didn't like Dillon, what was Caitlin missing? Sure, he could be abrupt and standoffish, and was often too busy to let himself be overly friendly, but he loved her. He told her so all the time.

But he doesn't show you . . .

That quiet little voice from deep inside her chest had her going still. Okay, that wasn't quite true. He took care of her. He always made her coffee and brought it to her in bed, just the way she liked it. And since that was an iced dulce de leche, it wasn't easy. He also never complained about her Amazon Prime addiction, even though at the moment she wasn't earning nearly the same amount of money he was. But maybe that was mostly because he enjoyed the fruits of her shopping, especially when it was lingerie.

She drew a deep breath. What else? Well . . . they were sexually compatible, but dear God, it had to be more than that.

But what if it wasn't? What if she'd been wrong about him being her person for life simply because he was good in bed? And now was a fine time to be wrong about something, with the *I do's* only four days away.

Suddenly both Heather and Jace were racing each other to the basket, missions clearly accomplished. They arrived at the same time, bumped into each other, and knocked each other down. They were laughing as Jace helped Heather up, and he gestured for her to drop her paper into the basket first, graciously offering her the winning spot. Heather grinned up at him, looking young, carefree, and happier than she ever had.

Caitlin wondered . . . did she ever look at Dillon like that? She turned to look for him and found him walking toward her. "Hey," she said with a smile. "What do you think?"

"Uh, that your friends are crazy?"

"You mean my siblings." She realized he was holding his arm to his chest. "What happened?"

"Walker and I arm wrestled for the last cold beer."

Walker was lethal. She knew that. She'd once gone to the gym with him and watched him spar in the ring. He was a lean, mean fighting machine, and she'd never bet against him. But she'd also bet her life that he'd never, ever hurt anyone on purpose. "He didn't hurt you," she said in disbelief. "He'd never—"

"Wasn't him, but nice to know you'll jump to his defense over me."

She grimaced. "Dillon—"

"I lost the round with Walker, and then Maze took his seat. She jumped the gun and slammed my arm down to the table, taking the win *and* the last beer."

"So you're saying that *Maze* hurt you."

"She's an animal."

Caitlin laughed, because in a way that was true. Maze, as well as Walker, was incredibly competitive and didn't recognize anything but the win. "She's like a hundred twenty-five pounds, and you're, what, two hundred?"

"One-eighty," he corrected. "I finally dropped my extra holiday weight, and you're missing my point. What are we doing here, Caitlin? Having a reception practice? It's silly and a waste of time."

"You don't understand," she murmured. "You can see your whole family whenever you want. For me, it's about spending time together with mine when I can get it."

"Is that why you've put more time into this week than you did the actual wedding?"

"Don't be silly." But that little voice, the one she was starting to hate, said he was right again.

"And I thought you were supposed to go shopping with Mom today," Dillon said.

"No, I left her a message that everyone was in town and staying here, and she said that she and your aunt would go together."

"For the last-minute wedding things," Dillon said doubtfully. "You're going to let them have full rein of anything wedding, Ms. Control Freak?"

"Hey, I'm not *always* a control freak."

He lifted a brow.

She rolled her eyes and moved off to go check on Maze, but her phone rang. Dillon's mom. She considered not answering, but she'd just promised Dillon to try harder with her.

"Darling," his mom said when she picked up. "The baker said your wedding cake is carrot, which can't possibly be right."

"No, it's right," Caitlin said. "They make the most amazing carrot cake, it's to die for. But why did they call you?"

"I called them. Just making sure to dot all your *i*'s and cross all your *t*'s since I know your mom isn't here in town yet to assist. But Dillon should've told you—my sister doesn't like nutmeg and my mother hates carrot cake. We were thinking of replacing it with something more . . . wedding-like."

Caitlin ground her back teeth together. "I understand it's not the most common choice, but my dad loves carrot cake and it's his birthday on Saturday. So we thought it'd be a lovely tribute, and since they're paying for the cake—"

"How about I get the baker to make you and your parents a few carrot cupcakes? And then you can pick a different flavor for the cake. Your choice."

"My choice is *carrot*." Yes, she'd just promised to play nice, but she wasn't going to lose this battle. "Uh-oh, I think we've got a bad connection." She imitated a crackling sound and then disconnected.

"Gotta put more phlegm into that crackle," Walker said, having come up beside her.

She rolled her eyes and looked over to find Dillon eyeing his phone with a familiar frown. *What now?* She went to him, and he gave her a quick kiss. "I'll be back."

"Where are you going?" she asked.

"Mom just texted, needs me to meet her at the cake shop. There's some sort of misunderstanding and she knows you're busy."

Misunderstanding her ass. "But the point of today was to spend it here, with me and my family."

Everyone was watching her, so she plastered a smile on her face.

"Everything okay with him?" Heather asked after he left. "When he and Maze were arm wrestling, he jumped the gun and I think he hurt himself."

Maze was looking worried, which meant she'd done nothing wrong. Because when Maze did screw up, she owned it. So Caitlin nodded. "Everything's fine," she said. "He just had to go to a meeting." And if he agreed to change the cake, she'd kill him. That should solve the problem. "Maze? What's next?"

Maze consulted her itinerary. "Music! More dancing!" She hit Caitlin's reception playlist. "Uptown Funk" came on.

Heather squealed and ran toward the makeshift dance floor, happily dancing with Sammie in her arms, her little feet swinging off the ground, their laughter filling the air. Jace and Maze joined them, and when Sammie got too heavy for Heather, Jace took her. Maze and Heather danced together until they realized Walker was still in a chair. Heather tugged him toward their little circle, and he good-naturedly let himself be dragged to the others.

It was one of Caitlin's most favorite things about him, actually. He adapted to everything life threw at him, fitting in seamlessly no matter what. Dancing was probably close to the bottom of his list of favorite things to do, and yet because Heather had asked, he'd done it.

He'd do anything for any of them, including being willing to lay his life down. Caitlin knew this because he'd done it.

Watching, she found herself smiling and relaxing for the first time all day, and it wasn't because she'd finally suddenly learned to relax. It was because with these guys, she could take a deep breath. She could let herself go a little bit, even fall, because someone would catch her. She turned to Dillon, before remembering he'd left. She'd wanted him to mingle with everyone and become a part of them. It was important to her, more than anything, and the thought had her chest tightening again, because he wasn't going to mingle, he didn't care to. Which meant that he didn't care how important it was to her.

She wasn't his first priority.

Cake was.

Chapter 13

Maze's maid of honor to-do list:
—Call the bakery to make sure the carrot
wedding cake is still carrot.

Maze walked around the mock-up wedding reception with a trash can, picking up the last of the mess. Darkness had fallen, but the night was unseasonably warm, and she was sweating as she worked and thinking about taking a dip in the lake.

Heather had Sammie inside for a bath after getting cake . . . everywhere. Jace was on a run. Walker was in the kitchen handling the inside mess. Dillon hadn't come back from whatever he'd left his own practice reception to do, and Caitlin had gone inside a little bit ago for aspirin.

Maze worried about the look she'd seen on Cat's face after Dillon had left. She wasn't glowing, but worse, she didn't seem excited. Even Maze knew those weren't good signs.

The bride was in trouble, and Maze hated that. Hated it and felt guilty about it. Maybe if she'd been in touch more, around more, she could've . . . what? Encouraged Caitlin to find a better guy? What right did Maze have to judge Dillon? He seemed fine enough. It was just that Caitlin deserved more than fine.

She deserved *everything*. She knew that Cat had to be missing Michael more than ever during this time, and ditto. But she needed to find a way to reach the old Caitlin.

When she finished cleaning up, Maze found herself walking down the small dock to think. She kicked off her sneakers and sat. The night was quiet around her, and she let out a long breath and as much tension as she could. But the sudden prickle of awareness at the back of her neck alerted her that she was no longer alone.

Sure enough, Walker came up beside her, hands in his front pockets, staring down at her, an unfathomable expression on his face. He was good at hiding his feelings when he wanted to. She admired that. But even more, she admired the fact that he had feelings at all, and how he was perfectly willing and able to share them—when he wanted, that is.

Apparently now wasn't one of those times. "What?" she asked.

"I was putting the food away and saw you from the kitchen window. You looked like you could use a friend."

"I wasn't aware that we were friends."

"Actually, I consider you one of the very few real ones I have."

She sucked in a breath at that. Because in spite of everything, *same*. "We went years without speaking," she reminded him.

"Real friends aren't measured by time." He crouched at her side and met her gaze in the ambient glow of the moon's light. "What's wrong?"

"Nothing." *Everything* . . . "I guess sometimes it feels hard to be here with you all."

"Maze," he said softly, voice tinged with regret. "How long are you going to carry all the excess weight around? It's got to be getting heavy."

"Hey, everyone gains a little weight in their late twenties," she quipped, purposely misunderstanding him.

But he wasn't playing. Already barefoot, he sat at her side and tilted her face up to his. "You can't joke this away." He left his hand on her and studied her for a long moment. "You're here because you want something."

"Yeah? And what would that be?"

"Redemption."

She stilled, because that was actually true. Not that it was ever going to happen. "Don't you get it?" she whispered. "There is no redemption for me."

"Exactly, because what happened that night wasn't your fault."

For a second, she thought he meant their wedding, and her heart skipped a beat because maybe he was going to tell her that he'd made a terrible mistake and missed her so much that he couldn't go on without her.

But of course that's not what he meant, and she didn't want to talk about what he *did* mean. She moved to stand up, but he grabbed her hand. They played tug-of-war until she yanked free. "What's your problem?"

"Actually, the question is what's *your* problem," he said, annoyingly calm. "You're blaming yourself for Michael's death. You've got the biggest case of survivor's guilt I've ever seen, even though what happened that night wasn't even your fault."

"Of course it was!" she cried, tossing up her hands. "It was *my* impulsive behavior that started the whole thing. 'Let's sneak out,' I said. 'It'll be fun,' I said."

Walker caught her hands in his. "I was already going out that night." He held her gaze, his own steady. Open. "I only let you think it was your idea because I was going to walk there with you and Caitlin, then ditch you both to go hang out with my friends."

She jerked to her feet. "What?"

"Yeah." He stood as well. "Look, until a few days ago, I had no idea you were harboring all the guilt as your own. But, Maze, *I'm* the one who couldn't get Michael out of the house alive."

"No," she said, stepping toward him, looking him right in the eyes. "Are you kidding me? You were the only one of us who even tried!"

He was looking at her with a strange expression. It took her a moment to realize she had her hands on his chest, that they stood toe-to-toe, and that her feet had no intention of backing up.

He shook his head. "The effort doesn't mean jack shit, because I *failed.*"

For the first time since being back here, Maze could see pain in the depths of his eyes. She sucked in a breath, wondering how she'd been so clueless as to miss that he'd been suffering alone in silence. "Is that why you left when you turned eighteen?" she asked. "Going into the military and then the FBI? Because you couldn't save Michael? You felt you needed to pay penance by trying to save the world instead?"

He didn't say anything to this, which was as good as a yes.

"Oh, Walk," she murmured softly.

He reached for her. There'd been something heavy lodged in her chest for a long time, but it loosened a bit now as he pulled her in, and she slowly felt her resolve wavering. The need to keep touching him was overpowering everything else, including breathing. She could hear the air catch in his throat as she moved her hands over him and up to cup his jaw, feeling the warmth and the delicious roughness of his stubble beneath her hand for the first time in years.

"I remember running into the house," he said quietly, voice raw, "terrified you'd try to come with me. And then the next thing I knew, I was on a gurney and being taken away in an ambulance."

Her chest tightened at the memory. "It was awful. The house was an inferno and you just ran right into it." She could still smell the smoke, feel it burning her eyes and lungs. "We were terrified you were gone too."

She shook her head. "Why have we never talked about this?"

"Because you hate to talk about anything involving emotions, and I hate to make you sad. And remembering makes you sad." He paused. "For a long time, I thought you were angry at me."

"For what?"

"For not being able to get to Michael in time. For getting you drunk in Vegas and marrying you. For not making sure the paperwork didn't get filed. Hell, for breathing." He shrugged. "Pick one."

She was stunned. "I'm not mad at you for any of that, and I can't believe you'd think I was."

"Then what? Because you've definitely been avoiding me for a long time."

She drew a deep breath. "Truthfully?"

He nodded.

"Right now I'm not sure."

Careful, her inner voice of reason whispered. *It wasn't all that long ago that he'd shattered you into pieces . . .*

"What are we going to do about the divorce?"

His eyes had gone dark and sexy, but they cleared at her question. "I told you, the ball's in your court, and I meant it. If you sign the docs and give them to me, I'll take care of it."

I'll take care of it. That was exactly what he'd said the morning after their wedding. It had set her off then, and it set her off now. Because, oh yeah, she *did* remember why she was so mad at him. She was damn tired of being a mistake he had to take care of. And suddenly he was standing *way* too close. "Oh my God, I'm so stupid." She gave him a little shove, needing him to back up.

He didn't so much as budge.

"You're an ass."

"Undoubtedly." He paused. "But a hint would be nice."

Mental head slap, because on most things, he knew exactly what she was feeling. So how was it that when it came to this, to *them,* he never seemed to know? And why hadn't she stopped feeling things for him, *all* the things . . . Gah. She hated that, resented it so much that the ball in her chest was back. "I'll give you a hint," she said, and shoved him again.

He grabbed her hands. "Stop."

But she couldn't. She needed to go, needed to get past him, so she shoulder-checked him as she slid by.

"Dammit, Maze—"

Which was the last thing she heard before they both went tumbling off the dock and into the water. Plunging into the lake at night was scary because there was literally no perspective. It was dark above the surface and just as dark beneath it, so for one horrifyingly long beat, Maze couldn't figure out which way was up.

Then a set of strong hands shoved her to the surface.

"What the hell, Maze?"

"You made me mad!"

He looked at her incredulously. "So you dumped us both into the lake?"

"I didn't mean to! And since when are you not strong as an ox?"

"Since you got your bony-ass shoulder right into the exact spot where I was shot."

All the anger drained out of her in a single heartbeat. "Oh my God," she gasped, brushing her hands over his chest as if she could see the damage through the water and his clothing. "Walk, I'm so sorry!"

"Are you?"

"Yes! You think I like hurting you?"

Instead of answering, he pushed the wet hair from her face. Then his hand disappeared into the water and she realized he had a grip on her and was keeping them both afloat. The night air was cool and somehow made the water seem warmer than it was. Above them, the moon was nothing but a sliver, casting a blue glow just to the right of them, enough to see his eyes were dark, mouth unsmiling, and yet nothing about the lines of his body said anger or resentment to her.

So her own anger and resentment also drained. And that was when she realized something else: they were chest to chest, thighs to thighs, and all their good parts in between were touching. And here was the thing about Walker—from a distance, he was impressive. Up close, even more so. He had an air about him, an easy confidence that never tipped into cocky and a way of moving that reminded her of a cat. A big, feral cat. Although this wasn't what was making it hard to breath or giving her little tremors. Nope. She wanted to say it was adrenaline, but she knew better.

It was arousal.

Because damn. Walker up close and personal had always been her kryptonite, and apparently that hadn't changed. She stared at his face, utterly still, aware of him holding her close, treading water for both of them, their gazes locked, feet occasionally brushing.

Neither of them shifted away. It was the first time she'd been this close to him in three years, and even longer than that since they'd touched like this, and dammit, how was it that he was even sexier now than he'd ever been?

She didn't have many rules for herself, but the few she did have were necessary for her sanity. And one of them was to stay miles away from Walker—or if not miles, then about eight inches should do it.

"You okay?" he asked, voice low, husky.

A part of her felt more okay and more alive than she'd been in a long, long time. But another part of her felt confused at the closeness and the concern in his voice, not to mention her body's reaction to it. Unsure what to say, she reacted with predictable immaturity. She dunked him, then started swimming to shore.

He caught her in two strokes. "Are we racing?"

They'd always raced when they were younger. Everything had been a challenge between them, a dare. "*Yes*."

"Same rules?"

First to shore had always gotten to be ruler of the universe for a whole day, and the loser had to do everything the other one said. Only a problem if one intended to lose, and she *never* intended to lose.

"Say it, Maze."

"I'm going to win and you're going to call me ruler of your universe for a whole day."

"And a *night*," he threatened . . . or was it a promise? In either case, she was already hauling ass toward the shore.

Before she'd gone three strokes, a shadow passed her. Damn him.

By the time she stepped out of the water a minute later, dripping wet and breathless, Walker was standing there, casual as could be, also dripping wet, but not breathless in the slightest.

And he wasn't alone. Nope, the whole gang had appeared—Jace, Heather, and Caitlin—all of them looking boggled.

"Holy cow," Heather said. "Aren't you guys freezing?"

Walker shook his head. "The water's warm."

The water was *not* warm, so it was a good thing that annoyance burned hot.

"Were you . . . racing?" Caitlin asked in disbelief.

"Of course not," Maze said, and Walker actually laughed. She stared at him and found a slow smile curving her mouth too, because damn, his was infectious.

"Dude, you're supposed to let the girl win," Jace said.

"Are you kidding?" Walker asked, gaze still locked on Maze. "She'd rather lose than win by pity. And if you've spent the past . . . what was it? A year with her now? You'd know that."

"Okay, so who needs a drink?" Heather asked brightly. Slipping her arms through Jace's and Cat's, she turned them toward the house, looking back to give Maze a look that wasn't that hard to decipher.

Figure your shit out . . .

Right. Like she was so good at doing that. She eyed Walker and found herself wound up all over again.

He swiveled his gaze her way, arching a brow.

"The least you can do is pretend to be tired," she said with disgust.

"I don't pretend, Maze. Ever."

No shit.

"I won fair and square." He came close. Too close. "But it's cute you were so certain you'd beat me."

She snorted. "You think you know me."

"I *do* know you. More than anyone else."

True statement. Didn't mean it didn't piss her off. "If you're so smart then, claim your prize. What do I have to do tomorrow?"

His eyes dropped to her mouth.

She stopped breathing. "You could have me do anything, and you want what, a simple kiss?"

"Oh, there's nothing simple about kissing you. But I'm not asking for that. I wouldn't kiss another man's girlfriend."

She opened her mouth but then shut it, because what could she say? This was a mess of her own making. "So . . . I *don't* owe you a day?"

"Oh, you do," he said smoothly. "A day *and* a night. Twenty-four hours, Maze."

Gulp. "When?" she whispered.

"I'll let you know."

She crossed her arms, nervous. Worried. "But what do you want?"

He smiled and her stomach went squishy. And if she was being honest, that wasn't her only physical reaction.

"You'll just have to wait and find out," he said, and then followed the others, dripping water as he went, which didn't seem to bother him at all. In fact, he suddenly looked downright cheerful.

Chapter 14

Walker's man of honor to-do list:
—Work harder at staying away from the
maid of honor.

Walker woke up the next morning to Maze rushing into his room, then immediately hiding behind his door, peeking out at whatever she was running from.

Normally, he needed caffeine or an early run to kick his brain into gear. But Maze and her wild bed-head hair, which was also her just-had-sex hair, did it for him. "What—"

"*Shh!*" she whisper-yelled at him, waving a hand behind her, which he supposed meant to shut the hell up.

He wasn't much of a follower and rarely did as he was told, but he did indeed shut up, because she was in a T-shirt and . . . he wasn't sure what else. It was light gray and oversized and had been washed so many times it looked soft and buttery, clinging to all her curves.

She was cold.

He was enjoying that—which, note to self, was better than *any* caffeine in the land—when she opened the door a little bit more and leaned out, looking left and right. The T-shirt rose up a little bit, exposing a pair of black silk bikini panties, which had also risen up some, giving her world-class ass a wedgie.

He'd had his hands and mouth on that ass. He'd bitten it. He'd squeezed it. And for one glorious night, it had belonged to him.

But far more important, he'd belonged to her.

It'd been a feeling like nothing he'd ever experienced. He could count on one hand the number of times he'd actually been someone's. Actually, he could count the times with two fingers: Caitlin's family, in which he included Heather, and . . . Maze.

"Who are you evading?" he asked. *Please say Jace . . .*

"Heather. She's on a new get-fit kick, starting this morning apparently, and wanted me to run with her."

Maze thought running was the devil. She clearly caught sight of something, or more likely someone, coming down the hall and quickly and quietly shut the door before pressing her hands and forehead to the wood and letting out a soft laugh.

He slid out of bed. Normally, he slept in nothing, but he'd learned that in this house it was dangerous, so he'd worn knit boxers to bed.

Maze gasped in surprise when he came up behind her, not leaving any space between them. Setting his hands over hers on the door, he pressed up against her back.

"Wh-what are you doing?" she asked, voice soft and breathless, turning him on even more.

Good question. He'd gotten out of bed for a reason, but hell if he could remember it with her ass snugged up to the only part of his body that was fully awake. "Well, I *am* the ruler of your universe."

"You said not today."

Her T-shirt had slipped off one creamy shoulder, inviting him to lower his head and nuzzle the spot.

She moaned at the touch of his mouth and the sound went straight through him, heating him up. He turned her to face him and waited until she looked at him with hunger, letting out a needy little whimper that nearly had him doing the same.

She pressed closer to him and he whispered her name.

"I know," she murmured, and slid her hands into his hair before yanking him to her. Her mouth landed on his and for a moment he utterly and completely lost himself—which never happened. He was aware, always.

But Maze obliterated every single survival instinct he'd developed. Always had.

When they were both breathless, she pulled back and stared at him. Then they dove at each other again, and in zero-point-five seconds she was wrapped around him and he had his hands inside those silk panties. "You always smell so good," he said, mouth on her collarbone, working his way south.

She shook her head as her hands roamed over him, setting him on fire. "Less talking. More action."

They kissed again and his eyes crossed with lust.

"It's just one week," she whispered against his mouth. "We've almost survived it. We got this, as long as we remember that."

He stilled and pulled back. "Remember what exactly?"

"That this isn't real. Vacay feelings are never real." She looked at him like she couldn't imagine what was wrong with him that he wasn't following what she was saying. "We've only got a few days left before we each go our own way. Which with us is definitely for the best. Besides, I'm a one-and-done at best anyway."

"A one-and-done," he echoed slowly, dropping his hands from her and stepping back. He had to. Apparently, he couldn't touch her and think at the same time.

Her feet back on the floor, she had her hands spread out on the door on either side, like she needed the help to stay upright. "Why are you surprised?" she asked. "We talked about this on day one when we declared a truce until after the wedding."

"A lot has happened since then."

"It's been a week."

"It's been years," he countered. "And you're not a 'one-and-done,' Maze. Not by a long shot. Not for me."

She stared at him, then slowly let out a breath and shook her head. "We already tried it the other way. It didn't work out."

"We were young and stupid."

"Yeah, well, some of us are still stupid," she said, pointing to herself. She straightened her T-shirt and gave him one last look filled with both dazzling, erotic hunger and exasperation. Then she shook her head like she still couldn't believe he'd messed this up for them and slipped out of the room.

It took him a minute to gather himself and cool down parts of his body. He thought about going back to bed, but sleep wasn't going to happen, so he pulled on some jeans and left the bedroom, seeking a shower.

Someone had beaten him to it.

He waited outside the door for his turn, but whoever was in there didn't seem to be in a hurry. He knew that later was some fancy lunch at a restaurant in San Luis Obispo near where Dillon worked because his co-workers were throwing him a wedding shower. Caitlin apparently didn't like any of Dillon's coworkers, therefore she'd decreed they all had to go as well to keep her company.

Fine. He could use a distraction both from what had just happened and from wondering when Maze was going to sign the papers.

And if it bothered her or hurt her to do so . . .

Just like whoever was in the shower, he was in no hurry to get the divorce. It was important to him that it be *Maze's* decision, not his. As for what *he* wanted, well, that was simple. He wanted to never be hurt like that again. His whole life he'd been forced on people. He wasn't going to force anyone to love him.

But that kiss . . . Damn.

Moving down to the end of the hall, he looked out the open sliding glass door to the upper deck to take in the morning and found something totally unexpected.

Heather and Jace kissing.

Heather broke free with a gasp at the sight of him. "Oh my God, I'm so sorry!" She covered her eyes. "See, this! *This* is why I can't have secrets. I never learn! And now she's going to kill me. I blew the secret."

"Which secret?" Walker asked dryly. "The one where you and Jace have a thing for each other, or that Jace and Maze aren't really together?"

Heather winced. "To be fair to Maze, the first one might be *my* secret, not hers."

"This isn't on you," Jace told her, rubbing a hand up and down her back while watching Walker. "It's on me."

Walker shook his head. "Oh, I think you can both share the blame with a certain redhead."

"Are you mad at me?" Heather whispered.

Mad? That the woman he wanted beyond all reason or logic or sanity was in fact *not* involved with someone else? "I've never been mad at you." He proved it by hugging her to him, studying Jace while he did.

"Whatever you're thinking," Jace said, "I deserve it."

"You should've waited," Walker told him over Heather's head. "Maze had you here with her for a reason."

"You don't understand." Heather pulled back and looked up at him earnestly. "*I* kissed *him*. I did it because Maze had already admitted that she and Jace are only friends. She said he was one of the best men she knew and that I could do a whole lot worse. And we both know I *have* done worse, so . . ."

Walker shook his head. "This isn't any of my business. As long as you're good, I'm good." He looked at Jace, who wore an expression that said he knew he was going to get no such free pass. "So to clarify," Walker said, "you and Maze aren't—"

"Aren't. Never have. Never will," he said. "We're good friends and we work together. I've got her back, no matter what, but I have her okay on this, so maybe you can stop planning my murder now."

"I was never going to murder you." Walker paused. "Maybe cut off your balls and force-feed them to you, but you could've survived that . . ."

Jace looked like he was just managing to not cup said balls protectively in his hands.

"I'm so sorry," Heather said to Jace. "I know I jumped the gun. I shouldn't have kissed you like that, especially without asking first."

Jace smiled. "Are you kidding? It was the best thing to happen to me in months."

Heather smiled back. "So . . . we're okay?"

"Very," Jace assured her. "And as soon as my pretend girlfriend and I have a talk, I'm hoping maybe you'll even kiss me again."

"You do realize what I am, right?" Heather asked. "A single mom who's a hot mess almost all the time?"

Jace ducked a little to look her in the eyes. "I like you exactly as you are. Look," he said to Walker, "I don't know too much about what you and Maze have been through because she's so private, and I'd never pretend to speak for her, but I'd bet you everything I've got that she'd lay her life down for you, for all of you." He'd met Walker's gaze straight on, earning him some serious points. "So maybe you can try to understand what she did and why, and find a way to . . . I don't know, start over?"

Walker nodded, message received. For years now, he and Maze had been circling each other. Their pull, no matter how far apart they were, was strong. Their one night together had irrevocably changed things between them. They knew the power of it now, and as much as he hated to admit it, it'd scared him into retreating. His retreat had been physical.

Maze's retreat had been emotional. She'd shut him out.

He missed her. He turned to go, but Jace stopped him. "I might not know how to rip out a guy's gonads and feed them to him, but I'll figure something out if you hurt her again."

"*Again?*" Walker asked, not worrying about the threat. He was glad Maze had someone who cared so much. "When the hell did I ever break her heart?"

Jace shook his head, like Walker was a huge idiot. "Man, if you don't know, I can't help you."

Maze received a text at the exact moment someone knocked on her bedroom door. Fresh out of the shower and wearing only a towel, she dripped water everywhere as she glanced at her screen first.

Her heart stopped.

JACE: He knows.

Another knock. It was Walker—she could tell by the implied impatience.

Shit. "Give me a minute!" she yelled. Panic blocked her air passage as she frantically thumbed out a return text for Jace.

MAZE: He knows???????? What do you mean he knows??????

The bedroom door started to open. Leaping to it, she pressed her spine to the wood and, sliding down to sit on the floor, held it closed with her back as she stared at her phone, willing Jace to text her back.

"If you're trying to get ahold of your *boyfriend*," Walker said through the door, "he's busy getting his tonsils sucked out by Heather. Open up, Maze."

"Hold on!"

"Tried that."

And then it was out of her hands. The door cracked open. Yes, she was sitting against it, but Walker easily pushed her across the smooth wood floor enough to squeeze through the opening he'd made for himself. Then he shut the door and crouched low in front of her.

With an undignified squeak, she dropped her phone and very nearly her towel. He caught the phone for her but didn't even attempt to help her save the towel.

Grabbing it herself, she readjusted and then glared at him, her wet hair dripping down her shoulders, giving her a chill. Actually, the chill might be coming from her life. Caitlin was getting married. Heather had a baby. Walker had a career. They'd all moved on from the tragedy of their youth and losing Michael and had gotten themselves real adult lives.

And what did she have? A silly lie she'd told everyone about having a boyfriend.

Walker was looking at her, gaze serious now. Intense. "Truth," he said. "Are you scared of us?"

"Of course not," she said, a big, fancy lie that made her shiver.

He rose and grabbed a second towel from the bed, coming back to wrap it around her shoulders, pulling it tight to her, the backs of his fingers brushing her collarbone, giving her a body shiver for an entirely different reason.

They stood there sharing air, watching each other.

"Okay, tough girl," he said. "Let's have confession time."

"Or not."

"I'll start," he said as if she hadn't spoken. "*I'm* scared."

She scoffed. "Right. Nothing scares you."

"You're wrong," he said, eyes serious. "I'm scared of a lot."

"Like?"

"Like something happening to Cat or Heather. Or you," he said in a way that made her swallow hard. "I don't think I could survive that." He paused. "Now you."

"Okay." She drew a deep breath. "So . . . I'm not dating Jace."

"And?"

"*And?* I just gave you a *huge* confession. Isn't that enough?"

"No. Scoot over." When she didn't move fast enough, he maneuvered her himself, his big hands on her hips sliding her six inches across the floor to make room for himself. He sat next to her, his long legs out in front of him, both of them leaning back against the door.

"Who told you?" she asked.

"You." And when she sighed, he said, "And I've suspected from the beginning."

She groaned. "It's a good thing I never tried to be an actress. What gave me away?"

"I got suspicious whenever he touched you. Your reaction was always to give a short little laugh, the kind of laugh you always use when you're uncomfortable."

"I do not." But a small laugh escaped and she slapped her hand over her mouth. "Dammit," she said through her fingers.

He grinned. "The grand finale was when I caught him and Heather in a lip-lock just now. So he's either a first-class dick or you two were never together."

She groaned and slid her hand up to cover her eyes.

Gently, he pulled it from her face.

"He's not a dick," she said. "He's a good friend. And actually my boss."

"Now see, *that* makes a lot more sense. Because there was no way he was into you that way, or you'd have seemed a whole lot more satisfied. Instead, you look . . ."

She raised a brow.

". . . uptight." He leaned in, and his mouth brushed her ear. "And you and I both know that orgasms don't leave you uptight, they relax you into a boneless state of contentment."

She felt her face heat as memories flooded her. Them turning to each other for hours: him over her, under her, murmuring the sexy nothings in her ear as he'd taken her outside of herself again and again and again, until they'd been nothing but exhausted, sated husks of human beings.

He took her hand in his. "Tell me what's really going on, Maze."

She blew out a breath. What the hell, she had no pride left anyway. "I knew you were coming, and I also knew if you showed up without a date, I'd be tempted. Just like I always am."

She'd never seen Walker surprised or off-balance, but he was both now. He just stared at her, eyes a little wide, and she almost laughed. *Nothing* got past his guard, but apparently she just had.

"You're . . . *tempted* by me," he said, heavy on the disbelief.

"I thought you knew everything."

"Well, I didn't know that."

She had to laugh. "I figured the way I kissed you might've been a big clue."

He turned her, putting his hands on her hips to maneuver her to face him. Then he slid his hands up her body and into her hair to hold her still. "You're tempted by *me*?"

"You want me to say it again?" she asked, amused.

"Hell, yes."

She stared into his blue eyes. "It started a long time ago but really kicked in when you flew me to Vegas."

"Where I got you drunk and married you," he said, not looking happy with himself for that.

"Hey," she said. "I gave as good as I got. If anyone took advantage of anyone that night, it was me."

"I did try to resist you," he said with a flash of amusement. "I'd been trying to do just that for forever. Clearly not hard enough."

"As I remember it, you were plenty . . . *hard*."

He laughed a very sexy laugh that made her extremely aware of what she was wearing. And what she *wasn't* wearing. She let out a long breath. "Our bodies seem to have this weird . . . chemical reaction to each other."

"Yeah. It's called simple animal magnetism. So on a scale of one to gotta have me now . . ." He shifted closer and ran a finger down her throat. "Just how tempted are we talking?"

She shivered. "Three . . . -ish."

Lowering his head, he nudged the towel clear and kissed her shoulder. "Liar."

"Okay, a solid four."

His mouth found its way to the swell of her breast above her towel.

She sucked in a breath and her head fell back a bit, giving him more room to work with, along with tacit consent. "Make that a twelve."

He let out a low laugh against her skin. "Maze . . ."

"Yeah?"

"There's a whole houseful of people."

"And . . . ?"

He cupped her face in his strong hands, and when his lips touched hers, the rest of the world faded away. It was insane how every nerve in her body pulsed with need, how she craved him, and she scooted in even closer, moaning as his hands headed southbound on her towel, which was an inch from revealing a whole lot of Maze.

Walker groaned. "You're gorgeous. And you're killing me."

"Why? What's stopping you?"

"The fact that if I ever get lucky enough for a second chance with you, I'm not going to stop until you're panting my name."

"Again . . . what's stopping you?"

He dragged her into his lap, sank his fingers into her hair, and had her halfway to indeed panting his name when someone pounded on the door behind them. "That," he muttered. "*That's* what's stopping me."

"Breakfast!" Dillon yelled through the door. "Caitlin made pumpkin pancakes and says that the last one of you downstairs has to do all the dishes. In perpetuity."

Maze scrambled to her feet, making Walker laugh. "Nice to see you've got your priorities straight," he said. "Food over nookie."

"Hey, you've tasted her pancakes. It's no contest."

He caught her and pulled her to him, sliding his fingers into her still-wet hair. "I'm going to make you take that back later. When we're alone."

"We're *never* alone."

"Trust me. I'll make it happen. *Later,*" he said again, meeting her gaze with his own heated one.

Her breath caught. "Later," she promised.

Chapter 15

Caitlin's to-do list:
—Make it through the week without
  becoming an alcoholic.

Caitlin was late. Not to a meeting, because please. She'd never been late to anything in her whole life. Nope, this was a different kind of *late* altogether. Like nine months of getting a big belly late. It had her both excited and terrified as she went through the motions at the coed wedding shower luncheon with Dillon's co-workers. The whole thing was a stuffy, overdone waste of time and her face still hurt from fake smiling. She'd been asked at least ten times by ten different people what she did for a living, and when she said she managed a deli and prepped all the food, inevitably the follow-up question was what were her career goals.

Implying, of course, that she was surely working on bigger and better things.

And she was, in her own way. She loved to cook and would continue to do that in whatever capacity worked for her, and she wanted to build a family. Every time the question came up, her first instinct was to glance at Dillon, thinking he'd maybe deflect for her. She hoped he'd say, "Whatever she wants to do." But in each instance, Dillon had turned to her as expectantly as his friends.

So she started taking a shot every time she was asked, and then she added a new game: making up answers. Her favorite had made Dillon flush with anger, but she still thought "teaching exotic dancing" was pretty damn funny. And okay, maybe she went overboard because Sara called her no fewer than three times to ask questions that she'd have no need to ask if she'd only read the notes Caitlin had left.

In any case, by the time they got back to the cabin, she was pretty sure she and Dillon were no longer speaking, but he surprised her when they all gathered in the kitchen for snacks because the food at the shower had sucked.

With both Roly and Poly following him like he was the Pied Piper, he took out the plate of burgers she'd had in the fridge for dinner. "I'll light the grill."

Walker looked at Caitlin in surprise. "You're going to trust him to cook those?"

Dillon frowned. "Excuse me?"

"No offense," Walker said with a laugh, "but she never trusts anyone to cook anything."

Caitlin narrowed her eyes at Walker. "If you think you know everything, why don't you go help him?"

Walker pointed at her, but he started out the door, because at least *one* of her people knew better than to argue with the bride.

"Wait," she said. "If you're ruler of the universe today, shouldn't Maze have to do it for you?"

Walker's eyebrows went up. "You want *Maze* to barbecue your burgers?"

"You're right. What was I thinking?"

"Hey, standing right here," Maze said, tossing up her hands.

Dillon was staring at them like they'd all lost their minds. "What's wrong with Maze's cooking? Is she going to burn another house down or something?"

Everyone sucked in a shocked breath.

"Babe, I told you that in confidence," Cat finally said, horrified. "And it wasn't her fault." She turned to Maze, her heart stopping at the look on her face. "Honey—"

Maze shook her head and walked out of the room.

"*What?*" Dillon said when everyone glared at him.

"You know those double half lattes you love so much?" Walker asked him, voice very quiet—and as any of them knew, while most men got loud when they were furious, Walker just got quietly lethal.

Dillon nodded. "Yeah."

"Get in your car and go to town to get yourself one before I forget that I'm an off-duty federal agent and put my fist through your face."

Dillon turned to Caitlin in disbelief. "*These* are the people you want at our wedding? *In* our wedding? Seriously?" He tossed up his hands. "I'm going to catch up on some paperwork in the office. Let me know when the food's ready."

Caitlin swallowed her stress and turned to the doorway—not the one Dillon had gone out of, but the one Maze had. "I'm going after Maze to apologize."

"You're not the one who should apologize," Walker said.

But she was. She'd brought them all here. She'd expected Dillon to play nice, to not act like he was . . . indifferent to those she considered family. It steamed her that she'd done her best with his family and friends all year and he couldn't afford her the same courtesy for a week.

"I'll go," Walker said.

"Wait." Cat was torn. "Maybe Jace should go?"

"No." Jace met Walker's gaze. "I think it should be someone who was there that night. Someone who loves her."

Caitlin's eyes widened as they met Walker's. "Wait. What?"

Walker shook his head with a *not now* look and went out the door.

Caitlin turned to Heather.

"I didn't like that Dillon said that to her," Heather said softly. "It was mean."

"I know." Caitlin's stomach was in knots over it. "And the Walker and Maze thing?"

"If it happens, I think it'd be amazing for both of them."

Caitlin nodded slowly. Maze and Walker were both far overdue for having true love in their lives, and together they'd complement each other in ways that would be truly amazing to watch. But if things went south . . . what would happen? Would it break up the family she'd just put back together, for good this time?

And how was it that she felt far more worried about that than going after Dillon?

Walker searched the immediate surroundings—no Maze. Not a surprise. She was good at hiding in plain sight. She'd had to be. Standing at the water's edge, he let out a breath. In both his professional and personal life, he tried very hard not to do anything stupid. He also tried to learn from his mistakes, of which he'd made many. It was important to him, given how he'd grown up, to be a good guy. But at his core, he was also an opportunist. He had a chance here to right some wrongs, and he was going to take it.

He did love Maze. He always had. But he held no illusions that she could love him back. And yet the way she'd looked at him earlier, how she'd allowed her body to melt into his . . . He drew a deep breath. At the very least, she wanted him, and he could work with that.

All he had to do was find her and try to break through her thick skull that what had happened to Michael wasn't her fault, no matter what Dillon had insinuated. That's how he'd reach her, he thought, with a distraction. They could plan Dillon's slow, painful death together.

And then maybe everything else would for once fall into place.

He found her at the small cove a mile from the house, sitting on the tire swing, staring at the water as she kept herself in motion.

When he got within twenty-five yards, she stiffened, then put her feet down, stopping the swing.

Walker circled around to face her. "Hey."

Nothing. Not that he'd expected her to speak. For a woman who liked to talk, she clammed up when she felt things too deeply. Her eyes were thankfully dry, but . . . damn, filled with sadness and regret and guilt.

"Remember when you used to climb trees when you got mad?" he asked.

"Yes, because no one other than you would come after me."

A surprisingly revealing statement. Taking heart in that, he moved closer. "I'm glad you didn't climb one today. Don't think I have it in me right now."

She sighed. "What are you doing here?"

"You don't own this beach."

She smiled before she could stop herself, he could tell. Because that's what he'd say to her back then: "You don't own this tree . . ."

He moved behind her and gave her a push. She tilted her head back, closed her eyes, and let the wind roll over her as she soared. He gave her another, bigger push, and they stayed just like that for a while, her seeming to enjoy the peace and quiet, him pushing her to keep her in motion, just letting her have a moment without being alone.

"He's right, you know," she finally said. "I was the one who turned on the space heater that night."

"Because it was freezing. If you hadn't, I would have. Or Caitlin. Or any of us."

"Are you just telling me that to make me feel better?"

"I don't work that way."

She studied him for a long beat and then nodded. "Thanks." She got off the swing and turned to walk back.

"Maze."

She paused and faced him.

"Do you trust me?"

She drew a deep breath. "I don't *not* trust you, at least with my physical well-being."

"And your emotional well-being?"

She bit her lower lip. "I'm pretty sure you've never been anything but brutally honest with me. So yeah." She nodded with a very small smile. "I guess I trust that too."

"And your heart?"

She snorted. "Now you might be pushing it."

"Fair enough." He held out his hand. "I think what you need is to get out of here, and I know I could use a drive. Come with?"

"You need a drive? Are you okay?"

He nearly smiled. Most people saw him as un-approachable, much less vulnerable. Too tough to need protecting, too cynical to garner caring. That Maze still gave a shit about him warmed something in his chest that he hadn't realized was even there anymore. "I'll be okay after a drive with you."

"Same." She gave him a small, but very real, smile. "Truth is, I'd probably go anywhere with you."

He caught her and dragged her closer, kissing her, letting it linger and heat them both, even though he'd been heated since . . . hell, since he'd first seen her again.

"Am I hurting you?" she gasped, pulling her hands back from where she'd dug her fingers into the meat of his shoulders to hold on to him.

"Pain is not what I'm feeling right now."

She laughed as she wriggled closer. "No kidding."

Chapter 16

Maze's maid of honor to-do list:
—Pick up Dillon's wedding band and
   make final payment without letting
   Dillon know, since Caitlin was supposed
   to have done it weeks ago.

Maze had no idea what she thought she was doing, but she knew one thing for sure: She wanted this. She wanted Walker. They walked back to the house to get the keys to his rental car, trying to be stealth. But Roly and Poly sounded the alarm, barking so hard their back legs came off the ground, letting everyone within five hundred miles know that clearly there was an incoming zombie apocalypse and they were all going to die.

"*Shh,*" Maze whispered, trying to shut them up to no avail.

Finally Walker tucked a dog beneath each arm, lowering his head to talk to them in a quiet, low tone. The tactic worked. The dogs had to shut the hell up to listen to him, and listen they did, vibrating with intensity as they stared fondly and lovingly up into his face.

Then he gave them each a kiss on their smashed-in foreheads and set them in their beds, where they turned in circles and plopped down to go back to sleep.

"What did you say to them?" Maze asked, marveling.

"Told them they were my wingmen, and as such, they'd be entitled to half my breakfast in the morning if they'd just shut the hell up. They understand the language of food."

When they took off out of the driveway, Maze expected Walker to head west and maybe hit the highway to the beach. Instead, he turned east, which took them on a narrow road around the lake. Soon the road ended, and he turned onto a dirt fire road she didn't even know existed. They went straight up a hill.

And up.

The road was narrow and twisty, but Walker was calm and relaxed, which in turn kept her calm and relaxed. Well, sort of. Because watching in the ambient light as he maneuvered the car, the muscles in his shoulders and arms working, his hands corded with easy strength on the wheel, was definitely revving her up.

"This week must seem pretty tame to you," she said, "just hanging out and not doing much."

"The break's been good. Work's been . . ."

"Crazy?"

"More like unfulfilling."

She turned in her seat to look at him. "I thought you loved your job."

"It's been years since I told you that. Things change."

"What things?"

"Things," he said, shifting into a low gear as he took the next curve.

"So clearly, Cat didn't give you the same 'be open' speech she gave me," she said dryly.

He glanced over at her. "Cat said you need to be more open to me?"

"No." She laughed. "But good thing your ego is in check. She said to be more open in general."

He nodded but didn't say anything, and she had to laugh again.

"That's it?" she asked. "Seriously?"

"What?"

"You do realize that you're no more open than I am, right? I mean, you know everything about me: how I grew up, where, why . . . *everything*. And meanwhile, I know almost nothing about your past. And then there's how you've kept tabs on me. I can't do the same because you're impossible to follow. You've got a low social media profile, and it's not like I could just ask Caitlin or Heather. So . . . talk."

He slid her an amused look. "Isn't that usually my line?"

She shrugged. "I stole it."

He kept driving, and she thought maybe he was going to ignore her, but then he spoke. Not about his early years, which was what she'd been hoping for, but about later.

"The military was good for me," he said. "Gave me a sense of purpose and some badly needed discipline."

She snorted her agreement, which won her a smile.

"Yeah, yeah, smart-ass," he said. "I know you know. And after, when I went into the FBI, that was good for me in a different way. I thought I'd be helping people and fighting the occasional asshole, but . . ." He shook his head. "It's more about red tape and political careers and winning, and I don't think like that. The sense of purpose is gone for me. I need something else."

"I can understand that," she said quietly. "What else do you need?"

"I don't know."

The frustration in his voice was clear, and she realized he wasn't nearly as relaxed as he led everyone to think. When she looked at him, really looked at him, she could see the lines of his body seemed tight and tense, and she frowned. Again, how had she let him fool her? "Are you happy here?"

"In Wildstone, with the others? Or here in this car, with you?"

Caught off guard, she stared at him.

"Yes." He glanced at her, then turned back to the road. "To both."

The answer should've scared her but actually had the opposite effect. Something deep inside her loosened, allowing her to sit back and more fully enjoy the ride now, because she wasn't in this—whatever *this* was—alone.

Surrounded by the dark night and the utter lack of city lights, the interior of the car seemed to cocoon them, giving off a sense of intimacy she hadn't felt in a long time. Closing her eyes, she took a deep breath and inhaled the scent of leather seats and sexy male. She listened to the sounds around her. Music drifting from the radio, low but with a beat that seemed to match the pulse of her heart. Wind rushing past the windows. Tires gripping the dirt road. The engine humming beneath her. Her own breathing. And Walker's.

It was hypnotizing, leaving her body vibrating like Roly's and Poly's with a sense of anticipation she didn't want to put a name to yet.

The night was lit by a half-moon and some clouds that caught the moon's glow and amplified it. She could see the black outlines of trees against a sky littered with myriad stars. She could see the hills, mostly beneath them now. And then the black span of the lake far below. "It's all so beautiful," she said softly. "I always forget how much I love it here."

"You haven't been back."

"No." She heard the wistfulness in her voice, so she knew he heard it too, especially when he took another look at her.

"It's been a good week," he said. "Maybe things will change. Maybe you'll come back more now."

"Maybe." Definitely. "You?" she asked, holding her breath.

He nodded. "You and I haven't been okay since Vegas. But the things that happened there"—he glanced over at her—"I'm still feeling."

Her body quivered. "You mean the 'animal magnetism thing'?"

"You sure that's all it is?"

"Yes." *No . . .*

He laughed softly and made a turn where she couldn't even see a road. He turned again, and then once more, the soft vibration of the engine continuing to spread warmth through her. She let her gaze drift over his body and up to his face and realized he was watching her as well.

A few minutes later, he steered off the road and into what looked like a clearing of wild grass with a few oak trees around them, creating a little haven. He glanced over with so much heat in his eyes it stole her breath. Then he exited the vehicle, quietly shutting the door behind him. Walking to the front of the car, he rested his perfect ass on the hood.

Taking a deep breath, she got out as well and joined him. They were at the top of a bluff, the night sprawled out in front of them. They leaned against the car in silence, taking in the light wind and singing crickets, the hoot of an owl . . . and for Maze, the delicious scent of Walker's soap or aftershave, along with the undeniable strength and heat coming from him.

She wanted him. She wanted him bad.

"This wasn't exactly my plan when I asked you to come with me," he said quietly. "I really just wanted to give you a moment away from the house and thought a drive would do it."

"Thanks." She sent him a small smile. "I'm starting to think there's some sort of a chemical disorder between us."

His mouth twitched. "You make it sound like a bad thing."

She wanted that mouth on her so much that she was shaking. "I blame the vibrations from every time you revved the engine, not to mention all the bumps on the fire road. I nearly had an orgasm on the drive up here."

She'd meant to make him laugh, to lighten the heavy mood, but he turned toward her, eyes intense—oh so intense—and dark with desire. "The drive turned you on?"

No more than the low, rough timbre of his voice. "Maybe it was also a little bit the man driving." She shrugged.

He slid his hands into her hair and tilted her face to his. "Again, I want to say that this wasn't my plan for tonight."

She wrapped her hands around his wrists. "Then thankfully you're a man who knows when to deviate from your plan."

At that, he finally smiled, his playful, sexy smile. And it was a doozy. "Yeah. I'm a real flexible guy."

He lowered his head slowly, clearly giving her time to change her mind—which was not going to happen.

Unlike him, she worked from the heart, on impulse. Yeah, it'd gotten her burned before, but she still couldn't help herself. Not when it came to this man. "Walk?"

"Yeah?"

She stared at his mouth, still an inch from hers. "It'd be great if you could deviate faster."

"Sorry, I've been waiting a long time for another shot at you." Lifting her onto the still-warm hood, he leaned over her. "You're not going to rush me."

"I'm not?"

"No."

And then he finally kissed her, slow and deep. When their tongues touched, she moaned. At the sound, he pulled her even closer and looked into her eyes before dropping his gaze to take in the rest of her. She'd wrapped herself around him like he was a tree and she was a monkey getting ready to go for a climb.

"Maze."

"Hmm?"

"I'm going to kiss you again. Tell me that's okay."

She nodded eagerly. If it was any more okay, she'd already be naked.

"The words, Maze."

"It's okay. Please kiss me, Walk. *Now.*"

He obliged with a sexy thoroughness that stole her breath. She heard herself whimper and slid her hands under his shirt to rest on his chest, where she could feel the steady beat of his heart. As they kissed, that heartbeat kicked into gear. She affected him, and the knowledge gave her a surge of power.

She had no idea how long they made out, she lost all track of time and place. She was adrift in the sensations, his lips on hers, his hands on her body, teasing her, bringing her to life, the sound of the wind and the night around them, the feel of the car beneath her. When they came up for air, his mouth moved down her neck, sending shock waves straight to her good parts, and there were most definitely more good parts than she remembered. Her fingers shook when she unbuttoned his shirt and shoved it off his shoulders. She was going for the zipper on his pants when he caught her hands.

"Don't even think about stopping now," she warned him.

He searched her gaze, his own dark and heated and sexy as hell. "Here then?"

"*Here.*" She ran her hands up his chest, cupped his head, and pulled him back in for another kiss.

With a rough groan, he tightened his fingers in her hair. "Do you remember what I said I was going to do if we got here again?"

"That you'd stop talking?"

He gave a low laugh. "That I wasn't going to stop until you were panting my name."

"I'm not much for making a lot of noise."

"That's not how I remember it."

She opened her mouth to argue, but he unzipped the back of her dress and pulled the top down past her shoulders. He kissed the curve of her throat, her collarbone, moving southbound to the swell of her breast above her barely there bra. Then that was nudged down too, baring her to him and his mouth, which he used liberally.

She already knew that Walker loved to touch, loved to kiss and taste . . . *everything*. He was a tactile guy, and he could say more things with his body than his mouth ever could. He lifted her higher onto the hood. Then, standing between her legs, he ran his hands up her thighs, bringing the hem of her dress along with him, until the material pooled on his forearms, his hands vanishing beneath. His fingers played with the edge of her panties, teasing her through the lace until she gasped out his name in both entreaty and demand, which made him laugh low in his throat.

"It's a good thing you're sexy as hell," she muttered, her mouth busy on his throat. "Now stop teasing me and—" She broke off when he slid the lace aside and out of his way.

"And?" he murmured, not stopping anything he was doing. In fact, he lifted a knee onto the hood between her legs, adding a delicious pressure.

"And *do me*," she demanded breathlessly.

He laughed huskily, and she might have killed him there and then, but their eyes met, and the need and desire she felt for him, everything was matched in his eyes.

"Be sure, Maze."

"This is the one thing I *am* sure of."

At that, he gave her the sweetest, most loving kiss. Then he took that mouth on a tour south, stopping when he got to the small tattoo of Harry Potter's glasses and lightning bolt on her hip, along with the tiny script that said, HAPPINESS CAN BE FOUND EVEN IN THE DARKEST OF TIMES, IF ONE ONLY REMEMBERS TO TURN ON THE LIGHT.

He smiled and then licked it.

"Oh my God," she moaned.

"I was hoping for 'Yes, oh yes, please, more, ruler of my universe.'"

She'd never laughed during sex before, but then he switched things up on her, adding his fingers into the mix, keeping her on the very edge until she tightened her fingers in his hair, holding him where she wanted him the most.

He laughed softly against her, but she didn't have the bandwidth for anything other than what he was doing to her. Well, she did finally manage to get his pants open and her hands inside, which was a whole lot like opening a birthday gift that you already knew you were getting but wanted more than anything. "I'm going to cry if you don't have a condom."

"No crying necessary," he said. "But if you want to scream out my name . . . I'm up for that."

"You're *up* for anything," she said, the evidence in her hands.

He laughed and did something diabolical with his fingers and then she was flying, still gasping for breath as he protected them both and entered her.

They froze in shocked wonder at the incredible sensations.

Gathering her wits the best she could, she wrapped herself around him as the sensations took them both.

After, she had no idea how much time had passed before Walker lifted his head and looked at her with both tenderness and good humor. "I'm never going to go off-roading again without thinking about this." He helped her right her clothing before reaching for his. And then they stood there on the cliff, beneath the moon, staring at each other.

Reaching out, Walker took one of her hands in his, using the other to push her damp hair from her forehead. "That was even better than all the fantasies I had about you."

Yeah. Her too. But the anxiety he'd beat back with his magic body was slowly returning and she shook her head. "What are we doing?"

He held her gaze for a moment. "Whatever you want to be doing."

"I don't want to go back to the past." The thought of losing him again, now, as adults, had panic swirling inside her. "I can't—"

"I know." He gave her hand a gentle squeeze. "It's okay, Maze. If you want this to be nothing, it's nothing. You're in the driver's seat. You've got all the control here."

She huffed out a sigh. "Well, that's just great."

He looked amused. "You can't control yourself around me?"

She groaned.

"You can't." He was out-and-out grinning now. "Cute."

"Look, not all of us can be Mr. Control," she said, crossing her arms.

"Don't mistake my restraint for lack of emotion, Maze. I do what I think is right, not what's easy." He held the car door open for her as she got in. Then, instead of closing the door, he crouched down on the balls of his feet so they were eye to eye. "To be clear," he said, "I didn't see tonight coming, but I'm not going to lie to you. I don't have any regrets. Not then, not now. I'm sorry if you do."

She held his gaze. "You've never been a regret to me, Walk."

He didn't move, didn't so much as blink, for a long few seconds. "Good to know. But . . . ? Because I sense there's a big *but*."

"But what we did tonight?" She shook her head. "It stops here. It has to." She felt herself getting emotional and felt silly for it, but she couldn't contain her feelings, they were spilling out all over the place. "I can't handle more, not with you. It nearly destroyed me the first time." She gulped in some air. "Please don't ask me to go back to that place."

His eyes were dark and intense as he gently squeezed her hand. "I've never asked you for a single thing, Maze. I'm not going to start now."

They rode back in silence.

Chapter 17

Caitlin's to-do list:
—Buy more wine.

Later that night, Caitlin was at the kitchen table flipping through recipes. It was either that or take a Xanax. Dillon was already asleep. They'd fought about what he'd blurted out to Maze in the kitchen earlier, and Maze still wasn't back. She felt sick with worry.

Roly and Poly were curled up at her feet as she thumbed through her iPad, specifically Pinterest and her wedding board, where she'd pinned everything from dresses to flowers to lighting to table decorations—all of it simple, designed for a small wedding with a warm and cozy feel, just as she'd been dreaming about since she was a little girl.

Too bad that wasn't what she was putting on.

It'd started out so perfect. Dillon had gotten down on one knee, offered to love her for the rest of her life, and since there was nothing she liked more than a happy ending, she'd said yes.

But if she was honest with herself, over the past few months something was making her restless . . . and unhappy. Having her people here this week had been good for her. Watching her life with Dillon through their eyes had given her some perspective, not to mention a few hard realizations.

Somewhere along the way, she'd become the sidekick in her own story.

Not an easy admission, even to herself.

She was still sitting there sipping tea an hour later, when the back door opened and in came Maze. And Walker.

Together.

At one in the morning.

The dogs lifted their heads, eyes sleepy, and gave big yawns and a few squeaks. Walker pointed at them and they went back to sleep.

Walker and Maze weren't speaking or touching, which was par for the course. What *wasn't* par for the course: Maze holding her sandals in one hand, her other at her throat. She was missing her bra, which was obvious only because the dress she wore was thin and she was clearly chilled. Her hair was wild and clearly wind—or finger—tousled around her face.

And then she moved her hand to push her hair out of her face, which revealed a suspicious mark at the base of her throat that was maybe, probably, a hickey.

Caitlin turned her attention to Walker, in jeans and an untucked button-down. His body seemed loose and relaxed, but that was deceiving, because he always looked that way. "What's going on?" she asked.

Walker shrugged and opened the fridge, pulling out all the makings for a late-night snack.

Maze went straight for the bottle of Jack on the counter, poured herself two fingers, and tossed it back. "Going to bed," she said, and headed to the door.

Neither of them was acting particularly out of character, but Caitlin's radar was buzzing. Something had happened, and she wasn't an idiot. She could bet what that something had been, and she was happy for them, but why did they each seem to be pretending the other didn't exist?

"Hey."

Maze turned back.

"You okay?"

Maze softened. "Yes. And that should be my question for you. What are you doing up this late?"

"Not sleeping, that's for sure."

Maze drew a deep breath and let it out before coming back to the table. "You're stressed. What can I do? What else can I take off your plate?"

Caitlin thought of the pregnancy test she'd bought at the pharmacy earlier, the one she hadn't yet taken because she was a coward. Still, that was more of a solo project. "You've already done so much. Actually, you've done *everything*. I'm fine. Now *you*," she said meaningfully, glancing at Walker.

Maze carefully didn't look at Walker. "Nothing to tell."

"Looks like we're both big fancy liars," Caitlin said with a laugh. "Come on, what's going on with you guys? Where were you?"

Walker had three mile-high sandwiches going with everything on them but the kitchen sink. He brought them to the table. "Whoever doesn't want theirs, I'll eat it," he said as he began working his way through his.

All while both he and Maze still didn't look at each other.

Caitlin eyed Maze, who shrugged again and picked up a sandwich, taking a big bite.

"So . . ." Caitlin said. "Neither of you has anything to say?"

Maze pointed to her full mouth.

Walker chewed, swallowed, and paused in his mission of inhaling the sandwich to say, "We were off-roading up to Old Man's Bluffs."

Caitlin choked on her tea. "The make-out spot?"

"Is that what it is?" Walker asked innocently.

Maze turned to him and narrowed her eyes.

He kept eating like it was his job.

Caitlin just gaped at them. "Have you both regressed back to teenagers?"

"I blame the lake air," Maze said seriously.

Walker snorted and eyed Caitlin's sandwich. She waved for him to take it and he picked it up. "Are you going to say anything?" she asked him.

"You got any chips?"

Caitlin got up, dragged a chair to the narrow cabinet above the fridge, and pulled down her hidden treasure trove of salt and vinegar chips.

Walker reached for the bag, but Caitlin hugged it to her chest. "One question—and I'm not judging, because if the answer's yes, then I'm happy for you both—but did you just sleep with my best friend?"

"I was under the impression that *I* was your best friend," he said, and eyed the chips.

Caitlin held on to them and turned to look at Maze.

Maze shrugged. "If it helps, there wasn't any sleeping involved."

Caitlin sank back to her seat, gaping. Her eyes went to Maze's hickey again, and she felt the teensiest, tiniest little bit of jealousy. Not because she wanted Walker to give her a hickey like that. No, she was jealous that there was a hickey at all. She and Dillon had a healthy sex life, but it'd been a while since it'd been hot and hungry enough for a hickey situation. And after earlier, it might be a lot longer. "What does this even mean?" she asked.

Walker snagged the chips from her. He poured half the bag onto his plate and handed the rest to his partner in crime, who also dug in. When Caitlin gave Maze a pointed glare, she swallowed her mouthful and sighed. "Look, I don't want you to worry about this, okay? It's not a thing. I wasn't even going to tell you because you've got a lot on your plate, and also the attention and focus should be on you this week. Not me. Not him." She hitched a thumb in Walker's direction. "This isn't a big deal. It was a one-time thing, and it's over and done."

Caitlin eyed Walker.

He just kept eating, and something tightened in her gut. Worry. These were two of her very favorite people on the planet. They meant everything to her. But God bless them, neither of them would recognize true love or a real relationship if it smacked them in the face right between their eyes. So whether this was really just "a one-time thing" or not, odds were that at least one of them was going to get hurt.

Not that either of them seemed to care.

"You know what?" she said, tossing up her hands. "You're both adults."

Maze blinked. "That's it? That's all you're going to say?"

Caitlin stood. "Yep. I'm going to try to get some sleep." She headed to the door, but then paused. "Okay, so maybe there's one more thing."

"*There* it is," Maze muttered.

"I love you both," Caitlin said softly. "I don't want to see either of you get hurt. So I really hope that you know what you're doing."

"*Not* doing," Maze said. "You mean what we're *not* doing."

Walker still didn't say a word, which had Caitlin's bad feeling intensifying. She looked at him, but he was doing a great impression of an impenetrable rock, the stupid man. "Just . . . be careful," she said.

"Too late for that," Maze mumbled.

Caitlin got a whole four hours of sleep before she was up again. She went into the bathroom to begin her morning routine, extremely aware that it was day five of an MIA period. She pulled open her bottom drawer and stared at the pregnancy test. Then she shook her head and got into the shower. Just as she was getting out, Dillon slipped into the bathroom.

"Hey," he said with a smile. "I tried to wait up for you last night, but I didn't make it. Where were you?"

So he'd noticed she was gone but hadn't come looking for her. Didn't seem like a good sign.

He watched with interest as she wrapped her wet self up in a towel. "Maybe we should get back in bed to discuss this further," he murmured, reaching for her.

She put a hand to his chest. "We don't have time. We're supposed to meet your mom at the florist this morning, remember? My mom and I already got everything all picked out and paid for, but your mom is insisting on going over everything one last time, like she did at the bakery—which I still don't even want to know about."

"She likes to be thorough and wants to feel involved."

"I get that," she said. "But this is an unnecessary meeting away from my houseguests on a day I don't need one more thing to do."

"I'm happy to do this meeting without you," he said. "But either way, I'm sure your houseguests understand."

He really didn't get it, and she was starting to think he never would. "For the thousandth time, Dillon, they're my *family*. I don't get enough time with them. I didn't want to do this today, but I am. Now I've got ten minutes before I need to be downstairs."

He slid his hands down her body, pulling her to him. "I can make do with ten minutes."

Ducking out of his arms, she headed toward the door. "Well, I need at least twenty, and besides, I can't concentrate on that right now."

"Wait, you have to concentrate?"

Shaking her head, she headed out of the bathroom to go get dressed. She chose a loose, flowy tea-length sundress because she'd shaved only to her kneecaps instead of all the way up. Hell, at this point, Dillon would be lucky to see all the way up ever again. When she headed out of their room and into the hallway, Dillon had left the bathroom. She went back in there and once again opened the bottom drawer, reaching past her lotions and makeup to the pregnancy test.

It was time.

Ten minutes later she was downstairs, a little numb. But she was also stunned when she found Heather and Maze waiting for her in the kitchen, a lovely breakfast already spread across the table.

"Surprise!" Heather said. "A little birdie told me you might appreciate some help this morning."

Caitlin looked at Maze, who smiled her real smile, and it warmed Caitlin's heart. "You did this?"

"Well, with a lot of help," Maze said.

Heather nodded. "She woke me up early and here we are. Sit. You've still got five minutes before you've got to leave."

Jace came into the kitchen from the back door, ducking beneath the door frame so that Sammie, sitting on his shoulders and holding gleefully on to his hair, didn't hit her head. "Smells amazing. And here're the doughnuts." He dropped a bag onto the counter.

Caitlin's mouth watered. She hadn't allowed herself a doughnut since her disastrous dress fitting. "You went to the bakery?"

"Maze told me which ones to get. Chocolate old-fashioned, your fave, right?"

"Yes . . ." She shook her head. "Thank you. You guys didn't have to do all this."

"We wanted to," Walker said, coming in the back door on the heels of Jace and Sammie. He had a platter of sausages fresh off the barbecue. "Sit. Eat. Caffeinate. Sounds like you're going to need it."

He had no idea how much.

Neither did she. Not until she and Dillon got to the florist half an hour later. He parked in the lot and Caitlin took a deep breath.

He turned to her with a frown. "You're already braced for trouble. It's just a meeting to show my mom what's being done."

"With your mom, it's never just a meeting."

He sighed. "Look, I get that you're hypersensitive and overly emotional right now, but—"

Caitlin got out of the car and shut the door on his precious BMW harder than she'd meant to.

"You don't have to take your bad attitude out on the BMW," he said when he'd caught up with her.

She stopped and faced him. "Truth?"

His tense expression softened and he stroked a strand of hair off her forehead. "Always, Cat. *Always.*"

She thought of the test she'd taken and how she felt about the results. "I'm feeling . . . overwhelmed." There wasn't a more truthful statement to be had.

"Because you're doing too much," he said. "Can you at least admit it was a bad idea to have company this whole week? You should've put them up in a hotel like I wanted you to in the first place."

"It's not that."

He looked like he disagreed, vehemently, but he let it go. "Then let me help you," he said. "Let me take over some of the stuff. Gimme that crazy binder of yours."

"I gave my binder to Maze and she's done everything I needed."

"Then let me take this meeting for you," he said when her phone buzzed in her purse, as it'd been doing for the past twenty minutes.

She looked at the phone. "It's my boss," she said reluctantly. "I have to take it if I want a job after our honeymoon."

One thing Dillon understood was work responsibilities. He brushed a kiss to her temple. "No problem. Take your time."

The call with Sara took her fifteen minutes, after which she hurried into the florist shop. She found Dillon, his mom, his aunt Tootie, the florist, and her assistant sitting at a high-top table sipping tea and oohing and ahhing over an opened portfolio.

Caitlin joined the group and eyed the pictures. The centerpieces were lovely, as were the bridesmaids bouquets and the bridal bouquet, but they were not what she'd ordered. For one thing, there were roses instead of her central theme of white lilies. "Pretty," she said. "Whose wedding are these for?"

Her future mother-in-law reached over and patted her hand. "Ours. I took the liberty of making some changes. Dillon said you were too busy and needed help. And of course, I don't mind."

Caitlin turned and looked at Dillon.

"One thing off your plate," he said.

"I told you, my mom and I picked out exactly what I wanted."

"But you didn't have a single rose," his mom said. "I was sure that was an oversight. Roses are a wedding flower."

"Traditionally, maybe, but I'm allergic to roses."

"You could take an antihistamine," Aunt Tootie suggested.

Caitlin opened her mouth, but Dillon stood and smiled at the table. "Excuse us a minute?"

"Of course," the florist said smoothly, clearly sensing a battle. Probably nothing she hadn't seen before a thousand times. "Take all the time you need." She rose with her assistant and they moved off.

Dillon's mom didn't move, just looked at her son, concerned. "Is there a problem?"

"No," Dillon said.

"Yes," Caitlin said at the same time.

Dillon took Caitlin's hand in his and then pulled her aside, into a private hallway with mint-green walls and myriad wedding pictures, every one of the brides looking gorgeous and serene and magazine-ready.

She absolutely could *not* do gorgeous and serene and magazine-ready with roses.

"They're just trying to be involved," he said, and she realized, staring at him, at the pictures behind him, that *he* looked gorgeous and serene and magazine-ready.

Dammit. "I told you I had this," she said.

Dillon scrubbed a hand down his face. "Okay, listen. I know you don't want to believe it, but you're pushing yourself too hard. I'm worried you're going to have another breakdown."

She sucked in a breath at this. She'd told him about her breakdown in confidence. Okay, so she hadn't told him, he'd been there. A year ago, just as they'd started dating, she'd gotten stressed and completely over-whelmed. There'd been her dad and the cancer, the work pressure from her unsatisfiable boss, plus deeply miss-ing Maze, Walker, and Heather, all while not knowing where her future was going, not to mention life. Dillon had come by one night unexpectedly after their second date to bring her flowers—*not* roses, thankfully—and had found her prone on her floor contemplating life and the dust bunnies beneath the couch.

He'd gotten her to her doctor, who'd treated her for anxiety. Both the meds and therapy sessions had helped tremendously.

But it still embarrassed her that it'd happened.

Dillon was the only one who knew. He had urged her to keep her therapy appointments, had dragged her to the gym with him, and had encouraged her to cut back her insanely unhealthy work hours. And she would be eternally grateful to him for the support. It'd meant so much because she'd been far too humiliated to tell the people closest to her. Even now she couldn't stand the thought of them finding out that their pillar, their ringleader, wasn't as strong as they believed her to be. They were the ones who needed *her*, not the other way around.

"I've been off the meds for six months now and doing good," she said to Dillon now. "And we agreed to never bring that up again."

Dillon sighed. "It's just that you're really anxious and stressed, and I'm worried about you. I'm only trying to help, and my mom's good at this stuff. You were outside on the phone with work when she came up with this new plan, and I said she could run with it."

Caitlin stared at him. *Find your backbone,* Maze had told her. At the time, she'd been insulted, because dammit, she'd *never* lost her backbone. But in that moment, she knew she had indeed. "You know who else is really good at this stuff, Dillon? *Me.* And it's *our* wedding. You and I agreed on what we ordered."

He opened his mouth, but it was his mom who spoke from right behind him. "I was just trying to help."

Caitlin ground her back teeth together but did her best to smile. "We still need a minute."

"I know, and I get that you're the bride," his mom said quietly. Her voice sounded shaky with emotion. "But I'm really just trying to help make Saturday as special as possible. If you don't want my opinions, I get it. I'm not your mom. So I'll just back off and leave you both to it, staying out of your life."

Oh, great. Now she felt like a first-class asshole bridezilla. To make it worse, his mom produced a tear. A single tear that ran slowly down her cheek. She sniffled and opened her purse to look for a tissue.

"Mom." Dillon looked pained as he put his arm around her. "Don't cry."

"I'm not asking you to stay out of our lives," Caitlin said.

"Of course not," Dillon added.

His mom sniffed. "I'm so sorry. I really never meant to overstep."

"We know," Dillon said, and gave her a squeeze. Over his mom's head he looked at Caitlin entreatingly.

Oh, for God's sake. Caitlin took a deep breath. "Maybe we can find a compromise to make everyone happy."

His mom gave a tremulous smile. "That would be amazing."

"Mom, just give us another minute, okay? After this, we'll go get that coffee you love downtown."

His mom brightened even more. "With that sweet coffee bread from the bakery?"

"Yes," Dillon said. He waited until his mom had moved off. "Thanks," he said to Caitlin softly. "I know she can be a bit much, especially with my dad gone, but she's my mom, you know? She came in today for a nice time with us. You've been so busy that we've been ignoring her, and I think her feelings are hurt."

"Well, so are mine."

Dillon let out a deep breath. "Let's just go back to the table and sign off on this stuff and then get out of here. We can talk about this later."

Later. Quickly becoming the story of her life. She nodded and they moved back to the table, where the florist and his mom were still bent over the portfolio, oohing and ahhing. His mom looked up at Dillon with sweet love in her eyes. "Everything okay now, darling?"

"Of course."

He shifted aside for Caitlin to get in closer. While he was turned away, his mom's eyes landed on Caitlin. Not surprisingly, the sweet love in her eyes was gone, but she kept her voice light. "You know what the saying is, when you marry a man, you marry his family."

Yeah, she was starting to get that. "We're still not having roses," she said, possibly too loudly, because everyone in the shop turned to stare at her. Right. She needed to use her inside voice . . .

"I hear you on the roses and I'll handle it, but, babe . . ." Dillon leaned in and whispered, "you're making this really uncomfortable."

"*I'm* making this uncomfortable?" She stared at him, hurt, pissed off, and, worse, far too close to tears. "The wedding's supposed to be about the bride," she said, and when he opened his mouth to say something, she pointed at him. "*You* told me that, Dillon, right after you asked me to marry you. We talked about what kind of wedding we wanted. You said you wanted whatever *I* wanted, and I said I wanted something small, intimate, cozy, and simple."

Dillon nodded. "And that's what we're doing."

"Are you kidding me? The invite list is up to two hundred. How is that simple?"

"We've got a large family," his mom said. "There was no way to cut people out without hurting feelings. Look, dear. Look what our darling florist has available for the centerpiece at the wedding party's table. Isn't it gorgeous?"

Caitlin eyed the very large, admittedly beautiful, but *way* over-the-top, centerpiece—complete with roses—and lost track of her inside voice. "Yes, and you should use it if you ever get married again."

There was an awkward silence, and Caitlin drew a deep breath, realizing Dillon was right about one thing. She *was* feeling far too *overly* emotional. She'd worked hard on this wedding to give everyone what they wanted. And she'd done it; she'd actually managed to work in everyone's thoughts and opinions—well, except for the effing roses.

"You know what?" She shook her head. "I've got no idea why I'm so worked up over this, I really don't. It's just flowers, and they've got nothing to do with how our marriage is going to be, right? I mean, what does it matter that I'm probably going to walk down the aisle carrying the only flower I personally loathe because even the scent makes me sick—"

"Okay." Dillon stood and put his hands on her arms. "I think we might need another minute to collect ourselves."

"No. No 'we' . . . just *me*." She grabbed her purse. "I'm going to go collect myself by myself, thank you very much."

"Hey," Dillon said gently, following her to the door, pulling her around to face him. "I'm sure we can find a compromise. She's hurting right now, Caitlin. You know it's the tenth anniversary of my dad's passing."

Shit. No, she hadn't put that together, and now she felt like a complete asshole. "I'm sor—"

He kissed her softly. "No, don't be. I'm sorry too. We can talk more. After coffee with Mom."

She drew a deep breath. "You two go. I'll see you at home later, okay?"

He looked at her for a long moment, then reluctantly nodded. She stepped outside into the nice, warm, sunny day and slid on her dark sunglasses. She walked across the lot and eyed the dandelions growing in abundance out of a crack in the sidewalk. "You ladies would be more welcome than roses," she told them.

They didn't respond.

She thought she heard footsteps right behind her, so she slowed, thinking it was Dillon coming after her. He probably wanted to say of course she should have the flowers she wanted, but no one was there. She could see him, though, in the huge picture window of the shop. He was back at the high-top table talking to the florist and his mom.

Deep breath.

It was going to be okay.

She was marrying him because they were meant to be. He loved her. She knew how good she had it, that other than the unmeasurable loss of Michael, her childhood had been better than good. She'd always had people who'd loved her. Her life was practically a fairy tale.

So why then didn't it feel that way anymore? Why did she feel like she was the one struggling to belong? Why did she suddenly feel trapped in this life, that the wedding was happening *to* her instead of *for* her?

Pulling out her phone, she texted Maze with a 911. Because even though she and Maze were still finding their footing, she knew one thing for certain: she'd be there for Caitlin through thick and thin, through roses versus dandelions, through anything and everything, no matter what.

Chapter 18

Maze's maid of honor to-do list:
—Do not lose track of the flight risk—er,
bride.

When Maze's phone buzzed, she tossed it to Heather because she was busy driving, and her piece-of-crap 1972 VW Bug was acting up today more than usual. It always did after a rain, and it'd rained for a whole five minutes around dawn, which meant opening the hood and drying off the distributor cap before expecting the thing to even start. "What does the text say?"

"It's another 911 from Caitlin," Heather said, worried.

Shit.

"You should hurry."

Maze patted her dashboard. "She's going as fast as she can."

They'd hopped in the car as soon as Maze had gotten the first 911 text. Walker and Jace were watching Sammie. Maze and Heather were the cavalry. So she drove and tried to clear her mind of the images of Walker from the time she'd spent with him in the middle of the night. On the bluffs above the lake. On the hood of his car.

Good Lord. She didn't have enough brainpower to process any of that, including how she felt about it. She'd told him she was a one-and-done, and she'd meant it. But the memory of his hands on her . . . and his mouth . . . "Gah," she said out loud. That was absolutely the *last* time.

Heather glanced over. "What?"

"Nothing. Ignore me. But FYI, boys are dumb and confusing and too sexy."

Heather laughed. "Truest thing you've ever said."

Another text came in from Caitlin, this one even more confusing than the last. It was a pic of a dandelion, surrounded by a bouquet of what looked like a bunch of weeds.

"She's done it," Maze said. "She's finally cracked."

"She's never cracked. She's our rock."

"I'm telling you, our rock cracked." She pulled up to the florist shop and found Caitlin sitting on the curb holding the dandelion-and-weed bouquet, which was raining dirt clumps all over her pretty dress.

Maze parked and rushed over to Cat, who was crying and talking at the same time in a decibel that couldn't be understood by human ears. So Maze sat on the curb next to her and did the only thing she could. She wrapped her arms around her and hugged her hard. "Who do we need to bury?" *Please say Dillon . . .*

As she'd hoped, Cat stopped sobbing to laugh. Then she sniffed and lifted her head. By this time Heather was sitting on her other side.

"There's no dead body," Cat said. "But if there were, there'd be *two* bodies."

"Dillon and his mom?" Maze guessed.

Caitlin sighed and swiped at her tears, streaking dirt over her cheek. *Dirt.* On Caitlin's face. Maze had never seen such an incident before, ever. Cat was always perfect.

"These coming with us?" Maze asked about the very odd, very dead bouquet.

Cat nodded. Maze hoisted her up and directed her to the car. Heather slipped into the back, with Caitlin shotgun. Maze got behind the wheel and looked at her. "Before we go, can I go into the florist shop and beat the shit out of anyone for you?"

Caitlin bit her lip like she was tempted, but she shook her head.

Maze nodded and drove off—in the opposite direction of the lake house.

"Where are we going?" Cat asked.

"First you have to answer a question," Maze said. "You going to go through with this wedding?"

Cat hesitated and then nodded.

Maze reached for her hand. "I'm going to ask you one more time," she said softly. "Are you sure?"

"I'm not a quitter."

Maze looked into Caitlin's eyes, saw the determination, and swore internally, but nodded. "Okay then."

"Where are we going?"

"I know you said you didn't want a bachelorette party, but I don't think it was you who decided that."

Caitlin sighed. "Dillon and his mom think it's a trashy tradition."

"They think we're all trash anyway," Maze said. "So do you really want to go back to the lake house, or do you want to go into Wildstone and blow off some steam?"

"Steam, please, with a side of fast food and bad decisions."

Heather whooped and got on the phone. Maze knew that she was calling Boomer, the owner of the Whiskey

River Bar and Grill, to let him know they were coming in hot.

"You know what else they think is trashy?" Cat asked. "Tossing the bouquet." She rolled down her window and tossed her weed bouquet out into the wind.

And not five seconds later came the *whoop whoop* of a siren.

"Oh my God," Heather gasped, craning around in horror. "We're going to get arrested!"

"We're not getting arrested," Maze said, eyeballing the cop tailing her with lights going in the rearview mirror. Damn. "We haven't done anything wrong."

"Maybe we can make something up and get arrested, and I'll miss my own wedding," Caitlin said with actual hopefulness in her voice.

Maze looked at her. "Say that one more time and I'll make it happen, I promise you."

"I'm just kidding!"

The cop gave another blast of his siren. Maze gritted her teeth and pulled over.

The cop walked up to the car and knocked on her window, giving her a wiggle of his finger, indicating he expected her to roll the window down.

"Badge first," she said through the glass.

"Maze," Cat whispered. *"Just roll down the window!"*

"Hell, no. I've seen the scary movies. You don't just roll your window down unless you want to be murdered by a serial killer."

"Oh my God," Heather moaned in the back, covering her eyes. "I can't go to jail, who'll take care of Sammie? And plus there's scratchy toilet paper in jail, and I'm too short for the orange coveralls they make you wear!"

The cop knocked again, less patiently. "Ma'am, I'm going to need you to step out of the car. *Now.*"

Maze rolled down the window and looked up at him. He was around her age, but the tense lines of his face said he had zero sense of humor. Fine. At the moment, she had zero sense of humor as well. "What's the problem?"

The cop leaned down to eye the occupants of the car. Cat smiled at him. Heather squeaked and ducked down.

"She doesn't have anything to hide," Maze said. "She just doesn't like cops who pull us over for no reason at all."

"You were littering."

"It was just some dandelions and weeds that we pulled from the sidewalk. Biodegradable, nothing to worry about."

"First of all," he said, "you can't just throw things out the window, biodegradable or not. And second, did you pick those wildflowers from someone's yard? Because that's trespassing and stealing on top of littering."

"No one stole anything," Maze said. "They were growing on the sidewalk, which means we prettied up city property. You should pay us."

He ignored the snark. "License and registration, please."

"You've got to be kidding me—"

Caitlin put her hand on Maze's arm. "I've got this," she whispered, and pushed Maze back to lean over and look up at the cop. "Hi," she said with a smile. "Do you know what's happening here, Officer"—she eyed his name patch—"Ramirez?"

The cop pushed his cap up with his pen. "No, but I'm guessing you're about to tell me."

Caitlin gave him another smile, the one that, near as Maze could tell, was irresistible. There'd been many times she herself had fallen for it and given Caitlin whatever she wanted. Men typically fell even harder.

"See, I just left a florist shop," Caitlin said. "The one on Main. You know it?"

The cop nodded. "Bought a coworker a bouquet there just last week when her mom died. The owner is real nice."

"She is," Caitlin said. "I was there checking on my floral arrangements for my wedding on Saturday, making the last payment, et cetera. But my mother-in-law was also there."

The cop winced, either from imagining the horrors of his own mother-in-law or from the fact that once Caitlin started to tell a story, there was no rushing her along. Probably he was sorry he'd asked and even more sorry he'd ever pulled them over to begin with.

"She got there ahead of me," Caitlin went on. "And do you know what she did?"

Officer Ramirez sighed. "I really don't need the details, ma'am."

"She changed everything to roses. I'm allergic to roses, and do you know what my fiancé's aunt said to me? She said I could take an antihistamine." She paused. "Are you married, Officer Ramirez?"

The guy opened his mouth, but Maze gave him a subtle shake of her head. Indulging Caitlin would only make the story go on longer. Luckily Officer Ramirez could take a hint and kept his trap shut.

"Well," Caitlin said, undeterred, "if you are, I hope your mother-in-law is nothing like my future mother-in-law."

Officer Ramirez sighed, took his cap off, and scratched his head. "Truth is, I'm more afraid of my mother-in-law than I am of standing here and facing the rest of your story. I'm going to let your friend here off with a warning—"

"My sister," Caitlin clarified. "Maze is my sister."

There'd been a time when Maze would've done anything to be blood related to Caitlin. There'd also been a long stretch when she'd not allowed herself to go there. But in the past few days, she'd realized something. She didn't need to be actually related to Caitlin to claim her as her own. They *were* sisters. To the end.

"Your sister then," Officer Ramirez said. "But no more throwing things from the car."

"Don't worry," Maze said. "I'm taking the bride here straight to a bar."

Officer Ramirez put his cap back on his head. "Just don't go to the Cock and Bull in SLO, because that's where I'm going after my shift, and nothing personal, but I don't want to ever see you ladies again."

When he walked away, Heather let out a long, shuddering breath. "No jail today," she whispered to herself.

Maze slid Cat a look. "Well, that was fun."

"Better than the florist meeting, though."

Five minutes later, Maze pulled up to a dollar store. She gave Heather her credit card and Heather nodded sagely and got out of the car.

"What's happening?" Cat asked.

"Wait for it," Maze said.

Soon Heather was back in the car with two mystery bags. "Let the bachelorette party begin!"

"I'm not dressed for a bachelorette party," Cat said, looking down at her casual sundress.

"We've got you covered," Maze said. "Heather?"

"Yep." Heather gave a bobblehead nod and opened one of the bags, pulling out a bright, bedazzled tiara. "Sorry, the pickings were pretty slim."

Cat just blinked.

"It's from *Frozen*," Heather said. "I figured this way we can reuse it, because Sammie's going to want it." She handed it up to Caitlin. "Oh, and here. It's from a Bride of Frankenstein costume that was on sale for fifty cents, but a veil is a veil, right?"

Caitlin stared down at the tattered veil made of torn lace. "You've got to be kidding me."

"It's a rite of passage," Maze said. "Put them on."

Cat did and then pulled down the sun visor to look at herself in the mirror. "Dear God, I look like a zombie princess."

"I think it's kinda awesome," Heather said.

Cat pointed at Maze. "I'll get you for this. Someday when you're getting married—"

"Bite your tongue, woman." Been there, done that, and now she had a set of divorce papers to sign to prove it. But even as she thought it, her heart constricted. Because she knew something no one else knew. Something was happening to her back here in Wildstone. She was . . . softening. More than that— and this was the biggie—she didn't *want* to sign the papers. *And* she wanted to keep Walker.

How terrifying was that?

"Seriously," Caitlin was saying as Maze pulled into the bar's parking lot. "You're going to fall in love hard, I just know it. Maybe even with Walker—"

She paused when Maze choked on her own tongue.

"Hey, it's possible," Caitlin said stubbornly, having no idea how accurate she was.

Heather pulled a pack of plain white T-shirts and a rainbow of Sharpies from the bags, and they sat in the car decorating the shirts. Cat's said BRIDE-TO-BE, along with some design that was meant to be dandelions but actually looked like vaginas. Maze's and Cat's shirts said MAID OF HONOR.

They all pulled on their shirts, tying them at the waist so they fit better.

"Now we're ready," Heather said.

"Yeah." Maze nodded. "The question is for what?"

Chapter 19

Maze's maid of honor to-do list:
—Keep the gas tank full just in case
  Caitlin needs a getaway car.

M aze led the way into the Whiskey River Bar and
Grill holding Cat's hand.

"Thanks for not listening to me about no bachelorette party," Cat said. "But I'm not really feeling the
whole social thing."

"No worries. It's just me and Heather."

"God, I love you," Cat said with feeling.

A back corner booth had been decorated with
streamers, balloons, and a string of lights that, up close
and personal, Maze could see were shaped like little

penises. She slid a look at Heather, who just laughed and said, "You're welcome."

They were served by the owner of the bar himself, Boomer Nichols. He brought a large pitcher of strawberry daiquiris to their booth, smiling when Maze pointed to the string of lit penises with a raised eyebrow.

"Standard bachelorette party decorations," he said, hugging Caitlin. "We keep them handy for just such events. Wait until you see the cock cookies."

"Oh my God," Caitlin muttered, turning beet red. "Seriously?"

"Double grande, babe," he said. "Just for you."

Heather raised her hand.

Maze laughed. "What?"

"If I ever get married, I want double grande chocolate cock cookies at my bachelorette party."

Maze took ahold of the pitcher of daiquiris. "Before I pour, we need a quick game of Truth or Dare."

Caitlin shook her head. "I definitely need alcohol before that game."

"Just play along for a second," Heather said, knowing she and Maze needed a truth from Caitlin, a very specific truth.

"Fine," Caitlin said. "Dare."

"Are you sure?" Maze asked. "A truth will be easier, trust me."

Heather nodded sagely.

"Nope," Caitlin said, shaking her head. "I want a dare."

That was curious enough on its own, but given what Maze had found back at the house in Cat's bathroom trash, she was going to press the issue. "Fine. I dare you to get up on the bar and do stand-up comedy."

"But I'm not funny."

"Then you should take truth."

"Oh my God, truth then."

Heather leaned in. "Tell us a *secret*."

Maze nearly laughed, because seriously, Heather and her secrets. But she didn't laugh because Caitlin *was* holding a secret and it was scaring Maze.

Caitlin looked down at her diamond engagement ring. "Okay, truth." She drew a deep breath. "I wish I'd given this more thought, which I can't believe I just said out loud." She thunked her head on the table a few times.

"Careful," Maze said. "You'll knock something loose."

"I wouldn't mind knocking myself into another life. Hey, is it considered premeditated if you drink yourself into a coma on purpose?"

"So you *do* wish you weren't getting married," Maze said softly.

"Moving on," Cat said tightly. "Your turn, Maze. Truth or dare? And pour the damn drinks."

"Not quite yet," Maze said, holding on to the pitcher. "You've got a bigger secret. You have to tell us the *biggest* one."

Caitlin squeezed her eyes shut. "Okay, fine, so I had a little, teeny-tiny thing happen last year. And yes, maybe my doctor called it a breakdown, but I prefer the word *exhaustion* . . ."

Maze and Heather stared at each other because that was so *not* the secret they'd been expecting.

"You had a breakdown? A year ago?" Heather asked.

Maze reached for Cat's hand. "Are you okay?"

"Of course."

"Cat," Maze said softly.

"Look, it was just me holding everything in as always, and I finally burst. And Dillon . . ." She gave a small smile. "I know you won't believe this, but he was amazing. He got me through it. He took me to a therapist and I got on some meds, and I'm good now." She nodded earnestly to their faces. "Totally good."

Maze put a hand on her chest. "I'm so sorry. We didn't know, but that's no excuse. You were all alone."

"I wasn't alone. I had Dillon. And I know you guys aren't crazy about him, but he's really been very good to me." She paused, then cocked her head. "And why do I have the feeling that's not the secret you were expecting either?"

Again Maze and Heather looked at each other, Maze still holding on to the pitcher.

"Oh my God," Cat said. "I'm not a fragile little snowflake. Just tell me!"

"Right before your 911 text, we found a pregnancy test kit in the bathroom trash," Heather said, and then clapped her hands over her mouth.

Maze gave her a long look.

"Right," Heather said from between her fingers. "*Let Caitlin tell us.* I always forget the important parts."

Caitlin's eyes narrowed. "What were you doing in my bathroom?"

"I've been borrowing your good face cream," Heather admitted. "And Maze's been borrowing your magic mascara."

"Oh my God," Maze said to Heather. "Seriously?" She sighed and turned back to Caitlin. "So we're makeup thieves, get over it. Now spill about the pregnancy test."

"You didn't look at the results?"

"That would've been rude," Maze said.

Cat laughed and shook her head. "So there are boundaries then. Good to know." She drew a deep breath. "I'm not." She tugged the pitcher out of Maze's hands and poured them all very large glasses. "The end."

"Why doesn't it feel like the end?" Heather asked quietly.

"Because . . ." Caitlin's eyes went misty. "Because I *wanted* to be pregnant."

"So maybe you actually try next time," Heather said.

Caitlin shook her head. "You guys heard Dillon, he doesn't want to have my babies. Actually, I'm not sure he ever did."

"Cat." Maze gripped her hand tightly. "You know you have to talk to him about this, right? Like before you say 'I do'—the day after tomorrow."

"I know." She lifted her glass. "But I don't want to think about it anymore right now."

Maze nodded, but she felt sick with worry and couldn't zip it. "Because if you don't talk about it with him, and it turns out you're right, maybe you shouldn't—"

"Maze, I *know*. Believe me, I know."

"So—"

"Not right now." Caitlin downed her drink, waited for everyone to do the same, then refilled their glasses and flagged Boomer down for a new pitcher. "Now drink and be merry, or I'll find better drink mates."

So they drank.

Two hours in, they'd consumed the cookies, played pool, and were on their third pitcher of daiquiris. The tiara was no longer sitting straight on Cat's head. Maze didn't know if she was drunk or on a sugar high.

"Truth or dare?" Caitlin said with rum-fueled enthusiasm to Maze.

Shit. The last time Maze had played this game, it'd been with Walker in Vegas. They'd been at the bar, which was where all her problems always started, when he'd dared her to kiss him. Damn him for being such a good kisser . . .

"Truth," she said firmly. *How bad could it be?* But Caitlin was looking very pleased with herself, giving Maze pause. *"Dare,"* she corrected quickly.

"Too late. Are you ever going to let yourself fall in love?"

Maze closed her eyes.

"You gotta answer," Cat said. "It's the rules. And I'm the bride-to-be, you're not allowed to disappoint the bride-to-be. So. Are you? Going to ever let yourself fall in love?"

Maze opened her eyes. "Been there, done that, and it didn't end well for me."

Both Caitlin and Heather stared at her in shock.

"You were in love? Past tense?" Cat asked. "Like . . . with Jace?"

Maze avoided Heather's gaze, because of course Heather already knew what Cat didn't—that she and Jace had never been a thing. "Nope. Not Jace." Maze pointed to Heather. "Your turn."

"Oh no, you don't," Cat said, leaning forward. "No way. More info, *stat.*"

"Yes, more info, stat," Heather parroted.

Maze gave her a long look, silently reminding her that in spite of the fact Heather hated secrets, she was keeping one of her own, that she and Jace were exploring a relationship with each other.

Heather flushed and bit her lip.

Cat's gaze was on Maze, deep and thoughtful. "Does this have anything to do with you and Walker coming into the house in the middle of the night?"

Heather gasped and turned to Maze. "*Really?* And yay! 'Bout time!" She lifted a hand to high-five Maze.

Maze just looked at her, and Heather shrugged and high-fived herself.

"Come on, Maze," Cat said. "Talk."

"What is this, high school?"

Cat smiled. "Did you know that when you and Walker are in the same room, the tension's so high you could provide enough natural electricity for the whole town? Hell, the whole state."

"That's nothing new," Maze muttered.

"Maybe not, but the *sexual* tension is."

Maze grimaced. That others had seen it was more than a little bit embarrassing. And once again, memories of the previous night, alone with him up on the cliffs, washed over her. His hand fisted in her hair as he'd moved over her; his rough voice in her ear, making promises he'd absolutely kept. How she'd sunk her teeth into his muscled shoulder trying and failing to keep from panting his name over and over like he'd wanted, making him groan and lose himself in her every bit as much as she'd lost herself in him.

Here was the thing about being with Walker: He was *magic*. He knew when to be gentle, when to be . . . not gentle, and she hadn't been the only one who hadn't been able to keep quiet either—only he hadn't tried to hide from her, not one little bit. And hell if that wasn't one of the sexiest things about him. She sighed. "Fine. You want a real truth from me? I don't know shit about falling for someone, or if I'll ever feel it like I should, but yes, Walker and I were together last night, and it wasn't our first time. Years ago, we had a drunken night in Vegas. *There. Two* truths for the price of one."

Cat and Heather were gawking at her. Then Heather raised her hand.

Maze groaned. *"What?"*

"Can you repeat that?"

"Please don't make me say it again."

"You and Walker . . ." Cat said. "Together. In Vegas. *Without me.*"

Maze had to laugh. "I'm giving you my biggest, darkest secret and all you want to talk about is the fact that we did something without you?"

Cat winced. "Okay, that came out wrong."

"Uh-huh, let's just say the princess tiara isn't just a prop."

Their resident princess had the good grace to look embarrassed. "Okay, whatever. I'm selfish. But you don't get to stop the story there."

Maze knew it wouldn't be that easy. "What else do you want to know?"

"Only everything."

"It was my twenty-first birthday."

"Right," Caitlin said. "I remember that. I wanted to take you out and you said you had something you couldn't get out of."

"Yes, Vegas was that something. And I lied, okay? Obviously, I could've gotten out of it if I'd wanted to. And if foresight was as good as hindsight, I *would've* gotten out of it. Anyway, he flew me to Vegas to celebrate."

"Romantic," Heather said with a sigh.

"Wait," Cat said. "You and Walker were seeing each other back then?"

"No," Maze said. "We weren't at all actually, but we both knew that there was something there and had been for a while." If she was being honest, it'd always been there. "We'd been ignoring it. But what happens in Vegas stays in Vegas." She shrugged. "Seemed worth it at the time. End of story time. Your turn, Heather. Truth or dare?"

"Whoa, whoa, hold on just a minute, missy," Cat said. "There's *totally* more. It's all over your face."

Maze tried a light, casual smile. Not easy when she was at least half drunk. Maybe all the way drunk if she considered the fact that she'd actually spilled the beans about Walker. "So . . . it turns out that the bar we were at was serving free mai tais."

"Uh-huh. And what did drunk Maze and Walker do?" Heather asked, emptying the last of the pitcher into their glasses for another round.

Maze's stomach tightened because she was about to lie her ass off—by omission. "We woke up the next morning and knew it was a mistake, the end."

Cat's hand hit the table hard enough to make the drinks all jump. "Oh my God!" She held out a hand to Heather. "Pay up."

"What? Why?" Maze asked.

"Because I just realized I was right," Caitlin said. "All those years ago, I told Heather I thought you two had gone together to Vegas."

"Wait," Maze said slowly. "You . . . *knew*?"

Cat nodded. "Guessed. Walker had let me know he was going to be out of town for a few days. Then you posted a pic of yourself in a casino."

"Okay," Maze said. "But that didn't mean we were together."

"In your pic you were wearing a plaid button-down around your waist."

Heather nodded sagely. "Walker's. That's when I knew that one plus one equaled *sex*."

"Wait. So you guys bet on me?" Maze asked.

Cat's hand covered hers. "It's a compliment. I love how you live your life balls out. Well, minus the balls. You know what I mean. Every adventure I've had has been thanks to you. Jumping off the bluffs into the lake. Camping in the haunted parts of the woods. That weekend we spent in San Francisco at my first Octoberfest."

Maze snorted. "You twisted your ankle jumping off the bluffs, you got poison ivy when we camped, and in San Francisco, you almost got mugged."

"But I didn't! You clocked the would-be mugger right in the face with your purse."

"I was too young for those adventures," Heather said with a laugh. "But you always made it up to me, Maze. You'd make me forts with every spare sheet and blanket in the house and hang out with me for hours, pretending we were stuck on a raft or alone on a mountaintop, no rules. I've always thought you were the bravest, most badass chick I'd ever met. Still do."

Maze stared at them, saw the utterly genuine honesty in their faces, and relaxed a little. "Sorry. I guess I feel touchy about all the mistakes I've made."

"Whatever mistakes you've made, I've made more, I can promise you." Heather smiled. "And to be honest, regarding Vegas, I actually thought you and Walker would come home married. Because that's where my young, embarrassingly romantic, and still-unjaded-in-spite-of-everything mind went. And it's why I owe Cat the money, because I thought there'd be no way you'd fall for each other, go to Vegas, and *not* get married."

"And I said that you might be impulsive, but you'd never do anything that stupid," Cat said.

Maze took a big gulp of her drink. "You'd be surprised." She set her glass down. "Also, it gets worse. If all that isn't stupid enough for you, I'm pretty sure I *am* falling for him."

Cat's and Heather's mouths were both hanging open again, and Maze pushed her glass away.

"Dammit. Nobody refill me."

"I don't think you're stupid," Heather said.

Maze looked at Cat.

"Well, maybe I think you're a little stupid," she whispered, tears in her eyes. "But only because I love you so much and I want you to be happy. You're falling for him?"

Maze sighed. "I know, the very definition of stupidity, right?"

"Wrong," Cat said firmly. "I didn't mean anything by the stupid comment. You've *never* been stupid. And Walker is . . ." She shook her head. "Well, I think he's amazing, and there's no one who could ever deserve him more than you. Not that I can see you ever hitching yourself to a guy for life, but you know what I mean."

Maze closed her eyes. "Yeah."

"Oh my God," Heather whispered, her eyes getting wider. "There's still more, what is it? You did something crazy and got arrested, right?"

"Crazy, yes. Arrested, no." Maze paused. "We did get married." She covered her face. "I blame the endless mai tais. And this cute little chapel right next to the bar. It was closed because the guy who ran it was an Elvis impersonator and he had a gig that night, but then his gig got canceled. I still get flashes of saying 'I do' to Walker with a very happy Elvis serving more mai tais."

"And then?" Caitlin asked, both she and Heather leaning in for the rest of the story.

"And then it was over, almost before it began."

"Well, that's disappointing," Heather said. "Walker's always struck me as the sort of guy who'd take his time with a woman—"

"Not that," Maze said with a laugh. "Trust me, not that." She drew a deep breath. "I'm talking about the next morning. He let me walk away, never even asking why. In fact, we never talked about it again."

"No," Cat said. "That doesn't sound like Walker."

"Well, it's what happened."

Heather was frowning. "You walked away?"

"Yes. And I get that my own actions led to that, but people make mistakes, especially me. I screwed up, but he never came after me, never texted or called, nothing," she said, knowing the betrayal she'd felt was all over her face but utterly unable to hide her emotions from the sisters of her heart.

"Honey," Cat said softly. "He's a guy. You walked out. That's all he needed to know. He'll never ask."

"He said he'd fix it. 'It' being me and our marriage."

Cat was still shaking her head. "We're missing pieces. What happened that morning exactly?"

"We woke up hungover," Maze said softly, remembering every little detail in spite of telling Walker she did not. "But even dying, I was ridiculously happy." She shook her head. "So dumb, because he woke up quiet and somber and *unhappy*. He actually apologized for letting us make such a huge, stupid mistake. Then he went out to get me some aspirin and caffeine, and I . . ." She winced. She wasn't exactly proud of this part. "I was reeling over being a mistake. And we all know how well I deal when I'm reeling. But the bottom line was that I refused to be anyone's damn problem. I knew he was leaving for another tour of duty, which also made me a liability. Not wanting to hear it again in greater detail, I left him an *I'm sorry* note and sneaked out. I went and found drunk Elvis, who promised not to file the papers, which meant the wedding was as good as never happened. Then I let Walker know via text, and that was the last we ever talked about it."

"Wow, you really did walk away from him," Heather said.

"More like *ran*," Caitlin noted, sounding incredibly unimpressed with her.

"I was a *mistake* to him," Maze insisted.

"Not you," Cat said. "He never said you were a mistake."

Heather nodded in agreement.

"You weren't there, you didn't hear him say it," Maze said quietly, a little thrown that they weren't automatically agreeing with her. "And anyway, the mistake lives because Elvis *did* file the papers, meaning we've been married this whole time."

"Oh my God!" Heather exclaimed.

"Seriously?" Caitlin asked.

Maze nodded. "He told me a few days after we got here."

"And you're just now telling us?" Cat asked. "Wow."

"It took me until now to process," Maze said.

"Wow," Cat said again.

"It threw me," Maze said. "Don't be mad. I can't do this if you're mad."

"Do what?"

"Anything," Maze said truthfully.

Cat's eyes got teary. "Aw. But you've gotta promise you'll tell me stuff!"

"The next time I'm drunk and plan anything stupid, you'll be the first to know," Maze said.

"Thank you." Cat smiled. "You're married!"

Maze shook her head. "Don't get excited. We're filing for a divorce." As soon as she signed the papers . . . "And I really don't want to talk about this anymore," she said, pulling a page from Cat's book. "This is *your* night, we're moving on now. And it's Heather's turn."

"Fine, but this isn't over." On that note, Caitlin pulled out two twenties and slapped them into Heather's waiting palm.

"You're kidding me," Maze said. "My sex life's worth only forty bucks?"

"Back then, forty bucks was a lot to me," Heather said. "Still is, actually. I can feed Sammie and me for a week if we're careful."

Maze's heart squeezed on that, thinking about Heather working multiple jobs waitressing and bookkeeping to make ends meet. She pulled forty out of her wallet—her spending money for the week, because she wasn't much better off than Heather, but at least she had only *one* mouth to feed—and pushed it across the tabletop. "Seems only fair that I pay up too, seeing as I started the whole thing with Walker to begin with."

"What do you mean you started the whole thing?" Cat asked.

Heather read Maze's expression and smiled. "You made the first move."

"After he dared me to kiss him, yes." Okay, so she'd made the second move too . . . Not that Walker had been a slouch in that department. She might have started it, but he'd certainly finished it in ways that she *still* dreamed about at night. And though she'd long ago convinced herself that she remembered it being far better than it was, the other night on the bluffs had proven her wrong. *Very* wrong. He'd been everything she remembered.

And more.

"Truth or dare?" she said desperately to Heather.

"After what you two just went through? Dare," Heather said firmly.

"No." Cat shook her head. "New rule. Dares are out tonight. So truth." She softened her voice. "Tell us what's going on with you and your baby daddy."

Heather stared at her for a beat, then tried Cat's trick of dropping her forehead to the table and banging it a few times.

"Yeah, so that doesn't actually help," Maze said.

Head still down, Heather sighed. "He's not in my life."

Cat gasped. "But you said—"

"I lied. We met in a bar. He drove a motorcycle and had a wicked smile. We had a really great night, and in the morning his alarm went off at the butt crack of dawn. He said he had to work and that he'd call me later. Long story short—he didn't." She swallowed hard. "When I found out I was pregnant, I texted him, but he ghosted me. Walker came and visited me on a day that I was having a really hard time and was freaked out about doing this all on my own. So he went looking for the guy." Heather paused, drew a deep breath, and lifted her head, her eyes bright with tears. "He'd been killed on the way home the morning after our night together. He was sideswiped by a Mack truck."

"Oh my God," Caitlin said, and climbed out of her side of the booth to scoot in next to Heather before wrapping her arms around her. "You went through this all alone?"

Heather sniffed. "That's not even the worst part. His parents sued me for custody of Sammie. They didn't win, again thanks to Walker, but for a long time it made me doubt my ability to do the mom thing. I'm still on shaky ground. I mean, let's face it, I can barely take care of myself, much less two of us."

"I think you're doing amazing," Caitlin said softly, tearfully. "Sammie's amazing."

"And you're not alone," Maze said, also leaving her side of the booth to squeeze in with them both. "Not ever again. We need to stick together and keep each other from making stupid mistakes."

"Hey, at least you're both doing better than me." Cat wiped her tears away. "I'm about to marry into a family who thinks I'm not good enough for their son."

"You're perfect," Maze said.

Caitlin shook her head.

"Okay, so you're perfect just the way you are."

Caitlin snorted. "You don't understand. Dillon doesn't have any siblings, but there are cousins, and they're very close. And those cousins all married big— one to a stockbroker, another to a doctor. One's married to a former Olympic skier. They're people who do it all, babies *and* careers. I can't compete with that."

"You shouldn't have to," Maze said. "We like you just the way you are. And Dillon must agree. I mean, he put a ring on it."

They all looked down at Caitlin's admittedly gorgeous rock. "I know I'm lucky," she said quietly. "Dillon's got a great job, makes a solid living, and he's good to me."

"Um," Heather said. "Aren't you missing something?"

Caitlin blinked and thought about that. "Oh! Of course! He handles all the yard work, and he even puts the seat down."

"Nice," Heather said. "It's hard to get a man to do that. But I was talking about *love*. You didn't mention love, not even once."

"Sure, I did."

Heather shook her head.

"Huh." Caitlin raised a hand to gesture to Boomer for another round. "Maybe because I've got love right here." She smiled a little dopily and took Maze's and Heather's hands. "I love you guys."

"Me too," Heather said. "I love you both so much."

Maze smiled and sipped her drink, feeling happily snockered before realizing both Caitlin and Heather were staring at her. "What?"

"You love us too," Caitlin said. "Right?"

"Right."

Caitlin sighed. "Seriously? Even drunk you can't say it?"

"I'm not drunk." She paused and considered the fact that the room was sort of spinning. "At least not one hundred percent."

"One of these days," Caitlin said, "you're going to say it out loud."

Maybe. But Maze was pretty sure not. The last time she'd said it out loud had been right before CPS dragged her away from her mom. Maze had cried "I love you" to her mom, who'd been too wasted to say it back. Remembering that, she pushed her drink away from her.

"Truth or dare?" Caitlin said to Maze.

"It's your turn."

"No, it's not," Cat said, and Maze was just snockered enough to be unable to figure out if that was true or not.

"Aren't we done with this game yet? I mean, I'd much rather play Pin the Penis on the—"

"*Truth or dare?*"

Maze took one look at the seriousness on her face and said, "Dare," because no way was she doing truth again.

"Dares are forbidden," Heather reminded her.

"No, wait." Cat smiled. "A dare is fine," she said, and Maze got scared.

"I dare you to go for Walker," Cat said. "For real. For *keeps*."

Heather clapped her hands. "Yes! I double down on that dare! You two were made for each other. Two young kids given up by the people who should've loved you the most, screwed over by the system, and yet you found each other, you found something *real* in all that chaos . . ." She sighed. "It's so romantic. Plus, he's the most amazing man on the planet."

"Stop," Maze said. "I'm begging you. None of us are going to talk about this anymore, and I hereby forbid either of you to talk about it too. Not to each other and not to Walker. In fact, don't even think about him, okay, because I think he can read minds."

They both sighed dreamily.

"Oh my God." Maze pointed to Caitlin. "Pick another dare."

"Fine. I dare you to tell Walker you're in love with him."

Heather burst out laughing. "Wow, you're evil. I like it."

"It's the same dare," Maze protested.

"No, it's not," Cat said. "Trust me, I know what I'm doing."

"This is ridiculous. My life's ridiculous."

"Aw, honey, no," Cat murmured, hugging Maze. "It's not. Not even close."

"It's the universe telling you that you two are meant to be," Heather said, or sort of yelled. "Listen to me— you're awesome, and Walker would be lucky to have you. Now repeat that back to me."

"But—"

"No." Heather put her finger on Maze's mouth. Or probably that's what she meant to do, but she got Maze right in the eye.

"Ow!" Maze pushed her hand away. "And how can you still believe in all that mushy stuff after everything you've been through?"

"Because knowing someone loves you is the best thing in the whole universe."

"Whoever said that never had grande cock cookies," Maze said, and bit into one.

"I'm wearing my sexiest lingerie," Caitlin said, apropos of nothing. "And no one's going to be seeing it."

Heather hooked a finger in the top of Caitlin's T-shirt and sundress and peeked at her bra. "Ooh. Pretty. And now someone's seen it."

Caitlin smiled at her. "Thanks."

"Sure," Heather said. "I'm not wearing a bra or I'd show you mine."

They both looked at Maze.

Since she couldn't remember, she looked down her own top. "Oh yeah. I'm wearing my sexiest bra, but only because it's laundry day. Oh, and I'm commando for the same reason."

This set them all off on a case of the giggles, which for Heather turned into a case of the hiccups, the really loud kind that come from deep in the chest. Caitlin, cracking up, choked on her drink and nearly had to be resuscitated by Boomer. Maze laughed so hard she fell out of the booth and hit the floor on her hands and knees.

Just in front of her was a pair of long legs wrapped in well-worn, buttery-soft-looking jeans. She lifted her head and found Walker looking down at her, an unreadable expression on his face.

"Oh my God," Heather whispered from behind her. "He *can* read minds!"

Maze found herself being lifted off the floor and onto her feet, and she met his amused blue eyes as he steadied her because she couldn't find her sea legs. *Damn, he was hot.* When she could stand on her own, she glanced back at Heather and Cat. "Okay, which one of you thought about him too loudly?"

They both raised their hands.

"You guys suck," she said.

"Hey, at least *I'm* wearing panties," Heather said.

This set both Heather and Caitlin off on another round of uncontrollable laughter.

Maze sighed and looked at Walker. "What are you doing here?"

"I'm the man of honor. I can't join the bachelorette party?"

"Truth or dare?" Caitlin yelled, while also grinning at him.

"No, *dares* only!" Heather yelled. "We get sad at our truths."

Walker raised a brow.

"Oh, for God's sake." Maze yanked them both out of the booth. "It's time to dance," she said, feeling smug because she knew Walker wouldn't dance.

But the joke was on her, because he started to come along with them.

"Wait!" Heather yelled, and ran back to the booth and her bag. She pulled the fourth T-shirt from the pack, hastily wrote MAN OF HONOR across the front and then PROPERTY OF MAZE across the back, and made him put it on.

"Not even going to ask," he said.

"Okay, *now* we dance," Caitlin said, and tugged them all to the dance floor.

Chapter 20

Walker's man of honor to-do list:
—Make sure the girls get to do their thing
  during their bachelorette celebration,
  while at the same time keeping them
  safe from harm. Best of luck while
  you're at it.

W alker looked down at Maze's face as she danced in front of him. She was dewy, flushed . . . and sexy as hell.

"I'm awesome," she said, apropos of nothing. Actually, she yelled it over the music as she shimmied and shook her hot bod to the beat. "And also, you're lucky to have me."

This had him blinking in surprise. "That's one hundred percent true," he finally said. "But I wasn't aware that I . . . 'had' you."

She shrugged. "Just announcing my stance."

"Good to know. And . . ." He let loose what was first and foremost on his mind. ". . . you're commando?"

"Laundry day." Then she turned her back to him and kept dancing.

Walker had gotten a call from Boomer half an hour ago. He'd barely been able to hear over the noise in the background. All he'd gotten was "the girls" over a whole bunch of music and laughter and ". . . they're lit . . . might want to come get their drunk asses . . ."

Walker's plans for the night had been entertaining Sammie with Jace, but after she'd gone to sleep and Jace had taken over the baby monitor, Walker had been headed for a beer and eight hours horizontal without conscious thought. He'd gotten as far as cracking the beer when the call had come in. The drive had been easy. No traffic at the lake or in Wildstone at this time of night.

He'd nodded to Boomer as he'd entered the bar. They'd known each other for a very long time. In fact, Boomer was trying to sell him the Whiskey River so that he and his wife could move to L.A.

Walker had to admit he was damn tempted. It'd mean quitting his job at the FBI, though, and he'd put his life and soul into the work.

But then again, that job had nearly taken his life and soul more than once.

Laughter drew his eyes back to the girls. Specifically Maze. She looked . . . happy. Just the sight of her took down the walls he'd built up, proven by the fact he was on the dance floor. He'd never been able to resist her, not once since he'd met her as a defiant, wary, resilient, amazing, tough girl. At the moment, though, she and her two comrades were dancing and singing at the top of their drunk lungs to "Shake It Off" by Taylor Swift. Heather was boogying, her feet planted on the floor, rocking side to side and swinging her arms with abandon over her head. Caitlin was dirty dancing with the air, shaking her booty along with everything else God had given her. Maze was the only one of them with any rhythm at all, and he couldn't take his eyes off her as she worked her hips to the music, eyes closed, singing loud enough for people in the next county over to hear her. It made him laugh. As always, she made him laugh.

Heather and Caitlin caught sight of him and sent twin dazzling, drunken grins his way.

"Walker!" Heather yelled right in his face. "Dance with us!"

Caitlin pulled him in a little and went back to shaking her groove thing, looking more like she might be having a seizure than actually dancing. "We need more drinks," she announced.

Thank God. Walker turned and headed to the bar.

"Told you," Boomer said, and they both looked out at the girls on the floor tearing it up. Caitlin and Heather threw their arms around Maze and nearly took her out at the knees. They all staggered but managed to stay upright.

"How many drinks in are they?" Walker asked.

Boomer grinned. "Probably a full pitcher each."

Shit. "Switch to virgin for this last pitcher."

"Look at you, acting like the boss already. You making me an offer for this place or what?"

"Haven't ruled it out," Walker admitted, accepting the virgin pitcher. "Thanks for the call."

"It's nice to see them cut loose. Caitlin's not usually all that much fun."

"Yeah, well, hungover Caitlin's going to skin all of us alive if she's too sick for her wedding rehearsal tomorrow." He took the pitcher back to the party. Thirty minutes later, it was empty and Caitlin said, "I can't feel my feet."

"Do you want to go home?" Walker asked. "Or . . . ?"

"Home." She beamed. "I love it that you think of us as home." She threw her arms around him and squeezed the breath from his lungs. "I also love that I can always count on you."

"Always," he said, getting a grip on her wrist, then turned to gather the other two. He had no problem being the rescue squad for the night. Or ever. It was something that he'd done a thousand times for both Caitlin and Heather and would do a thousand more without conscious thought, because they were family.

He'd never rescued Maze before. At least not in a way she'd recognize as such, because Maze hated needing help or rescue. Feeling those things made her feel trapped. Worthless.

And that was the *last* thing he wanted for her.

As for what he *did* want, well, his brain and his heart were not on the same page. Neither were certain body parts, which twitched as he watched her, still out there on the dance floor, moving with easy, sensual grace.

As if she felt him, she opened her eyes. She didn't stop dancing, though, just kept swaying, watching him with those beautiful eyes of hers.

"Caitlin wants to call it a night," he said. "Your chariot awaits."

Heather and Caitlin both "Awwwwed" in sync and looked at him like he was the sweetest thing on the planet.

Shaking his head, he turned and eyed their booth. "Let's get your stuff." Since they all just kept dancing, he headed back to the booth and gathered three purses, which he slung over a shoulder. "What do you guys keep in here?" he asked, shocked at the weight.

"Stuff," Heather said. "I bet you'd make the best husband on the planet. Isn't that right, Maze?"

Maze pretended not to hear.

Walker reached for Caitlin's hand because she was usually the most reasonable. "Come on, honey, let's get you home."

She clapped her hands to his cheeks. "I love you, Walk."

"No, *I* love him," Heather said, pushing her way in, cuddling into his side.

Maze rolled her eyes. "No getting mushy at a bachelorette party, it's the rules."

"Hey, it's important to express your feelings," Heather said. She looked at Walker. "She loves you too."

He should be so lucky. "Yeah, yeah," he said. "We all love each other, but I'll love you more if you get outside and in the car."

He managed to wrangle them halfway to the door, but then Heather had to go to the bathroom and Caitlin wanted to hug and kiss Boomer goodbye. Maze, suddenly a little quiet and broody, wanted to walk home.

Feeling like he was herding cats, he ended up standing on the sidewalk waiting for Heather and Caitlin to come outside. Maze sat on the curb, something definitely wrong. He had no idea if it was last night or something that had nothing to do with him, but his luck wasn't that good so he figured that yeah, it was definitely last night. Aka *him.* "You okay?"

She lifted a shoulder.

Even he knew that was woman code for no. Taking off his sweatshirt, he wrapped it around her and sat at her side. "Is this about last night?"

"I don't want to talk about last night."

"Maybe we should."

She sniffed, and his heart stopped. *Shit.* He knelt down in front of her and zipped up the sweatshirt before meeting her gaze. "Did I hurt you?"

She let out a watery laugh, then wiped her nose on his sleeve. "I think you know you didn't. And it's not about that. It's about tonight."

"Tonight," he echoed.

"Yeah. It was . . . great." She gave a teary smile. "Cat and Heather and I talked, like *really* talked." A tear slipped out and she swiped it away. "Dammit. I always feel stupid weepy when I stupid drink too stupid much."

"So this really isn't about . . . me?" he asked cautiously.

"No! And seriously, dude, check your ego. You and I were *last* night."

"And . . . you don't want to talk about last night."

She shook her head. "Absolutely not. Because—"

"Don't say one and done," he said.

"Of course I won't. Because we're not talking about it."

Okaaay. He cupped her face, which was full of so much emotion, he felt his heart roll over. "You and the girls are really okay?"

She nodded and sniffed again. Her mascara had run and her nose was red. She was adorable.

"So these are . . . happy tears?" he asked, feeling like he needed to buy a vowel.

She nodded again.

"That's good then, right?"

"Right."

He nodded, but in truth, he was confused as hell. "But . . . you're not happy with me."

"Right."

"Even though thirty minutes ago you danced with me like everything was okay," he said, wondering if they were speaking the same language.

She shrugged. "I faked it."

"You . . . faked it."

"Yep," she said, popping the *P* sound. "Like I faked all the orgasms with you last night."

He stared at her and then laughed. Hard. When he got himself together, she was glaring at him.

"What's so damn funny?" she demanded.

"You weren't faking."

"I was so."

"Maze, your eyes rolled back in your head. You even passed out for a minute."

"Hey, my eyes were tired, okay? And I did not pass out. I . . . took a quick catnap, that's all."

He was still grinning. "Okay."

"Ugh, you're so full of yourself."

He twisted and lifted his shirt to show her his back. When she sucked in a breath, he knew she'd locked her gaze not on his burn scars, but on the angry scratches down his back, vanishing into his pants. He could've dropped them and shown her the ten nail indentions in his ass, but he figured she had enough evidence.

"Oh my God," she said. "I'm an animal."

He laughed at her horror. "Yeah. And I loved every second of it."

Boomer came out the front door, Caitlin in one hand, Heather in the other. "You forgetting something?"

Walker rose and relieved Boomer of his cargo. It took a few minutes to wrangle them all into the car. He got Heather and Caitlin into the back and seat-belted them up, and then Maze into the front. Once he slid behind the wheel, he leaned over and buckled her up as well.

The two in the back sighed dramatically.

"Okay," he said, craning his neck. "Seriously. What's going on with all the dreamy sighs tonight?"

"Nothing," Maze said, giving both back-seat occupants a long, hard look.

They giggled.

Aw, hell. He ran a hand over his eyes and then turned to Maze. "You told them about us."

"You went to Vegas and I won forty bucks!" Heather yelled cheerfully.

Walker raised a brow at Maze.

She pretended as if he wasn't in the car. In fact, she pulled up the hood on his sweatshirt and turned to face the window.

"She also told us you're married," Heather said. "And that you said she was a mistake."

"Heather!" Caitlin whispered.

"What, it's true!"

Walker glanced at Maze. "I said 'it' was a mistake, not that you were a mistake."

"Oh my God," Caitlin muttered. "News flash, Walk, any woman would have taken that as an insult. Why are men stupid?"

"I don't know, but it's so true," Heather said. "I tried to switch to women, but I didn't like them either. Too much drama."

Walker adjusted the rearview mirror to look at Caitlin and Heather. "You're telling me that Maze doesn't want the divorce?"

Cat turned to Heather. "He's getting pretty old. Maybe he's started to lose his hearing along with his wits."

Heather nodded sagely. "Good thing, or he'd be able to hear us now."

"I *can* hear you," he said. "And *she* wants the divorce." He turned to Maze, but her deep breathing and stillness told him she was no longer just ignoring him.

She'd fallen asleep.

He didn't get two blocks before the chatter in the back seat stopped as well. One glance in the rearview mirror explained why. Caitlin and Heather had also fallen asleep, curled up together like a pair of kittens.

Relieved at the silence, he drove home, his mind racing. Was what Caitlin and Heather said true—did Maze not want to file for divorce? And if so, *what did it mean?*

He hadn't realized she had taken, nor had he meant for her to take, the "mistake" comment to heart. He'd truly believed *he'd* been *her* mistake and had been operating from the knowledge that neither of them had been thinking clearly that long-ago night. That they'd been far too young to tether themselves to each other. That as much as it'd destroyed him, they'd done the right thing by going their separate ways. He, for one, had needed to grow the hell up, and he had.

And Maze had always been violently allergic to any sort of roots or ties, especially relationships. Hell, she still couldn't even say the words *I love you* to those she clearly *did* love, like the two in his back seat.

In fact, the whole reason he'd presented the divorce the way he had was so that she *wouldn't* completely freak and feel like he was trying to trap her into a commitment with him. He'd used the fact that she'd made it crystal clear she hadn't wanted to stay connected to him in any way as further proof.

And you'd walked away pretty damn quickly yourself, never bringing it up again, instead letting it fester between you like a dirty secret. Like she was your dirty secret . . .

But that was the past, he argued with himself. And now it seemed possible that he'd made decisions based on facts that weren't true. The thought sent an odd sensation running through his veins, a glimmer of something new.

Hope.

He glanced over at Maze again, so still in the passenger seat, head tilted awkwardly to the side. Reaching out, he nudged her into a better position, causing her to let out a soft snore, which made him laugh. Even snoring she looked good.

He had it bad.

He'd sent a quick text to Jace, so when he pulled up to the house, Jace was already there waiting. He peered into the window of the car and shook his head with a small laugh.

"Where's Dillon?" Walker asked. "I texted him too."

Jace shrugged. "I don't know. I knocked on their bedroom door, but he didn't answer."

Asshole. Walker got out of the car. "If you take Heather, I'll get the other two."

Jace nodded and scooped up Heather.

"Mmm," she whispered, throwing her arms around his neck, snuggling in, and setting her head trustingly on his shoulder without ever opening her eyes. "I love the way you smell. Where's my baby?"

"Asleep," Jace said softly, brushing a kiss to her temple. "Don't worry, I've got the monitor hooked to my belt."

"Aw. Hey, Jace?"

"Yeah, babe?"

"If we'd gotten married and then you offered me a way out with a divorce, I wouldn't take it. You should know that."

"Um, okay?" Jace sent Walker a questioning look.

Walker just shook his head. He wasn't going into that. Not now, not ever. He got Caitlin to her bedroom and went back for Maze. He laid her down on the bed, then went downstairs again, turning off the lights and locking up. When he got back upstairs, he realized Jace and Heather were in *his* room, presumably because Sammie was sleeping in Heather's.

Great. He peered into Maze's room. She wasn't on the bed where he'd left her. Then suddenly she came out of nowhere, yanking him all the way into the room, shutting the door behind him to press him up against the wood.

Jesus. "You're awake," he managed.

Her hair was . . . wild, her cheeks flushed. Her eyes were shining bright with intent and she was smiling at him, truly smiling at him for the first time in years, and he felt his chest tighten because he couldn't—wouldn't—take advantage of her. He'd kill anyone who did. But when she hugged him, he couldn't help but put his arms around her and hold her close. Closing his eyes, he breathed her in. *This is all you're doing.*

And then she rocked her hips against his and he knew he was a dead man walking. "Maze. What are you doing?"

"Trying to be irresistible." She'd already dropped his sweatshirt. She tugged off her T-shirt next and then started on her jeans, but Walker grabbed her hands.

"You're already irresistible," he said, never having meant anything more than those few words. "But you've got to stop—"

"You don't wanna kiss me?"

His low laugh was mirthless as he wrangled her in and pressed his forehead to hers. "More than my next breath, but I want you to remember it."

They stared at each other.

"I will remember it," she said, tugging her hands free to lose first her bra and then his shirt. "Yum. Naked Walker chest."

"Maze, I can't. I won't take advantage of you." *Again.*

"Mmm, that's actually kinda sweet."

God help him, she was shimmying out of her jeans now, and as promised, she was . . . sweet baby Jesus . . . commando.

"New plan," she said, and then shoved his jeans to his ankles. "I'll take advantage of you."

That was when her foot got caught on her pant leg and she toppled over like a felled tree.

"Shit." Walker rushed to scoop her up and against him. "You okay?"

"Yep. I meant to do that." She snuggled in closer and pressed her face to his throat, taking a little nip as she kicked her jeans away, smiling when he sucked in a deep breath.

His grip tightened on her, his voice a rough, warning growl. "Maze—"

"How do you always taste good?" she asked, licking her way to his ear, giving him an all-body shiver of the very best kind. "Seriously, though. How?"

"You need to get a grip."

She slid her hands to a most impressive erection. "Done."

He choked and manacled her wrists with his hands. "I was talking to myself."

She set her head on his shoulder and sighed.

"I'm going to let go of you now," he said cautiously as she became a deadweight in his arms. "Are you going to behave yourself?"

The only answer he got was a soft snore.

Chapter 21

Maze's to-do list:
—Make Caitlin and Heather pinkie
  promise to have regular girls' nights out
  for the rest of their lives.

One moment Maze was dreaming about eating pancakes, and the next she was awake and her head felt like it might fall off. Without opening her eyes, she groaned, then stilled at two realizations. One, it was still dark. Two, she was lying on something.

Correction: lying on *someone* . . .

Eyes still closed, she reached out and gave Jace a shove. "Dude, it's not your turn for the bed. Move over."

"Babe, you've got ninety percent of the bed already, I can't move over any farther without falling off."

Oh boy—*not* Jace.

Walker.

"Oh my God," she whispered, and then groaned again because dear God, her head.

"Shh." Walker ran a soothing hand down her back.

Her *bare* back.

"What the—" She blinked blearily, lifting her head with difficulty, but hey, at least it was still attached to her neck. "What are you doing here?"

"Sometimes I wonder that very thing."

"In my *bed,*" she clarified, ignoring his amused tone. "What are you doing here, in my bed?"

"Mine's already taken."

She blinked. "By who?"

"Heather and Jace."

"Oh my God," she said again, shocked. *"Why?"*

"Well, when two grown-ups like each other a whole lot, they—"

She pointed at him and he thankfully shut up.

To laugh. When he was done he said, "I put a glass of water and aspirin on your nightstand. How bad is it?"

She grunted and took the aspirin, chasing it with the water before lying back down with a sigh and closing her eyes. Apparently there were people who enjoyed having full conversations in the morning, and she was of the mind-set that it was okay to hurt those people.

But Walker didn't say another word. Probably because talking wasn't his first choice of morning activity either.

She lifted the covers and took a peek. Walker was in black knit boxers and nothing else. She wore a sports bra and cheeky undies. They'd come from a set of five, each with a pun on a different sport. At the moment, she was wearing the hockey ones, which had little hockey pucks and sticks all over them and said PUCK OFF across the front. "This isn't what I was wearing last night."

"Nope."

She swiveled her gaze his way. He was looking amused again.

"Where are my clothes?" she asked.

His amusement faded. "You don't remember?"

She frowned and gathered together some loose thoughts. Rescuing Caitlin from the florist shop. The bar. The penis cookies. Sharing secrets with Heather and Caitlin. Dancing. Dancing with Walker. Going home. Trying to execute a sexy striptease . . . "Oh God," she moaned.

"There it is."

"Tell me I didn't really try to do a striptease when we got home."

"Okay, I won't tell you."

She stared at him, suddenly remembering every-thing, including wrapping her hands around his goodies. Welp, there was no point in being embarrassed now, especially when she'd enjoyed every second of it. "But how am I wearing more—and different—underwear than I was last night?"

"I put them on you so you wouldn't kill me when you woke up."

"A sports bra. I'm impressed."

"Yeah, well, who knew how hard those things are to get on," he said with a low laugh.

She laughed because okay, so he was a good guy. A really good guy. "And *your* clothes?"

"You got me down to my skivvies before I could control you."

There was a little quiver in some of her good parts. Or all of them. And she wasn't the only one. He was . . . awake too, and she lifted the covers to take another peek.

"See anything that interests you?"

Yes. "Drunk Maze is losing her touch if you've still got a stitch of clothing on."

He laughed. "No, she's not. You were a lot of fun last night. You always are."

"Maybe we should forget about last night."

"Too late." He leaned back against the headboard, hands behind his head, the sheets pooled in his lap. "I've already filed it with my other favorite Maze memories."

He sat there in her bed looking so delectable she was nearly rendered stupid enough to forget why they weren't friends with benefits. *Nearly.* The truth was she needed a time-out, and fast. Reaching over the side of the mattress, she grabbed up his shirt from the floor. Pulling it on, she instantly realized her mistake. It smelled like him, which was to say delicious. She nearly pressed it to her face to inhale it, but he was still watching, so she flopped onto her back on the bed and stared up at the ceiling. "Are Heather and Caitlin okay?"

"Jace took care of Heather, but because Sammie was sleeping, he took her to my room, and when he didn't open the door again, I took it as man code to go away. So then I got Caitlin to her bed—"

"Where was Dillon?"

"He didn't wake up."

Asshole.

"Yeah," Walker said, watching her face. "I'm with you there. But we can't step in, Maze. This is her life, her choices."

"But what if she's basing her choices on things she believed to be true that might not be?"

"Such as?"

"A year ago she had a nervous breakdown." She waited for his reaction and didn't get one. "You knew?"

"Not until long after," he admitted.

"And you didn't tell me or Heather?"

"It was her story to tell."

She hated that but knew he was right. Knew also that if she'd been checking in with Cat as she should have, Cat would have told her herself. "Dillon was the only one there for her." That Maze hadn't been was something she'd have to live with. "And I think she feels a lot of gratitude to him for that. But she was also under the impression he wanted kids as much as she does."

"Again," Walker said softly, "her life, her choices. She's free to walk away, Maze. People do it all the time."

She ignored the dig, intended or not. "She's getting married *tomorrow*."

"Have faith in her."

She nodded. Sighed. Stared up at the ceiling some more, extremely aware that their bodies, side by side, were touching, and that his was big and warm and corded with muscles that she wouldn't mind tracing with her tongue. "Why aren't you out running, or doing something equally insane?"

"Because we have unfinished business."

"We always have unfinished business."

"Not that," he said with a laugh. "Not entirely, anyway."

"What then?"

He turned to face her. "I'm having a hard time piecing together exactly why you've been so mad at me."

She looked at him in surprise. "I'm not," she said. "I'm actually trying to remember why I said we weren't going to sleep together anymore."

His eyes darkened. "Hold that thought. Talk first. Can we start with Vegas?"

She nodded reluctantly.

His serious gaze held hers. "You left me there. You got on a plane and vanished. And please don't say it was because I said it was a mistake. That's a bullshit excuse and you know it. You're not shy, Maze. If that was all that tripped you up, you'd have said something to me right then. In fact, you would've gotten right in my face about it, and then *I'd* have said you misunderstood and explained myself, and we'd be fine."

Her heart was pounding in her ears. "This isn't something that can be fixed with a conversation, Walker."

"No shit. It's because you're scared and won't admit it."

She felt her spine snap ramrod straight. "No, you don't get to turn this on me. You made it clear that I was a problem that had to be handled, and I felt . . . stupid." *And humiliated and heartbroken. Fix that with a damn conversation,* she thought bitterly.

But Walker's face softened. "It wasn't like that, Maze. You weren't the problem, I was. I was going to be shipping out. I couldn't—"

"I understood that part. I was proud of you." She felt choked up. "So proud. But . . ." Her throat decided to close too tight to finish that sentence how she wanted, which was, *When you didn't even try to come after me, I knew the truth—you didn't love me enough to make it work . . .*

But she wouldn't beg for love, not ever again.

God, they were both so screwed up.

He studied her face and then closed his eyes, as if looking at her pain was too much for him to take. "That morning when I woke up with you, I felt . . . sheer joy." He shook his head. "I'd never experienced anything like it. Do you know how many people have walked away from me, Maze?"

She felt her heart squeeze.

"Just about everyone," he said. "But then you hitched yourself to me and promised forever, and . . ." He scrubbed his hands over his face. "We were so far gone that night. When you said you didn't even remember it . . ." He grimaced. "That's when I realized that I'd taken advantage of you. I hated myself for that."

Stunned, she shook her head. Because she remembered so much more than he thought. "Maybe *I* took advantage of *you*," she whispered.

He gave a head shake. "That's not how it works."

"You mean because you have the penis, therefore you get to decide what I think?"

His eyes flashed. "You know damn well that's not what I'm saying. You've got the sharpest mind of anyone I know. I was trying to make it easy on you. We made a mistake rushing things. We were too young. I knew we'd get there someday, but I also knew I was committing to a job that would take me away for long months at a time. The last thing I wanted was for you to be married to someone who wasn't even home. You've had enough family members disappearing on you."

"What I'm hearing is what I've always known," she said. "You regretted what we did."

"No." He stopped. "Okay, so I regret Elvis. But I could never regret anything with you."

She stared at him, a little surprised by how genuine he sounded. And more than that, how the words made her feel. A minute ago she'd been enjoying the view of him in nothing but those boxers, and maybe she'd also been thinking what could another hour in bed with him possibly hurt?

And she still felt all that, but now she also felt . . . *more*.

He didn't regret her. She hadn't been a mistake.

She thought about what Heather had said last night. From Walker's perspective, she'd walked out on him. End of story. He hadn't needed to know why; all he needed to know was that he hadn't been wanted.

Again.

She was the one who'd made a mistake, a big one. "You would've grown to resent being tied to me so early," she said.

"No. You don't get to tell me how I feel about you. Do you remember any of the conversation we had that night?"

Even now she could conjure up flashes of them together in bed, teetering on the edge of no return. Did she remember any of it? She remembered *all of it*. The warmth of his body on hers. The pull of his fingers in her hair. The taste of hunger and desire on his lips . . . "I remember you giving Elvis the *don't make me kick your ass* look."

"Because at the ceremony, he kissed you *way* too enthusiastically."

She had to smile. "He backed right off when you threatened to rearrange his doodles."

He grinned. "His doodles?"

"You know what I mean."

"No, tell me."

She pointed at him. "You're just trying to get me to talk dirty."

"Yes, please." He laughed but sobered quickly. "I remember all of it, Maze." He closed his eyes. "But I hate that you don't."

"Walk?"

"Yeah?"

"I lied," she admitted softly. "I'm so sorry. I blame my stupid pride." She scooted a little closer and crawled back under the covers and into his arms. "I remember all of it."

He stared at her.

"*Everything,*" she whispered. "You. Us. What we did. How I felt. I remember it all. You jokingly said you'd ruin me for all men, and you did. You ruined my heart."

He drew a deep breath and pulled her in tight. "Nothing to forgive," he said huskily, pressing a kiss to her shoulder. He lifted his head. "So what's the verdict?"

"That we were both young and dumb?"

"Good thing we're old now."

"Speak for yourself." She straddled his lean hips before bending down to rub her jaw against his scruffy one, then pressing her face to his throat and breathing him in. His skin was warm, and she hummed with pleasure as his hands slid down her body, taking their sweet time too, slowing to explore every inch. She did the same with her lips, brushing them back and forth just beneath his jaw, working her way up to his mouth, the whole while making sure to touch as much of him as she could.

"Is this going anywhere or are you just copping a feel?" he asked, voice thrillingly rough.

"Depends."

Leaning over him, she kissed his neck and he gave her a lazy smile as he wrapped his arms around her, seeking out her mouth, kissing her breathless. Then he pulled back and stared at her. As they drank each other in, she watched emotions flicker over his face: hunger, desire, aching desire . . . and the same wildness that had always drawn her to him like a moth to the flame.

He smiled first, and when she returned it helplessly, he whispered her name and drew her back down. He rubbed his jaw against hers, pressed his face into her hair and inhaled deeply, breathing her in like she'd done to him. "Do you have any idea what you do to me, Maze?"

"Show me," she whispered, and almost before the words were out, their clothes were gone and he'd rolled them so that she was flat on her back, covered in 180 pounds of lean muscle . . . the both of them unhinged, unglued, as he took them on a wild ride.

After, she lay there, stunned. When she finally managed to sit up, she took in the sight of Walker still kneeling in the middle of the bed, breathing hard, looking as dazed as she felt. "You okay?"

He gave a slight laugh. "I'm not sure."

He lay down beside her and propped himself up on his elbow while she ran a finger down his chest, lazily thinking about following that finger with her tongue. Walker caught her hand in his and squeezed, but he looked torn, like he was trying to use both heads at the same time and was failing because of blood loss. She took in his frown and stilled. "Did we hit a hard limit? Too tired for round two?"

He laughed. "Smart-ass."

"Then . . . ?"

His smile faded. "I need to know if you're sinking as deep as I am again."

She sagged back, shaken at his admission. "You want to talk about feelings? Now?"

His gaze never wavered. "Worried I'm going to say this isn't just sex?"

Suddenly she became acutely aware of her own heartbeat and how her stomach was tightening uncomfortably. "I decided a long time ago not to worry about things like that."

"Because you don't stick around long enough to care?" he asked.

That he was right didn't help.

He watched her for a minute. "I don't want any more misunderstandings between us, so to be crystal clear, just now wasn't a mistake, not for me. It was special, and if you run away, it's fear. You're afraid to do this."

"This?" she asked thinly, trying not to panic.

"Us."

Needing a moment, she rolled off the bed, realizing with surprise it was still dark.

"So I'm good enough to be married to, but not good enough to give a real shot?"

She turned and gaped at Walker, still in the bed, deceptively calm. "You want a real shot?"

"Yes."

She gaped some more.

"Wow," he said. "I guess I'm your one-and-done, huh?"

"Actually, technically, you're a two and done, but I'm not saying that's what this is."

"Then say what you mean," he said. "No more perceived wrongs, no more running instead of facing our shit. I don't ever again want to be the idiot standing all alone in a hotel room wondering what the hell just happened."

She was looking for her clothes, but at these words she turned and bumped right into a naked and pissed-off Walker. She stabbed a finger into his pec. "Want the truth?"

"Sure, let's try that."

She poked him again and searched for the right words to make him understand. "Truth—I've ruined every relationship I've ever been in. And I don't want to ruin this, that would kill me." She sucked in some air and told herself she absolutely was not going to cry. She was tougher than this. "Truth—I'd rather have you in my life from a distance than destroy this, and destroy it I will. I'm selfish, impulsive, and . . . Mayhem Maze."

Walker's hands slid up her arms. "Truth," he said softly. "There's only one of those three things that is true. I love that you're impulsive. I love the way your mind works, and you have *not* ruined all of your relationships. You haven't, Maze," he repeated when she gave a small, disbelieving shake of her head. Ducking down to see right into her eyes, he smiled. "I'm still standing here, aren't I?"

"Well, that's because you like morning sex."

He grinned. "I do. But to be fair, I like it at any time of the day or night. Not just mornings."

She tried to pull free. "You aren't listening to me," she said.

"I *always* listen," he assured her. "I just don't always agree. You're a lot of things, Maze, all of them pretty fucking amazing, making you who you are. I adore every part of you, even the parts that scare me just a little bit." He smiled again when she rolled her eyes. "Look, be impulsive. Be whoever you want to be. Just let me be there at your side while you're doing it."

"Like . . . a couple?"

"Yes, just like that. I want us to be closer." He paused. "And since you haven't run off screaming, maybe you want that too." He held out a hand. "Come with me?"

"Where?"

"Does it matter?"

She thought about that. "A little, but only because you're naked."

With a laugh, he tossed her some clothes and pulled his on as well. They tiptoed through the still-quiet house and down the wild grass hill to the water. He had her hand in his and a blanket tucked under his other arm as the sky was making the slow but dazzling shift from midnight black to a kaleidoscope of purples and blues. Nothing stirred except the occasional splash of a fish breaking the glass surface of the lake.

And there in the peaceful quiet of the predawn, alone with Walker and catching the sunrise, Maze let herself believe it could all be real.

Chapter 22

Walker's man of honor to-do list:
—Send a thank-you note to drunk Elvis.

That long-ago summer spent out here on the lake had brought Walker a happiness he'd never experienced before. It'd taken him years and a trip back here this week to make him realize something: It wasn't the place that made him happy.

It was the people in it.

Still a little off-balance from that newfound knowledge, he held Maze's hand as they walked to the hidden cove. The sky had shifted to a pale purple above the still water, the stars quickly fading away. They sat, their backs to a huge rock, wrapped up in a blanket against the predawn chill, and watched the sun come up over the rolling hills.

"I used to come out here that summer," he said. "Watched the sunrise, just like this."

"You did?"

"Yeah. Sometimes Michael came with me. We liked the quiet. When we'd get back, Caitlin would be making all of us a huge breakfast, even back then."

Maze laughed. "Yeah, she'd pretend we ran a restaurant. God, she was so bossy. She'd put us all to work, just so she could be in charge."

"She used to make us leave her reviews," he said. "Remember?"

"Yeah, because that's the summer I discovered my love of all things baked. Her cinnamon rolls still highlight my fantasies."

"Your yellow bikini highlighted my fantasies. Still does." She laughed, as he'd intended. "I liked playing restaurant with you."

She met his gaze. "You used to want to own one."

"With you guys, yeah," he said fondly. He still believed it'd be the perfect life and thought about Boomer selling the Whiskey River. "It'd be nice to be all together again."

Looking torn between wanting exactly that and being scared of it at the same time, she nodded.

Not wanting her to get bogged down by her fears of letting love into her life, he playfully tugged on a loose strand of her hair. "You know, I also have a lot of fantasies of you *without* that yellow bikini." This time he was prepared and was laughing as he caught her hands before she could punch him. Wrapping his arms around her, he hauled her onto his lap.

"The sun's almost up," she said, wriggling in a way that made his eyes cross with lust. "We are not doing it out here in broad daylight."

"Agreed," he said, mouth on her neck.

"You . . . do?"

She sounded so disappointed that he laughed again and nipped her jaw, working his way to her mouth. "Yes. Because we're going to *talk*," he said. "Like we're on a date."

"A date," she echoed, like the concept was foreign to her.

"Is that so odd?"

"Odd, no. Backward, yes." She smiled. "You don't have to wine and dine me, Walk. You know I'm a sure thing."

"Maze." He took a beat because he needed to find the words to make her believe him. "You're important to me."

"Uh-oh." She craned her neck to meet his gaze. "That's your very serious voice."

"Because I am very serious. You know how we both grew up. It was shit. It might have defined our childhoods, but I won't let it define my adult life. We're more than our circumstances. We deserve hopes and dreams and love like everyone else."

She swallowed hard but didn't take her eyes off his. "Actually, I don't."

"What?"

"I don't know how you grew up. You never discussed it, not with any of us. Everyone always jokes that *I'm* the closemouthed one about the past, but really, it's you."

He could see hurt lurking in her expression and also in her voice.

"You know everything about me," she went on. "Everything. But you hold back, Walker, even with the little stuff."

True story. But he'd thought he'd been doing her and the others a favor. Who wanted to hear another sob story? No one. And he sure as hell never wanted the pity that would go along with it.

But apparently he hadn't done any favors at all. The people who cared about him had shared everything, let him in, and in return, he'd built walls taller than . . . well, Maze's. "You're right," he said. "I'm sorry."

"And . . . ?"

"And . . ." He drew a deep breath. "I was given up by my parents when I was two."

She stilled, didn't move a single muscle, like maybe if she did, he'd stop talking.

"I don't know why, but I was left at a firehouse in Paso Robles." He shrugged. "Like a bad pair of shoes. No one knew my name or even my birthday, or where I'd come from."

He watched her eyes cloud over with fury. For him. "What happened?" she asked.

"They gave me a name—Walker, because I loved to be on my feet moving around. I ended up in the system, just like you."

"Yeah, but I didn't go in until I was a teenager. You were *two*."

"I had some good homes," he said. "Once I stayed with a family who owned and ran a café. We always had a ton of good food. It's where I learned to cook."

She sat straight up and stared at him in surprise. "Wait. You can cook? You buried your lede!"

He grinned. "I'm really good at it too, but I'd rather eat, so don't tell Cat."

She laughed. "You're sneaky and manipulative *and* talented? I like it."

"I know how to sew too."

She gaped at him, looking shocked and hugely impressed. "Get out."

"Serious. Once I lived with a family who made all their own clothes. I'd like to tell you I'm talented in that arena too, but I am most definitely not." He held up his fingers. "I stuck myself so many times, I still don't have much feeling in my fingertips."

Taking his hands in hers and massaging them, she asked, "Who steered you toward the military and FBI?"

"The cop I told you about? With the good search programs? He caught me on his computer. Instead of kicking me out as he probably should have, he took me under his wing." He smiled briefly, remembering. "Taught me how to *not* get caught. Suggested the military would be a great way to learn some respect for authority and a place where I'd learn to be a part of a unit. And he was right. I grew up a lot. As for the FBI . . ." He shrugged. "Felt right."

She smiled. "You're full of surprises."

And, he knew, she related to a lot of what he'd grown up with. The uncertainty, moving from family to family, not sure where she fit in . . . He couldn't believe he'd been so blind when it came to her. He never realized that the things that he'd shoved down deep inside and made so insignificant to him would have meant so much to her to know. How he'd gotten his name. Where he'd lived. His early experiences. And he wondered if he'd ever fucked up anything as much as he had his relationship with her.

He looked at her in the pale dawn light. Ran a finger along her temple, tucking a loose strand of hair behind her ear, needing to touch her. He'd missed this. He'd missed her. "I'm sorry I haven't shared more with you," he said. "I'm going to change that."

"Uh-huh." She smiled. "You, Walker Scott, are going to become an open book?"

"With you."

"Why?"

He had to laugh at the question. "Only you would question it."

"Humor me."

"Okay," he said. "I like being with you." He grinned. "In *and* out of bed."

She stared at him for a beat, then dropped the eye contact and turned to stare at the water and the streaks of color across the sky. "Spending time together was never our problem," she said. "For those few days in Vegas, I was so happy."

"What's stopping us from being that happy now?"

She looked at him as if he'd gone daft. "Besides the fact that this"—she gestured between them—"is over after tomorrow's wedding?"

"And why is that again?"

"Because I'm leaving to go home to Santa Barbara, back to the grind. And you're going back to the FBI three thousand miles away." She paused. "Aren't you?"

He drew a deep breath, needing to be honest but also not wanting to scare her off. Again. "It is where my life was only a week ago."

Crickets literally chirped.

"Right," Maze finally said, and tried to move off him.

But he held her in place. "*Was*," he repeated.

She studied him for a moment. "You really think this could work?"

"Pretty sure we proved that earlier." He smiled.

"You know what I mean."

"I do. And yeah." He ran his hand down her back, snugging her in closer to him. "I've always known it could work, Maze. But . . ."

"I hate the *but* already."

He palmed and squeezed her sweet ass. "But . . . it means getting rid of all the bullshit."

She was still for a long beat, so still he wasn't sure she was breathing. Then she carefully inhaled. "By bullshit, do you mean mine or yours?"

"Both," he said, and could almost hear her self-doubts. "Hey," he said softly, nudging her a bit to make her look at him. "*Hey*."

"What?"

"I wouldn't change a single thing about you, so stop thinking that."

"Get out of my head, dammit."

"I could only wish to be in your head, Maze."

"No, you don't. It's a scary place."

"Do you remember when we first met?" he asked.

"Yes." She gave a small smile. "I was in Caitlin's front yard when her parents pulled up with you."

He nodded. "You were in the middle of a brawl with the kid next door. Like actually rolling around on the grass in a full-out war."

"Not my finest moment," she admitted softly.

"Are you kidding?" He was smiling at just the memory. "He'd thrown a rock at Michael and beaned him in the head. You were standing up for him, giving the little punk asshole a badly needed lesson."

"That's not how the parentals saw it. I was grounded for a week."

"I don't care how anyone else saw it. I took one look at you, bleeding from your nose, hair wild—"

She grimaced, and he nudged her again, wanting eye contact for this.

"Your jeans were ripped and your shirt had dirt all over it. Your expression was fierce and unapologetic and . . . well, pissed off at the world. And I thought you were the most impressive thing I'd ever seen."

She looked embarrassed. "Come on."

"You were amazing and incredible, and I *still* think that."

She swallowed hard and her eyes skittered back to the view. "You see me differently than everyone else. They see the wild, feral kid, no plans, no dreams."

He squeezed her hand. "That was never true. Well . . . okay, maybe the wild, feral part is," he said, laughing when she rolled her eyes. "But you always had plans and dreams. You wanted to be a bartender. You used to make us fun drinks from stuff in the fridge."

"Some people think I should aim higher."

"What people?"

She lifted a shoulder. "People."

"Since when do you care what anyone thinks?" he asked.

She bit her lower lip. "Okay, it's me. *I* worry that I should be aiming higher. I guess that's why I'm in school too. Maybe I can be a business manager at a place where I can also take on some bartending shifts."

"Cat told me you volunteer at a women's shelter."

"Cat has loose lips."

He smiled. "She loves you. She's proud of you. And so am I."

She squirmed, uncomfortable with the praise, so he changed the subject.

"We all had simple dreams back then. Simple doesn't mean not good enough. And the way I see it, you're the only one of us currently following your dream."

"You were interested in owning your own place because you like people and also like to gather them around you. But more than that, you wanted something of your own that no one could take away from you."

"You remember all that?" he asked, surprised.

"I remember everything," she said softly. "Caitlin wanted to be the cook. Heather wanted to be in charge of the books because she likes numbers." She laughed a little. "God, we had it so good back then and didn't even know it. Why can't life be like that all the time?"

"It could be. With you, I know it could be."

She looked stunned . . . and uncertain. "How do you know?"

She was still in his lap, so he turned her to fully face him, wrapping his arms around her. "Because being with you now is as easy as it was back then. Don't you get it yet, Maze? You're the best thing that's ever happened to my life."

"You spent *one* year with me, and that was accidental. We could've landed at different houses, easily."

He raised a brow. "And now, this week?"

"Another freak accident that we're both here at the same time," she said.

"Caitlin's wedding is a freak accident?"

"Actually, it's a disaster in the making," she corrected him. "And if it hadn't happened, we wouldn't be here. So yeah, it's also an accident. And anyone who knows us is going to think this is ridiculous, that it's just an itch to scratch, that we have no business trying to make something of it."

That was fear talking. He knew because he felt it too. The only difference was that it wouldn't stop him from trying. "Your happiness is all that matters to those of us who love you, Maze. You can be you all the way to the bone, and we'll all still love you and support any choices you make."

"That's—" She broke off, looking shocked. "Wait. Did you just say you love me?"

He couldn't help the smile at her shock. "I said you can be who you are."

Her eyes narrowed. "You said you loved me."

He nodded, watching her carefully. "Scared?"

"No," she said. Hesitated. "Maybe."

He tugged playfully on a stray strand of her gorgeous, wild hair, currently the same fiery color as the sky. "Truth is, Maze, I've always loved you."

She didn't so much as blink. "Me too," she finally whispered.

He snorted and pressed his forehead to hers.

"I do!"

Her fervor spoke more of her feelings than words ever could, and equal parts affection and thrill went through him.

"I feel it, you know," she said earnestly. "I just . . . don't like to say it."

Since he knew why, he wasn't about to push the issue and dredge up any bad memories for her. "I know. And I get it, Maze." He smiled. "You're better at show than tell."

Her own smile was sweet and filled with relief, and she slid her fingers into his hair. Tightening her grip, she directed his mouth to hers. "Let me do a little show-not-tell right here," she murmured, straddling him to do just that.

"You were worried about broad daylight."

"Yes, but it's not all the way light yet . . . we've got a few minutes."

He smiled and tightened his grip on her. "Good thing I do some of my best work under pressure."

———

Caitlin slipped quietly out of bed and into the shower, but not before taking aspirin and cursing last night's alcohol for her pounding head. In the steaming water, she closed her eyes and let the hot water work its magic. But no amount of hot water could push back her problems and worries. They were simply becoming too big for her to manage with a smile and a few deep breaths. So she went with the facts.

One, she wasn't pregnant.

Two, she wanted to be.

Three, she no longer believed Dillon was on board for that.

On the bathroom counter, her phone was having a seizure. Sara, of course, with more work problems. "It's a deli," she said to the phone. "Not life or death." Which led her to fact number four: she wanted to leave her job and work for herself, but *again,* not sure Dillon was on board for that either.

And then there was the biggest fact of all. Number five: she now believed that she'd rushed into this wedding—a disaster of her own making. As someone who'd prided herself her entire life on always making smart decisions, she was horrified. And at that realization, her knees gave in to the nerves and she sat on the floor of the bathtub, letting the water pummel her.

"Caitlin," Dillon said quietly.

Her head snapped up and she stared at him.

He lifted his hands, signaling that he wasn't here for a fight. "You okay?"

"I just need a few minutes." Or another year . . .

"I understand." Reaching in past her, he turned off the water. Then he gently wrapped her up in a towel, picked her up, and brought her back to bed.

The dogs were in it, of course, but he did the unthinkable. He shooed them off and set her on the bed, therefore putting her ahead of his "babies."

"But you don't like it when the covers get wet," she said inanely.

"I don't like it when my future wife is sad." He tipped her face up to meet his. "Can you talk to me?"

She drew a deep breath. She'd tried everything else, so why not? "I'm, um . . . six days late."

"For making the last payment on the rental equipment?" he asked. "Yeah, I know. They called me and I took care of it."

"No." She shook her head. "I mean, thank you. I'd forgotten. But that's not the kind of late I was talking about."

He blinked. "Oh."

"Yeah."

He drew in a deep breath. "Are you . . . ?"

"No. I took a test."

He sagged with clear relief and smiled. "Okay."

She did not smile, and his slowly faded.

"You were hoping otherwise."

She nodded, and he grimaced and shoved his fingers into his hair.

"Aw, Caitlin. I'm so sorry."

Her eyes filled, but she swallowed hard. "Are you?"

"Yes." He pulled her to him. "Babe, you know I love you, right?"

"And I love you," she said. "I do. But, Dillon, this is a big problem for me, and it should be for you too. It turns out we want two very different things. How can we do this? How can we get married tomorrow?"

He took her hands and looked her in the eyes. "Look, I'm sorry I didn't jump right onto the baby train. And it's not like I don't want them ever, I just don't want them right now. This isn't something that has to derail us."

"But what if you never get on the baby train?"

Their gazes held for a long beat and then he let out a weighty sigh. "Can't we deal with that when the time comes?"

Yes. They could. They absolutely could. But . . . did she want to? Did she love him enough that in the end, if he decided it was never the time to have kids, that it would be okay? That she'd be okay?

He took in her expression and shook his head. "Caitlin," he said softly, squeezing her hands. "You're scaring me."

"Same. You're asking me to wait and see in good faith, no questions asked."

"And you're asking me to make you a promise on something I'm not sure about. I won't lie to you, Caitlin. No matter how much I want this, we can't start it out with a lie."

"So what then? Where does this leave us?"

"I don't know," he whispered.

"I don't think—"

He gently set a finger on her lips and shook his head. "No, please don't say it. Not yet, okay? Let's think about it."

She wrapped her hand around his. "The rehearsal dinner is tonight. The wedding's tomorrow."

He pulled their joined hands to his chest. "Yes, and come tomorrow, I want you to do what you think is right. You follow your heart, and I'll accept it either way."

He was telling her it was *her* choice whether they did this or not. On the surface, that was incredibly gallant. But just beyond that came another, darker inkling. He wasn't sure about getting married either, or he'd never have given her an out. Not only wasn't he sure, but he didn't want to be the bad guy. "Dillon—"

"Shh," he whispered, and pulled her in close, warming her up in the way that they communicated best.

She didn't know what would happen tomorrow, what she'd do. All she did know was that *he* wasn't going to make the decision, that it was all on her to do so, to either show up . . .

. . . or not.

Chapter 23

Maze's to-do list:
—Be there for Caitlin no matter what.

Late that afternoon, Maze stared at herself in the mirror. She was in a pale rose dress that was more demure than she'd normally wear, but Caitlin's rehearsal dinner was not a place where she wanted to stick out.

In fact, if she could get away with not going at all and continuing to avoid Cat's parents—who, let's face it, she'd severely disappointed over the years—she would. But she always knew she'd have to face the music at some point, and tonight was it.

She drew in a shaky breath. Maybe it wouldn't be so bad.

Cat had been acting off all day, so when earlier she'd asked Maze to make sure everything ran smoothly during the wedding rehearsal, she'd readily agreed without thinking it through.

Being in charge of everything running smoothly was going to be interesting in its own right, but that task was nowhere near the same anxiety-inducing level as knowing that in less than an hour she'd be walking into a room and coming face-to-face with Caitlin's parents for the first time since she'd walked out of their anniversary party all those years ago.

The adult Maze understood that all of it, including her reaction to the Walshes' move after the fire, wasn't their fault. But the angry, hurting, devastated teenage Maze hadn't understood a damn thing. All she'd known was that she'd had to once again pack up her bag and start over.

Her reaction embarrassed her now. They'd lost a child. Michael was gone forever, and she'd had a hand in that. Cat's parents deserved more from her than what they'd gotten, at the very least a sincere apology. That she hadn't managed to do so before now meant she clearly wasn't nearly as grown up as she liked to believe. The truth was Shelly and Jim had saved her. They'd given her a home when she'd never really had one she could trust before. They'd given her so much, and all she'd done in return was hurt them.

They took two cars to the restaurant. Caitlin and Dillon went together, and then Walker, Heather, Jace, Sammie, and Maze in a second car.

Originally—as in before Heather had shown up with Sammie—there wasn't going to be a flower girl. But Caitlin had decided that Sammie belonged in her wedding, and no one even tried to argue otherwise. Once Caitlin made a decision about something, not even God could change her mind.

Walker parked and Jace pulled Sammie from her car seat. "I've got her tonight," he told Heather. "You do what you have to do for Caitlin and enjoy yourself. We'll be fine." He smiled down at Sammie and gently booped her nose. "Right?"

Sammie let out a stream of garbled words no one could understand, but she seemed enthusiastic about it.

Heather got out with a sweet, thankful smile for Jace. Maze loved that Jace could calm Heather, who deserved someone like him in her life.

As far as herself, Maze had convinced herself over the years that she didn't need anyone. She'd been wrong of course, but she had been proud of herself for hiding it from everyone.

Walker held the door of the restaurant open, letting Jace, Sammie, and Heather through, but then held Maze back. He was dressed in charcoal-gray pants and a slightly lighter charcoal button-down that complemented his leanly muscled build in a way that could almost take her mind off her troubles.

Almost.

"What?" she asked, finally meeting his gaze to find him taking her in as well, a small sexy smile telling her he was every bit as appreciative of his view of her. Her heels put her at eye level with his mouth, which she couldn't help but stare at. After all, it was a pretty great mouth, and she should know. It'd had its merry way with every inch of her body—

"You okay?" he asked.

"Why wouldn't I be?"

"That's not an answer." He searched her gaze. "You're freaking out."

"I'm freaking out," she admitted softly.

"Jim and Shelly are going to be thrilled to see you."

"You don't know that." She shook her head and looked around for a way out. "I don't know what I was thinking."

"You were thinking that you wanted to be here for Caitlin, but you've just realized you're so far outside of your comfort zone that you can't even see the comfort zone."

"Yes!" She grabbed him by the shirt. "I can't do this. What made me think I could do this?"

He covered her hands with his warm ones. "Because when someone you care about needs you, you give them your all, no matter the personal cost."

She dropped her forehead to his shoulder and took the comforting hug he offered, sighing in pleasure at the feel of his arms closing around her. "Thanks," she whispered.

"Any time." He lifted her chin and looked into her eyes. "And I meant that. *Any* time."

She'd never really believed in a forever sort of love, but somehow Walker was making it feel possible. Which was momentarily terrifying enough to bank her panic over the evening ahead. "Okay," she murmured. "I'm good. Let's get this over with."

He gave her a small squeeze. "That's no way to live, Maze, just trying to get through all the moments."

"Not *all* the moments," she said, even though she knew he was right. "Just some of them." Or, you know, a *lot* of them . . .

They walked in together and were greeted by a hostess with a tray of filled wineglasses. Walker took two and handed her one as they met up with the others.

"To pregaming," Maze said, and clinked hers with first Heather's, Jace's, and then Walker's.

The hostess pointed them to the big open room in the back that had been set aside for the dinner. The entire back wall was sliding glass doors that were opened to the property. The plan was to walk through the wedding ceremony first, then eat after. As she knew from her trip here earlier in the week, the property had a huge grassy area, trimmed and landscaped beautifully with oaks lining the sides, flowers planted to add color, and, far off to the west, a stunning view of the ocean. Tonight the crowd would be small, the gathering intimate—family and wedding party only. Tomorrow, with two-hundred-plus people, it'd be a zoo.

Caitlin and Dillon were at the open doors, greeting the various wedding party members. Dillon had a grip on Caitlin's hand as if she were a flight risk. But Caitlin broke free to hug Maze, then pulled back to look into her eyes. "What's wrong?"

Maze shook her head with a smile. "Nothing."

Caitlin searched Maze's gaze and sighed. "Maze, they're going to be so happy to see you. Please, don't worry."

"Who, me? Worry?" Maze managed a laugh. "Why would I worry? You're the one getting married."

Caitlin rolled her eyes but squeezed Maze's hand before being tugged away by Dillon to greet some of his family.

Maze turned to eye the room as a warm mouth brushed her ear. "You've got this."

Maze sagged a little. "I just don't know what to say to them."

"How about 'It's good to see you'?"

Caitlin's mom and dad were standing in front of a pretty wood high-top table showcasing framed pictures of Caitlin and Dillon, warmly greeting people as they walked by, smiling, laughing.

Not too late to run, Maze thought, but then Shelly turned to hug someone and her gaze snagged on Maze from across the room and she smiled.

Maze froze.

Walker followed her gaze. "She seems happy to see you again."

"She has to pretend to be happy to see me."

Walker turned his head and looked at her, eyes serious. "Do you really not know?"

"What?"

"How we're *all* happy to see you again. Like to-the-bone happy, Maze."

"You also have to say that. You're sleeping with me."

He snorted. "There's been almost zero sleeping involved, and I don't ever say anything I don't want to. Neither do they." Then he gave her a little nudge in their direction, which actually was more like a shove.

There was no way out of this now, and her stomach sank and hit her toes. She didn't want to do this— God, she so didn't want to—but she was no longer that wild teenager who ran from . . . well, everything. This weekend was about Caitlin, not Mayhem Maze.

Besides, they'd already seen her.

Caitlin's mom gave her a wave and then a little finger crook to come over there.

Somehow feeling cold yet also sweating at the same time, she started walking.

Everything else—the other people, the low music, the talking and laughing around her, even Walker—all faded away as she drew a deep breath and moved like she was walking to her own execution. Because this was going to be hard. Shelly had been the first positive female role model in her life. She'd made Maze cookies, let her use every freaking sheet and blanket in the house to build forts for Michael and Heather, coaxed her into participating in family events, and expected her to be civilized, all while cocooning her in safety and unconditional love. She'd single-handedly turned Maze from a feral, lost kid into a real person.

And just like that, her feet stopped working. Just stopped, as if she'd stepped into a vat of cement. It'd sucked her in, drying around her, making movement impossible. In contrast, her heart pounded in her ears and she couldn't get enough air.

Nodding her understanding of the situation, Shelly took the last few steps for her, closing the distance between them. "Maze." Her voice was the same as it'd been all those years ago: soft, warm, genuine. "I'm so happy to see you. I was worried you wouldn't come because of me."

Maze's stomach twisted, and all she could do was hope she wouldn't be sick until after. She figured she'd smile, bear the hugs, look Shelly and Jim in the eyes and give a genuine apology for basically pretending they didn't exist, then move off. Instead, her eyes filled, and she heard herself whisper, "I'm sorry. I'm so sorry—"

"No, darling, no." Shaking her head, her eyes shiny, Shelly said, "No apologies necessary." She smiled through unshed tears and cupped Maze's face. "I've missed you so much."

Maze nodded, because words were beyond her now, and she hoped Shelly knew she meant she'd missed her too.

Caitlin had come close, and she snorted at Maze not repeating the words, but she didn't interfere. Which meant that Maze stood there feeling like an idiot. A frozen-in-anxiety idiot. Looking into Shelly's damp eyes made it impossible to pretend everything was fine. Everything was not fine, and she was tired of the pretense. "Please let me say I'm sorry," she managed.

"Honey, *we're* the ones who are sorry. There were things we could have handled better. When we lost Michael, we were so devastated that we were barely hanging on by a thread. We weren't thinking clearly. But the truth was, between losing him and the house, it wasn't just that we couldn't have taken on the extra responsibility; they actually wouldn't allow it. And by the time we were ready, you'd already been settled with another family."

Shelly was by now somehow holding both of Maze's hands, which Maze felt really bad about because her hands were sweaty. And shaking. She could also feel the weight of Caitlin's gaze, along with Heather's and Walker's, who'd made their way over and stood close to her, at her back, aligned with her. She took a deep breath. "I understand. No, wait." She grimaced because she needed to tell the truth, needed to get it all out once and for all. "It took me a while to really understand, to get that it wasn't about you not wanting to fight for me but that your hands were tied. I was terrible to you both, and I'm . . ." She had to swallow hard, but she still felt like she was choking on unshed tears. "I'm so sorry for that."

Shelly lost the battle with her own tears as well. "Oh, honey, we did fight for you. But by the time we jumped through all the system's hoops and got the paperwork handled, a year had gone by and you were already settled in a new school. We didn't want to uproot you again. I couldn't do that to you after all you'd been through."

"You . . . fought for me?"

"So hard." She squeezed Maze's hands. "That's what family does, they fight for each other."

"But I didn't even come into your lives until I was a teenager."

Shelly hugged her tight. "You don't need to be in the beginning of a child's story to change the ending."

Maze felt Walker's hand on her shoulder, could feel Caitlin and Heather by her side. Her heart swelled until it felt too big for her chest. Pulling back, she searched her pockets for a tissue, which was ridiculous because she never kept tissues on her. Heather came up with a few spare napkins from her bag.

"It's a mommy thing," Heather said. "I also have crayons and crackers if you need."

They all laughed and cried and hugged again.

Maze swiped at her tears and suddenly her senses kicked in again. She became aware of the fact that they stood in the middle of the wedding rehearsal and that there were others around, a lot of others. "I'm sorry." She squeezed Caitlin's hand. "I'm so sorry. Tonight's supposed to be about you."

"It *is* about me," Caitlin said, wiping her own tears away and hugging Maze hard. "You're my family. And this is all I've wanted—everything out in the open so we can move on."

"We're doing just that," Maze assured her. "Now let's shift this over to you and Dillon. *Please.*"

"Yes," Shelly said, giving her daughter a sweet, soggy smile. "Let's move on to getting you married."

"Right," Caitlin said with a nod. "Sure. Yep." She suddenly looked a little . . . green?

Maze squeezed her hand. "Hey, you okay?"

"Of course." Caitlin waved her concern off. "Just a little headache. I've had it for weeks, but I'm fine. Totally fine. Like completely, totally, one hundred percent fine."

"One more 'fine' and we just might believe you," Walker said dryly.

Caitlin tossed up her hands. "Look, I'm just tired, okay? I mean, what else could it be?"

"The roses?" Walker asked.

Maze looked around and caught sight of Dillon's mom placing a vase of roses at her table.

"It's the groom's family who plans the actual dinner part of the rehearsal dinner," Caitlin said tightly. "I have no control over that, nor do I have any illusions of *ever* having control over her."

Shelly turned to the table just behind them, the bride's family table, and pointed to the gorgeous bouquet of wildflowers in the center. "I wrapped the stems with the ribbons from the gifts you got at your work friends' shower last month. Thought you could walk down the aisle with that as your bouquet tonight."

"Mom," Caitlin said, looking undone, "how did you know?"

Shelly looked at Maze. "A little birdie told me."

Caitlin's eyes filled again as she looked at Maze. "You called her?"

"Texted," Maze admitted, and found herself in another tight Caitlin hug. She thumped dramatically on Caitlin's back. "Can't. Breathe."

"Shut up and love me."

"I do," Maze said, and sighed when Caitlin laughed.

"Can we do the run-through now?" Maze asked, desperate to get out of more hugs.

Thankfully, the wedding officiant waved her hands for everyone to gather around.

Walker pulled Maze back by the hand and looked into her eyes. "Proud of you," he said quietly. "I know that was hard."

"Almost as hard as letting you win the swim race to shore a few days ago."

He laughed. "I won that fair and square and you know it. Which reminds me, you still owe me twenty-four hours of servitude."

"Dream on," she said, even as her body quivered. "And haven't you learned by now a woman's always right?"

He smiled. "You are right." He lowered his head and kissed her. "Actually, you're more than right. You're perfect."

She'd never been anything close to perfect a single day in her life. But hell if she was going to be the one to fill him in, so she tugged his face down for another kiss.

"We need the maid of honor at the back of the aisle to line everyone up in the bride's preferred order," the officiant said.

"Give them another minute," Shelly said. "This was a long time coming."

Maze jumped back guiltily, but Walker was much

slower to drop his hands from her, not seeming guilty in the slightest. He smiled at Shelly.

Shelly beamed back. *Everyone* beamed at them, and while Maze was not ashamed of what she'd found with Walker this week, she'd barely just admitted to herself that they had something at all, so she sure as hell wasn't exactly ready to have the whole world know about it.

And yet . . . no one was looking shocked. Instead, they all seemed happy. She tried not to panic about that, about knowing they now all had expectations, when the truth was no relationship had ever worked out for her, not once. *Panic later,* she decided, and she pulled out her iPad to access her notes. "Okay," she called out. "Heather lines up with Walker, and I line up with . . . Dillon's childhood BFF, Eddie."

Caitlin gasped. "Oh no! I forgot! He got sick and missed his flight." She turned in horror to Dillon. "I didn't even think about how that'd affect the wedding processional."

Dillon shrugged. "Maybe Maze can walk by herself?"

"Of course not!" Caitlin whipped around and surveyed her group of friends and family. "You," she said, pointing to Jace. "You've just been upgraded from Maze's plus-one to someone Dillon can't live without in his group of groomsmen. You'll walk Heather down the aisle."

"But Walker's walking Heather down the aisle," Maze said, staring at her screen.

"No, Walker's walking *you* down the aisle," Caitlin said. "It's perfect."

There was that word again.

"Remember," Dillon's mom said from the sidelines. "Step, pause, step, pause. Rushing is undignified."

Maze thought undignified was trying to stage a coup and take over the wedding, but she kept her thoughts to herself. Not successfully, apparently, because at her side, Walker laughed low in his throat. "Easy," he said. "Too many witnesses."

Her heart fluttered, because he not only knew her to the very depths of her soul, he also understood her. Two minutes later, she walked down the aisle with the evening's wind blowing in her hair and Walker at her side, sure and strong and steady, looking like the best thing that had ever happened to her.

Sammie was next. She had a little basket of flower petals. She started to run down the aisle, but Jace laughingly intercepted her, crouching down to her level. "Okay, so remember last weekend on the TV when we were watching a little football?" he asked. "Here's our play. You're going to take the ball—in this case the basket—and walk it straight up the field to make the touchdown. Got it?"

Sammie grinned and nodded.

They started the music again, and Sammie turned to Cat.

Cat smiled tentatively, obviously prepared to be rebuked by the toddler, but Sammie didn't do her usual deadpan stare. Instead she threw her short little arms around Caitlin's legs.

Cat's eyes filled and she squatted down and hugged Sammie. "Thank you, baby."

"I *three.*" But she grinned, wriggled free, then did just as Jace told her. She walked the basket up the aisle . . . and slammed it down to the grass. Then she executed a sweet little touchdown dance, complete with a case of the giggles.

"Thank God she wasn't the ring bearer," Walker said with a smile.

At dinner, Maze somehow ended up sitting next to Walker.

"We aren't seated together on the seating chart," she said, checking her notes again.

Walker took her iPad and set it facedown on the table. "I switched with Jace so he could sit next to Heather."

"That was nice of you."

"Nice had nothing to do with it," he said. "I wanted to sit next to you."

She squirmed in her chair and his smile faded.

"What's wrong?"

She sighed. "Earlier you said I was perfect, which has me thinking that you've lost your marbles and don't know what you're doing."

His smile came back. "You're still freaking out about that?"

"Among other things."

He shook his head. "Maze, I meant it. You're perfect— for me."

Something deep inside her warmed, but she also felt . . . worried.

He tipped up her face to his. "What else?"

She squirmed again. "I just don't think we need to be shoving this down people's throats."

"This?"

She looked away. "You know what I mean."

He waited until her eyes met his again. "I've got no intentions of being your dirty little secret, Maze. I'm not hiding us. If that's what you're hoping for, tell me now."

"I'm trying to be logical," she said. "What happens after tomorrow? We go back to not speaking for years?"

She had no idea why she said that. Maybe because she knew what she secretly wanted to hear—that no, they would not be going back to not speaking for years.

But Walker just looked at her for a long moment. "That's entirely up to you."

"Great," she said with a soft, sarcastic snort, because when she self-detonated her life, she usually jumped in with both feet. "And let's be clear—you did more than your fair share of avoiding me as well. At least own that much."

He brought their joined hands up to his mouth and brushed a kiss to her palm, his eyes dark and solemn. "I do own it. I've been with you, and I've been without you. And I learned one thing with absolute certainty: my life's better *with* you. You know where I stand. I love you, Maze. There are no doubts for me. All that's left is for you to get off the fence, on one side or the other."

Chapter 24

Caitlin's to-do list:
—Survive the day.

Caitlin stood in front of the mirror in the bridal dressing room staring at herself. Her wedding dress was admittedly beautiful, her hair and makeup were done up to perfection, and she was confident enough to know she looked like she had walked off the cover of any of the million wedding magazines she'd read over the past few months.

But . . .

She sighed. So many *but*s. First, it'd rained heavily earlier, a huge sign if she needed one. Second . . . well, everything else was tied for second. All the worries, concerns, doubts . . . "What are you even doing?" she whispered to herself.

Herself didn't answer.

Her gaze drifted to the earrings she was wearing. They were simple sapphire studs and not even real. But Michael had given them to her on her sixteenth birthday. He'd been seven at the time, which meant her mom or dad had helped him, and they weren't worth any sort of money. But they were still one of the most valuable things she possessed.

He should be here today.

She drew a deep breath. Through all the feverish planning these past months, she'd been so sure it would all work out. She'd just kept thinking if she buried herself into things 100 percent, she'd outrun the doubts chasing her and the doubts that kept trying to tell her this wasn't right.

But she hadn't outrun them at all. They were right here in the room with her.

Everyone had just left to make their way to their places for the ceremony. Her mom. Heather, Maze. For this one last minute she was alone while Maze and Walker made sure everyone was ready to go for the processional.

It was quiet. So quiet she could hear those doubts incredibly clearly now, and they'd multiplied. Exponentially. In fact, they were screaming at her.

But she wasn't a quitter. She didn't back out of things. She didn't flake. She came through on her promises, and she'd made one to Dillon when she'd accepted his ring.

Yes, her doubts whispered, *but he'd made promises too,* and he'd changed his mind on a few key things, which in turn changed everything for her.

The light knock at the door nearly had her leaping out of her skin. It was Maze, who stuck her head in the door. "Walker's got everyone lined up, good to go. Your dad's waiting for you." She smiled. "You look gorgeous. Are you ready?"

"Yes," Caitlin's mouth said, but at the same time her body—acting independently from her brain—shook her head in an emphatic *no.*

Maze paused, studied her, then slipped inside the room and shut the door behind her. "We running for the hills?"

Caitlin stared at the sister of her heart and bit her lower lip.

Maze blinked. "Oh shit. I was just kidding. Okay. Okay, talk to me. What's the plan? Out the window?"

Caitlin felt a hysterical laugh bubble up in her throat, but she couldn't draw a deep enough breath for it because the dress was too tight. "No. I'm just kidding too." She tried to smile.

Maze narrowed her eyes. "Okay, now I'm even more worried." She came closer, the peach floor-length bridesmaid dress she was wearing looking more like a dull orange beneath the lights.

How had Caitlin missed that? The color was awful. "It's fine. Everything's fine. I . . . just need a minute."

"Sure," Maze said. "Use it to talk."

Caitlin shook her head. Because suddenly she couldn't get enough air into her lungs. "It's this dress." She pulled at it, or tried, but there was no give in the fabric. It was fitted within an inch of her life. But she couldn't breathe, at all, and she turned her back to Maze. "Unzip me."

"Um . . ."

"I can't breathe!" She tried tugging her little cap sleeves down and couldn't get them to budge either. "Oh my God, Maze, I'm going to die in this dress!"

"I'm trying to get to the zipper behind all these damn buttons, give me a sec!"

"Second's up!" Caitlin tugged harder. There was a tearing sound, but who cared because suddenly she had room to breathe. Gasping for air, she let out a sigh of relief.

"Oh my God, Cat."

"I just needed a minute."

"Well, I don't know how many minutes we have, but there's sure as hell not enough of them to fix this dress."

Caitlin looked down. She'd ripped the dress wide open in the front. Her breasts were barely contained in her pretty white lace demi bra.

Maze eyed the damage. "Looks like your girls are making a run for it whether you're with them or not."

Caitlin laughed and cried at the same time.

Maze narrowed her eyes. "Are you drunk?"

"Okay."

"Okay? What do you mean, okay? It was a yes or no question!"

"Oh, I thought you were making me an offer." Caitlin plopped down on the floor and began working on unbuckling her complicated high-heeled sandals with shaking fingers that were not working. "But yes, please, let's get drunk. That's the only way I'm going to get through this day."

"You no longer have a dress to wear. I think it's a forgone conclusion, you're not getting through this day, at least not on plan A." Maze dropped to her knees in front of her, gently brushed Caitlin's hands aside, and unbuckled the sandals for her. "We need a plan B, pronto."

"Plan B," Caitlin said. "Run like hell. I believe you suggested the window?"

Maze shook her head, looking shocked. "Why didn't you get out of this sooner? Like any time before I had to spend two hundred bucks on this orange monstrosity?"

"I'm sorry. I didn't realize how god-awful it was. *And I don't know!* I'm not like you, Maze, I've never done anything impulsive in my life! And now there's a whole bunch of people here. And cake."

"Cat, honey." Maze grabbed Caitlin's hands and looked into her eyes. "Those aren't reasons to get married when you're not ready. Tell me this. Do you love him?"

Caitlin searched for the right words. "You know when Girl Scout cookie season starts? You love the Thin Mints so you buy like twelve boxes, but somewhere around box eight or nine you start to feel a little sick. Only you still press on because you paid five bucks a box. But somewhere around box ten, you never want to eat another Thin Mint again. Except you're committed now, so you just plow through."

Maze blinked. "Are you comparing Dillon to a box of Girl Scout cookies?"

"Yes, but specifically box ten."

Maze stared at her. "He gave you a ring and you said yes."

Caitlin sighed and massaged her already aching feet. Why had she chosen looks over comfort? She'd give just about anything for a pair of sneaks right now. "I know I said yes. He ticked off all the boxes. He's got a good career and an involved family."

Maze, kneeling in front of her in that horrid orange dress and a pair of beat-up red sneaks, stared up at Cat like she'd grown a second head.

"Okay," Caitlin said, grimacing. "I just listened to what I said, and I heard it."

"Good, because his mother's so involved that she literally took over your wedding."

"Can I have your sneakers?"

Without question, Maze kicked them off and handed them to Caitlin, which for some reason made her eyes fill with tears.

A knock sounded at the door and they both jerked around to stare at it.

"Honey?" came her mom's voice. "Everything okay in there?"

Caitlin, who *always* knew what to do, found herself just gaping wide-eyed at Maze.

Thankfully, quick-thinking Maze calmly went to the door and opened it a crack. "Hey, so it turns out we need an extra few minutes here."

"No problem," Caitlin heard her mom say. "I'll tell

everyone. You two take your time." She took a beat, lowered her voice. "Seriously. As in take as *long* as you need. You get me?"

Oh God, her mom knew. She knew and she approved . . .

Maze shut the door and raised a brow. "We've got an ally. Okay, babe, your call. What are we doing?"

Caitlin drew a deep breath. "There really are reasons why I like being with Dillon."

"Name them."

"He makes great coffee." She searched for more. "Oh, and he's really good in bed."

"You do realize you just ranked his coffee-making skills above his sex skills, right?"

Caitlin sighed. "He was there for me when no one else was, and that means a lot. *And,*" she went on when Maze winced and opened her mouth, "I don't blame you for not knowing. That was on me, not you. Please don't feel bad for me, because I don't. My point is that Dillon and I got close during a time when I was particularly vulnerable, which I hate to admit. And I really did think things were good between us, or at least had the potential to be good. But last night I watched you and Walker slow dancing after the rehearsal dinner, swaying in a loose embrace, staring at each other, and even from across the patio I could see how much he loves you. He kissed you, and his hands slid up your arms and cupped your face, and you nearly melted into a puddle. You probably would have, but he caught you and held on to you." She shook her head. "I've never melted like that, not once. And I want to melt, Maze."

Maze drew a shaky breath. "Look, I'm no example. Last night Walker asked me to get off the fence about us one way or the other. And the thing is, I want him. I want him for . . . forever, but did I tell him that? No. Because I'm stupid."

"You'll tell him. When you're ready."

"Yes. But I'll probably wait too long and mess it all up, so please don't use me as your ruler. And also, you're still forgetting something vital when you list the reasons for marrying Dillon. The L-word. Pretty big omission, don't you think?"

Starting to feel a little defensive, Caitlin stood up and shoved the torn wedding dress to her hips. "How relevant can it be when *you* can't even say the word? Maybe I should take a page from your book and run from it at every turn. Or *sit on the fence about it.*"

"Hey, don't turn this on me," Maze said. "I can totally say it."

"Yeah?" Caitlin tossed up her hands. "Then say it. Say 'I love you, Cat.'"

Maze opened her mouth, hesitated, then closed her mouth, looking shocked. "Oh my God," she finally said, shaking her head, putting a hand to her mouth. *"What is that?"*

"Told you!"

Maze's eyes narrowed. "Why do you always have to be right?"

Caitlin went palms up. "I don't know, probably the same reason you always run from love. We're both so stubborn it makes us stupid."

Maze stepped back like Caitlin had slapped her. "And why can't you just let a person be who they are? We're not all fixer-uppers, you know, Cat. Some of us are fine just as we are."

Caitlin shoved her dress to the floor and punted it across the room.

"If you take off any more clothes, this conversation is over."

Caitlin looked down at her white lace bra and undies. "Well, excuse me, but all I've got to put on is a short silk dressing robe. I need some more clothes. Why didn't I think ahead?"

Maze sighed and shrugged out of her bridesmaid dress. "And you want to know what I know about the L-word? I know how to blow it up." She threw her dress at Caitlin and it hit her in the face. *"As you already know!"*

Caitlin caught the dress and stared in regret at Maze, also now in nothing but her bra and undies. "That's not true."

Maze drew a deep breath. "Look, the truth is I *do* know things about . . . those three little words everyone likes so much. For example, I know it's too easy to say for most, but I also know it's almost impossible to follow through on. Think about it, Cat, how many people have followed through for you?"

She stared at Maze, who was standing there furious and worried in nothing but her undies because she'd literally given Caitlin the clothes off her back. "You," she reminded her BFF softly. "Plus my mom, my dad, Walker, Heather, Michael . . . *everyone*, Maze."

"Well, of course everyone follows through for you. You're Caitlin effing Walsh. You're sweet and kind and don't make stupid choices."

Caitlin lifted her hands and gestured to herself. Her half-naked self.

"Well, *one* mistake doesn't count," Maze said.

Caitlin stared at the stubborn, loyal, incredible, always honest Mayhem Maze and felt her heart melt. "You mean everything to me. I hope you know that. I love you, and I know damn well you love me back, even if you're afraid to say it because love's been hard on you."

"I am not scared. Take that back."

"So you've told Walker you love him then?"

"You know I haven't."

"Because you're afraid he's going to leave you."

"That's not why."

"Why then?" Cat pushed.

Maze went hands on hips. "We don't have time for this! Put my dress on."

Caitlin shoved herself into the bridesmaid dress. It was a better fit than her wedding dress had been, mostly because she had breathing room. Well, except in the chest. Her breasts were bigger than Maze's and still making a run for it, busting out of the thing.

"Uh . . ." Maze said, pointing to a nipple, which had escaped both the demi bra and the dress.

"Dammit." Caitlin tucked herself back in. "I've got too much boob."

"You've got great boobs, though they look bigger than I remember."

"They should. I bought them."

Maze gasped. "What? When?"

Caitlin shook her head. "Dillon's dad's best friend is a plastic surgeon. Look, I don't want to talk about it. I want to get out of here. Now."

"Are we going to go on your honeymoon to Bali?" Maze asked, sounding hopeful.

Caitlin both laughed and cried. "Just get dressed."

"Problem," Maze said. "I came here in that dress. I don't have anything to put on."

They both eyed the torn wedding dress on the floor.

Gritting her teeth, Maze stepped into it. Thanks to the new rip, the dress was open from neck to belly button, but otherwise it fit Maze's enviable curves far better than it had Caitlin.

"Tell me you have a sweater I can pull over this so I don't get arrested for indecent exposure," Maze said.

Caitlin tossed her the pale champagne-colored cashmere cardigan that she'd planned on wearing if she got cold at the reception.

Maze pulled it on and buttoned it up, swearing the whole time.

Caitlin snorted out a laugh at her creative use of words, then covered her mouth, because she was about to walk away from a man she'd thought she loved. And damn if that didn't kill her. How could she have believed this could work? Unlike Maze, Caitlin had always had a family at her back; she *knew* love, she should've followed her instincts. Now, for the first time in her life, she no longer trusted herself. It was shocking, honestly. She'd always been the rock, the steady one, but she was suddenly anything but. She looked at

Maze, who'd never claimed to be steady or a rock. And yet here she was, helping Caitlin, standing at her back, willing to do whatever she needed.

"I'm ready."

Maze met her gaze, her own very serious. "You know if you do this, if you run, and then later decide you were wrong, it's never going to be the same. Trust me."

Caitlin felt her throat close at the pain in Maze's eyes. "I know. Can you go find Dillon for me? Ask him to come here? I need to see him before we go."

"Of course. But I'm going to call for him, because . . ." Maze gestured to herself in the wedding gown.

"Right." Caitlin handed over her phone.

Maze hit Dillon's number and put the call on speaker.

"Hello?" a female voice answered.

Not Dillon.

Maze and Caitlin stared at each other.

"Hello?" Dillon's mom said again. "Caitlin?"

Shit. "Yes," Caitlin managed. "Hi. Um, can I talk to Dillon?"

"Now? With everyone waiting on you?"

Caitlin grimaced. "Yes, please."

There was some rustling as presumably Dillon's mom brought him his phone, and Caitlin's heart skipped a beat. If he sounded even slightly devastated, she'd walk down the aisle. Sure, she didn't have a dress, but she would find a way—

"Caitlin," he said, not sounding devastated but . . . cool. Distant. "What are we doing?"

Caitlin closed her eyes.

"Is this about . . . the test?" he asked. "The one that you . . . didn't pass?"

That he had to speak in code about this told her everything she needed to know. "Yes." She swallowed the lump in her throat. "I'm sorry, Dillon. I love you, but it's not enough. Not for me. I'm so sorry."

There was a beat of silence, then maybe a sigh. "Can't say I didn't see this coming," he finally said.

"Dillon?"

Nothing.

She stared at the phone, eyes swimming so that it was hard to see the screen. "What happened?"

Maze looked at the phone. "He disconnected."

Caitlin sucked in a breath. "*Please* get me out of here."

Maze swallowed her fury at Dillon and nodded. "Text your parents, just so they don't worry we were kidnapped or something."

Caitlin nodded. "Honestly, I think they'll be relieved. Let's face it, Dillon will too once he thinks about it. He's dodging a bullet."

Maze nodded, though she was of the opinion that it was *Caitlin* doing the bullet dodging. "And Walker and Heather? We can't just leave them."

"I'll do a group text," Cat said.

Maze nodded, her heart squeezing at the thought of Walker. A good kind of squeeze. Last night after the wedding rehearsal, they'd gone to bed together and had a magical night. She'd woken up with a smile on her face that she could feel even now just beneath the surface.

Caitlin was right. Love did scare her. But she was starting to think that what she and Walker had could transcend her fears and her walls, that they might actually have a shot at something real.

"Oh my God. This isn't happening," Cat murmured, bent over at the waist, hands on her knees, hyperventilating. "Can't. Breathe," she gasped, like she might be less than a second from utter meltdown.

"Okay," Maze said. "I've got you." She pulled out her phone to text Walker herself so he'd know where she was and what was happening, knowing he'd be there for Heather and Cat's parents. But her phone was dead. She looked around. No paper, no pen, nothing. She could hear Cat wheezing, the sound getting worse. They had to go, so she quickly grabbed Caitlin's lipstick and turned to the mirror. She got out I'M SORRY before Caitlin grabbed her by the hand, her crazy eyes reminding her of Roly's and Poly's.

Maze squeezed Cat's hand and eyed the door. Too risky. She pulled Cat to the window.

Unbelievably and thankfully, it opened easily, and better yet, no one was out there. Shelly had come through for them, buying them extra time. The woman was smart and there'd been a tone of understanding in her voice, telling Maze she wouldn't be at all surprised at what they were up to.

"Hold on," Caitlin said, and grabbed an unopened champagne bottle with each hand. "Okay."

Maze looked into her eyes. "You're sure, right?"

Caitlin climbed out the window.

Okay, so she was sure. Maze followed after her, and they ran—the bride in the bridesmaid gown and red sneakers, the bridesmaid in the wedding gown barefoot—through the parking lot.

"Where the hell did you park?" Caitlin asked, breathless.

"In the way back."

"Why?"

"Because my car's a bitch to start after it rains. Gotta dry off the distributor cap first and it's embarrassing. You'll see."

At the car, Caitlin headed for the driver's door. "This is *my* great escape. I get to drive."

"You can't breathe."

"I can now."

"Fine." There was no time to argue with the crazy almost-bride anyway. Maze tossed her the keys, then ran to the hood and popped it open. She pried off the distributer cap. "Toss me the towel in the back seat!"

"Why?"

"Just do it!"

Caitlin tossed her the towel, and Maze dried the inside of the cap and disappeared under the hood again to put it back on. "Okay, start it!" she yelled, and Caitlin cranked the engine. It turned over just as Maze jumped into the passenger seat.

"You're right," Cat said. "That was embarrassing."

Maze had bigger problems. She couldn't get the door to close, the wedding dress was too big. She started tugging yard after yard of white satin fabric in, swearing the air blue. Caitlin had to lean over her and add her two hands to the cause.

"Jesus," Maze said breathlessly. "Remind me to never get married."

"You're already married."

"Oh shit," Maze said. "I keep forgetting. *Drive!*"

Caitlin hit the gas, the veil still attached to the top of her head, waving out the open window behind them. "I hope Officer Ramirez isn't on duty."

Maze winced as they took a turn on two wheels. "Slow down. We're not Thelma and Louise."

Caitlin laughed, and it sounded a little hysterical.

"Are you okay?" Maze asked worriedly.

"For the first time in months, I can take a deep breath. Remember when we were listing all the people who love me?"

"Yeah."

"All those same people love you too, you know."

"Thanks," Maze said. "But we're running away from your wedding, I'm wearing your wedding dress, and your veil just flew out onto the highway behind us. I think we should concentrate on you right now."

"Yeah." Cat sucked in a breath. "Is it bad that I know I made the right decision?"

"It's good that you know. It's good that you did it now instead of an hour from now."

"Thanks for being with me," Caitlin said softly, "for talking me through it."

Maze shrugged. "Well, I am the master of doing stupid shit that you can never take back."

Cat took one hand off the wheel and squeezed Maze's. "We're all still here, aren't we?"

"Yeah, but only because you guys won't go away."

Cat smiled. "We are a stubborn lot. And hey, there's one good thing to come out of this week. Us. We're back together. Forever this time."

Forever. It had a ring to it that Maze had never wanted before. But she wanted it now, desperately, and the realization formed a huge lump in her throat. "Where are we going?"

"I don't know." Cat's expression crumpled. "Someplace that matters."

Maze thought about it. "I know just the spot."

Cat looked at her, searched her gaze, and then nodded in accord. And not thirty minutes later, they were at the graveyard, drinking champagne straight out of the bottle with Michael.

Chapter 25

Walker's instincts were usually dead-on, so when he woke up with a feeling that the day wasn't going to go as planned, he took it as gospel. Which meant that several hours later, standing at the back of the wedding aisle with two hundred people seated and waiting for the procession to start, and with no maid of honor or bride in sight, it wasn't a huge surprise.

He watched, along with all the other wedding guests, as in the front row, Dillon's mom stood up and brought Dillon his phone.

Dillon listened, said something quietly, then handed the phone back to his mom. He held up a finger to the crowd and came back down the aisle to Walker. "Caitlin's not coming." He paused. "Do you think the roses were the final tipping point?"

"No," Walker said, "I don't think it was the roses."

"My mom?"

"Getting warmer."

Dillon nodded and looked away. "My last fiancé said it was me. That I don't listen. That I railroad people to get what I want."

Dillon's mother came down the aisle. "What's happening? We're late starting." She looked at Walker. "Where is she? And the other one, the one with the bad attitude. Go get them." Then, before Walker could respond, she stormed off.

Because Caitlin had planned to walk herself down the aisle to be greeted by both parents before turning to Dillon, Jim and Sherry were seated in the front row. Walker made eye contact with them, and both stood up as if to come over. He gestured that he had this, and they sat back down. With a deep breath, he headed to the bride's chambers. When no one answered his knock, he let himself in. The room looked like a cyclone had hit, but it was empty. The window was open, and, more telling, the flowers in the window planter box were crushed, and there was a piece of torn silk on a nail on the windowsill.

He turned in a slow circle and froze when his gaze landed on the mirror.

I'M SORRY

He actually staggered back a step, instantly transported to a certain morning in Vegas, when he'd found a note with the same message. His chest actually hurt and he rubbed it. Logically he knew this wasn't about him, but there was nothing logical about the road his brain had just gone down.

He pulled out his phone.

No messages.

He called Maze, but her phone was either dead or off, and that's when he knew the real reason for the way his gut had turned itself inside out. It wasn't just Caitlin on the run. He couldn't explain it, but deep inside, he knew. Maze was on the run too.

Again.

And he knew why. Over the past week, they'd connected on a level deeper than they ever had, and he'd forgotten to hold back, to keep himself from opening up to her. Instead, he'd told himself when and if Maze got cold feet and wanted to run, they'd run together.

He'd been an idiot.

His mission had been simple: get the divorce. But he should've known that nothing was ever simple with Maze. Now the mission had gone FUBAR, and he was back at square one, grieving her all over again.

But hell if he'd do it.

He strode out of the room. Jace and Heather both looked at him and he gave a very slight head shake. There'd been a low-level hum of quiet talking among the guests, but at the sight of him, all two hundred went silent. One hundred and ninety-eight of them he couldn't care less about. Walking straight to Shelly and Jim, he crouched down and took Shelly's hand. "Cat's not coming," he said quietly.

Whatever he'd expected, it hadn't been for them both to smile. "We know," Shelly whispered. "She texted."

Jace came over. "What can I do?"

"Take Heather and Sammie home," Walker said.

Shelly stood up and grabbed Walker's hand before he could turn to go talk to Dillon. "The cake."

"The cake?"

"I swapped it out for the carrot cake Caitlin wanted. I want that cake, Walker."

"Then I'll make sure you get it." He looked at Jim. "You've got her?"

"Absolutely, son." He squeezed Walker's shoulder. "You got our girl?"

"Absolutely," Walker said grimly. He turned and came face-to-face with Dillon.

"So . . . I guess we should tell people," Dillon said, looking like he wasn't sure how he felt about it.

Walker knew how he felt. He knew because something not so unlike this had happened to him, which was almost enough to make him feel bad for the guy.

"My mom's going to blow a gasket," Dillon said.

"Listen," Walker said, "I'm going to offer some advice you didn't ask for. I didn't know my mom, so I can't say how I'd react if she walked all over my life at every turn, but I can say that the woman you loved enough to ask to marry you should probably be higher up on the totem pole than your mom."

Dillon closed his eyes and nodded. "Getting that."

"You need to make the announcement."

"No. I can't. I've gotta get out of here," Dillon said, and spun on a heel and left.

Walker looked out at the waiting guests and rubbed his jaw. Shit. He moved to where the officiant stood in front of the microphone, looking shell-shocked. He leaned toward the microphone. "Ladies and gentlemen, I'm sorry, but love's not going to happen here today."

Not for anyone . . .

Maze watched Caitlin take a long pull on her bottle of champagne. "You should eat something," she warned. "Or you're going to get drunk."

"Too late," Caitlin said, and let out an involuntary hiccup. She covered her mouth and giggled and hiccupped again. "You should join me."

"I'm your DD." Maze was having a serious moment of fear and regret, because everyone was going to think this was all her fault. But really, what could she have done differently? She wasn't about to advocate for a marriage that Caitlin clearly didn't want. Yes, she could've made the decision sooner, but who was Maze to judge?

Cat looked down at herself. "Seriously, these boobs are far more trouble than they're worth. Kind of like men."

"Well, I've had a serious shortage of both, so I wouldn't know."

"You've got a good guy now," Cat said.

Maze felt a smile cross her face at the thought of Walker. For the first time, she believed in this thing between them and that it could actually work. Even more shocking, she realized her worries and fears about how much she felt for him had gone, leaving a huge warm glow in her chest for him. God, she was so sappy. She closed her eyes, remembering the peek she'd gotten of him in his dark navy suit earlier, looking good enough to eat.

"I know love's never worked out for you before," Cat said, "but this time it will." She emphasized her words with a little wave of one of the champagne bottles and fell over. She stayed down, staring up at the sky.

"You've got a real shot at something, Maze, something real. I promise you it'll work out."

"I don't need promises. Promises aren't real."

Caitlin shook her head, getting grass in her lovely updo that was no longer all up but half in her face. She blew a few strands out of her eyes and turned her head to point at Maze. "I've *never* broken a promise to you, not once."

Maze looked down at this woman who was one of the most important people in her entire life. No matter how long they went without speaking, it didn't matter. Nothing would change; Caitlin would always be there for her, and she would always be there for Caitlin, no questions asked. "It's true, you've never broken a promise to me."

"Damn right." Caitlin fought to try to right herself and ended up just bicycling her hands and legs in the air. "Dammit!" She gave up and flopped back. "You've been the best friend and the best sister I could hope for. I mean, I dragged you into staying this whole week and you never even complained."

"Oh, I complained."

"Okay, maybe a little," Caitlin said with a rough laugh. "For a minute. But then you dug in, took my hand, and walked me through everything. Every single thing. You did whatever had to be done, even if it meant facing your past, like Walker, and my parents. You were there for me, Maze. Just like when you first lived with us and I needed someone to love. You let me love you."

"Well, it's not like you gave me much of a choice," Maze muttered, uncomfortable with the praise.

Cat laughed at her. "Stop making it weird. You're my person, Maze. And . . . shit. Where was I going with this? Oh!" She rolled to her hands and knees and finally managed to sit up, legs crossed, hair wild, boobs bulging. "Promises. I don't break promises."

"Um, this might be a bad time to bring this up, but you just walked away from a pretty *big* promise."

"Nope. I promised to get married today, and I *am* getting married today."

Maze laughed. "Once again, I'm already taken. And plus, nothing personal, but you don't have the equipment I usually prefer."

"Good thing then that *I'm* my type!" Caitlin said exuberantly, waving the champagne for emphasis. "I'm marrying myself!" Still sitting on the grass looking like a hot mess, she wrapped a blade of grass around her ring finger. "I, Caitlin Walsh, promise to love, cherish, and *never* obey myself! I promise to always eat a chocolate chip cookie before bedtime and to be there for myself through thick and thin."

"Just a chocolate chip cookie? Like a *single* cookie?"

"Yeah, don't you remember?" Cat asked. "When we'd sneak them late at night?"

"Oh, I remember. But we always ate more than one."

Caitlin sighed. "That was before I gave up carbs to fit into that dress you're wearing. I wish I could get Mom to give me that recipe."

"First, be honest. You never gave up carbs. Nor should you. Carbs make the world go round. And also, I have the recipe if you want it."

Caitlin stared at her, mouth open. "You have the recipe? How? Mom never gives it to anyone."

Maze shrugged. "She gave it to me that summer we all stayed at the lake. I think because it's supposedly so foolproof that even I can make them." She paused. "Well, probably. I never actually tried. And honestly, I don't think she'd be surprised by that. She just wanted me to have it in case, because . . ." Maze felt herself get choked up. "Because she had more faith in me than I had in myself."

"Oh my God. She *does* like you better!"

"But *I* like *you* better," Maze said softly.

Caitlin gave her a drunken smile. "No, I like *you* better." And with that, she fell onto her back again and stared up at something that made her frown. "Uh-oh."

Maze lay back as well and peered up to see what Caitlin had seen and sucked in a breath. *Uh-oh* was right.

An upside-down Walker was staring down at the both of them, face quietly intense, mouth grim.

Caitlin pointed at him. "You're upside down."

"And you're MIA."

Caitlin sat up and took another swig from her bottle. "I'm not marrying Dillon today."

"No shit," Walker said. "And what the hell are you wearing?"

Caitlin looked down at herself in Maze's bridesmaid dress. "We switched."

Walker turned his attention to Maze, and she felt herself smile helplessly at him. "Hi."

He just stared down at her, hands on hips, taking in the disaster that was her: the sweater that had fallen open, revealing the wedding dress split to her belly button; her lack of shoes and her undoubtedly crazy hair. "I know," she said. "Impressive, right? Like you can't wait for more of this?"

He didn't smile. He didn't blink. And when he turned back to Caitlin without a word to her, her smile faded.

Caitlin offered Walker her nearly empty bottle of champagne. "I know it's really annoying to be around a very slightly tipsy person if you're not imbibing, so—"

"Do you want to know what's *really* annoying?" he asked, not taking the bottle. "When you have to tell two hundred strangers expecting a wedding that the bride went AWOL."

"I just married myself to myself."

"Congratulations," he said, sounding unimpressed.

Caitlin frowned. "That's your mad voice."

He blew out a breath. "I didn't know where either of you were, if you were okay." He paused and looked right into Maze's eyes. "Or if I'd ever hear from you again."

"Cat texted you," Maze said.

"No, she didn't."

Maze looked at Cat.

Cat gasped. "Oh my God. I forgot to text you and Heather! I'm so sorry!" And then she burst into tears.

Maze didn't cry. She was . . . stunned. Shaken. *Guilty*. Because Walker overreacting wasn't Caitlin's fault. It was *hers*. She was the one who'd left him behind all those years before, and she was starting to get that he'd believed she was doing a wash and repeat here today. That she'd walked away from him. "Walk—"

Sending her a fulminating look, he turned his back on her and crouched down at Caitlin's side. "Don't cry, Cat."

"But you're mad at me," she sobbed. "You think I made a rash decision."

"No," he said. "The rash decision was to go through with this when your instincts told you not to. And then to run away from the problem, which isn't like you." Again, he was looking right at Maze, and you know what? She was starting to get pissed off.

Cat dropped her forehead to Walker's shoulder. "I panicked."

"Love makes us stupid," Walker said.

Cat choked out a laugh and sniffed.

"Did you just wipe your face on my shirt?"

"Yes," she said soggily. "I ruined my life!"

He sighed and ran a hand up and down her back, pressing his jaw to the top of her head. "No, you didn't. You protected it. It's going to be okay, Cat. You know that, right? It's all going to be okay."

Watching him comfort Cat gave Maze a pang so deep it hurt her soul. It wasn't jealousy. She wasn't worried that Cat and Walker would take up with each other. Their bond was as family, and it was real.

The pang was . . . yearning. Because she could only *wish* love came as easily to her as it did for them. Watching them, listening to Walker talk to Cat in that low, steady voice of his, reassuring her . . . she wished she could be more like that, so sure and steady in his feelings, not ashamed of having emotions, and certainly not willing to bury them.

So. There she had it. She *was* jealous after all. Jealous of their ability to be human, to believe in love blindly.

Caitlin finally lifted her head and sniffed. "What did Dillon's mom say? Did she freak out? Did she take all the roses home with her?"

"I was too busy worrying about you two to notice anything else. If you were okay or"—again he looked at Maze—"ever coming back."

Caitlin looked at Maze and grimaced. "Okay . . ." She pushed to her feet. "I think that's my cue to give you two a moment to talk. I'll get an Uber."

"Jace is in the parking lot waiting to drive you home," Walker said.

"I don't wanna go home," Cat said. "I want to go to the Whiskey River and celebrate marrying myself."

"Jace will drive you wherever you want to go," Walker said.

Cat bent and kissed the top of his head, then staggered off, holding up the tattered hem of the bridesmaid dress like she was royalty.

Awkward silence descended.

Maze tried to wait Walker out, but waiting had never been her strong suit. "So . . ."

Walker said nothing.

"Are you ever going to talk to me again?" she finally asked.

"I hope you know what you did today," he said. "Because even though I don't think Dillon's the one for Caitlin, when she sobers up, she may never forgive you."

"Wait." Maze shook her head. "Back the hell up. You think this is *my* bad?"

He just looked at her.

"Wow. Okay." She stood up to walk away, but was apparently unable to help herself from getting the last word. "I wasn't the instigator on this."

"You're always the instigator, Maze."

She let out an exhalation of stunned breath, hurt to the core. "Good to know what you really think of me."

"I'm not telling you anything you don't already know. You blow everything up and then don't even seem to realize the damage you leave in your wake because you're already gone, while the rest of us are left to pick up the pieces."

She nodded. "And . . . we're no longer talking about the wedding."

"Depends on which wedding you're referring to."

Another direct hit. She'd worked hard to change, and she'd thought she'd proven it. But he still saw her as that destructive girl she'd once been. "I'm no longer Mayhem Maze," she said quietly. "I thought you knew that."

He turned to Michael's grave, a muscle clenching in his jaw. "You're still trouble with a capital *T.* You left a note on the mirror with nothing more than an 'I'm sorry.' Do you have any idea what that reminded me of? What it felt like to be stupid for a second time when it came to you?"

"Walker—"

"Don't, Maze."

"Are you serious?"

"Very," he said. "I can't talk to you right now."

Well, tough shit. She stepped between him and Michael's gravestone. "Look, you're right, okay? I didn't think about how you'd feel seeing the note."

He shook his head. "There's the problem, Maze. You don't think. And words are cheap."

"Not these words. I really am sorry, Walker."

He didn't move an inch. Only his eyes slid from Michael's gravestone to hers.

She blew out a breath. "Seriously. Why are you being such a hard-ass about this?"

"Because I'm tired of being the idiot standing there by myself while others walk away from me. This time, *I* walk away."

And that's just what he did.

Chapter 26

When Walker got to the parking lot, he realized Jace and Heather were still parked and getting Caitlin into the car. Pulling out his phone, he turned and started walking in the opposite direction as he called Heather.

"Hey," she said. "Where are you?"

"Change in plans. Wait for Maze so you can caravan back to the house together."

"Sure, but where are you—"

"I've got a ride. Take care of them, okay?"

"Of course," she said. "Walker—"

"Gotta go." He disconnected the call.

Yeah, it was a dick move, but he needed a few moments. Probably more than a few.

He got an Uber to his car and then headed to the Whiskey River, where he found Boomer sitting at a high-top table swearing at his laptop.

"You know," Boomer said in disgust, "just once I want a username and password prompt to say 'close enough.'" He looked up. "Interesting wedding."

"Yeah." Walker helped himself behind the bar, grabbing two water bottles.

"Practicing for when you buy this place from me?" Boomer asked hopefully as he accepted one of the bottles.

"Right now?" Walker sat across from him. "Just working on surviving."

Boomer clinked his bottle to Walker's. "I'll toast to that." He drank and then cocked his head. "You looked messed up."

Walker lifted his first finger and thumb about an inch apart, and Boomer laughed.

"Let me guess. Woman problems."

"How did you know?"

"Because only a woman could put that look on a man's face. Been there, man."

"Yeah?" Walker took a long pull of his beer. "You ever get messed up by the same woman twice?"

Boomer laughed long and hard over that. "There's only ever really been one for me, and she's messed me up so many times I've lost count. Still married her, though." He shrugged. "The heart wants what it wants, and at the end of the day, no matter how much of polar opposites we are, no matter how crazy we drive each other, the love never fades."

The love never fades . . .

Walker was still thinking about that an hour later when he ended up back at Caitlin's cabin. He had no idea what he was doing or why he'd lost his shit over a note from Maze that hadn't even been directed at him.

Okay, so that was a lie, because he *did* know why, and it was called fear. The same old fear that lived deep inside him, eating at everything good in his life. The fear that he was easy to walk away from.

He let himself into the house and instantly knew it was empty. He pulled out his phone and once again called Heather.

"I've got Caitlin, no worries," Heather said in lieu of a greeting. "Dillon took their honeymoon without her, so she and Jace and Sammie and I are having takeout on Avila Beach and pretending it's Bali. Join us?"

"Where's Maze?"

She hesitated.

"Heather."

"She left."

He couldn't say he was surprised. She'd been compelled to leave—by him. That was the thing about fears. You could use them against yourself to make them actually come true. And he didn't see a way to change that.

Two hours later he was on a late-night red-eye heading east. Getting back to work was what he needed. Real life was what he needed. It was how he'd always lived, in the present. When one assignment was over, he had always needed to move on to the next as fast as possible, taking control of his future in a way he'd never been able to do in his past. It was a good, solid decision. He needed to make more of those.

He made it back to D.C. and handled his reentry into "real life" by doing what he always did after a rough case at work: he slept, losing all day Sunday.

Monday morning, he hit the ground running, getting into the office just as his team's morning meeting was starting up.

Red, his boss, gave him a long side-eye but didn't say a word as Walker dropped into a chair waiting for his orders. After addressing everyone else but Walker, Red cleared the room. "You look like shit."

"Good to see you too," Walker said. "What do you have for me?"

"Depends on why you look like shit."

"Not talking about it."

Red studied him. "Is your head in the game?"

"It will be."

"When?" Red asked.

"When you give me my next case."

Red nodded slowly, then shook his head.

"What does that mean?"

"You're on paperwork, backing up the other on-going cases."

Walker narrowed his eyes. "You're making me a desk jockey?"

"Until you can tell me your head is totally in the game, yeah."

Walker scrubbed a hand down his face. He wasn't stupid enough to call his boss out, though. And besides, the truth was his head *wasn't* on straight. Not even close. The weight of his sidearm after eleven days away—and how was it that it'd only been eleven days? it felt like years—was heavier than it used to be. And it somehow matched the heaviness in his heart.

Yeah, this time *he'd* messed up. He'd convinced himself that no matter how much he wanted Maze to lean into a relationship with him, she'd eventually run.

So he'd just beaten her to it.

Asshole move, and he knew it. And the things he'd said to her . . . He let out a shaky, shuddery breath, because he wasn't proud of it. He'd said shit he didn't mean and then he'd run, all to avoid *her* running. Yeah, he was some catch.

He tried to bury himself in work while he figured out what to do. By noon, he'd provided intel for some of his team's cases. Important work, but his eyes were bleeding from boredom and the knowledge he needed to be somewhere else.

Like back in Wildstone.

He was in the break room fighting the piece-of-shit coffee maker, and was two heartbeats away from pulling his gun and shooting the damn thing, when someone came into the room.

Jeff was a special agent whom Walker had worked with on many cases. The guy took one look at Walker's coffee situation and laughed. "The big badass Scott, taken down by a coffee maker."

Actually, he was being taken down by a damn broken heart, which he'd done to himself, but hell if he'd admit that.

"So, how's it being back?" Jeff asked. "Anything exciting going on?"

"From behind my desk? Not exactly."

"Come on, man," Jeff said. "Even behind the desk you're lethal. You saved my ass earlier. Thanks for providing the missing intel. I've researched that file a thousand times and I never found it." He clapped Walker on the shoulder. "It's good to have you back where you belong."

Walker couldn't echo the sentiment. He was going through the motions, and he wasn't invested, not even close. Turned out Red had nailed it—his head was most definitely *not* in the game.

And he knew it wouldn't ever be.

Up until last week, his attitude had been simple. There was never a need to look back, at anything. All he had was forward.

But Maze had changed him for the better. He'd let it scare him into running, but he'd been wrong.

He knew that now.

He needed to go after Maze and right his wrongs. He also wanted to move back to Wildstone, buy the Whiskey River, and, if they were interested, hire Caitlin and Heather in whatever capacity they wanted, hopefully giving them a new future as well.

"I'm heading out on assignment later today," Jeff said. "See you in a few weeks when I'm back."

Walker nodded, but he knew he wouldn't be here in a few weeks. By the end of the day, he'd given his notice to Red. He took the elevator to the lobby and headed across the floor, only to stop short at the sight in front of him.

Maze was sitting on one of the reception chairs, and his knees went weak with relief. She was sitting next to . . . *Elvis?*

When she saw him coming, she stood up. She didn't have many tells, but her hands were clasped together and, though the smile on her face was real—if not exhausted—she was white-knuckling it.

Elvis stood too, and Walker realized it was Jace in a costume, making the ugliest Elvis he'd ever seen. Caitlin and Heather were also there, along with Sammie. The toddler caught sight of Walker and started bouncing up and down in Heather's arms, clapping her hands in delight.

"What are you all doing here?" he finally managed.

Maze smiled a little nervously. "Waiting for you."

For the first time in days, he felt a ball of heat swell inside his chest. Hope. Because no one had ever waited for him.

Heather hugged him tight. Sammie too, wrapping her little arms around his neck and brushing a very wet kiss to his cheek. He hugged them both back, then tugged lightly on Sammie's ponytail, making her giggle. He shook his head, boggled. "What's going on?"

Everyone looked at Maze. She was wearing dark jeans and a white button-down, which, if he wasn't mistaken, was one he'd accidentally left in Wildstone.

Her boots gave her an extra three inches, and so did her hair, since it was piled up on top of her head.

"They came as my support group," she said.

She stepped close, and he had to force himself not to touch her, not to haul her into him and hold on far too tight, because he wasn't sure if he could let her go again. "Maze—"

She shook her head. "I hope you don't mind, but I've got to go first, and fair warning, I haven't slept in two days, I've had six cups of coffee since we landed, and I think I've got a Cheerio in my bra." She took Walker's hand and pressed it to her heart. "When I left you that lipstick note, it wasn't like Vegas. I was just in a hurry. I never meant to hurt you. I didn't actually fully understand what you must've gone through until we ran by the church to pick up Caitlin's stuff and I saw the message again."

He opened his mouth, but she shook her head.

"I've got more, and there's even some groveling." She spread her hands out at her sides. "This is me, Walk. I screw things up, *especially* matters of the heart. I promise you to work harder at it, but this is who I am. I react without thinking, especially with the people I love. On Saturday, all I could think about in that moment was getting Caitlin out of there."

"She said the L-word," Heather whispered. "We all heard that, right?"

"Shh!" Cat said. "I wanna hear the groveling."

Walker ignored their audience and kept his eyes on Maze. "I don't want you to grovel," he said. "I don't deserve that. In fact, you deserve it from me." He cupped her face, so damn happy to see her he could scarcely breathe. "The things I said to you before I left . . ." His throat felt tight. "I was wrong, about all of it. I didn't mean any of it. I overreacted. I was scared." He shook his head. "No, make that terrified. I thought you'd walk away eventually, and I used the excuse to beat you to it."

"But—" Maze started, but this time he put a finger to her lips.

"I acted on impulse," he said, "like someone else I know." He felt a small huff of amusement against his finger. "And then I went from terrified to . . . crazy." He shook his head. "When I saw you at Michael's grave, smiling and laughing . . ."

She closed her eyes. "I swear, that wasn't about you."

"I know that now. And I knew it then too. I was just too far gone to admit it. I was a complete idiot."

Wrapping her hand around his wrist, she pulled his finger from her lips. "Well, I don't know about complete idiot . . ."

450 · JILL SHALVIS

"Complete," he repeated. "But luckily I'm still capable of learning from my many, many mistakes." He pulled out his phone and showed her his boarding pass for his flight out in two hours.

"You were coming back," she whispered.

"I was coming back. But that didn't mean I took this"—he gestured between them—"as a given. In fact, it was the opposite. You have a choice here. You always have the choice."

"See?" she said, her eyes shiny. "Definitely not a complete idiot."

With a rough laugh, he hauled her in tight for a long, deep, *desperate* kiss. When he pulled back and looked into her gorgeous eyes, he said, "I love you, Maze. I have since that day I arrived in Wildstone to find you fighting a bully for Michael."

Jace shook his head. "So I borrowed this stupid Elvis costume and got on a plane for nothing?"

"Not for nothing," Walker said. "Because you look pretty stupid, and that's very amusing." He looked at Maze again. "We're really doing this, right? You're mine, and—"

"Um, excuse me," Heather interrupted, leaning forward to Walker. "Sorry, I don't mean to hold up the negotiations, but that whole 'you're mine' thing is a little alpha, and alphas aren't exactly in vogue right now."

Walker never took his eyes off Maze. "—and I'm yours."

"Oh, well, that's okay then," Heather said, nodding, backing up. "Carry on."

Maze smiled up at Walker with her entire heart in her eyes. Or maybe it was *his* heart . . . "I love you too," she said, voice sure and firm. "I've always loved you. And I'm not afraid of it anymore."

He slid his hands into her hair. "Say it again."

She smiled. "I'm not afraid."

He tightened his grip on her. "Not that."

She laughed and stepped into him so there was zero space between them. "I love you, Walker."

His heart caught and rolled over. "Enough to stay married to me?"

"I burned the divorce papers, so yes, and even though I have no idea what I can offer you other than adventure and great toast, I want to stay married to you."

"How about your heart? You offering me that?"

She smiled. "Already yours. Has been for as long as I can remember. And I think we need a honeymoon this time that lasts longer than a few hours."

"God, yes," Walker said fervently. "And a lot farther away than Vegas. I'm thinking somewhere private and warm enough so that clothes are optional."

Caitlin looked at Heather. "Should we tell them we can still hear them?"

"They don't care." Jace tugged off his Elvis wig. "They're too busy trying to swallow each other's tonsils."

This was true. Walker was now kissing Maze like his life depended on it, loving how she made that soft, needy, just-for-him sound from deep in her throat. Lifting his lips from hers, he smiled into her eyes. "Do you hear talking?"

"No." She laughed and nipped his jaw. "How fast can you get me cleared and into your office? And does your door have a lock on it?"

"I don't have an office anymore. I just gave notice."

She stilled. "What?"

"I'm moving back to Wildstone."

Their audience cheered.

"There's more," he told Maze, who was standing there looking at him like maybe he was better than Christmas morning. "I'm going to buy the Whiskey River. We can run it together, or if that doesn't work for you, we can put these guys in charge and live wherever you want."

"But . . . you love your job. It's your life. Your home."

"Yeah, I was wrong about that," he said. "Turns out, home's not a place, not for me. It's you, Maze. You're my home."

Epilogue

Cat's maid of honor to-do list:
—Keep any Elvis impersonator away from
the ceremony.

Maze stood in the hotel suite staring at her reflection. For a woman who'd spent most of her life trying to shove all her emotions in a box with a lock and no key, she had no words. Because that box was open and every feeling had escaped. Excitement. Happiness. Giddiness.

Love.

And not a single drop of fear.

She was in a simple white silk sheath dress with spaghetti straps that showed off the tan she'd gotten over the past week in Hawaii. Her makeup was as usual minimal, her hair long and loose so that the wild waves were doing their thing. She looked like herself, which was important to her, but there was something very new. The happy. "Wow," she whispered at her reflection.

Caitlin's and Heather's faces popped in on either side of her, grinning. "Right?" Heather said.

"I've never seen you look more yourself," Cat said softly, "if that makes sense."

Maze turned to face them and wrapped her arms around them both. "Thanks for being here with me."

"Are you kidding?" Cat asked with a laugh. "Where else would we be except with you on a day like this?"

"It's not too soon for you?" Maze asked quietly, very serious. It'd only been six months since Cat and Dillon had gone their separate ways. They'd talked a few times, had considered going back to dating each other, but had ultimately decided that was a bad idea. Cat had just recently stuck a toe into the dating pool, but was still happier on her own for the time being. That didn't mean that Maze wanted to shove her and Walker's happiness down her throat.

Cat grabbed Maze's face and gave her a smacking kiss right on the lips, leaving some of her red gloss on

Maze. "Honey, it's not a day too soon for me to see two of my favorite people finding each other in love. And now you have the perfect amount of color on your lips to go get married."

"They're *already* married," Heather reminded her. "It's a renewal of their vows. Sober this time." She laughed.

A knock came at the door and Maze's stomach curled, but it was a pleasant sensation that warmed her from roots to toes.

Heather opened the door to Jace.

"Ready?" he asked.

"So ready," Heather said, and jumped into his arms, wrapping her arms and legs around him.

Laughing, he easily held on to her. "I hear you, and we're most definitely next. But Maze first."

With her heart in her throat and sweet butterflies in her belly, Maze walked out of her hotel suite's sliding glass door, the people she loved following as she headed down to the private beach Walker had booked for them.

Walker stood waiting for her beneath a wood arch wrapped in wildflowers, the light wind ruffling his hair, face tanned, eyes crinkled with love and acceptance and good humor. As she stood there ready to walk to him, the "step, pause, step, pause" decree suddenly came into her head, making her laugh.

Dignity wasn't needed here. Walker loved her as is. And with that knowledge warming her heart, she kicked off her heels, grasped the hem of her dress, and ran down the aisle toward the rest of her life.